They BLED ORANGE

MICHAEL REIT

MICHAELREIT.COM

ISBN (eBook): 978-3-903476-03-5
ISBN (paperback): 978-3-903476-04-2
ISBN (hardcover): 978-3-903476-05-9

DISCLAIMER

Title Production by The BookWhisperer.ink

Cover Design by Patrick Knowles

Part One

AMSTERDAM
JULY, 1943

CHAPTER ONE

Nora hardly recognized the figure hunched on the bed. Drawing ragged breaths, Floris Brouwer lowered his eyes as she closed the door of the musty cell. A single light bulb hung off-center, occasionally flickering. Nora shivered as she took a step closer.

"Hey, it's me." She spoke in a low voice and set down a plate with crusty bread, a sliver of margarine, and a cup of weak tea. "You should eat something."

The man on the bed's composure changed, and he looked up. Floris silently acknowledged her with bloodshot, tired eyes. He swung his legs out of bed, his bare feet touching down on the cold concrete floor, took two steps, and greedily lunged for the hunk of bread.

Nora sat and watched her husband chew furiously while she rubbed her thighs and inhaled deeply from the opposite bed. Four months of captivity in this Amsterdam basement had reduced the strong, healthy Nazi police officer to a pitiful heap of a human. His face was gaunt, making him look ten years older than the twenty-seven he was. His ragged clothes were dirty and hung loosely around his thin frame. Nora shook her head. *He brought this on himself. But has the punishment fit the crime?*

Floris took a large gulp of tea before setting the cup down with a clang. He wiped his mouth with the back of his sleeve and turned to Nora. "Why are you here? I haven't seen you in weeks." His voice was raspy, like that of someone who'd spent a lifetime smoking. "Have you come to gloat at my situation?" He spread his arms, shirtsleeves flapping. "Well, this is it, Nora. You've got me caged like an animal."

Nora frowned and shook her head. "It's not like that, Floris. I'm here to bring you news." She swallowed hard and forced herself to meet his cold eyes. She steeled herself, opened her mouth, but he spoke before she could.

"What could you possibly tell me that would change my situation? News about more victories of your resistance?" He scoffed. "Please, I get enough of that from those idiots you have guarding me. They seem to have no purpose in their lives but to fill my head with their incessant babbling and lies." Nora narrowed her eyes as Floris sat next to her. "But sure, Nora, tell me your news."

"You don't get it, do you, Flo?" He grimaced at her use of his nickname. "Four months down here, and you haven't changed a bit. More and more people are fed up with the occupation. They're done seeing their neighbors hauled off to God knows where on made-up charges, losing their jobs and going hungry." She paused for a moment, meeting her husband's eyes in the vain hope that she would find something resembling understanding. Instead, the resentment had only grown, his eyes reduced to thin slits glowering in the semidarkness.

"But most of all, they're done with people turning their backs on their country. People who will turn in their neighbors for a few Guilders or Reichmarks. People who help Nazis. People like you, Floris." Her voice trembled, and she cleared her throat. "You're a policeman. You're supposed to protect us from criminals. Instead, you've become one."

Floris didn't immediately respond. The buzzing of the light

above their heads seemed to grow more intense in the silence of the cramped room. Floris began wringing his hands before he stood, took a step, and towered over her.

"Criminal? That's rich coming from you!" He jabbed his finger at her face, a vein on his forehead throbbing as he raised his voice. "I've listened to the wild stories of your guards." He thrust his thumb up at the ceiling. "They're rather proud of their acts of sabotage. Those Jews you insist on hiding will betray you at some point. Just you wait, Nora."

Nora opened her mouth but struggled to respond. She had never felt more detached from him; those four months *had* changed her husband. "You've gone completely delusional," she whispered.

He didn't react. "I'm not keeping a police officer locked in a cell. You realize once this place is found, and it will be, you and everybody involved here will be punished?" Floris sat down on the bed again, eyeing her challengingly, his chest heaving.

Nora stood and straightened her back. She clasped her hands together and looked down at Floris. "You know why I really came down here? I wanted to see if you'd come to your senses. When I leave this room, it will be the last time you see me." He raised his eyebrows, and Nora continued at pace. "I hoped I could go back up there and tell them they're making a mistake. That you're not the evil Nazi, that there is still a trace of the man I fell in love with." She looked him in the eyes and saw confusion. She wavered for a moment as she felt her stomach churn. "That there was another option."

"Another option?"

"You're going to die. Tomorrow morning."

Floris stared at the wall opposite, processing her words. Nora stood silently near the door, confident the guard on the other side would open it well before Floris could do anything. But as she looked at him, the idea of him assaulting her seemed distant at best. The news had floored him, his face growing paler by the second. Nora pitied him. She cleared her throat. "I'm leaving now, Floris. Farewell. I hope you find peace."

He nodded absently, his eyes fixed on the wall opposite. Nora knocked on the door and turned back one more time. Gone was the confident, brash police officer who'd made it his mission to hunt down every single Amsterdam Jew in the past years. As the guard's key clicked into the lock, Floris looked up.

"If I am to die tomorrow, could you do me one last favor?"

Nora stopped in her tracks. She had expected him to get angry, plead for his life, or attack her, but not this. "What is it?"

"Could you bring me some fresh clothes? I don't want to meet my maker dressed in these rags."

The door swung open, revealing a burly guard. Nora considered Floris' request for a moment. *There's no harm.* "I can do that. I'll leave them with the men upstairs."

In a rare display of grace, Floris bowed his head. "Thank you."

"Farewell, Floris." She stepped out of the cell without looking back, her eyes stinging as the door shut behind her.

CHAPTER TWO

The lake glistened in late-afternoon sunshine, but the man hurrying across the small bridge paid little attention to the stunning scenery. Christiaan Brouwer rarely missed the opportunity to appreciate the beauty of Lake Geneva, but today there was no time. The summons from the consulate had been clear.

He felt a tingle of excitement as he swung open the door, startling the young man behind the desk.

"Christiaan, you're here quicker than I expected." The man stood from his seat. "Can I get you some water? You look winded."

"I'm fine, thanks. The call sounded urgent." Christiaan sat on the creaking chair, thankful for the breeze coming in through the window behind him. "Do you know what this is all about, Willem?"

The man shook his head. "Jean arrived in the morning and has been in his office ever since. He only came out to grab a coffee and asked me to call you."

"He's here?" Christiaan's excitement shot up another notch. He hadn't seen Jean Weidner since arriving as a refugee from the Netherlands with his girlfriend, Lisa, more than four months ago. Weidner had orchestrated their escape through Belgium and France and finally into Switzerland. From their first night in Antwerp, he and Lisa had been on the escape route set up by Weidner. Christiaan owed his—and Lisa's—life to the man who sat in the office beyond the simple door to Willem's left.

"Christiaan!" A strong voice boomed through the room. Christiaan looked up as a tall, wiry man moved confidently toward him. He quickly stood and shook Weidner's outstretched hand, tightening his grip to match the other man's firm handshake. "It's great to see you again, and thank you for coming so quickly."

They stepped into the sparsely furnished office, and Weidner waved him to a chair near the window. Outside the fifth-story window, the weathered copper-green roof of the church opposite glistened in the sun. It reminded him of the grand Tuschinski theatre in Amsterdam sporting similarly colored twin copper domes. The thought of home passed as he sat and turned to find Weidner studying him with interest.

At thirty, Jean Weidner was only seven years older than Christiaan, but he could easily pass for another ten. His dark hair was brushed back expertly, exposing a receding hairline, emphasizing his pale face. The dark rings around his eyes showed a man who worked too much. The eyes, however, shone, betraying the youthful energy befitting a man who spent every waking moment thinking of ways to outsmart the Nazis across Europe.

"How are you and Lisa doing?" Weidner asked. "I hear you've both done great work welcoming the newcomers."

"We both know what it feels like to arrive here and know nobody. It's been thankful work."

Jean nodded. "And they will keep coming. I've just returned from Paris, and our safe houses are full of people waiting to make the journey south." He shook his head. "We're struggling to get them papers quickly enough. You know how it is."

"I think we were lucky. Unfortunately, life in the occupied countries is getting worse, and the streams of people trying to escape are only growing."

"And we're only seeing the ones who succeed," Jean said, the usual glimmer in his eyes fading momentarily. "There are plenty of people who don't make it. They end up going in the other direction, to the camps in the east."

A silence passed as Weidner's heavy words filled the room. Christiaan knew the Gestapo had stepped up its efforts to hunt down people in hiding in France. He looked to Weidner, who also had a considerable bounty on his head. Despite that, the man was always on the move, maintaining his escape routes and connections across multiple countries. The threat of capture or betrayal was always looming, but it hardly appeared to affect him. Christiaan suspected it only drove Weidner on harder; every successful escape provided more motivation to continue.

"You must wonder why you were asked to come to the consulate at such short notice."

"I didn't expect to find you here," Christiaan said. In truth, he had been terrified that something terrible had happened back home. To Nora, the sister-in-law he cared for deeply. He'd been forced to leave her behind as he fled the Netherlands with Lisa. Even though Nora's abusive husband, Christiaan's brother Floris, had been missing for months, Nora's resistance activities were high risk. As soon as Willem told him he was meeting with Weidner, he knew it was something else.

"You described helping those people coming to Geneva as thankful work. Is that also how Lisa sees it?"

Christiaan frowned. "You'd have to ask her, but to be honest, we're both just grateful to live in freedom and do our bit for the people arriving." He shifted in his seat, fumbling with his hands, and looked away.

"But? It sounds like there's something else." Weidner sat patiently on the other side of the desk, leaning back in his chair. His eyes sparkled with interest, and Christiaan felt his confidence grow. *I've asked to speak with him for months, I should grab this chance.*

"When I was in Amsterdam, I felt like I was making a real difference. I was hiding people, making sure they received their food coupons. I was sabotaging the occupation, fighting the Nazis. When Lisa was no longer safe, and my brother learned about my involvement in the resistance, it made sense to leave. We were both in danger." Weidner listened without interrupting, and Christiaan felt a sliver of doubt about speaking the next words. *Out with it, Chris. You need to tell him, or nothing will change.* He took a deep breath. "Yet, these past months, something has been gnawing at me. I keep thinking of the people back home. My friends in the resistance. Nora. I've abandoned them." Sharing the feelings that had gradually been building in his mind felt oddly liberating, and he continued. "They risk their lives every day while I'm hiding here. I feel like I could, and should, be doing more."

Weidner didn't immediately respond. Instead, he stood and moved to the other side of the desk, sitting down next to Christiaan. "Your feelings are perfectly understandable. I can't say I've never felt the same."

"How? You're the reason so many people make it to safety. Despite the Gestapo's bounty, you travel across Europe to make sure your network of safe houses remains operational. I don't know of anyone more involved in the resistance."

"But I didn't start out like that. I also fled my home at the start of the war, leaving my friends and family behind. I struggled with the same feelings as you, Christiaan. You worry about those closest to you, and you feel like you're betraying your comrades in Amsterdam." Christiaan nodded, and Weidner continued. "And after a while, you convince yourself every bad thing that happens back home is your fault. You tell yourself if only you had still been around, you would be able to stop it. It's the guilt that consumes you. But only if you let it."

"Don't get me wrong. I'm proud to be a part of your organization, but I'm all the way at the end of the line. By the time these people arrive in Geneva, it's about getting them on their feet, to show them where they can buy their groceries. At best, I help them find a job."

Weidner moved from his chair and sat on the edge of the narrow wooden desk. "I understand what you're saying. Most people arriving are happy to find a safe place to hide. But you're different. I noticed it from the moment you arrived. And listening to you just now confirmed what I suspected. You want to do more. You need to." He looked thoughtful, and Christiaan held his breath. "Willem says you've been asking about operations for weeks now. I'm sure that's why he suggested I meet with you today. And you know the risks. You've made the journey across Europe before, you know what it's like."

Christiaan felt his throat go dry. "Do you want me to return home?"

"No, I don't want you to go back." Weidner raised his hands and shook his head.

Christiaan lowered his head in disappointment. *Then what?*

"I want you to head farther south."

CHAPTER THREE

Floris woke to the familiar creaking of the stairs. The cell was pitch dark, but he sat up in his bed wide awake. Soft, patient footsteps came his way. Whoever was coming down the stairs had made it into the small hallway.

This is it. They were coming for him. Nora's promise didn't materialize. She hadn't shown up with his clothes. He was going to die in these rags, after all. *Treacherous bitch.* His temples throbbed as a bout of rage built up. Even after he'd caught her at the crèche, he'd still allowed her to save the child she was carrying. And look where it brought him. Now she wouldn't even let him die with dignity.

Floris listened to the footsteps and recognized the gait of Andre. It was then that he realized there was only one person on the other side. Without another thought, he jumped off the bed and crossed to the door. *I might have a chance, after all.* He held his breath as the guard put the key into the lock and turned. *Even if I'm wrong, it doesn't matter. I'm dead either way.*

The door slowly opened, and a small stream of light entered the cell. The marginally fresher air from the hallway crept in, a cool and welcome touch on his cheek. Then he heard the breathing of the man on the other side of the door, closer than expected. For a second, Floris hesitated, but the grunt of surprise sprung him into action. Without another thought, he burst through the opening. Andre had taken a few steps from the door. Floris felt the blood rush from his face. The hand at Andre's side held a gun. All of Floris' experience as a police officer took over in that moment. Seizing the initiative, he threw himself at the other man, not giving him any time to lift the weapon.

They hit the dusty concrete floor with a dull thud. Andre took the brunt of the impact and looked up at Floris with groggy eyes. The impact had knocked the gun from his hand and it slid a few meters down the hallway. Floris did the only thing he could do. Ignoring the other man's hands, he launched a flurry of punches to his face. His fists connected with Andre's nose, and Floris felt an odd sensation as the guard's face quickly turned into a bloody mess. He felt energized as his punches increased in velocity, then caught himself when Andre's hands fell limply to the sides of his body. He looked at the bloodied face—Andre's eyes had rolled into the back of their sockets. Only the soft, ragged breathing confirmed he was still alive.

Floris stood and picked up the weapon from the floor. Inspecting the gun, he was relieved to find it loaded. The basement was deathly quiet, and he let out a long sigh. He looked at the unconscious man on the ground and wondered whether Andre would've had the guts to shoot him in the basement. He smiled wryly; he would never know. *Time to get out of here.*

He stalked toward the stairs and strengthened his grip on the gun, lifting it to eye level and keeping it aimed at the open door at their top. As he ascended the stairs, the steps creaked, sounding much louder here than in his cell. He grimaced as he forced himself to keep moving. *No sense in slowing down now. They're expecting us upstairs.*

His heart was in his throat, and he forced himself to take deep breaths as he continued climbing. A shadow crossed the faint light in the hallway above as Floris stood halfway up. He instinctively held his breath, loosely rested his finger on the trigger, and waited.

It didn't take long. The shadow increased in size, and then transformed into a large man in the doorway atop. It was the other guard, Peter. The man was a giant, and there was no way Floris would beat him in a fight. The guard's confident and relaxed expression changed instantly as he looked into the barrel of Floris' gun. His eyes went wide with fear and surprise. He opened his mouth to shout, but the words never had the chance to form.

Floris expertly adjusted his aim and squeezed the trigger twice. The explosion of the gun was deafening in the confined space, and Floris had to control himself to keep from dropping the gun as his ears protested. The sweet scent of gunpowder drifted up his nostrils as a high-pitched ringing overwhelmed all other sounds. He looked up to see Peter was—amazingly—still on his feet, clutching his stomach. His hands were red with blood pouring from two rapidly growing spots. Despite that, the big guard appeared determined to block Floris' only exit. Grunting in pain, Peter reached for the door.

Floris cursed. *He's going to lock me in.* He rushed up the stairs as the guard grabbed the door and, with an immense effort, prepared to slam it shut. As the door swung, Floris knew there was only one way he would make it out of the basement alive. He pulled the trigger twice in quick succession, aiming at the spot where he estimated Peter would be. The sound of the gunshots was as loud as before, but Floris kept squeezing the trigger until the gun clicked empty.

The bullets had torn through the door with ease, the impact at such a short distance leaving large, splintered holes. Through the ringing in his ears Floris tried to catch any sounds coming from the other side. He heard nothing. He pushed the door and managed to open it far enough to squeeze through before encountering resistance. Holding his now useless gun in front of him, he stepped into the hallway. The sight that greeted him turned his stomach.

Sprawled on the floor, head leaning against the door, was Peter. His shirt was soaked in blood, a pool forming on the ground near his groin. His eyes were fixed in surprise, and Floris was about to say something when he noticed the bullet wounds in his neck. Floris shook his head. Two of his rapid-fire bullets had found their mark. Peter would no longer pose a problem.

The ringing in his ears subsided, and the silence of the house washed over him. He looked at the gun in his hands. He'd never killed anyone before, and apart from the relief of being freed from his captors, it gave him no pleasure. He stepped over Peter's body and headed for the front door. Through the small window he could make out it was still dark outside. To his relief, the door handle turned and gave way as he swung the door open.

The cool summer night air drifted in, instantly clearing the fog in his head. He was outside for the first time in four months and took a deep breath of fresh air. He quickly shut the door, leaving his former captors behind. Stepping into the street, he heard the gentle sloshing of water in the canal opposite. The water was dark, but the sound calmed him. He crossed the street, and as he moved from the house, he casually tossed the gun into the canal.

CHAPTER FOUR

The clear sky turned blood red as the sun rose beyond the rows of canal houses. Nora would have a spring in her step on any other day, anxious to get started. She clutched her small bag a little tighter as she approached the bridge. It felt odd to be out this early, and she'd only run into factory and dock workers. However, she'd been told to arrive just after sunrise, and she was well on time.

It had been almost half a year since she'd last seen Christiaan, her brother-in-law, in the back room of Bet van Beeren's Cafe 't Mandje. When Christiaan and Lisa left, Nora prayed for their safe passage every day—and she wasn't even religious. News of their safe arrival in Geneva came a month later, and she couldn't remember ever feeling more relieved. After that, it had become quiet, but she knew no news was good news in this case. *If only you knew what was about to happen to your brother, Chris.* She felt a lump in her throat as she approached the safe house. She took a deep breath, cleared her throat and knocked on the front door. To her surprise, it gave way. *That doesn't make sense.* The hairs on her arms stood up, and she scratched the back of her neck involuntarily.

Nora gently pushed the door open, peeking inside the hallway. An odd, coppery smell filled her nostrils. It took her a moment to recognize what it was—blood. She pushed the door open farther and, as she stepped inside, suppressed a shriek, dropping her bag. She slammed the front door closed and leaned against it. She was breathing hard, her eyes fixed on Peter's body sprawled on the floor only a few meters away. His pale face offset by the dark pool of blood around him, lifeless eyes frozen in surprise and anguish.

Floris. Nora fought off a wave of nausea as she controlled her breathing. She took a step toward Peter, then stopped. *What if he's still here?* She looked around, unable to regulate her breathing, her heart throbbing in her ears. Nora's feet remained rooted in place, her eyes still on Peter but her ears listening for any sounds in the house. It was eerily silent, and after a few seconds, she decided she was alone.

She knelt next to Peter, inspecting the giant's face. Apart from the bullet wounds in his neck, his face looked the same—serene and calm, just like him. Peter had protested against Floris' execution, but in the end, the decision wasn't his. *He didn't deserve this.* She ran her fingers over his face, closing his eyes.

Nora rose, unsure what to do next. If Floris had escaped, she needed to get out. He might return with a squad of policemen—seeking revenge on those who had captured and vowed to execute him. Nora shivered as she considered the damage Floris, and the other men of the Bureau could cause. *I need to warn the others.*

She turned and took two steps to the door when she heard something. *A cough?* She stopped in her tracks and turned to the source of the sound.

"Help." There was someone in the basement. Nora was undecided for a second. What if it was a trap? What if Floris had waited for more people to arrive, only to take them out as well?

"Please, whoever is up there, help me. I can't move." This time, the voice was stronger. Andre's, the other guard. She tentatively opened the door to the basement, gently nudging Peter's face aside as she did, and carefully descended the stairs. She found Andre in front of Floris' open cell door—or at least what was once Andre.

She recoiled at the sight. Andre was still alive, but his nose was caked in blood, and both eyes were reduced to thin swollen slits. She marveled at Floris' strength despite his months of captivity. Then she remembered what he used to do to her, and she shuddered. Clearly, he hadn't forgotten how to inflict damage with his fists.

Andre's eyes flickered when he recognized Nora. "He's gone, isn't he?" he croaked. Nora realized his shouts for help had exhausted him.

She helped him sit upright. "I found Peter upstairs. What happened?"

"He jumped me when I came to collect him this morning." He touched his face, wincing as he felt his nose. "Is Peter okay? Floris took my gun! Did he let Floris go?"

Nora looked at him with compassion. "Peter didn't make it. He must've surprised Floris on the way out. He's at the top of the stairs. I'm so sorry."

Andre looked at her in disbelief. "Peter's dead?"

She nodded, not knowing what to say next. Andre's face went from shock to anger. "Why couldn't he just let him go? Only someone as stubborn as Peter would try to stop a man with a gun." He turned his face away, tremors shooting through his body as a soft wail escaped his lips. "He was my best friend, Nora."

"He did what he believed was his duty." She put an arm around his shoulder, carefully avoiding his bruised face. "There's a lot of pride in that."

They sat together for a moment, and they didn't immediately notice the sounds from upstairs. Andre nudged her.

"Do you hear that?"

Nora froze as footsteps in the hallway padded over to Peter's body. Had Floris come back with reinforcements that quickly? It wouldn't be long until they came down the stairs now. She looked around, searching for a window. But that would mean leaving Andre behind on his own. She looked at him, and he appeared to read her mind as she shook his head.

"The stairs are the only way out."

Shit. They were trapped. "Any weapons down here?" she asked, already knowing the answer. "Well, at least we'll be going down together, then."

Nora could hear them move Peter's body out of the way. Light streamed down the stairs and into the basement as they opened the door wide. Nora's throat constricted, her breathing shallower. She squeezed Andre's hand a little tighter as the first boots came down the stairs.

Nora closed her eyes, resigning herself to the harsh commands and strong hands lifting her from the floor any moment now. More boots stomped down the stairs, and then she felt the presence of someone hovering over her. She opened her eyes and gasped.

"When did he escape?" The man addressing Andre wore regular clothes, his brow creased with concern. Two other men appeared alongside him, both wearing the uniforms of factory workers. Nora recognized Toon, one of the leaders of the resistance group.

"I went to get him around four. That's when he knocked me out," Andre managed.

Toon addressed the men in factory clothing. "It's only been an hour. We still have time." He gestured at Nora and Andre. "Get them out of here, quickly."

"What about Peter?" one of them asked as the men helped Andre to his feet. Nora got up by herself.

Toon hesitated for a moment, then turned on his heel. "We'll have to leave him here. It'll be light out soon." The men supported Andre as they ascended the rickety stairs together. Toon turned to Nora, gesturing to the stairs. "Come, we should go. Are you okay?"

Nora rubbed her temples. "I'm not sure. I don't know what to do. I can't go home. Floris will be waiting for me."

"He'll be looking for you all over town. Is there anywhere you can go? A friend's house? Someplace Floris doesn't know about?"

She shook her head. "No, I never expected this would happen." She felt cold. "I have nowhere to go." She took Toon's outstretched hand as he guided her up the stairs. As they reached the top, she looked at the lifeless face of Peter one last time—at least he looked peaceful.

"There's only one thing you can do now, Nora." Toon's voice sounded oddly distant, despite him standing less than a meter from her. She turned and focused on his strong, intent eyes. "You need to go into hiding. We will take you to the same house as Andre. You'll be safe there for now."

Nora followed him through the front door. Everything had changed in an instant. Floris would stop at nothing to find her.

CHAPTER FIVE

Floris followed the scent of coffee as he made his way down the narrow stairs. Hans and his wife, Maja, were sitting at the kitchen table. She reached for a large pot.

"Would you like some coffee, Floris? You look like you could use some." She poured without waiting for an answer, and he sat down gratefully.

"Thank you, you have no idea." He cradled the mug in his hands while he blew on the steaming liquid. "I haven't had a coffee in four months. Come to think of it, Hans, how did you manage this? I thought ersatz was all we could get these days?"

"Found some in a house we raided the other week. They had plenty of supplies in the basement." Hans grinned from across the table. "Grab some breakfast, Flo. I'm sure you're hungry. You look like you've lost quite a bit of weight. Didn't feed you properly there, did they, those savages?"

Floris helped himself to some bread and, a welcome surprise, cheese. "No, it was water and bread most of the time. If I was lucky, they would give me some margarine or a slab of bacon, but that was it." He gritted his teeth, thinking back to the musty basement cell. "I'd like to get to the station as soon as we can."

"No problem. We can head out as soon as you've eaten enough," Hans said. "I'm sure the chief will be interested in what you have to say. Should we check on the house?"

Floris shook his head. "No sense in going back there. You reported it when I came in this morning, right?"

"I did. They promise to send some uniforms down there."

"Good, although I doubt they will have found anything interesting. I'm sure they fled right after they found out I escaped." *Well, most of them.* He chewed the last bite of his sandwich and wiped his mouth. "Let's get to the station. We've got work to do." There would be revenge.

It was a short ten-minute tram ride from Hans' house to the Bureau of Jewish Affairs. Floris had a spring in his step as he stepped off tram 5 at Rokin. They followed the canal south, and he looked around, smiling as the shopkeepers put their meager selections of produce out on the streets. Months in dark captivity had given him a new perspective.

They crossed the canal, to Nieuwe Doelen Street. The headquarters of the Bureau of Jewish Affairs came into view. The building was much like the others on the street: a classic, narrowly built *herenhuis.* With large windows and a small flight of steps, it looked as inconspicuous as the adjoining buildings. But in the case of number 13, looks were very much deceiving. Housed inside was the special branch of the Amsterdam police dedicated to hunting down Jewish citizens. Once the men of the Bureau got their hands on them, they were sent to Camp Westerbork in the east of the country, where they awaited transport to the camps in Poland.

"Anything I should be aware of?" Floris said as they reached the front door. "Any big changes?"

Hans shook his head. "No, it's been business as usual, although the number of arrests has gone down in recent weeks. But that's mostly because there's hardly any Jews left." He sported a savage grin. "We got most of them."

"Very well." Floris opened the door and stepped inside. The familiar smell of cigarette smoke in the narrow hallway brought back memories—since joining the Bureau two years ago, he had worked himself up to the rank of lieutenant. Before his capture by the resistance, he was responsible for the arrests of hundreds of Amsterdam Jews.

He felt his confidence growing as he passed the common room, where he recognized some of his colleagues chatting in a circle. He peeked his head inside and greeted them in a pleasant voice. "Morning all."

They looked up, and there was a slight hesitance before they returned his greeting. One of them, a fellow lieutenant called Hendriks, managed to say, "Didn't know you were back, Brouwer. We thought you had left."

"You better believe I'm back and ready to continue doing my bit. *Heil Hitler!*" Floris saluted them crisply, his arm shooting into the air. The men returned halfhearted salutes before turning their backs on him. Floris turned to Hans. "What's wrong with them?"

Hans looked uncomfortable as they walked on. "Just people, you know. They talk."

"What do you mean, talk?" Floris stopped in the middle of the hallway. "What did they say?"

"Look, this is just what I heard, and I told them they were wrong, but—"

"Come on, Hans, out with it!"

"When you disappeared, people assumed something had happened to you. At first, they thought you had been killed by the resistance, but the rumors started floating around that you were involved with them."

Floris felt the blood rush to his face, the vein on his forehead throbbing. "Why would they think that? I'm a damned legend here. Nobody brought in more Jews than me!"

"I know, I know." Hans held up his hands. "But somehow, someone decided that since your brother left town, and it was clear he was part of the resistance, you were in on it, too."

"They thought I was a double agent?" Floris was fuming now, struggling to control his anger. "Who started those rumors? Tell me, Hans." He took a step closer to his friend and felt a vein throbbing on his forehead.

"I don't know, Flo. The others didn't really involve me because, at first, they thought I was involved as well. I told them you had gone missing and that something must've gone wrong. I told the chief about what we were working on and how I thought it was likelier you were caught by the resistance."

Two uniformed officers walked by and gave Floris an odd look. *Calm down. Talk to the chief.* "Okay, what did he say about that?" He forced himself to speak slowly, focusing on his breathing.

"At first, he told me to search for you. But it's difficult when you don't know where to start. Whenever we raided resistance houses, I was hopeful we'd find you. But after two months, I must be honest with you, Flo, I also gave up." He looked ashamed. "I'm sorry."

Floris grabbed his shoulder. "There's no reason to apologize. It sounds like you were the only one who believed in me." He looked around the empty hallway with a snarl. "Those snakes were probably happy to see the back of me. More bounties for them." *Nothing easier than spreading rumors about someone who's not around.*

"Let's go see the chief. I'm sure he'll be very interested in what you've found out." Hans had recovered some of his confidence and led Floris up the stairs.

The door to the office of the Bureau's commander, Rudolf Dahmen von Buchholz, was open, and Floris knocked enthusiastically.

"Come in," came the answer. Floris and Hans entered to find the chief thumbing through a filing cabinet in the corner. He had vouched for Floris when he was accused of looting a Jewish home after its occupants had been arrested. Floris had, in fact, done so, but Dahmen von Buchholz had kept the Germans at bay. Floris was indebted to him for that, and he couldn't wait to share his news.

Floris and Hans stood awkwardly in the middle of the room while the chief had his back to them and continued rustling through files. When he found what he was looking for, he slammed the drawer shut and turned to them. He almost dropped the folder when he saw Floris.

"Brouwer! Well, I never! I did not expect to see you here." He crossed the short distance to his desk and sank into his comfortable chair. Floris and Hans sat on hard metal chairs opposite. The chief turned his attention to Hans. "This call in the middle of the night now makes sense. Did you find him at a resistance house?"

"No, sir. Floris showed up at my house. He escaped from that house. But it's probably best if he tells you all about it himself."

Dahmen von Buchholz looked thoughtful, his eyes scanning Floris' face. "Well, I'm certainly interested in hearing where you've been. How long has it been?"

"Four months, sir."

"Yes, there have been some interesting theories about where you went." He pointed his finger at Hans. "He never stopped believing you'd come back, though, defending you whenever anyone suggested you'd walked to the other side."

Floris gave Hans a grateful look. "I'm glad someone was there to defend my honor in my absence, sir. I assure you it wasn't of my own choosing." He then proceeded to tell his chief about the crèche, his four months of captivity, including his suspicions that his brother was in the resistance but leaving out Nora's involvement in his capture.

"Well, that's quite the tale, Brouwer. I have to say, you look like shit, so that part of your story certainly checks out." The chief's dark eyes revealed nothing, and Floris felt himself getting flustered, a trickle of sweat running down his back. *Does he not believe me?*

"Sir, if I may speak freely?" The chief raised an eyebrow but nodded. "I understand you may be reluctant to believe me at my word, but given my escape last night, I think some things will be set into motion by the resistance."

To his surprise, Dahmen von Buchholz nodded slowly. "If you're speaking the truth, which I'd very much like to believe, I agree."

Floris saw the lifeline leading back to his old job and status and pounced. "I believe they will do everything they can to evacuate as many children and staff from the crèche as possible. I'm the only one who knows about it, and they know it." *Nora's job finally comes in useful.*

"Yes, that's what I'd do in their position."

"I'd like to organize a raid without delay, sir." As he spoke the words, Floris regained the confidence to act, to lead from the front. "I'm certain the people working at the crèche will lead us to more resistance fighters." He wasn't so sure, but he was willing to take that gamble if it meant leading the initial raid. He couldn't wait to send those smug women to the interrogation chambers of the *Sicherheitsdienst*.

Dahmen von Buchholz thought only for a few moments. "Get it done, Brouwer. But make sure you involve the Sicherheitsdienst and *Grüne Polizei*. They've been on our case about cooperating on raids these days."

Floris struggled to contain his excitement and practically jumped from his chair. "Yes, sir. You won't regret this." He saluted the chief before bounding out of the office. He was back, and he was going to show all those who doubted him he was no traitor.

CHAPTER SIX

Christiaan sat in a quiet corner of *Café du Centre.* The upscale yet friendly establishment where he and Lisa had their first freedom lunch. The cafe's high ceilings, clean white table linen, and old-world chandeliers had fast made it their favorite place in the city. He kept his eye on the door, awaiting her arrival, anxious to share his news.

"Another coffee, sir?" Christiaan looked up from the book he was having trouble focusing on to find a waiter standing at this table. He nodded, then saw Lisa enter through the open patio doors.

"Make it two, please," he said before the waiter disappeared, waving at Lisa as she scanned the room. She gave him a peck on the cheek and sat opposite him.

"Didn't prefer sitting outside? The weather's great."

"A bit too crowded for my liking. I wanted some quiet time with you."

The waiter returned with two cups on saucers. Having coffee served in such fancy surroundings was alien to them at first, but they had gotten used to it rather quickly. Christiaan felt a pang of guilt when he thought of his friends back home. They had no such luxuries, drinking weak tea instead or, if they were lucky, watery ersatz. It returned his focus to why he invited Lisa for lunch.

"You're brooding over something," Lisa said as she took a sip.

"I was just thinking about how fortunate we are to be living here."

She purposefully placed her cup down and leaned in closer, her eyes shining. "We are. But I know that's not why you asked me to come down here. I know you had a meeting at the consulate yesterday, and you've been acting odd ever since. Out with it, Chris." She spoke evenly, her lips curling ever so slightly upward.

He moved his hand across the table, slipping his fingers into hers. "I met Weidner yesterday. He's in town for a few days."

"That's great. You've been trying to get a meeting with him for ages." Lisa sounded genuinely excited. "Did he have any news from home? About Nora?" Her expression turned into one of concern when she realized news about Nora could also be bad.

Christiaan raised his hand reassuringly. "No news about Nora. He hadn't gone farther north than Brussels. The Gestapo are really ramping up their efforts in Belgium and France, and he wanted to check in on his connections."

Lisa looked slightly more relieved, but he could feel her hand tensing. "Then what did he want to talk to you about?"

"We talked about you and me, our life and work in Geneva, and how we play an important role in welcoming new people. He said we're making a big difference."

"It's good work, and I'm happy to help," Lisa said. Her eyes bored into his before Christiaan averted his gaze. "But that's not why he asked you to meet him, was it?"

He took a deep breath. *Out with it.* "No, we talked about home, about Amsterdam, the resistance." Lisa remained quiet, her eyes giving away nothing. "He said he could use my help."

"Does he want you to go back to Amsterdam?" Even though Lisa's expression hadn't changed, there was a slight tremor in her voice.

"No, he wants me to go to Spain."

At first, Lisa was surprised. "Spain?" Then it quickly dawned on her. She, too, had worked at the consulate for four months now, and she knew what it meant to go south. "Does he want you to go to England?"

Christiaan grabbed her other hand. "Yes. He wants me to escort a British pilot to Gibraltar—"

"And on to England from there." Lisa finished his sentence. "You could join the Dutch or British forces." There was determination in her voice. "It's what you wanted ever since we arrived here, isn't it?"

"Initially, it was. But now I'm not so sure."

"What are you talking about? This is a great opportunity! If Weidner secures you passage to England, you can link up with the Dutch government. With your knowledge and connections with the resistance in Amsterdam, you would be a vital asset to them."

"I'm not sure my knowledge is still as valuable as it was. A lot will have changed since we left Amsterdam. Besides, that's not why I'm reconsidering."

"Why, then?"

He looked her in the eyes. "Because it would mean leaving you behind."

"What are you talking about?" Lisa pulled her hands back across the table. Her eyes were locked on his. "Do you really think I'm going to let you go on your own?"

Christiaan shifted in his seat and reluctantly shook his head. "I can't ask this of you, Lisa. You're safe in Geneva. As soon as you cross the border into France, you're in danger."

"Chris, I've been in danger for most of the past four years. In the past year, I've gone into hiding, lost my parents, and trekked across Europe with you." She looked down at the table, fumbling with her hands. "I don't know for certain what happened to Mama and Papa, but I'm fairly sure I'm alone in this world now." She looked up, her misty eyes meeting his. "Alone, but for you. Chris, you've been the only constant in my life for the past year. You're why I'm still here. I'll be damned if I let you leave me."

He looked at the woman across the table, her bottom lip quivering, and his heart swelled. She was right. He was foolish for thinking he could leave Geneva without her.

"Let's go talk to Weidner."

They arrived at the consulate unannounced thirty minutes later. Willem told them to wait while he checked with Weidner.

"You're sure you want to do this?" Christiaan asked while they sat in the small anteroom.

Lisa grabbed his hand and squeezed hard. "Yes. I'm not losing you. I'm coming with you. If we can make it out of the Netherlands, through Belgium and France together, we can certainly get to Spain with Weidner's help."

"And a British pilot," Christiaan said with a chuckle. "That doesn't complicate matters at all."

"We'll make it work."

The door to Weidner's office opened and Willem appeared. "He's ready for you." As they passed the consulate worker, he whispered to Christiaan. "And I think he's been anxiously waiting."

Jean Weidner stood from his desk as they entered. His eyes shot to Lisa, and he masked his initial surprise with his trademark hearty smile. "Lisa! How lovely to see you. You look great. Geneva agrees with you."

"It's an easy city to get comfortable in, especially compared to Amsterdam these days, Mr. Weidner," Lisa said as she and Christiaan sat down.

He made a dismissive gesture with his hands. "Please, call me Jean. We're all friends here." He turned to Christiaan. "I'm glad to see you again so soon. I take it you've considered what we talked about yesterday?" His eyes shot between Christiaan and Lisa.

"I have, and I've decided I want to take the mission. I'll go to Spain with the British pilot."

The relief was evident on Weidner's face as he stood. "That's wonderful, Christiaan. I can't tell you how happy I am to hear that. You've kept me in suspense ever since you left yesterday."

"There's one condition, though." Christiaan cleared his throat, turning his face to Lisa. "She's coming with me."

Weidner, still standing behind his desk, opened his mouth, then sat down again. He looked at Christiaan in surprise. He rubbed his face in silence, as if pondering his response. Finally, he managed, "Ah. That changes things."

"I can't leave her behind, not after everything we've gone through. I don't want to lose her. It's either both of us going to England, or neither." Christiaan was surprised at his own determination. He glanced at Lisa, who looked at him with determination. She took hold of his hand, and he felt the warmth spread through his arm. *I'm making the right decision.* He turned back to Weidner, who looked at him with a curious expression.

"I'm not a fan of large groups traveling across the continent, Christiaan. Smaller is better, and two is better than three. Especially with a British pilot. You don't want to attract too much attention. It's too dangerous."

"Mr. Wei—Jean, if I may say something," Lisa said.

There was a twinkle in Weidner's eyes, and he waved his hand. "Of course, Lisa. I'm sorry, I'm talking about you like you're not here. Go ahead."

"I understand your concerns, and I would agree if it were anyone else. But don't forget Christiaan and I have traveled across the continent before. We know how to act at border crossings or with German patrols. We both speak German, and I've picked up quite a bit of French here."

Weidner's eyebrows shot up. "Have you, now?"

"I'm not fluent, but I have a lot of time on my hands, and I decided if I'm living here, I might as well learn the language. Besides, traveling as a couple meant nobody questioned us. We talked ourselves out of quite a few situations in Belgium." She placed Christiaan's hand on her lap. "And I'd say we've perfected the couple situation since."

"That you certainly have. You make a strong case, and I can see why Christiaan doesn't want to leave without you. There's only one problem. The Dutch and British governments don't provide passage to Jewish refugees."

Christiaan felt his skin tingle, and Lisa's face dropped. "But . . . why?"

"It's quite outrageous," Weidner said while shaking his head in apparent frustration. "It's mostly the Brits worrying they'll be swamped with refugees."

"Do they make any exceptions?" Lisa asked, her voice softer and less confident than a minute prior.

Weidner stood and paced the small room, rubbing his chin. Christiaan gave Lisa his most encouraging smile. *We'll make it work.* Weidner stopped and gazed out the small window behind his desk, then turned around. "I think I've got an idea. It's hard to argue you're coming to England purely as a refugee, Lisa. You've got experience at the consulate here, and you've helped dozens of people since arriving. I'm sure they could do with a capable office worker at one of the ministries in London. From what I've heard, the workload is only increasing."

Lisa's face lit up. "You think they'll go for it?"

"I'll need to lean on some of my connections, but if you safely escort a British pilot home, I'd say you've got some leverage. Let me make some calls. I should know more by tomorrow morning." He held out his hand. "I'll have Willem send a courier to your home as soon as I know more."

CHAPTER SEVEN

Nora was restless in the small attic. She listened to the sound of the Berken family going about their business downstairs. It sounded like the usual morning rush before setting off to work. Nora envied their relatively normal life. After the Germans invaded, Floris had been quick to take the Nazis' side. She'd suffered silently until Christiaan asked her to join the resistance.

She stood from the bed and paced the windowless room. Nora was grateful for the quick actions of the men the previous day. They hadn't hesitated in taking her to the Berken's home. Even though the space was cramped, she knew this was as safe a place for her as could be. But she knew she couldn't stay here for long. *I can't sit here and hide for the rest of the war.* She balled her hands into fists, frustration building as she thought of Floris roaming around freely, terrorizing the people of Amsterdam while she hid in this attic.

But worst of all, she'd spent most of her almost twenty-four hours alone worrying. She'd browsed the books lined neatly on a bookshelf, even picking one out. However, her mind didn't give her any peace, and she was quickly distracted back to her worries. *The crèche.*

Before the men left her on her own, Nora insisted they inform the leadership about the threat to Henriëtte Pimentel's crèche on the Plantage Middellaan. It was where two of the men working in the school next door had overpowered Floris, after which they locked him in the basement. *He will be out for revenge, and the crèche is an easy target.*

Nora sighed, knowing there was nothing she could do but wait. Footsteps sounded on the stairs. Her ears perked up, and soon she heard additional, lower voices mixed with those of the Berken family. Men's voices. She felt a tingle of excitement as the muffled voices spoke for another minute before there were sounds on the narrow staircase leading up to the attic. *They're here for me.*

There was a quick knock on the door, and a few seconds later, it opened. Two men entered, and Nora was relieved to recognize Toon was one of them. She quickly rose and shook both men's hands, squeezing Toon's a little tighter than she intended. The air in the room felt a bit lighter.

"Not easy hiding in here for a full day, is it?"

Nora shook her head. "No, but I know this is nothing compared to what some other people have gone through. I'll manage, for now. Do you have any news? Did you warn Henriëtte?"

Even in the dim lighting of the room, the change in Toon's demeanor was obvious. His shoulders dropped ever so slightly, his forehead creasing as he frowned. "You should probably take a seat, Nora." He waved at the bed while he grabbed a stool from the corner. The other man stood behind him, silently observing her.

Nora didn't move. "What happened? Tell me." She rubbed her hands together, her fingers feeling cold.

The other man stepped between Nora and Toon, raising his hand before the latter could speak. "You know, Nora, the past twenty-four hours have been interesting, and I've been thinking."

Nora frowned. *What is he talking about?*

The man's jaw tightened, the tone of his voice hardening as he continued. "And I believe what happened is all just a bit too much of a coincidence."

"What is?" Nora snapped. "Who are you, anyway?" She stepped forward and looked at Toon. "What's going on?"

"How come you made it to the basement so quickly, right after your husband escaped?" The man was now scowling, no longer attempting to hide his suspicions. He wagged his finger at her. "And look at you. You came out of this scot-free while your husband walks the streets."

Nora felt light headed as the words hit her. *He can't be serious. And why isn't Toon saying anything?* Toon looked at her apologetically. *I'm on my own.* She turned back to the unnamed man and gritted her teeth, struggling to conceal her anger.

"If you're suggesting I had anything to do with Floris' escape, you obviously don't know me very well, or my relationship with my husband." The man looked at her, his expression unchanged. Nora stole another look at Toon, who now looked back at her encouragingly. She pushed on. "I've risked my life many times for this organization. First by spying on my husband, then by smuggling children out of the crèche. And while you're accusing me of helping Floris escape, we should be evacuating the crèche, saving as many children, as well as the women working there, as we can. Before it's too late."

The man folded his arms. "People do crazy things for their loved ones. You wouldn't be the first to betray the organization for a husband or wife. I've seen people turned for less."

Nora's anger almost bubbled over, but with an effort, she contained herself. "I have no allegiance to Floris anymore. Haven't for quite a while. Not since he decided to use me as a punching bag."

The man's expression changed instantly, the scowl on his face replaced by a look of surprise. Suddenly, his eyes showed a hint of compassion, but there was still some uncertainty left. "But you were in his cell the afternoon before he was to be executed. What were you doing there if you didn't care for him anymore?"

"I didn't say I didn't care for him anymore. I've spent most of my adult life with Floris, so of course, I still care for him. And I could've forgiven him for the abuse, eventually." She was silent for a moment, remembering the early days of their marriage. Floris had swept her off her feet, saving her from the brothel. The first months had been like a dream. Until she miscarried. She winced at the painful memory. When she was unable to get pregnant again, Floris' attitude drastically changed; he blamed her. Then he started staying out late, coming home reeking of alcohol. That's when the beatings started.

She looked back at the man across from her. "But I can't forgive him for what he's done to the Jews of Amsterdam. Hunting them down, willfully sending them to their deaths, and enriching himself by robbing their houses. He would've arrested his own brother if he'd been given a chance. You know about this, don't you?"

The man nodded silently, the doubt in his eyes fading. Nora felt her anger dissipate as she continued. "And now that he's escaped, he'll be coming for me. The night we caught him at the crèche, when I was leaving with that baby, he was going to arrest me as soon as we took the baby to safety." Her eyes stung at the memory. "Letting it go would've been the only good thing he did in the past years. But if you believe I helped Floris escape, you couldn't be more wrong. There's no one in the country with more to lose than me."

It was quiet as Nora's words hung heavily in the air of the cramped room. She sat on the bed. The unnamed man turned away from her, looking at Toon. "You were right." He then turned to Nora. "I apologize for questioning your loyalty. I'm suspicious by nature; it's how I've survived in this position for so long. Toon told me you had nothing to do with Floris' escape, but I had to hear it for myself."

Nora let out a deep sigh. She felt the tension flow from her neck and shoulders. "I understand. I might've been a bit suspicious if I were in your shoes." Her thoughts went back to the crèche. "Please tell me you reached out to the people at the crèche yesterday, though."

A pained look appeared on the man's face, but it was Toon who broke his silence. "The crèche was raided by the Grüne Polizei and Sicherheitsdienst yesterday morning. I'm sorry, Nora. We didn't make it in time."

Nora felt faint, her head spinning. *It can't be. How did Floris move so quickly?* "Are you sure?"

Toon stood, crossed the small distance to her, and sat down next to her. "I was there. They had the entire street blocked, and by the time I arrived they were loading up all the children into the trucks."

Nora's heart felt heavy, remembering some of the children's faces. She had spent many evenings helping out at dinnertime, reading books and playing. They were all so optimistic, dreaming of the future, waiting for the day it would be their turn to leave through the back door. Now, she could see them hauled through the front door by stern soldiers shouting harsh German commands at them to hurry up. Tears welled in her eyes. "What about Henriëtte? Was she there?"

Toon winced. "She was always there, you know that. She fought tooth and nail to stay with the children." He lowered his eyes. "But she was taken to Euterpe Street instead. The children were taken straight to the train station, to Westerbork."

Nora felt like her head was underwater. She heard Toon's words, but they were coming through at a delay. She thought of Henriëtte Pimentel, the headmistress of the crèche. She shuddered to think of the treatment she would receive if she was taken to the Sicherheitsdienst's headquarters on Euterpe Street.

Toon's voice snapped her back to the present. "Nora, I know you're hurting. But there's nothing we can do for them anymore. We need to focus on what this means for you."

"Yes, of course," she said, wiping the tears from her eyes. She looked at the man across from her and saw him looking at her with compassion. Nora steeled herself. This was no time to appear weak.

There would be time to grieve for Henriëtte and the children later. "Floris won't stop until he's found me."

"And once he does, he'll look to bring down our whole operation," the unnamed man said. "We'll need to keep you out of sight."

Nora looked at her surroundings, her throat tightening as she spoke. "I'd need to stay here?" The thought of hiding for the rest of the war, not being able to do anything for the resistance filled her with dread. *I can't sit on the sidelines. Not now.* "I can't. I want to be useful. I would go crazy in here."

The man focused on Toon, who shrugged, as if to say, *"I told you so."* Then his gaze returned to Nora, a sparkle of admiration in his eyes. "I thought you might not be thrilled about our proposal, but it's too dangerous to have you out on the streets of Amsterdam. I'm sure Floris will have every police officer looking out for you. And where would you go? You can't go home."

Nora nodded. She'd thought about where to go after this, but she didn't have an answer. She no longer had a home.

"What if I don't stay in Amsterdam?" Christiaan and Lisa had made it out when Floris was onto them. *Why not me?*

The two men looked at each other, and Nora's eyes darted between them. Toon had the same, almost mischievous, look on his face. *There's something he's not telling me.* The other man looked thoughtful. "Where would you go?"

"Anywhere but here," Nora said. "Anywhere I can be useful. Maybe up north, where the children are taken?" As soon as she spoke the words, she knew that was going to be nigh on impossible. An outsider in the smaller villages and towns would stand out. The man's doubtful expression confirmed her thoughts, and she changed tack, glancing at Toon. "Or south, perhaps?" *To Christiaan and Lisa.*

"Out of the country," the man said, stroking his chin. "That might be an option."

"I think we'd be wasting Nora's talents by keeping her hidden in a stuffy attic or basement." Toon spoke up, and Nora's heart jumped.

Finally. "She's proved to be an invaluable asset in the past year. Maybe she could join up with the government-in-exile in London?"

England? Really? Nora hadn't considered the option. She knew of people trying to reach England by crossing the North Sea in rickety boats, but never considered it a realistic option. Now Toon was suggesting she would make for England via Spain?

The other man looked at Toon and then Nora. "Are you sure about this? The route south is heavily guarded these days. The Germans have increased their patrols on the Swiss and Spanish borders." He clicked his tongue. "And that's not even considering your journey through Belgium and France."

A tiny flutter of doubt crept into Nora's mind, but she quashed it as she answered resolutely. "If it gives me a chance to be useful, I must try it." England was free and resisting Hitler.

The man didn't immediately answer. Instead, he paced the room for a minute, then stopped abruptly. "You've got character, Nora, I'll give you that. The journey south is not one to be considered lightly. And you won't be able to do this on your own. A woman traveling alone might attract the wrong kind of attention." He paused and pursed his lips. "But you're not the only person looking to make it to England through the southern route. Let me talk to some people and see if we can arrange something for you. I must warn you, though, if you do make it to Switzerland or Spain, you'll be waiting a long time before you have a chance to get to England. The Brits are quite selective about who gets a visa."

"If there's even a remote chance for me to reach England and reach our government, maybe even support the Allied war initiative, I need to try. It beats hiding and waiting here. I joined the resistance because I want to do something."

The man looked amused. "All right, Nora. I can see you're determined. Let me see what I can do. I can see why Toon told me to come and speak with you." He turned to leave, and Toon stood from the bed and winked at her. She gave him a thankful look. As they stepped toward the door, a thought struck. “Wait. Could you do me a favor?”

Both men looked back inquisitively.

“I may have a way to cripple Floris. It might not work, he may have taken care of it, but it’s worth a shot.”

CHAPTER EIGHT

Floris was whistling as he crossed the bridge into Nieuwe Doelen Street, to the headquarters of the Bureau of Jewish Affairs. The sun glistened on the water of the canal below, improving his mood even further. He walked on, a pretty blond-haired woman on a bike catching his attention. He winked at her, and she flicked her hair out of her face as she walked on.

He climbed the steps to the Bureau's office building, the large white wooden door open. Even the normally stuffy air in the hallway felt different, and Floris made his way to his small office on the first floor. He took the stairs and enjoyed the memory of the events the day prior. As soon as he'd left the chief's office, Hans had made a couple of calls to the Sicherheitsdienst and the Grüne Polizei. At first, the man answering the phone at the Sicherheitsdienst refused to take his claim seriously. Floris had taken the receiver and challenged the man to call Dahmen von Buchholz. At the mention of the chief of the Bureau's name, the man acquiesced. An hour later, Floris and a combined team of Sicherheitsdienst and Grüne Polizei troopers pounded on the door of the crèche.

It had been one of the easiest raids he'd ever partaken in. The Jew women and children just stood there as they entered. Securing the place had been easy; Floris had been the first one in and made sure the back door was blocked. From that point on, it had been a matter of getting all of them into the trucks outside. He was especially pleased to catch the woman running the crèche, Henriëtte Pimentel, completely unaware of the danger. The look on her face as she raced down the stairs was etched in his memory. She would be singing in the basement of the Sicherheitsdienst by now, along with the other women. The arrests would likely lead to more names of those involved being revealed. He hoped it would lead him to Nora, who had—predictably—gone missing. *Never mind, she won't be able to hide forever.*

Floris had made no mention of Nora's role in the resistance, not even to Hans. His friend would likely ask about her sooner or later. The best way to avoid the issue was to pretend everything was fine at home.

Floris entered his office and was surprised to find Hans waiting for him. "You're in early! And in my office." He caught the condescending annoyance in his voice and quickly added, "Feeling energized from yesterday's raid?"

Hans either didn't catch Floris' annoyance or ignored it. "I'd say the celebratory drinks at *De Bever* afterward sapped most of my energy. I was up early, so I figured I might as well get to work."

"Now that you mention it, you do look a little rough," Floris said with a chuckle as he sat in his comfortable desk chair. "What's on your mind?"

"Just wanted to let you know Dahmen von Bucholz has an early visitor today. Someone from the Sicherheitsdienst. I caught them in the kitchen getting coffee. Looked like an important man, lots of stripes on his shoulder straps."

"Sicherheitsdienst big shot?" Floris sat up, on full alert. This could only mean one thing. They were assessing yesterday's raid. "Did you hear anything?"

Hans shook his head. "As soon as I came in, they went quiet. The chief gave me a look, so I made myself scarce. They looked pretty serious, though. I hung around in the common area outside the kitchen a bit, but they only spoke about the recent developments on the eastern front. Nothing we wouldn't know from the papers. What do you think is happening?"

"Must be about the raid," Floris said, almost to himself, as the options shot through his brain. "Maybe they got some intelligence from the interrogations, and the SD man came to share it with Dahmen von Bucholz?" *Although the SD wouldn't share information with them unless they needed something.* Floris paused, then looked at Hans. "Maybe they need our help with something?"

"That would be a first," Hans said, looking unsure. "They seem quite happy with us minding our business, hunting down Jews for them while they take the credit with the top brass in Berlin. I'm not even sure the chief gets much credit outside Amsterdam."

"Maybe it's different this time. Why else would a higher-up make such an early call to the office?"

"I suppose we'll find out soon enough," Hans said, getting up from his chair. "I thought you'd like to know about it, considering you led the raid. And you're right; it does seem too much of a coincidence to have that SD man here the day after. It would be quite exciting if they did obtain useful information from our efforts."

Floris nodded absentmindedly, hearing his friend's words but already thinking ahead. Hans took the hint and left the room. Floris leaned back in his chair. *I need to know what the chief is discussing. What if they uncovered more connections to the resistance?* He rubbed his hands in anticipation; this might lead him to Nora, or Christiaan, even. The thought of his brother momentarily soured his mood, and he wrung his hands. He had no doubt Christiaan was involved in the resistance, especially after he had disappeared after Hans and Floris searched his house a few months ago. He wondered how connected Christiaan and Nora had been. *Patience. You'll find them.*

"Floris?" He looked up to find Dahmen von Bucholz's secretary in the doorway. "The boss wants to see you in his office now if you can."

Floris' temples throbbed as he sat opposite his boss. The unexpected summons had unnerved him. Following the secretary, he calmly convinced himself they probably wanted his firsthand account of the previous day's events. Perhaps they even wanted to congratulate him.

But when he had entered the office, he sensed something was awry. The SD officer stood in the corner to Dahmen von Bucholz's left, who greeted him with a curt "Sit down."

The SD officer glared at Floris while Dahmen von Bucholz sank into his chair. Despite his calm demeanor, there was thunder in his eyes; this was not going to be a congratulatory chat. Floris forced himself to stay calm. *You've done nothing wrong.*

"I suppose you're wondering why you're here," his boss started, then turned to the SD officer behind him. "This is *Obersturmführer* Vogel. I don't suppose the two of you have met before. He had some *interesting* news for me this morning."

"Sir, pleasure to meet you."

Vogel acknowledged him with a barely perceptible nod, then started without preamble. "After your successful raid yesterday, your name was everywhere in our offices. I heard you spent a few months locked in a basement. The resistance scum held you?"

"Yes, sir. I was overpowered near the crèche, and they held me for four months. After I escaped, I was surprised to find they were still operating from the crèche. I think we got there just in time, sir." His hopes rose. Vogel was here to talk about the raid, after all. Both men's stern faces stared in his direction. "The interrogations at Euterpe Street were fruitful?" He looked from Vogel to Dahmen von Bucholz, who looked back impassively.

Vogel stepped forward and leaned on Dahmen von Bucholz's

desk. "We haven't spoken to all the women yet, but I'm sure one or two of them will have something interesting to share."

"The old lady running the place should know more. From what I gathered, she was involved from the start." Floris was so eager to assist that he realized—too late—he had spoken out of turn. "Apologies for interrupting, Herr Obersturmführer." He inclined his head.

"We'll find out whatever they know and act accordingly," Vogel continued, ignoring Floris' apology. "The raid was a great success, Brouwer, a real blow to the underground." The scowl on the man's face faded, and Floris let out a quiet sigh of relief. "So, you can imagine my surprise when your name came up again later that day. I was just about to head home, when one of my agents came in with a troubling report." His eyes fixed on Floris. "About the same man who had done such great work that morning."

Floris squirmed in his seat, unsure how to respond. He looked to Dahmen von Bucholz, whose passive expression had turned into an openly hostile glare.

"We received a call about ill-gotten loot in your home, Brouwer. The agent who took the call initially didn't think much of it, but when he checked your file, as is customary, he found last year's report."

Floris' stomach dropped. They had found his crate of stolen Jewish goods. He closed his eyes and rubbed his forehead. There was no denying it, especially after two SD officers caught him looting houses last year. Dahmen von Bucholz had been able to keep him out of the wind back then, claiming Floris was one of his top agents, but the banknotes, jewelry, and other valuables found in his attic proved last year was no one-off incident.

"So, he sent two men to your home to check on the tip. I guess I don't need to tell you what they found. You've been busy these past few years, setting up a nice retirement account for yourself." Vogel's tone was accusatory.

Floris sat up in his seat. "I realize it looks bad, sir. But I assure you I haven't taken anything since that incident last year." He faced

Dahmen von Bucholz with a guilty expression. *I've let him down.* "I took the chief's warning to heart."

"I'm afraid that's not good enough, Brouwer." Vogel folded his arms and sat down on the side of the desk. "When he warned you, it was assumed this was a single incident. What we found in your attic is worth tens of thousands of Reichsmarks, if not more—you've been stealing from the Reich for many years. And to be perfectly frank, I don't believe your claim that you stopped your illicit activities after the warning. Once a thief, always a thief. Your boss agrees with me."

Dahmen von Bucholz looked disappointed but said nothing. Floris desperately racked his brain to come up with a plausible excuse. He stared at Obersturmführer Vogel, waiting for the man to announce the penalty for his supposed crimes. Instead, it was Dahmen von Bucholz who spoke next.

"Brouwer, I'm mostly disappointed. When you came back yesterday, I was skeptical of your use in our organization. But you proved me wrong with that raid. And then I come in this morning to find you've been looting homes for years, accumulating a small fortune." He shook his head. "I'm sorry, but you can no longer work for the Bureau."

Floris let out a deep sigh, feeling utterly deflated but relieved it would just be his job he'd lose. However, Dahmen von Bucholz wasn't done yet.

"As I told you last time, stealing from the Reich is a serious crime. Obersturmführer Vogel is here to take you to Euterpe Street, where you'll await transfer to stand trial."

Floris' body went rigid with fear. Euterpe Street housed the very people he arrested. Standing trial for crimes against the Reich as a Dutch person could only mean prison. Or worse, he could end up in a concentration camp as a criminal prisoner. The blood drained from his face as he stared at the two men opposite him in utter dismay, unable to speak.

They looked back at him for a few moments, as the air appeared to get sucked from the room. Floris felt his throat constrict as he imagined himself stuck in one of the camps. He'd heard the way the SS spoke of the prisoners. They didn't care whether they lived or died, Jewish or otherwise. He'd laughed with them at parties when they spoke of the type of *sport* they had the prisoners participate in, their exhausted and malnourished bodies breaking as the guards rained down blows on them when they failed to keep up.

"But there is another way." Vogel interrupted Floris' macabre thoughts. "You can avoid the whole ugly matter of jail time."

Floris' eyes shot toward the man. *Is he leading me on? Has the abuse already started?* Despite his reservations, he heard himself asking, in a voice that sounded nothing like his own, "How? What must I do?"

Vogel glanced at Dahmen von Bucholz, who kept his face neutral. "You can volunteer for a new position."

Floris saw a glimmer of light in the very dark tunnel. Eager as he was to avoid the possibility of Dachau, Buchenwald, or even Auschwitz, he cleared his throat and straightened his back as best he could. "Volunteer for what?"

Two days later, Floris stood at Amsterdam Central station, carrying nothing but the duffel bag slung over his shoulder. Groups of excited men much younger than him stood scattered around the platform. The optimistic conversations were about fighting Bolsheviks and earning Iron Crosses.

Floris didn't share their glee as he stared down the tracks, waiting for the train to arrive—he felt only remorse and anger. Getting fired from the job he cherished so much was pitiful. He'd spent his life climbing the ranks of the police force, finally catching his big break when the Germans took over. Now, all of that was lost. He gazed around at his fellow men, and could barely look them in the eye.

The train appeared in the distance, the steam bellowing from its engine—a new life was approaching.

He gritted his teeth as he thought of his old life. He didn't doubt it was Nora who had somehow thought of reaching out to the Sicherheitsdienst about his crate in the attic. Even from the shadows, she had found a way to trip him up. The train pulled into the station, and Floris saw the cars packed with young men. Finally, it came to a stop, the wheels of the cars creaking and the engine in the front letting out a loud hiss. Floris took a step toward his new future. *Nora may have won this round, but I'll be back.*

CHAPTER NINE

The regular drumming of the train's wheels calmed Lisa's nerves as she looked out the window. As the sun rose, she could make out the magnificent sight of the Pyrenees rising in the distance. She looked at Christiaan, still asleep across from her. His mouth was slightly open, and her heart surged. Slouched in the seat next to him was Gareth, the British pilot they were escorting to Spain, his face hidden behind a small cap.

Lisa readjusted her blanket, pulled it up to her chin, and enjoyed the changing scenery outside. Yesterday afternoon they had left Geneva, and she was surprised by the ease at which the train crossed France. There had been no problems entering the country. A few French border guards had boarded the train and, after a cursory glance at their papers, continued down the train. Christiaan had mentioned they probably didn't care much about people entering the occupied country. The real test would be when they wanted to leave. As they neared the Spanish border, Lisa started to pick at the skin around her nails. Would their papers hold up to the increased scrutiny they would surely experience? Would Gareth be able to sneak out in time? They had gone through their approach multiple times. Gareth's best chance at crossing the border was to hide underneath the train while they stopped at the border station. It was risky, but Weidner had told them hiding in a narrow space underneath the car was the only way to make it. Lisa agreed; in the worst case, she and Christiaan could get by in their German. For Gareth, the game would be up as soon as he opened his mouth. His English Midlands accent was too heavy to pass for anything but the obvious.

Christiaan stirred opposite. He opened his bleary eyes. "Morning," he said groggily before looking out the window. "Any idea where we are?"

"Can't be too far from the border now." Lisa pointed at the mountains fast approaching. "Those must be the Pyrenees."

Christiaan turned and nodded. "Let's get Gareth prepared. He must be ready before we get to the station."

On cue, the pilot lifted the cap, exposing his dark brown eyes. He shielded them from the rising sun and gave a mock salute. "Morning. How long have you been awake?"

"Just woke up, but you better get ready. We're near the border."

Gareth's eyes flashed in anticipation. "Good, I'm ready to get to Spain."

Lisa appreciated his optimism. From their meeting in Geneva, Gareth had been easy to get along with. Despite his situation—crashing into occupied France and barely making it to Switzerland, far away from home—he had a positive outlook on life that was infectious. He spoke openly about his wish to return home as soon as possible, and he didn't flinch when Christiaan asked him about the risks of getting caught on their way there. "I won't go down without a fight," he'd said, and Lisa believed him. She wasn't sure if his confidence came from youthful ignorance—he was only twenty years old —or from the thirty-plus successful missions he'd completed since joining the Royal Air Force. Either way, they had quickly warmed to their young companion and he to them.

They had told Gareth about their journey south, and he had listened with obvious fascination when she spoke of their near run-in with the Gestapo in Paris and their escape from the French border guards when crossing into Switzerland. Even though they'd met less than twenty-four hours ago, Lisa felt she'd known Gareth for much longer.

The train slowed, and Gareth reached for his jacket. The grayish-brown color was unassuming and boring—precisely what they were going for. Weidner had picked it out for him, saying it would blend well with the train car's undercarriage. All the small details mattered.

"Are you ready?" Christiaan asked as Gareth looked out the window. The brakes squealed as the train rolled into Narbonne, the last stop before the border crossing at Perpignan.

"Ready as I'll ever be." Gareth grinned sheepishly.

The station's platform appeared to their right, and nothing but a fence to the left. Lisa sighed in relief; Weidner had been right when he said Gareth could climb into the space underneath the car without being seen. If they had come in on another track, he would've been in full view of the people on the platforms. *Not that we must worry, there's hardly anyone around.*

Gareth stood as the train came to a stop and held out his hand. "I'll see you on the other side. Don't worry about me. I'll be quiet as a mouse."

Christiaan clasped his hand, and to Lisa's surprise, Gareth pulled him in for a quick hug. They clapped each other on the back, and then Gareth shook Lisa's hand. "Look after him, okay? I need you both to get me to Gibraltar. I don't speak a word of Spanish."

She chuckled. *Neither do we.*

Gareth slid open the door to their small compartment and slipped out. Lisa heard him open the door to the platform and resisted the urge to peek. It was up to him now, and she didn't want to draw any attention. Instead, she turned back to Christiaan, who looked oddly at ease across from her. "In less than an hour, we'll be in Spain. Don't worry, Gareth will be fine." Christiaan spoke calmly.

As the train slowly pulled out of the station, Lisa prayed the men's optimism didn't prove ill-founded.

The platform at Perpignan station was more crowded than Narbonne's. Lisa was dismayed to see plenty of uniforms among the passengers waiting to board the train to Spain.

"There are even a few German police uniforms," she said to Christiaan, a slight tremble in her voice. "Their uniforms look just like those of the Sicherheitsdienst at home."

"I know, but don't worry about it. We have the correct papers." He tapped the front pocket of his jacket. "We've done this before, remember? Just stick to our cover story. We'll be fine." He leaned forward and gently took her hand in his. Lisa squeezed it, relieving some of her stress.

The doors opened and the sounds of dozens of passengers embarking filled the car. Doors of the compartments around them opened and closed, people speaking in French and Spanish maneuvered through the narrow aisles. A few peeked inside their compartment, but they moved on when they saw there weren't enough free seats for them.

"They're inspecting the outside of the train." A shiver ran down her back as she noticed two French police officers walking along the car. They were followed by a tall man wearing the uniform of the Sicherheitsdienst. The three men were in animated conversation as they passed their window.

"That's odd, isn't it?" Christiaan frowned, his eyes following the men. "They don't seem too worried."

"They're just talking, it seems," Lisa agreed.

"Oh, wait." Christiaan's frown deepened. "They stopped at the end of our car."

Lisa's blood froze. *Have they discovered Gareth?* She didn't move, instead focusing on Christiaan's pained expression. "What can you see?" she asked softly.

He didn't answer, leaning forward to get a better look. Then he sank back into his seat, letting out a low, nervous whistle. "They've moved on. It looks like they were talking to someone."

Lisa felt her blood pressure return to something resembling normal. "What are they doing now?"

"Just walking."

"Not checking the bottom of the cars?"

He shook his head. "Doesn't seem like they're particularly bothered. Do you see anyone else on the other side?"

"No, I think it's just them." A few people approached their compartment, but thankfully walked on. "Looks like everybody has boarded. I hope we start moving soon." Lisa's nerves were frayed, and she considered taking off her sweater but decided against it. *Just focus on your breathing, you'll be fine. We'll be in Spain soon. Keep it together.*

A shrill whistle sounded at the front of the train, and their car doors closed moments later. Lisa couldn't help but exhale audibly. The train pulled out of the station, slowly picking up speed as they rolled out of Perpignan. They left the city behind, and soon the landscape became hillier. Where they had seen plenty of farms up to Perpignan, the area south of the city was arid, with only a few fig trees dotting the landscape flashing by.

"I think Gareth made it," Christiaan said. "Apart from the people boarding, it all seemed pretty quiet back there."

"We'll find out soon enough. The border can't be far, right?"

He shook his head. "It shouldn't be more than forty kilometers to the border. We should reach the first station in Spain within an hour, Weidner said."

"I can't wait," Lisa said, trying to get comfortable, keeping her eyes on the Pyrenees closing in.

They had sat quietly for fifteen minutes when the train slowed to a stop. Lisa frowned; they weren't near a town or city, and they hadn't crossed into Spain yet. *What's going on?*

Her question was answered seconds later when the doors to their car opened. A deep, confident voice called out in French: "Inspection, have your papers ready!"

Lisa's throat went dry. Somehow, as she worried about Gareth, she'd forgotten about their own situation. *Of course there would be an inspection inside the train.* She turned her gaze to Christiaan, who calmly looked back at her. He produced the papers and handed them to her. "We'll be fine, Lisa. These papers are good."

Their compartment was the second from the car's entrance, and she heard muffled voices in the area next door. At first, she only heard the same voice asking questions. Then, to her horror, a different voice. The man spoke German. Her eyes shot to Christiaan, whose confidence looked to have taken a small hit. He was still smiling, but she could see his shoulders tense. To his credit, he quickly recovered, and lowered his voice.

"We can handle his questions as well if we have to. Let's just wait and see. Stick to the story."

Lisa tried to make out what was being said next door. She couldn't, and she resigned herself to having to improvise.

The door to the other compartment closed, and two men appeared in the hallway. Lisa was taken aback to find them both much younger than she'd expected from the voices. In their late twenties, they didn't appear unfriendly. The German was wearing a Sicherheitsdienst uniform. The Frenchman's uniform didn't look anything like the clothes the border guards that had chased her and Christiaan up the mountain a few months ago wore.

The French man opened the door and stepped into their compartment. "Good morning, your papers and tickets, please," he said in French. The Sicherheitsdienst man stood in the doorway, his face passive.

Surprised by his polite manner, Lisa smiled and handed him their documents. He didn't appear to notice her slightly trembling hands. He leafed through the tickets with little interest, focusing on their identity papers instead. His gaze shot between their photos and faces with the trained eye of someone who'd done this a million times before. He handed the papers to the German standing behind him.

Lisa's heart was in her throat when he addressed her. "What's the purpose of your visit to Girona?" His voice was still pleasant, that of someone asking routine questions.

She took a deep breath to steady her nerves and responded in her best French. "My husband has some urgent business matters he needs to attend to in Barcelona, and I'm accompanying him." She nodded at Christiaan, before adding. "The beaches near Girona are much nicer than in the city, so we've found a nice hotel there."

The border guard's eyebrows shot up as she spoke, and Lisa felt her neck burning. *He's not buying it.* She quickly repeated the words in her head; she was certain she hadn't made a mistake.

"Girona's beaches are indeed *fantastique*," the guard said, his eyes narrowing a bit. "And where did you say you're from, again?" He peeked over his shoulder, where the German was studying their papers, not showing any interest in their conversation.

"Geneva," Lisa said with as much confidence as she could muster. "We've lived there for seven years now."

The guard turned his attention to Christiaan. Lisa's palms were sweaty, but she didn't dare wipe them on her skirt. She kept her face neutral as the man's gaze returned to her. He looked at her with a curious expression. "You know, *Madame*, your papers do indicate you're from Geneva, but I'm having trouble believing that."

Lisa struggled to keep her face composed. *He's onto us.* She dug her fingers into the soft leather of her seat, swallowing hard to rid herself of the lump in her throat. "I'm sorry, sir, but what makes you say such a thing?"

At that point, the German interrupted their conversation, pointing at one of the documents as he addressed the border guard in German, "Ask them why they're stopping in Girona."

The guard repeated Lisa's earlier answer, and the German appeared satisfied with it, returning his attention to the papers. The French border guard turned back to Lisa.

"You speak atrocious French for someone who's lived in Geneva for such a long time." His eyes narrowed, and Lisa averted her eyes to the floor, dreading what would happen next. *It was all over.*

"It's a good thing my companion doesn't speak a word of French, though." Lisa's eyes shot back up to find the French man grinning. "I don't know what your real business in Spain is, but I'm pretty sure it's not what you say it is. And I would bet he doesn't speak a word of French, either." The guard's eyes went to Christiaan.

Lisa looked at him open mouthed, while her eyes shot to gauge the response of the German. There was no visible reaction. She blinked hard, unable to speak. The border guard held up his hands. "Don't worry. My job is to keep people of interest from crossing the border and leaving the Reich." He paused and, with a grin, added, "You're of no interest." He turned back to the German. "Are you ready to move on?"

The German looked up and observed Lisa and Christiaan for a few seconds. His eyes bored into her, and she dug her nails a little deeper into the side of the seat that was outside his field of vision. Then he stepped forward and handed the documents back to Lisa, adding, "*Gute Reise nach Spanien*—have a good trip to Spain."

With that, he turned and left the compartment. The French border guard tipped his hat. "Bon voyage, and good luck to both of you." He closed the door, and Lisa felt like she could finally breathe again.

Fifteen minutes later, the train crossed the Spanish border, passing small villages. The buildings were slightly different from those on the other side of the border, and Lisa could feel the change. The low houses were built using a mix of colorful stones, whereas those north of the border used more neutral concrete bricks. Lisa felt the Spanish side looked more traditional.

"You were incredible back there. I'm not sure we would've made it without your French," Christiaan said as they entered the outskirts of a larger city.

"We wouldn't have," Lisa said emphatically. "But we were also lucky with that border guard. If we had run into someone more loyal to the Germans, we would be in a French cell now, awaiting God knows what horrors."

"Maybe it was meant to be."

Lisa was still tense. A sign flashed by. They were entering Figueres, the first city of significance—and the train's first stop—in Spain. This was the moment of truth. "I hope Gareth made it."

"I'm sure he did." Christiaan sounded confident. "They didn't find him in Perpignan, and I didn't see anyone check outside the train when we stopped near the border."

"I hope you're right." After the border guard had left, Lisa and Christiaan looked out for any activity outside the train. There had been none. Despite that, she couldn't help but shake and keep looking out the window. *Maybe something went wrong along the way?*

"Lisa, please stop worrying," Christiaan said, leaning forward. "We'll know soon enough. No sense in torturing yourself over it now. We've done all we could. He'll show up soon enough, and we'll get him to Gibraltar."

The train slowed to a snail's pace, and a few moments later, the platform of Figueres station appeared alongside. The wheels creaked as it came to a stop. Lisa was pleasantly surprised to find the platform crowded. The doors opened, and people jockeyed to get on, the strong pushing and shoving the weaker people aside. This would be a perfect place for Gareth to climb out and blend in.

It took less than five minutes for calm to return to the platform. It was now empty, but for the French border guards who had disembarked. Lisa spotted the man who inspected their compartment smoking a cigarette among two similarly dressed men. The German man stood on his own a few paces away.

The sound of the conductor's whistle indicated that the train was leaving. Lisa looked at Christiaan. *Where's Gareth?* She could see he was starting to worry as well. *Something went wrong.* If they lost Gareth, they would have little chance of making it to England. They needed him.

The train left the station, and they sat in silence as their plan was falling apart. *What will we tell Weidner?* Will we have to return to Geneva? Lisa stared out the window, the landscape flashing in a blur, her vision unfocused as she racked her brain about what went wrong.

She didn't hear the door.

"Hey folks, what's up? Somebody die?" Lisa jumped at the familiar voice. In the door opening stood Gareth in his dirty, dusty jacket.

CHAPTER TEN

Nora fumbled with the straps of her small backpack while she eyed the faces of the other three travelers. Sitting in a small shed, far from the main road, Nora worried about someone wandering past their hideout and finding them. Or worse, that the Germans knew about the shed's function. *What if they're just waiting for us farther down our route?*

"Wasn't Wim supposed to be here by now?" The other woman, Katja, spoke softly, but the strain in her voice was evident. She peered through a crack between two of the planks. "It'll be dark in an hour, if not sooner. He won't risk coming out here in the dark, will he?"

"Or that's exactly what he's waiting for, the cover of dusk and then darkness?" Lars' Rotterdam accent took Nora some getting used to at first, but she'd come to appreciate his assured, no-nonsense approach since meeting him that morning. Whereas Katja and Arthur, the final member of their party, were jittery from the moment they met at Amsterdam Central station, Lars seemed confident about their journey ahead. "Whatever happens, there's nothing we can do about it now. We'll just have to wait for him to show. And if he doesn't, we best get comfortable here. We've got nowhere else to go." Lars opened his bag and produced an apple. He took a bite, then turned to Nora. "Say, while we're waiting, maybe we can get to know each other a little better? What's your story, Nora?"

"Nothing special, really. Just needed to get away from Amsterdam. Too much trouble there," she said, not wanting to reveal too much. It was always better to volunteer as little information as possible. And to know as little as possible about the people you traveled with. *In case things go wrong.* She caught her pessimism and forced a smile. "Yourself?"

Lars returned her smile. "Easy. Didn't want to sign the oath, and I'm not going to work in Germany, that's for sure. I'm not helping those Kraut bastards build bombs that they'll drop on England." He took another bite of his apple and continued, small bits of apple escaping from his mouth. "Figured I might as well make a run for it to the south. Make myself useful in England."

Katja and Arthur both nodded. The Germans had mandated that every Dutch student sign an oath of loyalty to the German occupiers. It meant they would refrain from any act of resistance against the Germans, now or in the future. Only fifteen percent of the Dutch students had taken the oath. The Germans had been swift in their response. All those who didn't sign were to report to be put to work in Germany. It meant most students in the country had either gone into hiding or, like Nora's companions, fled. Most made for England, risking the arduous journey that would take them through Belgium, France, and Spain. Despite the detour, it was less dangerous than the direct route across the North Sea, where German submarines patrolled the waters.

Arthur spoke up, addressing no one in particular. "If we make it to England, what do you want to do?"

It was quiet for a few moments until Katja responded. "Do you think they'd let us join the army? I'd like to join the navy. Really make a difference, you know?"

Lars sat up with interest. "What would you do?"

"Anything, really. I heard they need volunteers on the merchant ships sailing between England and Portugal. Maybe they'll have me on board one of those. I can make myself useful, maybe help out in the kitchen or the communications area?"

"Those are two very different things," Lars remarked with a smirk.

Katja seemed unperturbed. "I'd have to start somewhere, but my German is pretty good, so perhaps I could listen out for German communications, the U-boats and all?"

Lars looked like he wanted to say something else, but Arthur beat him to it. "What about you, Lars?"

"Don't know yet; I haven't thought that far ahead yet. I'll be happy once we make it to Spain and find a boat or plane to England. From what I've heard, there's plenty of work in Britain. If they'll have me, I'd like to join the RAF."

Arthur appeared amused. "Do you have any experience flying?"

"Not really, but I'll learn. And otherwise, I'd make a fine mechanic. Either way, it's something I'll worry about once we get there. For now, we're still stuck here."

Nora looked at her three companions. They really couldn't be more different, but she had a feeling they were going to need each and every one of their qualities in the next few weeks. Toon had made it clear the journey could take anything from a couple of weeks —if they were very lucky—to as much as a year. He told her of a friend who left Amsterdam in the fall of 1941, only to make contact from London a few weeks ago. She swallowed hard. *Hopefully we'll make it there a bit quicker.*

The attention of the other two had turned to Arthur.

"I was studying medicine until a few months ago, so I'd like to continue working in that field in England," he said softly. "Even if I was only in my third year, I'm sure I could make myself useful."

"I think they can use all the hands they can get. They'll be happy to have you," Nora agreed. Between the four of them, Arthur probably had the best chance of getting a visa to Britain. Even though

Hitler's *Luftwaffe* wasn't bombing London as furiously as at the start of the war, they still rained down enough bombs to keep British homeland casualties high. They would welcome Arthur with open arms, of that she was certain.

A quick rap on the door startled them, and Lars almost choked on a piece of apple. Nora felt her heart beat faster as they sat in the semidarkness of the shed. Someone wriggled the door—Nora remembered it jamming a little when they entered—before cautiously opening it.

A tall man with scruffy hair entered the room, the soft light of dusk accentuating his frame. He stepped inside confidently and met each of the four travelers' eyes as the door closed behind him. His eyes settled on Nora, and he spoke in a soft but self-assured voice.

"You must be Nora." He held out his hand. "I'm Wim, and I'm sorry if I kept you waiting. There were rumors of a patrol coming through the main road, so I had to wait a bit longer." He spoke with the soft accent of the south, and Nora found it oddly comforting.

She shook his hand, relieved to meet the man who would secure their passage into Belgium. "We were worried something might've happened to you."

"You best get used to waiting, I'm afraid. Things change all the time, so patience will be necessary." He looked around the room. "You're living in the shadows now."

Nora thought he was being a bit dramatic, but she let it go. "So, when do we leave?"

"Now's as good a time as any," Wim responded, sliding the straps of his backpack from his shoulders and setting it on the floor. He opened it and took out four small packages. "The border is less than two kilometers away, and you can use the cover of darkness and the trees to make it there without being seen." He patted the packages in front of him. "Even in the unfortunate event you get caught, these packages are your way out."

"What's in them?" Lars asked, raising the question that was also on Nora's mind.

"Sausages, a pound of coffee, a bit of chocolate, and cigarettes." When he saw the uncomprehending faces staring back at him, Wim explained. "You're going to smuggle this across the border. That's your cover if you get caught."

Nora saw the genius in the idea. "They'd just send us back, right?"

"That's what usually happens," Wim said, a slight frown betraying that sometimes things didn't go that way. Nora decided not to ask about the alternative outcomes. *We're going to make it across without getting caught.* "You better get moving; you'll still have some daylight for a good hour." He proceeded to give them detailed instructions on their crossing.

"When you get to the cafe in Belgium, look for a man of around fifty, wearing a red beret. You won't be able to miss him. Tell him you've brought the goods from me, and he'll give you shelter for the night. His name is Nicolas, and you can trust him."

Nora followed Lars through the darkening woods. Wim had sent them in the right direction some twenty minutes ago, and Lars had taken the lead to Nora's relief. Wim had told them to follow the small stream next to the hut and to keep going south when it branched off in two directions. Nora wasn't sure which way they should go in the impending darkness, but Lars had confidently decided. Nora didn't protest, and she was glad to see the Rotterdammer had been right when the tree line thinned and they faced an open space.

"This must be the meadow Wim told us to look out for." Lars crouched down and spoke in a whisper while he checked his watch. "Not a bad start, two kilometers in less than half an hour. And in darkness, no less." Nora wasn't entirely sure if he was mocking them, unable to make out his face as he stood in the shadow of the trees. The new moon was setting in the sky ahead, casting a faint glimmer of light on their path ahead.

"So, shall we?" Nora spoke softly, anxious to get to the other side of the meadow. "That's where the border is, isn't it?"

"Yeah, there should be a ditch on the far side. Let's move across the meadow quickly but watch out for the water. You don't want to get your feet wet."

Nora looked over her shoulder and saw Katja and Arthur's heads bob in agreement. *They're anxious to get across as well.* Nora couldn't explain why, but she had a bad feeling about crossing the meadow. "Should we go around?"

Lars looked at her with big eyes. "Why would we do that? It's less than fifty meters across. Let's go." He stood and took a few steps into the open, making the decision for them. Nora reluctantly got up as well when a hand on her shoulder pulled her down and back into the bushes.

"Lars, get back!" Katja hissed in a whisper barely loud enough for the man ahead of her to hear, but he turned around quickly enough, surprise in his eyes. Katja pointed to his right. Lars' eyes followed her hand, and he dropped to the ground in the meadow without another word.

Nora turned her head in the same direction, and her heart skipped a few beats. Only a hundred meters away from them danced the beams of three flashlights. They moved slowly but methodically as if they were searching for something. *Or someone.* Nora pricked up her ears and made out baritone voices speaking softly. *A patrol. Just our luck.*

Her eyes shot to Lars, who lay exposed a few meters away. To his credit, he hadn't moved a muscle since dropping to the ground, and she could only make out the outlines of his body in the darkness, his soft breathing the only evidence of his presence. However, if the patrol moved their flashlights a few meters to the left, it would all be over. Nora silently prayed the men's attention would be focused on the area more in the vicinity of the border.

To Nora's dismay, the man leading the group turned in their direction. They kept their light beams aimed at the area directly in front of them, illuminating their path. With one move, they wouldn't be able to miss Lars in the open.

The patrol continued their course for another twenty or so meters and then stopped. They were now close enough for her to make out some of their conversation. They were German, and they sounded bored. *What are they stopping for?* The sound of her heart pounding in her chest was so loud that she feared they would hear. The distinct click of a lighter being flicked open was almost deafening in the quiet of the night. The men were enjoying a cigarette break less than twenty meters away from them. Nora didn't dare turn her head to check on Katja and Arthur, but she could hear their nervous breathing.

"I don't know why they make us do these patrols," the tallest of the Germans said. "Have you ever heard of anyone catching Jews in this area?"

"It's not just 'bout the Jews, Hansi. There are smugglers active in these parts."

"Smuggling what? These people have nothing," Hansi responded.

"You'd be surprised at how resourceful some of these people are. They might not have a lot, but if you've saved a bit of chocolate, it's worth its price in gold these days."

"Enough to slog through the fields and woods around here and risk a bullet to the head?"

Nora shuddered. Wim hadn't mentioned anything about getting shot.

"It would be a nice distraction; this area is more boring than the end-of-the-world town I grew up in," Hansi said, drawing laughs from the other two men.

The orange lights faded, and the men picked up their flashlights again, quickly scanning the area around them, but not far enough to make out Lars. Yet.

"Okay, I think Hansi's right, though. It's getting dark, and I didn't like the sight of those clouds earlier. I'd like to be back inside before the rain hits." A new voice exuding confidence spoke. *Must be the leader of the group.* "Let's check the little bridge and head back."

Nora's heart jumped at the sight of the men turning in the other direction, the deadly beams of light dancing away until they disappeared. She didn't dare move for another minute, and it wasn't until Lars crawled back to the safety of the bushes that she dared to breathe out loud again.

"Damn, that was close." Lars was shaking, his eyes betraying genuine fear. "Let's wait another fifteen minutes just to be sure, shall we?"

There were no protests from the others.

They didn't run into any more patrols as they traversed the meadow and found the bridge Wim had mentioned. After they crossed it, it took them half an hour to find the road leading to a small Belgian village. The moon provided little illumination, and none of them carried a flashlight. Not that they would consider using it, not after what they heard earlier.

After finding the road, they followed it—their eyes trained for threats in the darkness surrounding them—until they reached Essen, confirming they really were in Belgium.

Nora felt a weight lifted from her shoulders as she followed Lars into the town. He stood taller as they entered the main square, and she was silently glad to have him alongside her on this journey. Despite his foolish bravado in the meadow earlier, he had expertly navigated them across the border in the darkness. She would never have made it here without him.

"I think this is the place," he said as he stopped at a dingy-looking building that had seen better days. The windows were blacked out, but the sign outside said this was *Cafe D'n Manke Bok—The Lame Buck.* It was a fitting name.

"Well, let's go see if Nicolas waited for us," Nora said, opening the door. Inside, the smell of stale beer and cigarettes greeted her. The one room establishment was practically deserted, but for a couple of old-timers nursing half-empty glasses of beer at the bar. They looked at the newcomers without interest. Nora felt a stab of panic as neither of the men wore the red cap that Wim had mentioned. *Nicolas must've left already.*

A door to the right of the bar opened and Nora could have almost screamed with relief. Out came a shoddy-looking man of about fifty, wearing a red cap. He looked at them and without missing a beat said, "Well, it took you long enough. Didn't think you'd make it tonight. Did you bring the goods?"

Nora pointed at her backpack. "Wim sends his regards."

The man opened the door next to the bar again. "Come with me. You must be exhausted. How about we get you something to eat?"

Part Two

LONDON
AUGUST, 1943

CHAPTER ELEVEN

Christiaan's arrival in England was not what he had expected. Gareth had become more restless with every passing minute after the plane took off for its three-hour flight from Gibraltar to England. As it started its descent, he could hardly contain his delight. "Almost home, I'm almost home!" Gareth said, and Christiaan couldn't blame him—he would've been just as excited if he were in Gareth's shoes.

Throughout the flight, Gareth assured Christiaan and Lisa they would be welcomed with open arms. "I wouldn't have made it back home without your help, and I'll make sure my superiors know this."

When they landed at the Whitchurch airfield, just outside Bristol, a small delegation greeted them on the misty tarmac. As soon as the door opened, Gareth jumped out and saluted two of the men wearing RAF uniforms. After that, he embraced one of them, shaking the hand of the other, obviously familiar with them. Christiaan and Lisa followed at a distance, happy to see Gareth back on safe, familiar ground. One of the men motioned for Gareth to follow them, but the young pilot held up his hand and turned back to Christiaan and Lisa.

"I know I've said this many times, but thank you so much. Now that you're in my country, please let me know if there's anything I can do for you." He caught himself and nodded at two men approaching from the small terminal building. "Although I'm not sure of how much use I'll be. Those gents over there seem keen to get me to my squad and back in the air."

"That's what you wanted," Lisa said, returning his smile. "Hopefully they'll clear you to return to the skies soon. From what you told us, they can use every capable pilot up there."

"True, but I wish I could get you started well, find you a place to stay in London, that sort of stuff."

"Don't worry about us, I'm sure we're not the first people to arrive in England without anything to their name," Christiaan said, slapping the young pilot's back. The two men wearing dark raincoats rapidly neared. "Besides, it looks like these men are here for us."

Gareth frowned. "Those chaps look an awful lot like policemen."

"Whatever they are, they're not Nazis, and we're on the same side," Lisa said, sounding confident.

The way the men in raincoats walked made Christiaan feel uneasy, but he decided not to mention it. *We'll find out what they want soon enough.* "I'm sure they're just here to take our details and direct us to the Dutch government," he said. Despite his best efforts to hide his worries, he felt Lisa glancing at him sideways. He focused his attention on Gareth. "All the best, ace, I'm sure you'll be back shooting down Jerries in no time."

Gareth laughed. "You picked up the lingo, Christiaan. I'm impressed. Keep it up and you'll be able to pass as a fine Englishman yourself in a few months." He leaned in for a hug just as the men in raincoats reached them. Gareth ignored them as he spoke to Lisa. "You take good care of your man, okay? Something tells me he's going to need you to save him one of these days."

"I'll try my best," Lisa said with a grin as they hugged.

Gareth gave them a nod of respect, then addressed the men in raincoats who stood by awkwardly. "I trust you'll take good care of my friends? They're the reason I'm back." He walked off without waiting for a response, catching up with the RAF uniforms waiting near a car. They got in and quickly sped away.

Christiaan turned to the men. "I assume you're escorting us to the embassy?"

They looked at him with serious faces, not immediately responding. They were both clean-shaven and of medium build and looked to be in their late thirties. Their raincoats were open, revealing the same dark gray suits underneath. *Government?* Their only distinguishing features were their faces. One round, almost pudgy, while the other's sharp jawline accentuated his harder features.

"Welcome to England. If you would be so kind as to come with us," the man with the round face said. "We're to take you to London, where some of our colleagues would like to hear all about your journey here." The men turned and gestured for them to follow them to the small terminal. Christiaan grabbed Lisa's hand and took a step in their direction.

"Will you take us to the Dutch embassy?" Lisa remained fixed in place on the tarmac.

The men turned around as one, surprised. "All in due time. Please come with us." The man with the hard features took a step toward them, his voice surprisingly soft. "This is all part of the process for foreigners arriving from occupied territories. I apologize for the inconvenience." From his tone, it was clear he wasn't apologizing for anything, and Lisa didn't move.

"Are we suspected of anything? Are you arresting us?"

The man's neutral expression started to crack, impatience and annoyance filtering through. "It's nothing like that, and you are certainly not arrested. But it's wartime, young lady, and we'd like to know who's entering our country and on what pretense. I'm sure you'll check out fine and be on your way to the Dutch embassy in no time. But for now, you're stuck with us, and if you don't mind me saying, it's mighty chilly out here, so I'd like to get inside and to the train station."

Christiaan grimaced at the man's overly polite phrasing. They had no choice but to follow along. He gently pulled on Lisa's hand and spoke softly in Dutch. "Come on, let's go and answer some questions. We're in England, Lisa. We're on the same side. They just don't know it yet."

Lisa looked at him and squeezed his hand before turning to the British police officer, or whatever he was. "All right, let's get this over with."

As they walked off the tarmac toward the small terminal, Christiaan glanced back at the plane. The sun was rising steadily and clearing the mist off the runway and adjoining fields. He took a deep breath of fresh air and exhaled heartily. Despite the frosty reception, he felt energized and optimistic about the future. They'd made it to England. Soon, he'd be able to help in the war effort, of that he was certain.

Christiaan had been stuck in the cramped interrogation room for well over an hour. He was tapping his foot impatiently and was about to knock on the door when it swung open. The man entering was in his early to mid fifties, with an athletic build and an especially prominent nose. His hair was neatly parted to the left, exposing a receding hairline. He took off his jacket and draped it over his chair before sitting down. Christiaan placed his hands on the narrow wooden desk between them as the man addressed him in Dutch.

"According to your papers, you are Christiaan Brouwer of Amsterdam, correct?"

"Yes, sir, I have confirmed this multiple times."

It was the second time Christiaan was in the room with Oresto Pinto, who had introduced himself as an intelligence officer of the Dutch government working alongside MI6. His job was to vet the new arrivals, he had explained. In other words, making sure no German spies entered the country on the pretense of being refugees.

At first, Christiaan agreed it was a reasonable precaution to take. Still, Pinto had turned suspicious halfway through their first interview and told him he needed some time to check some of Christiaan's answers.

Even though Christiaan and Lisa were placed in comfortable surroundings, they weren't allowed to venture beyond the building's small inner courtyard, and after three days, he was starting to get fed up. Especially since Lisa had a completely different experience. Pinto had told her they would prepare housing arrangements for her, and she should make sure she was ready to leave soon. *We didn't come all this way together to get separated at the first hurdle.*

When Christiaan was summoned for another interview that morning, he was hopeful Pinto would only need him to verify a few details. Instead, as Christiaan confirmed his place and date of birth, it appeared the agent wanted to repeat the entire first interview. *He's suspecting me of something, but what?*

"Agent Pinto, if you don't mind, can I ask you something?" The intelligence officer looked up from his file in surprise. "What is it you really want to know from me? I've told you where I was born, where I went to school, which, to be perfectly honest with you, seems pointless at this stage. I've told you about my work for the resistance, and my journey to Geneva and then to Gibraltar and England. What is it you don't like about me? Do you think I'm a German spy? You know I escorted a downed British pilot across Europe, don't you?" Christiaan kept his voice calm and composed, but the palms of his hands were a little sweaty.

Pinto leaned back in his chair, cupping the back of his head with his hands while the edges of his mouth curled up ever so slightly. "Wouldn't you agree, Mr. Brouwer, that the Germans sending one of their own to escort a pilot back to Britain would be the perfect cover? After all, who would suspect someone assisting in such a heroic act?" Pinto clipped his words, and Christiaan couldn't place where he was from. His measured manner suggested he'd been in intelligence well before the war. "Do you know what happens to German spies attempting to infiltrate Britain, Mr. Brouwer?"

There was no mercy for spies. They were responsible for supplying the coordinates for the Luftwaffe's bombing runs, killing hundreds—if not thousands—of innocent British civilians. Christiaan was about to say something, but Pinto held up his hand. "But no, after speaking to your companion, Miss Abrahams, I don't think the Nazis have sent you. I'm not worried about that. I think the problem might be a bit closer to home."

Christiaan frowned. "I'm not sure I follow. If you don't think I'm a spy, then what's the problem?"

"I didn't say you weren't a spy." He opened a manila folder and unsheathed a single piece of paper, sliding it across the table.

Christiaan looked down at his brother's face smiling for the camera at what looked to be a party. The swastika banners in the background were hard to miss, as were the men wearing neatly pressed SS uniforms. Displayed prominently on Floris' chest was the insignia of the NSB.

"That's your brother, Floris Brouwer, correct?"

Christiaan met Pinto's inquiring eyes without flinching. *I have nothing to hide.* "Yes, that's my brother."

"It would've looked better for you if you had mentioned your brother was a Nazi in our first chat," Pinto said in an even voice. "You see, I felt something was off with you when you spoke about your past, like you were leaving something out. That's when I started digging. It's better if you volunteer all information rather than have me find it myself."

The insinuation was clear enough, and Christiaan almost felt like laughing at the absurdity of the situation. Here he was, coming to fight the very people Floris worked with, and they thought he was in cahoots with his Nazi brother. He shook his head and cleared his throat. "Floris is the reason I fled the country, Agent Pinto."

Pinto's eyes sparkled. "I'm listening." He reached for a pencil and turned to a fresh page in his notebook.

"My brother and I were close when we were young. And when I say young, I mean when we were growing up. That started changing when he decided he wanted to become a police officer."

"How so? Nothing wrong with serving your community, is there?"

Christiaan understood the message and quickly shook his head. "No, except when he joined the academy, the Dutch Nazis were gaining popularity among many cadets."

"The NSB, you mean?"

"Yes. We saw him changing when he returned home for the occasional weekend. He spoke about what was happening in Germany and how they were taking care of what he called the problem of the Jews owning all the wealth. He said it was the same across Europe and that we hadn't been paying attention to them taking over everything. He announced he'd joined the NSB."

"And how did you feel about this?"

"I detested the NSB then, as I do now," Christiaan scoffed. "But it was all relatively harmless until the Germans invaded. That's when Floris really changed. He pledged allegiance to the Nazis to keep his job, but that was just a welcome bonus for him. His early membership to the NSB ensured a privileged position in the police force." Christiaan took a sip of the lukewarm water in front of him, and Pinto patiently waited. "When he got the chance to join the Bureau of Jewish Affairs, he pounced. This was when he went off the rails, hunting down Jewish Amsterdam residents for bounties. After that, we stopped talking, and I decided to join the resistance."

"Because of your brother's actions?"

"No, that was a nice addition. I joined the resistance because I wanted to save the community from people like Floris, from the entire organization. I wanted to fight back, to not stand by idly while people were sent to their deaths. Being a messenger, and later delivering food coupons to safe houses made me feel as if I was making a difference. I was saving lives."

Pinto stopped scribbling on his notepad and met Christiaan's eyes. "And then he found out about you?"

"He raided one of the safe houses, arresting Lisa's parents. He was snooping around my home, and I knew it was only a matter of time before he would arrest me. We needed to flee and made for Switzerland." The memory of his brother searching his home and preparing to arrest him made him both sad and angry. How had they grown so far apart so quickly? He wondered how Floris felt about it.

"Switzerland," Pinto repeated, taking him back to his current predicament. "Where you joined the Dutch consulate."

"Yes, and where Mr. Weidner asked us to escort Gareth, the British pilot, to England. And that's how I ended up here." He followed Pinto's furious scribbling and waited for the agent to meet his eyes. "I'm no spy, Mr. Pinto. I'm here because I want to continue fighting the Germans. I want our country to be free again, and I know my best chance at helping with that starts here in London."

Pinto put his pencil down and stood. He brushed a hand through his hair and walked to the small window on the far side of the small room. He stood there for a minute or two, evidently engrossed in his thoughts. The only sound in the room came from the regular tapping of his right foot. Christiaan closed his eyes for a moment and opened them to see Pinto return to his seat. The intelligence officer put his hands on the table, the pencil rolling off the desk and clattering onto the floor.

"Tell me something, Mr. Brouwer. In the past few years, between working for the resistance and making your way across Europe, when was the time you were most afraid to die?"

Christiaan didn't hesitate. "Right now, in this room, to be honest."

Pinto looked taken aback for a moment, then raised an eyebrow. "Why's that?"

"Because if you decide I'm a spy, I know I don't stand a chance in whatever happens next. And that terrifies me, sir, because I've told you everything I can to prove I'm here with the right intentions."

"You know what's interesting, Mr. Brouwer? When I found the file on your brother yesterday, I was almost certain you were a spy, lying to me to get into the country. But something didn't seem right. A German spy arriving in England with a Jewish lover escorting a British pilot?" He shook his head. "No, the Germans would know that would set off alarm bells everywhere. I mean, you couldn't make it up." Christiaan listened silently, and Pinto pointed at Floris' picture on the table between them. "And surely, they would've anticipated that we would start digging into your past and find your NSB brother. That's just too much to believe, isn't it?"

Christiaan felt a flutter of hope in his stomach. "That makes sense."

"But that could also be the plan's brilliance," Pinto said with a grin. "You appear to be so obviously a spy that we would think you can't be."

Christiaan felt his hopes crashing down again. *What?*

"But when I summoned you this morning, I spoke with Miss Abrahams one last time. I told her that I thought you were a spy. Would you like to know what she said?" He didn't wait for an answer. "She said I must be off my rocker. I've never had someone in custody speak to me like that."

Christiaan suppressed a grin. He could picture Lisa calling out the tall man, despite his position. "She can be like that, sir."

"She told me about what you've done for her and her parents. She also told me about your brother's wife and their fractured relationship."

"That's a polite way of saying it, sir. He abused her."

"Lisa also told me you were there for your sister-in-law when she most needed it."

Christiaan flinched at the painful memories, and his thoughts went to Nora. *I hope she's okay.* "She's very dear to me."

"Clearly." Pinto leaned forward, his tone softening somewhat. "After listening to Miss Abrahams and your account of your relationship with your brother, I don't believe you would work with him to undermine the resistance or our efforts from Britain." Christiaan looked up and met the man's gaze. "Mr. Brouwer, I believe you are telling the truth and that you would be a valuable asset to the Allied cause."

Christiaan felt weak and fought back tears of relief. He stared at Pinto's face, looking for a trace of deceit, a final attempt to entrap him. But there was no malice on the older man's face as he offered him the first genuine smile.

Oresto Pinto adjusted his papers and stood, inviting Christiaan to do the same. He grabbed his notebook last and extended his hand. "Welcome to England, Mr. Brouwer. Shall we go and find Miss Abrahams?"

Shaking his hand, Christiaan had never felt so relieved in his life. Then, as they walked to the door, Pinto stopped. "One more question." Christiaan felt his heart skip a beat. It wasn't over yet. "If you could pick any job here, what would it be? Army? Navy, air force, perhaps?"

"If it's all the same to you, sir, I would like to go back and assist the resistance again. But this time, with connections to London."

"Naturally," Pinto said as he reached for the door handle. He looked at him knowingly. "So, you'd like to be an actual spy, then."

CHAPTER TWELVE

Floris trotted back to the main square of the camp. Alongside him were two dozen new recruits, dressed identically in black shorts and white shirts. It was a quarter past eleven in the morning, and they had just finished a grueling ten kilometer run during which Floris and plenty of other recruits found their fitness levels severely lacking. Only the incessant barrage of insults hurled at those who dared to stop and take a breather kept him going.

It was Floris' third day at Sennheim, a Waffen-SS training camp in the east of France, some twenty kilometers from the German border. Not that the border mattered, as France was just as much part of the Reich these days. The journey by train had taken almost a day, and Floris was pleasantly surprised when they entered the camp. Where he had expected drafty barracks and purely functional common areas, Sennheim was located on the grounds of a former nursing home. This meant most of the buildings were rather stately, with the administration building resembling a small castle. While there were some newly built wooden barracks in the back, Floris was pleased to find himself in one of the main buildings with comfortable bedding and running water.

The men assembled in the square, where their training officer informed them they had exactly one hour to change and have lunch. After that, they were given an hour to rest. At first, Floris found this odd, but he had soon learned to take full advantage. The afternoon was filled with military exercises, classrooms lessons, and cleaning duty. The training officer dismissed the men, who hurried to the showers. They would need to jockey for a spot with the other groups returning from their morning exercise.

When Floris finished his shower, he walked to the mess hall on his own. It had taken all his energy to keep up with the activities, and he hadn't made much effort to mingle with the other recruits yet. He had spoken to some on the train, but he soon grew bored of their juvenile interests and unrealistic expectations about life in the Waffen-SS. He'd been surprised to find most of the young men believed they were going on an adventure, one that would pay them handsomely and have them return home as heroes. Floris had no such illusions.

He grabbed a bowl of soup and a hunk of dark rye bread and studied the faces of the men at the tables. He passed tables of men speaking Danish, French, and German. On arrival, Floris' training officer had informed the men Sennheim was set up with the sole purpose of integrating all the Germanic brother nations to the ways of the Waffen-SS. He encouraged them to speak German, and to mix with their brothers from other countries. Predictably, most preferred to band together with their own countrymen, meaning the tables were heavily segregated by nationality. Floris found a free spot at one of the Dutch tables. Nobody noticed him taking his seat as two men on the far end of the table were involved in a heated discussion.

"So, you think you're better than me?" A burly man leaned forward menacingly; the palms of his hands flat on the table. "Just because you chose to come here. At Sennheim, we're all the same."

Floris followed his gaze to the other side of the table. A man, about half the size of the burly one, held a look of barely veiled contempt. "Not at all. I'm wondering how motivated those forced to come here really are."

The man stood up in a flash. "So you *are* saying you're better than me, you scrawny little shit. I'd like to see you on the front lines. I bet you'll be running at the first sign of trouble. I don't think you'd even make it there. You'd find somewhere to hide when the fighting starts."

"I'm here by choice; you didn't have one, did you? What did you do to get sent here? I bet you're only here to avoid prison." Floris' ears perked up at the accusation, and he paused to gauge the other man's reaction. Before the man could say anything, someone intervened.

"Come on now, boys, we're all the same here. It doesn't matter how we got here; we're brothers now."

"Screw that brotherhood bullshit. Save your SS doctrine for someone else. I'm here to serve my time and stay alive," the larger one spat, pointing at the man across from him. "He can pretend to believe in the Reich, but we'll see when we face the Red Army. See how that protects you from their bullets."

Floris found himself shocked and angered by the man's insolence. He checked the room for training officers. There were none.

The smaller man shook his head in disgust but didn't respond, ending the argument. The others returned their attention to their soup. Then, after a minute, conversations started around the table, and the man next to Floris turned to him.

"You arrived on the train from Amsterdam a few days ago, didn't you?"

The man didn't look familiar. "I did. I'm sorry, did we meet on the train?"

"No, I've been here for two weeks, but it's easy to pick out the new faces. My name is Anton." The man held out his hand, and Floris shook it, introducing himself. "How did you end up here, Floris? That was an interesting discussion just now, wasn't it?"

"Sure," Floris said, quickly taking another bite before answering.

He decided he wasn't going to tell this stranger the truth. "I volunteered. I want to do my bit."

Anton looked pleased. "Nice. Me too." He lowered his voice a little. "Most men aren't necessarily here for the right reasons, though." His eyes went to the burly man who had spoken earlier. Floris followed his gaze and studied the man while he ate. It was difficult to pinpoint what made him stand out, but over the years Floris had developed an additional sense to spot potential troublemakers. The man looked up from his bowl and caught Floris staring at him. His nostrils flared and his face darkened.

"What are you looking at? You got something to say?" His deep voice silenced the rest of the table. "You're new, aren't you? How did you end up here, then?" All eyes were on Floris, who gently put his spoon down.

"I applied."

The man scowled at him. "Oh, so what, you're looking for an adventure like this clown?" He glanced at the man across the table, who ignored him. "Or you're here for the money? An Iron Cross?"

"Not at all," Floris said, forcing himself to speak calmly. He looked around the table, trying to read the faces of the men looking at him. "I'm here because we need a strong Reich." He saw a few men agreeing but also took in plenty of hostile glances.

"Oh, you're one of those," the man said. "Let me guess; you're NSB?"

Floris nodded. "Is that going to be a problem?" The table was deathly quiet by now, and Floris fixed his eyes on the burly man.

The man held his gaze for a moment, then shrugged and broke the stare. "I suppose not. Just don't look at me like that again." He returned his attention to his soup.

Floris looked around the table, where some stares lingered on him a bit longer. Then, ignoring them, he took his soup bowl and drained its contents. Anton did the same as he stood and followed him to the tray return, where they handed in their spoons and bowls.

"I'm NSB as well," Anton said with no small amount of pride in his voice. Rotterdam."

"Amsterdam myself. Glad to hear it. What about the other men? I saw some of them looking at me."

Anton shook his head. "There's a few, but most of the men are only here for the money, or they're like that piece of shit you challenged. Criminals."

"Well, Anton, then I'm glad we've met. We should stick together. Heil Hitler."

"Heil Hitler. Say, Floris, how about we grab a drink in town after dinner? I can tell you all the things you need to know about this place."

"Sounds like a plan." Floris couldn't wait to have a drink.

The center of Sennheim was nicer than Floris had expected. He'd found an outside table at a tavern in the village square. Anton was trying to get the attention of the young waitress attempting to keep up with the clientele on the crowded terrace. Most of the other tables were occupied by those wearing the uniforms of the SS training school. A mix of different languages filled the square, the recruits enjoying a glass of wine or beer as the sun disappeared behind the houses. Anton finally caught the attention of the waitress and ordered two beers. Floris' mouth watered; he hadn't had a drink since his capture in Amsterdam.

"So, tell me about your life back home." Anton turned his attention to Floris. "What made you decide to sign up for this?"

Floris frowned. "What do you mean? I want to be here." He could hear the reluctance in his voice as he spoke the words.

"Okay, I'll play along." Anton leaned back in his chair. "You know what, I'll go first, and then you decide whether you want to tell me your story. Because I don't believe you joined just because of your beliefs."

"Why not?" Floris said hesitantly.

"Because nobody signs up for the front line willingly and out of the goodness of their heart." Anton looked at him knowingly. "Nobody wants to die on the eastern front just because they support the Reich, or Hitler. Not even the Germans. Not that much, anyway. You'll find out soon enough."

"So why did you sign up? Money?" *Is he just like those men back in the barracks, after all?* Floris eyed the man sitting across from him and found it hard to believe he was here just for the pay or the glory.

"No, not just the money, although it helps. You need to know one thing about the men at Sennheim, Floris. They all have good reasons for being here." He nodded at a group a few tables away. "Those boys, they're from Antwerp. I spoke to them the other day, and they signed up because their situations at home had become so difficult that they needed to get out of the country."

"Nazi supporters?"

"They discovered some safe houses along the escape lines, sheltering Jews and such. So they informed the Gestapo, who promptly raided the places and picked up, according to what those boys said, half the Antwerp resistance."

"That's great," Floris mumbled, looking at the men with admiration. He knew the challenges.

"Oh, of course, it's great," Anton said, pausing as the waitress set down two large mugs of beer. He raised his mug in salute. "*Proost*—Cheers." Floris took a large swig, the alcohol instantly relaxing him. Anton set the mug down and continued, "But the other half of the resistance found out about what they did. So, they had to go into hiding, much like the Jew pigs they had uncovered."

"Didn't the Gestapo help them?"

"Sure did, eventually. Told them they could get them out of the city, out of the country."

"To Sennheim," Floris said as he took another sip. Anton nodded, and Floris looked at the Flemish men with a newfound sense of camaraderie. He scanned the men at the other tables and wondered how many more were here for the very same reason. He looked at Anton. "Is that also why you're here? Did you upset the wrong people back home?"

"No, nothing quite that spectacular, I'm afraid. Back home, I worked at the docks. I was fortunate that I kept my job even when much of the docks were destroyed by the German air strikes." Floris nodded. During the invasion of the German forces, the Luftwaffe had hit targets across the country; Rotterdam had been hit particularly bad. "But it wasn't until the Americans hit the shipyard in March that I was told I no longer had a job. I suppose I was lucky to have one for as long as I did. I can't remember how many times I had to scramble to a bomb shelter in the past two years." For the first time, Anton looked shaken, and he quickly took a large swig of his beer.

"And that's when you signed up for the Waffen-SS?"

"Pretty much. I tried getting other jobs, but it was impossible. Everywhere I went, hundreds of men lined up for a few positions. Then, one day, an SS recruiter showed up at one of our NSB meetings, looking for people to join the SS. At first, I didn't realize it was the Waffen-SS, but it soon became clear when they handed me my contract." He shrugged. "Things at home were getting desperate, with my wife threatening to leave me if I couldn't provide for our family, so this seemed like a good opportunity to get away from her, make some money, and fight for the good cause." He looked into the distance for a few seconds, his lips resting on the rim of his beer mug. "So, that's my story. Tell me how you ended up here."

Floris considered telling Anton the truth. He was an NSB brother, and his heart seemed to be in the right place. Before he could open his mouth, a group of men headed straight for their table. Floris looked at their faces and recognized the burly man from lunch. His glassy eyes were focused on Floris for as much as they still could. Floris placed his hands flat on the table. Anton turned his head, following Floris' gaze. His shoulders tensed as he set his mug on the table.

"Look who we have here. The righteous ones!" the burly man

said, drawing laughter from the half-dozen men accompanying him. Heads at nearby tables turned. Even though most of the men sitting at the other tables weren't Dutch, the newcomer's threatening tone and stance were impossible to miss. The murmur of voices died down. Floris felt his pulse quicken, adrenaline shooting through his veins.

The large man sat next to Anton, leaning forward toward Floris. "You thought you were pretty smart at lunch, didn't you? You signed up because you wanted to, isn't that what you said? All high and mighty." The other men crowded around the table, three of them behind Floris.

Floris looked to Anton, who put up a calm face, but determination burned in his eyes. *He'll have my back if this goes wrong.* Despite that, the odds were stacked against them if it came to a fight. They weren't going to hold off seven men between the two of them. He decided he wouldn't let the man bait him into doing something reckless. "Didn't you sign up for the same reason? You seem like a reasonable man."

The man seemed thrown off by Floris' response, looking at him with confusion. Then his beady eyes narrowed, and a smirk displaying crooked teeth appeared. "Sure, let's go with that. I'm here because I want to be." Then, in a move that surprised everyone, he slammed his fist onto the table, tipping over Floris' half-full mug, its contents spilling over the side. Floris quickly moved back but was too late, most of the beer landed in his lap. The men crowded around the table laughed, mocking him. A jolt of anger shot through Floris' body as he balled his hands into fists and turned to lash out at one of the men behind him. He controlled himself at the last moment as the burly man spoke up again.

"I'm only here because of some bullshit police work back home," he spat, his eyes narrowing further, and Floris felt a chill running down his spine. *This isn't a chance encounter.* The man must've spotted the look in Floris' eyes as he nodded. "That's right. Some asshole policeman thought I had helped the resistance back home.

As if I would do such a thing. But it didn't matter, for it got me a one-way ticket to the Gestapo basement. They told me I could die like a dog or try my luck on the battlefield. Said they needed fresh flesh for the eastern meat grinder."

The tables around them had gone quiet, the language barrier doing nothing to hide the tension from the bystanders. The burly man stood and pointed a finger at Floris. "So, imagine my surprise to hear that you are a copper yourself. And one that was working with the Nazis as well." *How did he find out about this?* "What happened to you? Can't imagine you really signed up voluntarily. Not if you knew what this place is really about. I bet you're as crooked as me."

Floris looked around. All eyes were on them now, and some of the men at the other tables had moved closer. They looked on with interest, some grinning, excited to see what would happen next. Floris sized up his opponent. The man was drunk, or at least tipsy. He stood unevenly, supporting himself by holding onto the table with one hand. Floris looked to Anton, who had moved slightly, making room between the burly man and himself. *I can take the bastard. But what will happen once his friends join the fight?* He looked around and realized he had few options. *Perhaps the others will intervene.* Either way, he knew walking away wasn't a possibility: he would look weak, if they would even let him walk off. There was only one way to end this.

"What do you want from me, an apology?" Floris said, standing purposefully and moving away from the table.

"No," the man said with a remarkably clear voice. "I want you to admit the truth. Tell the rest of the men here that you're here because you screwed up at home, and you're just as much a failure as me." He moved toward Floris and jabbed his finger at his chest. "Stop pretending you're better than us."

Something inside Floris snapped as he swatted the man's finger away. After that, things moved very quickly. The man looked at him with glee, then threw a clumsy punch. Floris easily dodged it and connected a fist to the side of the man's face. The man's expression changed to surprise, then fury, as he launched himself at Floris. An instant later, Floris landed on the ground, the much heavier man now on top of him, knocking the wind from his lungs. In the background, excited voices shouted encouragement. Floris focused on the man on top of him, his mind drawing up memories of that night in the garden of the crèche. *Never again.* Mustering all his strength, he arched his back and pushed himself from the ground. It caught his opponent off guard, and they rolled on the terrace. This time, however, Floris was on top. He didn't hesitate and launched a flurry of punches at the man below. The punches connected, blood pouring down the opponent's nose, confidence draining from the man's eyes. Floris pulled back his right arm, preparing for the knockout blow, when strong hands grabbed his wrist, jerking him off the bloodied mess of the man underneath him. He tried to break free, wishing to lash out at the men dragging him away when he heard the piercing whistles around him.

"Stop resisting! This fight is over—you're only making it worse!" an authoritative voice yelled at him. He turned to find it came from a man wearing a uniform. His heart sank when he saw that uniform and those of the two men pulling him away from the town square. Military police.

I'm in real trouble now.

CHAPTER THIRTEEN

Christiaan checked his watch as he stood waiting on the corner. He looked up at the clouds hanging menacingly overhead. In the two weeks he'd been in London, he knew the wailing sirens of the air raid alarm always preceded the most significant danger from the skies. Besides, it was uncommon for the Germans to carry out daytime bombings. The first time he'd heard the siren was in the middle of the night. He and Lisa had scrambled to the basement of Mrs. Green's home. He had been surprised to see their host saunter down almost carelessly, telling them the basement only offered marginally better security.

"If a bomb hits the house, we're all goners. No need to rush," she had said with genuine indifference.

Somehow, their host's fatalistic attitude had calmed their nerves. She was right, after all. Their room in Mrs. Green's Victorian house was basic but very comfortable. Lisa loved sitting in the front room, looking out into the street through the high bay windows. Mrs. Green had lost her husband in the Great War, and she loved fussing over Christiaan and Lisa. She had been especially interested in their stories of the resistance in Amsterdam. Christiaan was certain they were fortunate to have been placed in her home, and it was a perfect opportunity to practice his English.

After Oresto Pinto cleared him they had been moved to Mrs. Green's house. Lisa and Christiaan had been told someone would soon be in touch about their assignments. Lisa was contacted two days later, and she now worked as a typist at the *Bureau Inlichtingen*, the Dutch government's intelligence agency. Even though she wasn't allowed to speak about the details of her job, she shared enough for him to know she was working with the messages coming in from across Europe. He was proud of her, but he was also frustrated that he hadn't heard from anyone yet. *It has been two weeks. Have they forgotten about me?* With every passing day, Christiaan worried more that his journey to London might've been for nothing.

"Ready to go?"

He looked up to find Lisa in front of him. She was wearing a light blue summer dress with a matching hat. She was beautiful, and Christiaan smiled as she leaned in for a kiss. "You are ravishing," he said.

Lisa beamed and gave him an appraising look. "You're not too shabby yourself, Mr. Brouwer. But it's not every day you get to meet Queen Wilhelmina now, is it?" She moved closer and they locked arms. "Let's get going, we don't want to be late."

"We have plenty of time," Christiaan said as they crossed the street. "Where did you get that dress?"

"Someone in the office loaned it to me. She said the queen loves blue."

"That's nice of her. Anything interesting happen at work today?" He glanced at Lisa and saw a twinkle in her eyes.

"Many, many things. But you know I can't tell you anything about that." She gave him a small poke, then her face turned serious. "Don't worry, I'm sure you'll hear from them soon. I can tell you that they need every able person to assist in the war effort on this side of the pond. Unfortunately, not too many people like us make it through to England, you know?"

"They're still having trouble getting them visas?"

"Well, the Brits are focused on getting their pilots and soldiers back home, and then they'll consider other nationalities. And then there are the many Jewish refugees trying to make it here. But that's not the worst of it. The Spanish and Portuguese are stopping people at the border."

"How so?" Christiaan recalled how easy it had been for them to get into Spain.

"Most people arriving in Spain don't have the right papers. So when they're caught, they're taken to concentration camps or prisons."

Christiaan stopped. "What? Spanish concentration camps?"

"Yes. But not like those in Germany. Although the conditions aren't great there, either. Once they end up there, the Madrid consulate reaches out to get them to Portugal and then England."

"And I suppose the Portuguese aren't helping much?"

Lisa shook her head. "No, they'll only give them a visa to enter if Spain gives them permission to leave. And neither country will start the process without the document from the other country."

"So those people are caught in bureaucratic limbo."

"Afraid so. Even though they're neutral countries on paper, neither Franco nor de Oliveira Salazar are willing to risk upsetting Hitler by providing a safe passageway to refugees." She squeezed his hand. "Don't worry. You'll have a job soon enough."

They walked on, the wind picking up as they neared the river Thames and Chelsea Bridge. Christiaan took a deep breath as they stepped onto the bridge, looking over the river. Waterways in cities always made him feel at ease, and the river Thames was no different. Of course, it was quite different from the narrow canals of Amsterdam, but it calmed him nonetheless. *Lisa's right. They need all hands on deck. They just didn't get 'round to processing me yet.*

They reached the middle of the bridge, and he felt it gently swaying underneath his feet.

"What do you think she's like?" he asked.

"The queen? Well, from what I've heard at the office, she takes much interest in the people visiting her. It's made me a bit nervous, to be honest."

"I feel the same," Christiaan said. "But at least you'll be able to tell her all about the work you're doing at the Bureau Inlichtingen."

"I'm sure she'll be more interested in your resistance work back home. Prince Bernhard and she are especially keen to hear about the fight back home."

"They told you that, too?" Christiaan felt a swell of pride.

"For sure. So, you better get your best stories ready. I'm certain we'll only have a few minutes with her, if that."

They reached the other side of the bridge and continued north. The consulate should be a short five-minute walk away, and Christiaan felt a nervous sensation welling up in his stomach. *I'm going to meet the queen.*

They passed a long queue stretching around a corner. Christiaan was surprised to find it populated with children and teenagers no older than fourteen, fifteen maybe. Some of the younger ones were accompanied by their grandparents. "I wonder what they're lining up for," he said casually to Lisa as they walked down the line.

"Must be something rather valuable. And fun, considering their ages. Can you imagine kids back home queuing up this well? If this was Amsterdam, I'm sure they'd be fighting to get in."

They turned the corner and saw a sign outside a store: "Comics and boy's papers here today only!"

"Well, that explains it. I'd wait in line for that myself if I were their age."

"Not much fun to be had these days. This is almost as valuable as food for these kids. I hope they'll all get something," Lisa said, looking at the children, their faces filled with anticipation. A strong man stood at the store door, expertly managing the flow of the queue: one child out, another in. There was no pushing or shoving, as it was clear from the man's stern expression that this would result in eviction from the line. Christiaan was impressed as he eyed some of the comic books in the store window.

"Come, let's keep moving, or we'll be late," Lisa said, tugging on Christiaan's sleeve.

"Don't worry, it's just up the street from here," he said confidently.

"Hey, what are you two doing here?" A voice boomed behind them. Christiaan turned back to the queue to find a muscular man leaning on a cane looking at them. His eyes were burning with indignation, a snarl on his face as he hobbled toward them. "What are you bloody Krauts doing in London? You have some nerve, prancing around here with your filthy language." He spat on the ground. Heads turned in the queue, and another man shuffled closer.

"Is that right? Krauts, in London? Bloody hell. You better have a good reason for being here," the other man said.

Christiaan looked at them in horror, not immediately sure he understood them correctly. He looked at Lisa, who took a step back. *Germans? Are they mad?* Then he understood and regained his composure. He responded in his best English. "We're not German. We're Dutch."

The man looked unconvinced. "Sounded German to me, all right." Some of the boys in the queue slipped closer.

Christiaan shook his head. "No, no. We fled the mainland a few weeks ago. She's Jewish, and the Nazis were after us at home." He pointed at Lisa, who straightened her back.

"Prove it, then." The man stepped toward them, his face growing more menacing. He looked ready to throw a punch.

Christiaan looked around; there were no friendly faces here. If the man decided they were German, it could turn into a lynching. "Okay, one moment, let me grab my papers." With trembling hands, he reached into his jacket pocket. *This is ridiculous, I've done nothing wrong.* The man's steely eyes remained fixed on him as he took out the papers and held them up to the man. *I'm not handing those over.*

The man leaned forward and inspected the papers, squinting as he did. His eyes went between the photograph on the papers and his face, and Christiaan forced himself to hold the man's stare. Then the man looked away. "Fine, I suppose you're not German, then."

The energy around them changed instantly as people understood they weren't the enemy. Christiaan suppressed a sigh of relief. *No lynching today, then.* He turned away, replacing his papers in his pocket. Lisa gripped his hand tighter.

"Not so fast." The man wasn't placated. "If you're in your twenties, why are you strolling the streets today? You should be fighting the Krauts."

"If you're not fighting them, you have no place here," the other man chimed in. He looked pleased with himself. The boys in the queue had grown bored of the argument, their attention returning to the gentleman manning the front of the queue instead.

Christiaan felt a flash of anger as he looked at the two men. *Who the hell do they think they are?* He took a step back, letting go of Lisa's hand in his haste to confront the men. "You think I don't want to fight? You think I want to walk around the streets of London without purpose?" He felt his face flush as he continued, the expressions on the men's faces changing from gleeful to surprise. "I'm ready to fight; I need to be assigned. The only thing I want to do is fight the Nazis!"

"Okay, okay, settle down, lad," the man with the cane said. "We thought you was German—"

"No, I won't settle down!" Christiaan interrupted. "You have no idea what it's like having to flee your home country." He pointed at Lisa. "If they'd found her, she would be dead now. We are not the enemy." He glared at the men, whose earlier cockiness had completely disappeared. Christiaan was breathing hard when he felt a soft touch on his shoulder.

"Come, Chris. We should get going. She's waiting for us." Lisa looked at him with affection. "Don't waste more time on them. They're not worth it."

Christiaan turned back to find the men had already scurried off, rejoining the queue.

Located on a quiet street, in unassuming building, Queen Wilhelmina's offices at 77 Chester Square weren't quite as grand as Christiaan had expected. They were welcomed and escorted to the parlor in the back with little ceremony. There they found six people already anxiously waiting for her Majesty. All were refugees, dressed in the best clothes they could find. Christiaan was pleased to see Lisa was the best-dressed lady in the room, the other two women struggling to contain their thinly veiled envious glances.

They sat around for five minutes, some people making quiet chitchat, but most of them were eyeing the door every few seconds. When it finally opened, they all rose to their feet, only to be disappointed by a man wearing a plain gray suit.

"Her Majesty will join you shortly; she has urgent matters to attend to first. I apologize for the slight delay," he said, his voice indicating he was anything but sorry. "Please make yourselves comfortable." He disappeared as quickly as he came, softly closing the door.

Christiaan felt Lisa's eyes on him. "You shouldn't get so worked up about people on the streets, Chris. They're just scared and angry. They don't know the difference between German and Dutch."

"I know, I know. It's just not right. They have no idea what we went through to get here."

"Exactly." She grabbed his hand. "They don't know. But their city has been bombed to smithereens. They've lost loved ones. Put yourself in their position. You'd be fuming as well, looking for someone to blame. We were just in the wrong place at the wrong time."

The man sitting next to them overheard. "Did you have someone yell at you? Say you were German? Don't take it personally. Happens all the time. I've had it twice this week alone, and I've been here for over a month. If I can give you one piece of advice: walk away. And learn to speak proper English. That helps."

He was about to say more when the door swung open, the same man with the gray suit now holding it. He gestured for them to stand and announced in a loud voice, "Her Royal Majesty, Queen Wilhelmina."

Christiaan felt his heart beating in his throat as he kept his eyes focused on the door. Moments later, the queen walked in, and Christiaan first noticed her lack of official attire. Instead, she wore a long blue skirt with a sober white blouse and a light blue jacket. There was no sign of the jewelry he'd seen in the pictures of her in the newspapers. There was only a silver brooch on her jacket's pocket. Despite her modest attire, her presence instantly changed the atmosphere in the room, her aura radiating royalty, as did the broad smile she flashed as she made eye contact with her guests.

"Good afternoon, and welcome to Chester Square," she said as she moved toward them. "Please sit down and let me pour you a cup of tea. You must be thirsty, having had to wait a bit longer than expected."

Christiaan awkwardly remained standing, as did the other people. *Wasn't the queen supposed to sit first?* And did he hear that correctly? *Is she going to serve us tea?*

Wilhelmina sensed their unease. "Come on, sit down." She turned away to a side table with two large porcelain teapots. The man in the gray suit gave them an impatient nod, indicating they really could sit down.

The queen carefully poured tea into delicate cups on saucers, handing them to her guests. From their faces, Christiaan could see they were all equally surprised to have their monarch serving them tea.

Wilhelmina poured the final cup, her own, and sat down among them. Christiaan pinched himself. It was surreal to be in London, sitting in a small circle with the queen. She took a measured sip, placed the cup down, folded her hands on her lap, and cleared her throat. Everybody had already put their cups down.

"Firstly, I want to thank you all for coming. I know your journeys to England have been long and filled with uncertainty. You decided to leave home and come here, to help fight the Germans. For that, I am most grateful." The queen purposefully made eye contact with them all, and Christiaan thought he saw a twinkle of excitement. "As *Engelandvaarders,* England sailors, you now have a duty to serve in our navy, air force, or army."

She picked up her cup and took another sip, letting the words sink in. Christiaan looked at the other people in the room. They looked at Queen Wilhelmina with awe. *They came here for the same reason as I did.* He met Lisa's eyes, and he was surprised to see them glisten. *This means just as much to her.*

"Before you set off for your duty, I'd like to speak to everyone. It has been a long time since I've set foot in our homeland, and even though we have a decent intelligence network, I'd like to hear about the situation firsthand from all of you." She pointed to a table in the corner and nodded at Lisa. "If you would join me there, please."

Lisa looked startled to be picked first but quickly recovered as she stood. "Yes, your Majesty." She followed Wilhelmina to the table while two women entered the room carrying trays with small sandwiches and an assortment of cakes. Christiaan couldn't remember when he'd seen such a delectable spread of food, and his mouth watered. The women set the trays down on the table in front of them. The others at the table seemed unsure until the gray-coated man said, "Please, take something to eat. The queen will call for you when she's ready." They all dug in, and soon they were softly chatting. Christiaan kept his eyes on Lisa and the queen, who appeared to be having a very engaging chat. At one point, he saw Wilhelmina put a hand on Lisa's wrist.

After about ten minutes, a beaming Lisa returned. "She wants to see you, Chris."

"How is she?" Christiaan asked as he stood, his legs a little wobbly.

"She's lovely and very well-informed. Go, don't keep her waiting."

Christiaan took a deep breath and turned to walk to the queen's table. He felt queasy as he thought of things to tell the queen. *If I only have five minutes, I need to make them count and not make a wrong impression.*

He reached her table, surprised to see Wilhelmina rising from her chair. "Mr. Brouwer, I've been inside all day. Would you mind if we walked and talked in the garden? It appears to be quite nice outside."

"Of course, your Majesty," he said, slightly bowing.

They reached the back doors, where the man in the gray suit opened them. Breathing in the fresh air, Christiaan instantly felt better as they entered the garden. It was larger than he'd expected, resembling more of a courtyard than the traditional English back garden he was accustomed to from Mrs. Green's home. The queen caught his look. "When I'm in the city, I don't get to go out much, so I like to stretch my legs here when I can."

"It's lovely, your Majesty," Christiaan managed as they left the house behind them, heading farther into the garden. It was in full bloom, with magnolias, zinnias, and daisies vying for attention.

"Mr. Brouwer, let me get straight to the point. I've heard of your journey, and I'm most impressed. Making your way across Europe, not once but twice, to ensure someone else's safety is a level of selflessness and courage I've not often come across. And I've met quite a few people with impressive stories."

"Thank you, your Majesty. I just did what I considered right."

"Not so modest, Mr. Brouwer. I was also told you were involved in the resistance in Amsterdam?"

"Yes, ma'am."

"Tell me some more about that." Her keen eyes studied him as they strolled along the wall separating them from the street.

"I did what a lot of other people did. Hide people, ensure they're fed and safe, and try to keep them from the grasp of the Germans."

"And your brother."

Christiaan turned to the queen with a look of surprise. She gave him a knowing look. "I like to know whom I'm meeting. I know all about your brother. That must've been hard, turning against your own blood."

He pondered her question for a few seconds, then shook his head. "If I can be honest with you, I don't regret the decision. He betrayed his country and willingly sent fellow Dutch men and women to their deaths. He would've handed me over to the Germans if given half a chance. I feel no loyalty to my brother anymore." As he spoke the words, he felt his throat constrict. Even though he'd thought about Floris many times, cursing him for what he'd done to Lisa's parents, Nora, and himself, he'd never spoken those words out loud.

The queen seemed to sense the weight of the words, for she acknowledged them with a nod. They walked in silence for a minute, and then she continued. "I asked you to come outside with me because I wanted to make sure we were completely alone when I make my next request." She stopped and turned to him. They were in the back of the garden, and Christiaan suppressed his surprise.

"Ma'am?"

"You must be wondering why it has taken so long for you to be assigned a job," she started, and Christiaan nodded. "Well, it is because you've been selected for a mission that is very dear to my, and my husband's, heart. We believe the resistance in the Netherlands is the key to freeing our country."

Christiaan looked at the queen and waited in silence, as the weight of the sentence hung in the air. "Your Majesty, I agree, but can I speak freely?"

"It's just the two of us here. Speak your mind."

"When I left Amsterdam more than eight months ago, the Germans and the corrupt Dutch police were getting stronger. They managed to infiltrate a number of resistance organizations, and I saw many of my brothers and sisters get caught." He paused, unsure whether he should continue with the pessimistic view he was sharing with the queen, but her eyes urged him on. "I fear this has only gotten worse since I left. The Germans are a mighty adversary, even without the help of Dutch informers."

Wilhelmina slowly started walking back toward the house, her face pensive. She took calculated steps while she scratched her nose. Christiaan followed half a pace behind her, now worried he had upset the regent. She turned toward him. "I appreciate what you're saying, but that is exactly why we need you." Christiaan was taken aback, and it must have shown, for Wilhelmina gave him a warm, reassuring smile. "You still know people in the resistance, right?"

Nora's and Bet van Beeren's faces flashed through his mind. *They're the reason I'm here.* "Yes, as far as I know, my sister-in-law is still there, and another friend I trust with my life."

"Very well. They can get you back in touch with whoever is in charge now, wouldn't you say?" The queen didn't wait for an answer. "The fact is, Christiaan, that only with a united resistance will we be able to free our country. We need our countrymen and women back home ready to fight when we push to liberate ourselves from the Nazis." Christiaan felt the hairs on his arms stand up.

"What is it you ask of me, your Majesty?"

Wilhelmina stopped, turned to him, and—to Christiaan's shock—took both of his hands. Her grip was firmer than expected. "I need you to go back home and unite our resistance. Rekindle your relationships with your friends in Amsterdam." Her eyes shone with passion.

Christiaan was overwhelmed as he considered the queen's request. In that interrogation room with Oresto Pinto, he had asked to make a big difference in the fight against the Germans. Going back to Amsterdam would give him that opportunity. He would see Nora again, and together they would carry out this mission. But his heart felt heavy at the thought of leaving Lisa behind, and the dangers lurking back home. If his brother found out about his return, he wouldn't rest until he found him.

"I realize this is a big decision, but I would appreciate an answer from you, Mr. Brouwer." The queen's voice interrupted his thoughts, her bright eyes studying him inquisitively.

Christiaan glanced back toward the large windows of the house, where he could see Lisa chatting amiably with the two other women. She was smiling, in her element. He then returned his gaze to Queen Wilhelmina, thinking her nickname Mother of the People couldn't be more apt. He inclined his head. There was only one thing he could say. "I would be honored to accept this mission, your Majesty."

CHAPTER FOURTEEN

The atmosphere at the table was electric as Nicolas scooped ladles of soup into their bowls. Lars didn't wait for the rest to receive theirs as he slurped the first spoonful.

"Didn't your mother teach you to wait for everyone to be served?" Katja said, but Lars ignored her. She rolled her eyes at Nora, who shrugged. She was too excited about Nicolas' earlier news. He had received word from Brussels that they had space in one of the safe houses. The previous occupants had secured papers to travel south, which meant it was now ready to receive Nora and her companions.

It had been an anxious few days as they spent most of their time in Nicolas' basement, staying out of sight during the day, not coming up until Nicolas closed the blackout curtains. She took her bowl from Nicolas gratefully. Nora had been slightly concerned when she met him at the cafe, but his gruff exterior was all show. As soon as they reached his house, he transformed into the perfect host, ensuring they were as comfortable as they could be in his basement. He had kept them fed and relatively warm, all while risking his life. Men like him were worth their weight in gold.

When Nicolas finished distributing all the bowls, Nora raised her glass of water in salute, and even Lars paused eating. "I don't think we've properly thanked you for your hospitality yet. We're grateful for what you've done for us these past few days."

Nicolas gracefully inclined and shook his head. "I'd like to believe you would do the same for me if the roles were reversed. I'm happy you're moving on tomorrow. I'll feel much better knowing you've safely made it to Brussels. They'll arrange papers for you there, and then you should have no trouble making it through France." He set down his glass and picked up his spoon. "Now, eat, before it gets cold."

They ate in silence for a few minutes, Nora enjoying the warmth of the soup. She wasn't particularly looking forward to another night in the chilly basement, but Nicolas' blankets kept them warm enough.

"Remember, walk to the safe house when you get to Brussels. Don't take public transport, for the Germans do spot checks all around the city. Don't walk around in a group. Keep your eyes peeled for checkpoints."

Lars grunted something about being used to this, and Nora gave him a reproachful look. "Thank you, Nicolas. I'll feel a lot better when we have our identity papers."

"Don't worry. The train between Antwerp and Brussels is of little interest to the Germans. You'll be fine." The older man leaned forward, elbows on the table. "But stay vigilant and keep an eye on the platforms of the stations you're passing. The Belgian conductors are easily identifiable and won't ask any questions as long as you have your train ticket. But if you spot a German patrol boarding, get off the train."

Nora shivered at the thought. This wasn't the first time Nicolas mentioned the remote possibility of German patrols on the train. The idea had haunted her for the past few nights, as this would be the only train ride where they would be without any form of identification. She'd spoken to the others about it, and they all agreed it was a risk they'd need to take.

"Plenty of others have taken this train before, right?" Lars said, pushing his empty bowl away. "We'll be fine." His usually confident voice cracked slightly, betraying a trace of nerves.

"Just stay alert, that's all." Nicolas stood, cleared their bowls, and placed them in the sink. In the same movement, he opened a cupboard and took out a bottle and five small glasses. Returning to the table, he placed them down with a thud. "This has become a bit of a tradition, a fond farewell, I suppose." He poured them a shot each.

Nora sniffed her glass but couldn't identify the clear liquid. "What is it?"

"Just something I distilled myself," Nicolas said with a cheeky grin. "It's a bit like your Dutch *jenever.*" He raised his glass, and they did the same. "To a safe onward journey. May you go to England and give those Krauts hell!"

They downed their shots in one go, and even though Nora wasn't a big fan of hard liquor, she enjoyed the sensation of the homemade alcohol burning its way down her throat.

"You better get some sleep," Nicolas said. "You have a long journey ahead of you tomorrow."

They stood and each said their goodbyes to their new friend. Nora waited for the others, and when it was her turn, she hugged the Belgian.

"Thanks again for everything, Nicolas. I hope we'll see each other when all of this is over. You should come visit me in Amsterdam."

Nicolas looked back at her with a wistful expression, a slight tear in his eyes that he quickly blinked away. "I would love that very much, Nora. And remember, when you leave tomorrow morning, use the tunnel I showed you."

"We will. Take care." She was the last to disappear down the basement steps and looked back up one more time to see the Belgian's friendly face before he closed and locked the door.

Nora had already packed her bag that afternoon and left it on her mattress in the corner. While she waited for the others, she moved to the cabinet on the far side of the basement. A solid oak piece that Nicolas' grandfather had crafted—the wood had aged beautifully, making every line and crease unique.

When she'd asked why it was stashed away in the basement, Nicolas replied it had always been there, and served a purpose. Moving the clothes to the side, he'd shown her the hidden door in the back, revealing a narrow tunnel.

"We've used this tunnel ever since the house was built. When my country rebelled against the Dutch in the early 1800s, my grandparents worried about the violence against Belgian Catholics by Dutch Protestants. They had heard stories of people getting dragged out of their houses at night." Nicolas had looked thoughtful. "Much like what's happening today, I suppose. My grandfather decided to build a small tunnel, hiding it behind this cabinet so they would always have a way out."

"And did they ever use it?"

"No. It's never been used for its original purpose. I used to hide in there when I was growing up, when I was unhappy with my parents, and I wanted to be left alone. They would leave me be, pretend that they didn't know about my hiding spot."

"Are you nervous about using it?" Nora was startled to find Katja behind her.

"Not really. It's only fifty meters." Nora saw the concern on Katja's face and closed the cabinet. "Don't worry about it; we'll be at the train station before you know it. Besides, the other people passing through the house also used the tunnel, and they made it out just fine."

"If you say so. I get nervous in narrow spaces."

Nora changed the subject, stepping away from the cabinet. "Have you ever been to Brussels?" She sat down on her mattress, and Katja did the same, shaking her head.

"I've never been outside the country. The farthest I've been is

Valkenburg, which is quite close to Belgium. My parents would take us to the coast most of the time. We'd rent a small house near the dunes for a couple of weeks, and my brother and I would bike to the beach daily." Her eyes were glassy, as if she was reliving the happy days of yesteryear.

"That sounds lovely." Nora's childhood had been nothing like that. Her parents had left her at a crèche as a baby, and her life had been filled with struggle ever since. She bit her lip and put her hand on Katja's. "You should treasure those memories."

"What about you? You must've been in Belgium before."

"I spent most of my life in Amsterdam. Hardly got out of the city, really." She shook her head and stole a glance at Lars and Arthur, who were getting ready for bed. "The trick is to make it look like you know what you're doing."

"A bit like Lars?" There was mischief in Katja's eyes.

"Maybe slightly less brash, but yes, a bit like Lars," Nora said, relieved to see Katja smiling. "I'm going to turn in."

Nora bid the two men good night and was asleep as soon as her head touched the pillow.

Nora woke up with a start. The room was dark, and the only thing she heard was the soft, rhythmic breathing of Katja on the mattress next to her. She sat up and perked her ears. Lars readjusted himself in his sleep and let out a deep sigh. Nora thought she saw the flimsy curtains near the small window move a little, letting in a sliver of moonlight. She shook her head; it was just a draft. She was reluctantly putting her head back down when she heard the unmistakable sound of rustling grass by the window above her head. *There's someone in the garden.*

She held her breath as she lay still in her bed, not daring to move, keeping her eyes on the window. Fear gripped her throat as she considered who would be out stalking about the house at this time.

Nicolas. I need to warn him.

Before Nora could rise, there was a tremendous crash upstairs. The others woke up with a start, Lars leapt to his feet. There were quick footsteps in the upstairs hallway, a voice calling out for Nicolas to make himself known. *I'm too late.* Katja sat upright on her mattress. Nora was close enough to see the whites of her eyes.

"What's going on?" Katja whispered.

"It's a raid." Nora spoke in a hushed voice, calculating their options. "We need to get out of here."

"And just leave him here?" Lars stood next to them, his voice a little too loud.

"Keep your voice down!" Nora hissed at him. Upstairs, whoever had come in had now made it to the kitchen, located directly above their heads. Voices filtered through, but not Nicolas'. She turned to the others—her eyes had adjusted to the darkness, and she could make out their faces—and whispered, "What if Nicolas has made it out? We should get out as well."

"We don't know that," Lars said. "He might still be hiding somewhere. I say we wait and help him if something happens."

Nora looked at Arthur and Katja. Surprisingly, she saw Arthur nodding. "Let's wait. It feels wrong to run away and abandon the man that's kept us safe."

Katja looked torn but eventually said, "I'll do whatever you decide, Nora."

Nora shifted her eyes between Katja and Lars, her fingertips tingling. She wanted to help Nicolas but worried about what they would find behind the basement door. To her dismay, Lars moved to the stairs, Arthur in tow. *They're serious about this.*

Reluctantly, she caught up with them before they reached the first steps. "Lars, let's wait a few minutes and listen to what's happening up there. We don't know if there's more of them outside." The memory of Floris' escape from the resistance safe house made her shiver. She would never forget Peter's lifeless eyes staring up at the ceiling. "And they're probably armed." *Unlike us.*

Her last words made Lars pause for a moment. He looked to Arthur, who suddenly seemed less confident. They stood at the foot of the stairs, the three of them listening closely. Katja was still on the mattress, her eyes fixed on the door atop the stairs.

It was quiet for a minute or two, and for a moment, Nora thought the men might've left through the back door without them realizing it. But then one of them spoke again, indicating they should check upstairs. From the footsteps, it was clear there were only two of them. Lars looked back at her.

"We can take them," he whispered, and put his foot on the first step. "We can surprise them when they come back down. It doesn't matter if they have Nicolas or not. We have to assume they'll also check the basement."

Lars looked confident, and Nora had to admit his reasoning was solid. The men would search the entire house, and the door to the basement was hidden in plain sight. There was no doubt they would come down here. There was nowhere to hide in the open space. Their only chance of an ambush was from behind the basement door. She looked back to the cabinet. "But we can still leave now."

"I won't abandon Nicolas, and neither will Arthur," Lars said, determination etched on his face.

Nora was surprised to see the men agreeing. She'd completely missed their bonding these past few days. Then she felt the presence of Katja behind her and chuckled. *Much like me and Katja.*

As the men ahead of her ascended the stairs, she looked to Katja. "Are you okay with this?"

Katja had opened her mouth to answer when two earsplitting explosions shook the house's foundation. Lars and Arthur almost tumbled down the stairs but managed to grab onto the railing just in time. Pieces of plaster and dust fell from the ceiling, and for a moment, Nora feared the house would collapse. It didn't, but seconds later, the unmistakable sound of gunfire erupted upstairs.

Lars and Arthur stood frozen on the steps. The gunfire stopped, and the same voices they'd heard earlier shouted at Nicolas to surrender. Nicolas must've booby-trapped the stairs, but somehow the men had avoided the brunt of the force. Now he was stuck upstairs, fighting off men with guns. She turned to Lars and Arthur.

"There's nothing we can do for him anymore! We can't fight men with guns," she said, hardening her voice as she realized that abandoning Nicolas had become unavoidable. "There will be more Germans swarming the house soon." Lars and Arthur looked shell-shocked, her words not registering as they stared at her with hollow eyes. She raised her voice, despite the danger of the men upstairs hearing her. "We have to go. Now!"

Lars snapped out of his stupor. He looked at Nora and nodded, grabbing Arthur's shoulders and maneuvering him down the stairs. Katja was already at the cabinet, holding her backpack. She opened the doors, feverishly pulling clothes onto the floor. Nora quickly grabbed her bag and looked on approvingly. It didn't matter anymore; the Germans would find the tunnel soon. They needed to get as far away from the house as possible. She reached the cabinet, where Katja had opened the back compartment, exposing the tunnel.

"You go first; we'll be right behind you," Nora said, handing a flashlight to Katja. To her surprise, Katja didn't protest and instead quickly crawled in. She shone her flashlight ahead, exposing the sandy tunnel. Nora turned to find the two men waiting impatiently behind her. Arthur went first, but Lars paused at the entrance. He looked at Nora with a seriousness she hadn't seen on him before.

"We might not know what happens to Nicolas, but I would be dead now if it weren't for you. Thank you." Nora could only nod as he entered the tunnel. She stood alone in the basement and realized it had become deathly quiet upstairs. She prayed Nicolas would find a way out. As she climbed through the tunnel's entrance, Katja's beam of light dancing farther ahead, she whispered a soft farewell to the man upstairs. "We will never forget your sacrifice."

CHAPTER FIFTEEN

Floris stepped out of the mess hall and took a deep breath. One of the things he appreciated most about his new surroundings was the feeling of being close to nature. Marching through the French countryside, with its rolling hills and thick birch tree forests, he'd come to appreciate the rural surroundings.

Anton appeared by his side. "Some of us are going to play a game of football. Care to join?" His friend was another reason Floris felt more at home in Sennheim; since his fight in the town square, they had become close. The man had his back, which was crucial for someone he'd most likely be spending time in the trenches with.

"I'd love to, but I have to report to Officer Degen."

Anton's face soured. "Is this about the fight again? I thought you'd handled that last time."

"I did." The morning after the fight his training officer had summoned him. Degen had been surprisingly interested in hearing his side of the story, but he made it clear Floris' behavior was grounds for dismissal from the Waffen-SS. In Floris' case, that meant getting sent home to the Netherlands, where he would be required to appear in court for his past transgressions of stealing from the Reich. He would end up in a concentration camp. Floris had gone pale at the mention of this scenario. He'd made it clear he was provoked. When Degen said there had been more complaints about the man, Floris felt a flutter of hope. His training officer then said that other recruits corroborated Floris' version of events, and that he would not be sent home. Before letting Floris leave his office, he emphasized this should serve as a stern warning.

"I'll catch up with you later." Floris spoke casually but in truth he couldn't feel his feet. The past two weeks of training had gone well, and he felt himself growing. He was comfortable with the long early morning runs now, easily keeping up with the front of the group, and he especially enjoyed shooting practice. He was very capable handling an MP40, scoring especially high marks in the exercise where they were required to quickly disassemble, clean, and reassemble the gun. Keeping his gun clean and functional could mean the difference between life and death on the battlefield, and he spent many free hours practicing in his barracks. He wondered what the training officer would want as he stepped inside the castle serving as administration building.

A young man with the rank of *Junker*, officer aspirant, sat behind a desk, greeting him with a slightly condescending look. "Yes?"

"*Soldat* Brouwer to see *Untersturmführer* Degen, sir," he said confidently, ignoring the man's rude behavior. Ever since interacting with the arrogant Germans in the Amsterdam branches of the Sicherheitsdienst and Grüne Polizei, Floris had learned it was better to go along with their sense of superiority.

The man scanned a piece of paper on his desk, his finger moving down the names in the first column. "Ah yes, Brouwer. Did you say you were meeting Degen?" He looked up with a frown.

"Yes, he's my training officer."

"Well, something must've changed, because, according to this, you're meeting with *Hauptsturmführer* Sacher instead. Follow me." The man got up from his chair and headed toward the stairs at the end of the hallway. He didn't look back as he climbed the stairs, and Floris silently followed him. His heart pounded in his chest. When Degen told him to report to the officers' building after lunch, he expected to meet his own training officer. For Hauptsturmführer Sacher to be involved, something else must be going on. *Is it about the fight after all?* As they reached the top of the stairs, Floris felt a trickle of sweat roll down his back. *This can't be good.*

"Wait here," the young officer-in-training said as he pointed at a small stool in the hallway. He walked ahead and knocked on an unassuming door down the hall. He entered and then closed the door, leaving Floris alone in the quiet hallway.

Floris' thoughts drifted back to the fight. That was almost a week ago now, and he couldn't imagine someone as high up as Sacher would care about that. He considered the past few days; he'd kept his head down, fully focused on staying on his training officer's good side. He shook his head. He couldn't think of any good reason why he was sitting here. *If they decide I'm to return home, I'll find a way to make it work. It's a long journey home, a lot can happen between here and Amsterdam.*

"He'll see you now." The Junker's voice down the hall took Floris from his thoughts. Floris stood and quickly crossed the distance to where the man was holding the door.

"Thank you," he said to the young man as he entered a spacious office.

"Soldat Brouwer, have a seat," came the booming voice from the tall man behind an ornate desk on the far side of the room. Floris felt very conspicuous as he made his way to the chair opposite Hauptsturmführer Sacher. The large windows behind the desk let in a generous amount of light, making the space look bigger than it actually was. A large Nazi Party flag was draped prominently on the right wall, a framed photo of the führer on the opposite wall. Underneath it hung multiple photos of military men in uniform posing at various rallies. Floris was certain the man he was about to speak to was featured in many of them. He waited for Sacher to sit first, then sat, his knees feeling like jelly.

Hauptsturmführer Sacher leaned back in his chair, his eyes studying Floris, without a word. Floris moved in his chair and folded his hands on his lap.

"You appear nervous, Brouwer. Tell me why." Sacher spoke German, like all officers in Sennheim. Floris had witnessed several recruits struggling to understand the commands, and he was pleased he had invested in learning German early on.

"Sir, to be honest with you, I'm a little unsure why I'm here," Floris said.

"How so?"

"I was under the assumption I would be meeting with Untersturmführer Degen, sir."

Sacher pursed his lips. "Is that so? Well, you were misinformed, then." Floris held his tongue. "You were involved in a bit of a fracas earlier this week, weren't you?"

Shit, so it is about the fight. I knew it. "Yes, sir. There was a misunderstanding. I did speak to Untersturmführer Degen about it."

Sacher looked impatient, his brow furrowed. "Yes, yes, Degen told me all about that. But when he told me about you, some of the details caught my interest."

"Sir?"

"He told me why you got into this fight—the other man questioned your loyalty to the party, to our führer. Is that correct?"

Floris raised an eyebrow in surprise. "Well, I suppose so, yes. We disagreed on why we were here, in Sennheim, sir."

"How so?" Floris was unable to read the expression on Sacher's passive face. *What is he getting at?*

"He accused me of only being here to escape a prison sentence, sir." Floris felt his cheeks burn as he spoke the words but forced himself to retain eye contact with the Hauptsturmführer, who picked up a file from his desk.

"But isn't that exactly why you're here?" He tapped the file. "You were dismissed from the Amsterdam police force, and that's when you opted to join the Waffen-SS. I don't have all the details, but I can put the pieces together. You're not that unique."

Floris' cheeks burned deeper but from indignation. In a controlled voice, he responded, "Sir, I made a mistake in the police force, for which I lost my job. But when the option to join the Waffen-SS came along, I grabbed it with both hands, for I truly believe in the Reich. Yes, I would indeed have gone to prison had I not come here, but that doesn't mean I won't do whatever is needed to serve our great leader from my new position." Before he realized what he had done, he stood and shot out his right arm. "Heil Hitler!" He quickly sat back down. "Apologies, sir."

Sacher looked at him with an amused expression, eyes twinkling. He rubbed his chin before speaking. "When I said I didn't have all the details, I wasn't being totally honest, Brouwer. That little outburst of yours just now seemed genuine. It was what I expected, what I hoped for. From what I've heard from the people witnessing the fight in the town square, you snapped when he compared you to a common criminal." Floris listened, not knowing what else to add. "And this is what makes it interesting. Do you know what happened to that man?"

"I haven't seen him at Sennheim since, sir."

"That's because he was sent home. Or, well, not home, but to serve his prison sentence. But you probably came to that conclusion yourself." He paused and, when Floris nodded, flashed his teeth. "In the Waffen-SS we care about certain values. Degen fought to keep you. Is it true you were one of the top Jew hunters in Amsterdam?"

A burst of adrenaline shot through Floris' veins. *He wants to know about the Bureau?* "Well, my team was responsible for almost a third of the arrests in the first year, sir."

"Interesting. And did you volunteer for this position, as you did for your current one?"

The remark caught Floris off guard. "I'm not sure I understand, sir."

"It seems mighty convenient to join a division that focuses on tracking down Jews when that's one of the best ways to move up the ladder."

Floris fervently shook his head. "Sir, I was a member of the Dutch Nazi Party well before the Netherlands was incorporated into the Reich. Joining the Bureau of Jewish Affairs was completely aligned with my values."

"And what are those?"

"To carry out the cleansing of our society and rid it of unwanted elements." He felt his pulse racing thinking back to his days at the Bureau. "The Jews have oppressed us for long enough. That is why I joined the Bureau, sir."

Sacher kept his gaze on Floris for a few seconds, then stood abruptly and turned to the window behind him. Floris remained seated, twiddling his thumbs, unsure of what was expected of him. *Did I answer his question correctly? What does he want to hear from me?*

"It wasn't just your past that convinced me to keep you here." Sacher turned and returned his attention to Floris. "You're one of the top marksmen in your unit, even after your short time here. Degen says he's never seen a recruit work an MP40 the way you do. Come, let me show you something." He moved to a large table in the corner that Floris hadn't noticed on the way in. A large map of Europe was held in place by heavy paperweights. The map was populated with small markers strewn across Europe. They were marked with numbers, and Floris quickly realized they were divisions of the Wehrmacht and Waffen-SS. The areas bordering the Soviet Union were densely populated, with many divisions stationed across eastern Poland and Ukraine.

"It's impressive, isn't it?" Sacher said, not without a hint of pride in his voice. "Those green markers are all Waffen-SS. Your brothers, pushing the Bolshevik devils back every day."

Floris nodded. His training officers had been keen to share stories of the Waffen-SS' success in the east. Most of them had fought the Russians themselves and spoke about their time on the front lines nostalgically.

"You'll soon have the opportunity to make the difference, Brouwer," the Hauptsturmführer said, pointing at one of the green markers. It was labeled "Wiking" and was positioned near a city called Charkov in the Ukrainian area of the Soviet Union. "You've heard about the Battle of Charkov, haven't you?"

"Of course, sir." They had been taught all about the strategies employed by the Wehrmacht and Waffen-SS in the recapture of Charkov earlier that year. The German army's disciplined flanking of the Red Army meant they celebrated a comprehensive victory. His training officer had made it clear this was what was expected of them in the future. "It was glorious, wasn't it?"

"It was." Sacher's face turned serious as he gestured at several markers pointing south, toward Italy. "But when the Allies landed on Sicily last month, many of our men were diverted there. It means we must reinforce our eastern divisions with capable men. Men like you, Brouwer."

Floris studied the markers on the map. He imagined losing the armies heading south was a significant blow to the eastern battle lines. *No wonder they're keen to get us out there.* His eyes fixed on the Wiking marker again. "Sir, are you saying I'll be deployed to the eastern front?" He felt his stomach churn. *I've only been in training for a little over two weeks.*

"Yes. You and the rest of the recruits will join up with the divisions on the eastern front. You'll be part of SS Panzer-Division Wiking, where you'll join Regiment Westland."

Suddenly everything fell into place. SS Regiment Westland was made up exclusively of Dutch volunteers like Floris. He would be fighting alongside his countrymen, alongside well-trained and supremely equipped Aryan brothers from Belgium, Denmark and, of course Germany.

"You'll soon be fighting the Bolshevik Jews of Russia, Brouwer. How do you feel about that?"

Floris scanned the map one last time, his eyes lingering on the Wiking marker. *My brothers are waiting for me.* He looked back up and met Sacher's eyes. He cleared his throat, then spoke with a voice tense from anticipation: "When do I leave, sir?"

CHAPTER SIXTEEN

Christiaan sat hunched against the side of the cold and dark fuselage. The wind howled outside as the Whitley aircraft tore through the night sky, its engines roaring at full power as they cleared the clouds. He looked to his left, where he could make out the face of Jackson, an affable Canadian paratrooper he'd met around the training base. Opposite sat a man who hadn't introduced himself and looked entirely at ease, minding his own business as he played with his lighter, flicking the top open and closed without actually lighting it. Unfortunately, it was too dark to identify the faces of the other eight men packed into the back of the narrow airplane.

Even though Lisa had been excited for him, she'd asked questions he didn't have the answers to. Now, almost two weeks later, sitting in the back of an airplane, he had to concede he was no more the wiser about his exact mission. The only thing he knew was that he needed to jump out of this airplane in a few minutes.

On boarding, Christiaan noticed he was the only one not wearing full paratrooper's gear. Instead, he wore a flight suit and a reinforced gear backpack strapped to his stomach. He checked to find it secured properly; he knew his landing needed to be perfect, so as not to damage its contents. If he botched the landing, his mission would be for nothing.

The aircraft steadied, the twin engines' roar subsided to a more gentle humming. The wind still tore at the aircraft's tail and wings, resulting in occasional bumps. Christiaan shifted his eyes to the back of the plane, where the small hatch would soon open, and they would be instructed to jump. He swallowed but comforted himself that this was not his first jump. He'd jumped out of the Whitley more than a dozen times in the first week of training, and then stopped counting. Yet, the anticipation remained the same, and it was enough to get his heartbeat up quite a few notches.

The metallic voice of the pilot boomed through a speaker. "Approaching target. Get ready to jump, lads. Good luck." Seconds later, the aft hatch opened, the cold air rushing in, immediately sharpening Christiaan's senses. The men got up and stood in their crouched positions, clicking their static lines to the steel cable running along the roof of the airplane. The static line would ensure their parachutes would open shortly after the jump. Christiaan was fourth in line, and when the signal to jump was given, he would be out of the airplane in a matter of seconds. He took a deep breath as he stood only meters away from the hatch, an occasional cloud rushing by below the only break in the vast darkness outside.

A crackle on the speaker preceded what all men knew was next. The pilot's voice. "Over drop zone. Go! Go! Go!"

Without delay, the first man ahead of Christiaan disappeared into the darkness. The two others ahead of him stepped forward, and one jumped with a triumphant roar. Christiaan felt the pressure of the six men behind him as he was pushed forward automatically. He tapped the shoulder of the man in front of him, confirming he was there, and the man flung himself into the night sky. Christiaan stood at the hatch, the sky tearing at his feet. He felt a lump in his throat, adrenaline pushing up his heart rate. *So this is what it's all about.* The tap on his shoulder signaled it was time. He closed his eyes and jumped, the icy night sky rushing up at him, the sound of the plane's engines quickly fading as he soared back down to earth.

The light of dawn came through the clouds above as Christiaan packed up his parachute. The field he landed in was damp with morning dew, but his thick boots and leather gloves kept him warm and dry. The temperature on the ground was certainly better than up in the sky, and the first rays of sunshine warmed his face. He spotted Jackson a hundred meters away and waved. Somehow, the Canadian had already finished packing his parachute and made his way over.

"It was proper chilly up there tonight, wasn't it?" he said, grabbing one side of Christiaan's parachute and helping him fold it. It was the one thing Christiaan struggled with during training, and he was grateful for Jackson's help.

"Was it? Hardly noticed. I was too busy keeping this bloody backpack in position," Christiaan said, pointing at the heavy pack a few meters away. It was covered in mud.

Jackson raised an eyebrow as they stuffed the remainder of the parachute in its pack. Then his eyes focused on Christiaan, whose flight suit was just as muddy as the backpack. "Did you have a tough landing?"

Christiaan shrugged. "Barely managed to avoid that little waterway there. Had to pull up at the very last minute."

"You know, if they send you back home, you'll have plenty of little waterways to look out for." He grinned. "This was perfect practice!"

"I suppose so. You think they planned it this way?"

The Canadian slapped his back. "Naw, that's giving too much credit to the planners." His face turned serious as he picked up and handed Christiaan his backpack. “But seriously, did you check your merchandise? They won’t care as much about a muddy flight suit as they do about what’s in here.”

“Let’s see.” Christiaan opened the bag and took out a container the size of a small briefcase. He opened it up and smiled. “They’re all good.” He showed the box to Jackson. It contained ten eggs, all perfectly lined up in the little box.

“That’s the second time you managed that, isn’t it?” The Canadian observed as Christiaan closed the box and replaced it in his backpack.

“Third time, actually. They’ll be well pleased back at the base.”

“Speaking of which, let’s get to our rendezvous. I could do with some grub.”

It took them fifteen minutes to reach the road, where an army truck was waiting. They were among the first to get to the rendezvous and handed cups of coffee, which they heartily slurped away. One by one, the other jumpers reported, and soon they were on their way back to base. It was an hour’s drive back to Royal Air Force Base Ringham, where Christiaan had been stationed for the past two weeks, and a few men nodded off.

Christiaan found it impossible to sleep while keeping a firm grip on the backpack on his lap. Successfully landing with his fragile cargo intact for the third time in a row meant he completed the final test of his paratrooper course. It would allow him to return to London and await further instructions. He was now ready to start his mission.

They passed the outskirts of Manchester and Ringham soon came into view. He was looking forward to leaving the northern city and returning to London, and not just because he missed Lisa. There had been little opportunity to get off base and explore the city. While most of the pilots and paratroopers stationed at Ringham had plenty of time to go off base, Christiaan was the exception. He was enrolled in a special program where time was of the essence. After basic theoretical training the first two days, he jumped from planes twice, sometimes three times a day.

The truck pulled up in front of one of the training buildings, and the men disembarked for their debriefing. A junior staff officer stood waiting at the entrance, signaling at Christiaan. "Brouwer, follow me, please."

"Guess you've got your own debrief again, huh?" Jackson grinned. "Come find me when you're done, okay? I have a feeling you might not be hanging around here much longer."

"Me neither, Jackson." They shook hands and went in different directions. Christiaan followed the staff officer inside the building. The man hurried through the corridors, almost flying up the stairs to the second floor. Christiaan struggled to keep up with him in his baggy flight suit. He only paused when he reached an open door halfway down the hallway. "In here, please, Mr. Brouwer; they're waiting for you."

They? Christiaan frowned, used to going through his debrief with squadron leader Murphy. He entered the room to find two other men sitting beside Murphy, who pointed at a single chair opposite. "Take a seat, Brouwer." His voice was overly formal, which was unlike Murphy. Nevertheless, Christiaan had built up a good rapport with the man overseeing his training. *Something's up.*

Christiaan sat and noticed the men flanking Murphy didn't wear RAF uniforms. They were dressed eerily like the men who greeted him on his arrival in England at Whitchurch, now almost a month ago. *More questions? More complications?* The hairs on the back of his neck rose.

Murphy was quick to notice his unease and held up the palms of his hands. "These men are MI6, Christiaan. They're here today to receive a status update on all their linked assets." He nodded at him reassuringly. "One of which is you, of course."

"Yes, sir," Christiaan answered, still unconvinced about the newcomers. He eyed them, and one of them gave him a curt nod. The other's face remained impassive, as he studied Christiaan's muddy flight suit.

"We went through your training progress, and I informed them that you've passed nearly all the tests required to become a field operative." Murphy glanced at the backpack Christiaan had placed next to his chair. "How did today's jump go?"

"Quite well, sir." Christiaan picked up the backpack, produced the small box containing the eggs and placed it on the table. "Why don't you have a look."

Murphy carefully pulled the box toward him while explaining to the MI6 men, "Master Brouwer's final test consisted of jumping from 10,000 feet with that backpack and landing softly enough to keep the eggs inside intact. If he can keep these eggs from breaking, we're comfortable sending him off into enemy territory with more valuable cargo."

"Such as transmission equipment," one of the men said. "Well, let's see it, then." He leaned forward, genuinely interested.

Murphy opened the box and immediately his eyes shot to Christiaan. For a moment, Christiaan's heart was in his throat. He could not make out the expression in the squadron leader's eyes. *Did some of the eggs break on the ride over? I was so careful.* His head suddenly felt very heavy and warm.

"Are there supposed to be ten eggs?" The MI6 man asked. Christiaan's temples throbbed.

Murphy nodded. "Yes, just like this. Well done, Brouwer. Three jumps in a row, that's impressive."

Christiaan's shoulders sagged with relief as he spotted the cheeky grin on Murphy's face. *Bloody British humor.* "Thank you, sir."

The other MI6 man spoke for the first time. "Well, Mr. Brouwer, you're ready to go back to London, then."

"The mission is ready?"

The man held up his hand. "Well, I didn't say that, and frankly, it's not up to me. All I know is that a lot of things are in motion, and your superiors at Dutch intelligence are keen to have you back." He turned to his companion. “How many more meetings do we have here at Ringham today?”

“Just the one.”

“Splendid.” He turned back to Christiaan. “Better pack your bags. We have a spot for you in the car back to London.”

CHAPTER SEVENTEEN

Lisa rushed to her spot in the typists' room at Bureau Inlichtingen, the Dutch intelligence agency. The other four women were busy at work, the clacking noises of their typewriters echoing through the room. Lisa caught a look through the window from her supervisor in the other room, and she made an apologetic gesture. He answered with a frown and a shake of the head, and she took off her light coat and hung it over the back of her chair before sitting down. *Not the best start to the day.*

"You all right, Lisa?" The young woman opposite looked over her typewriter, her large brown eyes filled with concern. "It's not like you to be late and come rushing in like this. I can't remember being here before you."

Lisa sighed but put up a brave face. "I'm fine. Just had trouble getting out of the house, Femke. Christiaan came home late last night and had a lot to share about his training up north."

"That's exciting! Has he finished training already? That's pretty quick, isn't it? He's only been away for a week or two?"

Lisa had been surprised when Christiaan appeared home. He said he'd be away for a month when he left. They'd spent the night talking about his training at Ringham, with Lisa especially captivated by his stories of parachute training. She couldn't imagine jumping out of an airplane, let alone doing it in the dark of night. She was proud, but reality was setting in. When they went to bed, she found sleep hard to come by. Now that he was fully trained, he would soon be placed in the field. To carry out a mission. Queen Wilhelmina's message had been crystal clear; Christiaan would return home to operate behind enemy lines. As he slept soundly beside her, it dawned on her that she'd have to live with the uncertainty of not knowing how he was doing.

She loaded a sheet of paper into her typewriter, ensuring it was properly aligned. Her eyes darted across the room, and she thought of the messages she and the other women processed every day. Besides a stream of messages coming from consulates across Europe and North America, there were messages from agents operating back home. It was always obvious when one of those arrived, for their supervisor would come into the room and request for the message to be processed with priority. When that happened, it didn't take long for the other women to find out what was in the message. The rules forbid them from sharing the contents coming across their desks, but it was a silly rule. The women in the typists' room knew everything.

Nevertheless, it was the one thing that gave Lisa some hope that when Christiaan did leave, she would be able to read his incoming messages. She might even be allowed to send something herself. She shook her head at the thought. *They're not going to waste valuable transmission time for me to check up on him.*

"Lisa."

She hadn't heard her supervisor enter and turned to him with a startled expression. His eyes went between the pile of handwritten notes to her left and the empty page waiting in her typewriter. *He's going to tell me off for being late and not having done anything yet.* Lisa quickly grabbed the sheet of paper atop the pile. "I'm sorry, I'll get these done before the morning's over."

He shook his head and produced another sheet he was holding

behind his back. "Please work on this one first. It just came in, and Somer will want this ready for his meeting with the Brits at noon. It's just a short message, but I want it to look neat."

Lisa took the paper and scanned the hastily scribbled words. That meant it was most likely a message from one of the agents across the North Sea. With the Germans operating radio trucks in their search to pinpoint transmissions, these messages were sent under extreme time pressure. It resulted in radio operators scrambling to decipher the agents' updates in a single transmission, with little room for error. It was up to Lisa and the women in the typists' room to make sense of the letters and make them presentable to the higher-ups. Chief of the Bureau, Colonel Somer, preferred to receive easy to read messages in English so he could share them with his British counterparts at the Special Operations Executive, the SOE. The Dutch and British agencies worked closely together in all intelligence-related issues.

"I'll get it done right away, sir," she said, but he had already disappeared back into his office. With a sigh, Lisa read the message. Unlike what she'd expected, it was quite coherent. She read it once, then twice, before placing her hands on the keys of her typewriter. As the words appeared on the clean white sheet of paper, she wondered how the agent in the Netherlands was feeling. His message was almost too neat, with too much detail around a German weapons transport arriving by rail next week. She frowned and stopped typing, staring at the words in front of her. She peeked over her typewriter, waiting for Femke to finish typing. When there was a pause in the clacking sound, she spoke up.

"Hey Fem, can you have a look at this message? I think I might be missing something."

The woman stood and walked to Lisa's side. She read the two neatly typed paragraphs, then cross-checked them with the handwritten message. Finally, she let out a low whistle. "This is quite the intel. I'm sure Somer and SOE will be well pleased with this."

"Yes, but look at this sentence." She pointed at the end of the first paragraph. "I know this operative, and he's supposed to use a safety check here."

Femke read the message again, then frowned. "I see what you mean. But maybe it just got lost in the rush of sending the message? You know how it is. It wouldn't be the first time."

"That's why I'm worried. This is the third message this month where there's no safety check. It's becoming too common. I should flag it with Bakker." Her supervisor was slouched in his chair, leafing through a thick file.

"I don't know, Lisa. The message looks genuine enough, and it's not up to us to judge its validity—you know that, right?"

Lisa felt frustrated. Femke wasn't taking her seriously. She pulled the sheet of paper from the typewriter and stood. Then, masking her frustration with a smile, she said, "Maybe you're right, I'll just ask him if he's happy with this before I translate it." Lisa didn't wait for an answer and briskly walked to her supervisor's office. She knocked and entered. "Sir, would you mind looking at the message before I translate it?"

"That was quick," he said, taking the piece of paper. Lisa watched his eyes as they traveled across the sentences. After a minute, he handed it back. "Looks fine. Let's get it ready for the Brits." He turned back to the file on his desk, but when Lisa didn't leave his office, he looked back up. "Something else you wanted to ask?" He sounded slightly impatient.

Lisa took a deep breath. *You need to tell him.* "I'm a little concerned at the lack of a safety check in the message, sir."

"How so?" He put the folder down and sat up, his hand outstretched.

She handed back the paper. "Sir, I know this agent. I've processed several of his messages since he started transmitting a month ago." Bakker gave her a curious look but indicated for her to continue. "He'll always make a deliberate mistake at the end of his second or fourth sentence, depending on the length of the message. But, recently, his messages have been without error."

"How recently?" He was scanning the message intently, his fingers running over the lines in the first paragraph.

"His past three transmissions in a row, sir."

Bakker didn't respond, his attention on the piece of paper. Lisa shuffled on her feet and looked through the window, where she saw Femke glance at her with a questioning expression. Lisa looked away. "I suppose you believe he's been compromised?" Bakker finally said, tossing the paper onto his desk.

"I'm not sure, sir, but I thought you should be aware of the irregularity."

"Thank you, I appreciate your efforts," he said neutrally, and Lisa breathed a little easier. He then continued, his voice taking on a somewhat condescending tone. "But you should also know that it's not your place to worry about this. We have competent people in our transmissions department and intelligence officers at the SOE who inspect all messages in detail."

Lisa felt her face flush. "Yes, sir." *He's not taking this seriously.*

He pointed at the sheet of paper. "I suggest you stick to your job and translate this so we can send it off to the experts. I'm sure they'll take action if they find anything unusual with the message."

"As you say, sir." Deflated, Lisa picked up the piece of paper and left the office.

"He told you not to worry about it, did he?"

"He did," Lisa said, aggressively jamming another sheet of paper into her typewriter. She pounded the keys with fury, unable to let this go. *Certainly not with Christiaan leaving soon.*

Christiaan looked at her from across the table, his plate still half-full. "You're sure it was the same agent?"

Lisa had just told him about the message, and he listened without interruption. "Yes, I recognized his call sign, and I thought it was odd that he didn't use his safety check in the previous two messages. But this time, I couldn't ignore it any longer. Someone's not paying attention at the SOE, Chris; I know it."

He sat back in his chair, his face thoughtful. "You think they all missed it? That seems unlikely."

"Very unlikely. But what if I'm right? What if the agent has been compromised? Will the Brits act on this latest information and tell people back home to intercept the train? It's a trap."

"What if it's an honest mistake, either by the agent or the radio operators receiving the transmission? I'm struggling to send faultless transmissions from my training office. Imagine doing it under pressure." He looked at her with affection. "I know you mean well, but maybe Bakker is right, and we should leave this to the experts? They have so many people analyzing all the transmissions; they would know when something's off, right?"

Lisa straightened the folds in her skirt and looked up. "I'm sorry, maybe you're right. I'm just worried about you leaving. What if I'm right, and the Germans did catch one of our spies?"

Christiaan stood and moved to her side of the table. He crouched down next to her and placed his arm around her waist. "I'm sure they wouldn't send me back home if there were any indications that the network was compromised. They're struggling to recruit and train enough agents as it is. So why would they send us if they knew the network was compromised? It doesn't make sense, Lisa."

She looked at him and let out a long sigh.

"I'll tell you what I'll do," Christiaan said, rising and moving back to his side of the table. "I'll reach out to some of my contacts at the SOE and ask if they've heard anything unusual about the transmissions from our agents in the Netherlands, okay? If it turns out they're also worried, I'll ask to speak to my handler."

Lisa nodded and took a bite of her now-cold dinner.

The following morning, Lisa arrived at the office before anyone else. She opened the door to the typists' room, put down her handbag, and hung her coat over her chair before heading into the hallway. She was pleased to see the other offices were still dark. Lisa stopped in front of a nondescript door at the end of the hallway next to Colonel Somer's office. She took a deep breath and opened the door. She quickly closed it behind her before finding the light switch. As the lights flickered on with a hum, she was greeted by the sight of row after row of filing cabinets.

A week ago, Lisa had been in the room for the first time, when she accompanied her supervisor with a box of files that needed to be sorted. Although the door to the room wasn't locked, Lisa was not supposed to enter without permission. She nervously took a step down the path between two rows of filing cabinets. *Where do I start?*

It all seemed so easy when she hatched her plan the previous evening. Lisa wouldn't let Christiaan leave on a dangerous mission without getting some guarantees of his safety.

Now, standing in the room, she wasn't so sure anymore. Finding the evidence didn't seem so straightforward anymore, with the filing cabinets in the middle and the racks containing boxes to the sides of the room looking insurmountable. *Come on, Lisa.*

She decided her best chance was to check the most recent messages from the Netherlands. Thankfully, the most recent files were kept in neatly marked filing cabinets, and she was encouraged to find the months she was looking for, August and July, near the front of the row. Feeling energized, she opened the first drawer and was greeted with files marked by day of the month. *This may be easier than I thought.*

Lisa started leafing through, quickly skipping past weekly reports from various consulates and meeting notes of the various subdepartments within the Bureau, until she found a file containing an agenda of Somer's weekly meeting with the Special Operations Executive dated two weeks ago. Her curiosity piqued, and she pulled it from the cabinet and opened it. She scanned the pages looking for any mention of suspicious transmissions coming from the Netherlands. There were none. Disappointed, she replaced the file and continued her search. In the next fifteen minutes, she found more reports of meetings between the Bureau and the SOE, but she found no mention of questionable transmissions. Slowly, Lisa started to consider the possibility that she was wrong. Perhaps Christiaan wasn't in danger at all, and she had underestimated the capable analysts at SOE? She replaced another file and checked the time. It was almost half past seven; the first of her colleagues would be arriving soon. She had just closed the filing cabinet when the door opened. Lisa stood in the middle of the room, in full view of whoever was entering.

"They must've forgotten to switch off the lights again," she heard a deep voice mumble as a man entered the room. He shook his head, looked in her direction, and let out a cry of surprise. Lisa's heart dropped as she recognized him—Colonel Somer. He quickly recovered, his face set in a surprised but suspicious expression. "What are you doing stalking in here? Who are you, anyway?" His hands were on his hips as he remained near the door.

Colonel Somer was imposing, placed in this position by the queen herself, for she believed he was the only person able to run the military intelligence operation properly. Lisa wasn't sure how to respond.

"I'm sorry, sir. I work down the hall as a typist."

"You're in Bakker's team, then?" His face softened somewhat. "That doesn't explain your presence in this room. Did he send you? I haven't seen him yet." His words came at her as from a seasoned interrogator, and she took a moment to consider her response. It wouldn't do to make up a lie about being sent to the archives by Bakker; Somer would undoubtedly check with him, and she would surely be in more trouble. Then an idea occurred to her.

"Sir, I wasn't sent here by anyone. I'm here on my account." Somer's eyes narrowed, but he didn't say anything. "I prepared one of the messages from one of our Dutch agents yesterday and translated it for you to share with the SOE."

"I remember. That was quite the revelation about those weapons. Of course, the Brits were rather excited about intercepting the shipment. But why is that relevant?"

Lisa hesitated, but she knew she had to push through. "Sir, I believe our operatives didn't send that message."

"Really? How so?" Somer looked only mildly surprised, which was odd. She explained about the missing safety check. When she mentioned it was the third time in a row, Somer nodded slowly. "What's your name?"

"Lisa Abrahams, sir. I started a month ago."

"Well, Lisa, I'm glad you told me about this. It's not the first time I've heard of this."

"It isn't?"

"No. I've received messages from anonymous sources at the SOE claiming their Dutch network has been infiltrated. Officially, the Brits deny it, claiming everything is fine and that they'll continue acting on the information."

"And who do you believe, sir?"

Somer shook his head. "I can only act on facts. All our agents continue to check in according to their schedules." Despite his words, he looked uncertain as his eyes scanned the rows of filing cabinets. Finally, he returned his gaze to Lisa. "What did you expect to find in here, anyway?"

"Some indication that what I found wasn't an isolated incident."

"You knew you were taking a big risk coming in here. Why do you care so much?"

Christiaan's face flashed through her head, and Lisa didn't hesitate to answer. "The man I love is about to be sent on a mission back home."

"I see." There was understanding in Somer's eyes as he leaned against one of the filing cabinets. "What's his name?"

"Christiaan Brouwer. He's just finished his training and awaiting his mission."

"And you're worried he might be parachuting into a compromised network."

"Yes." The thought of Christiaan landing back on Dutch soil only to have German soldiers waiting for him terrified her. She knew the fate of captured spies.

"I can assure you we've done everything to make sure it won't happen."

Lisa was unconvinced. "How so, sir? What if the rumors are true?"

"I'm afraid that's all I can say for now." A smile crept onto his face, and he turned to the door, his voice more authoritative. "Now come, we should get back to work. I'll pretend I didn't catch you here, and you won't speak a word about what I told you."

Resigned and confused, Lisa followed her boss. Somer's words had done little to ease her worries.

CHAPTER EIGHTEEN

The train stopped in a field without explanation and had been there for forty minutes. The other passengers seemed undisturbed, but Nora had felt nervous, keeping her eyes on the door. Then the familiar sound of the engines fired up, and the Flemish countryside flashed by. As the train continued south toward Brussels at a steady pace, she relaxed a little.

Their hasty retreat from Nicolas' house had been nerve-racking. The tunnel seemed to go on forever. Katja had kept her calm, and when she shone her flashlight on the ceiling at the end of the tunnel, they had found a hatch concealed behind some overgrowing roots. The tunnel brought them well beyond the garden of Nicolas' house, and when Nora emerged, she saw the headlights of two cars in the distance, some two hundred meters away, heading toward the home. They had moved quickly, delighted to be making their way to the station.

When they had arrived at Antwerp Central station, Nora was immensely relieved to find plenty of people hurrying to catch their early connections. They had planned to be on the seven a.m. train, but Lars had suggested they try to exchange their tickets for an earlier one.

"When those Gestapo men head into the basement and find our mattresses and the tunnel, they might think of coming after us," Lars said, and he was right; the train station would be the first place they would search. *We'd be stuck in Antwerp, with nowhere to go.*

When Lars came back from the ticket kiosk smiling, Nora couldn't help but feel optimistic. Only the train was departing in five minutes. They had to sprint to catch it, and Nora was afraid they would be too conspicuous, but they made it without incident.

Once on board, they decided it would be safer to split up, and Nora now found herself alone in a car with bleary-eyed commuters. Nora yawned. The silence and the light rocking of the car on the tracks enticed Nora to close her eyes for a few seconds.

She opened them with a start when a loud voice sounded through the car, which had now stopped. "Get your papers out for inspection. Tickets, identity papers." Nora looked up and felt the blood in her veins turn to ice. The man confidently walking along the aisle wore the gray-green uniform of the SS. He glanced at some of the people but, to Nora's surprise, opened the door on the far side of the car and left.

Damn it. She had dozed off and had missed them stopping in Mechelen, halfway to Brussels. The people around her took out their papers in the careless way of those used to inspections. The door of the next car opened, and Nora heard the SS man issuing the same command to the people there. He would return soon. She eyed the other door and made a quick decision.

She grabbed her small backpack, clutching it to her chest as she edged out of her seat and stepped into the aisle. Without making eye contact with the other passengers, she moved toward the door the SS man had come from. Her back tingled. She felt glances from a few passengers in passing, but none said anything. The door was only a few paces away now, and she took the last steps in a hurry. She grabbed the handle and glanced at a middle-aged gentleman sitting next to the door. He looked up from his newspaper, and their eyes met. He looked at her kindly, encouraging her to step out. Nora opened the door and stepped into the small area at the front of her car, with doors on either side. The doors were open, the station platform deserted.

There was only one thing she could do, and it terrified her. She took a step toward the doorway, straining her ears to make out any sounds. When all remained quiet, she risked peeking her head outside, quickly looking up and down the platform. On both sides of the train stood a sentry, but the one nearest to Nora was talking to the train driver. Nora looked at the space between the platform and the train. *This is my chance.*

Without another thought, she jumped from the train onto the platform. Within another beat, she lowered herself into the tight space between the platform and the train, landing in the mud next to the tracks. She crouched and held her breath, waiting for the inevitable shouts of alarm from one of the sentries.

All remained quiet but for the soft hissing of air in the tubes running along the train's undercarriage. Nora crawled to the other side, disappearing from sight. She was no longer on the platform side, and she didn't spot any sentries ahead. Then, keeping her head low, she crawled to the front of the train, toward the noise of the running locomotive. She didn't know why, but she felt safest at the front, where she assumed the SS men must've started their patrols.

When she got to the first car, she crawled back underneath the train, between the tracks. There, surrounded by wires, connectors, and other hissing instruments, she saw the legs of the sentry on the platform side. She was well hidden. Her heart was in her throat. *If they do come down here, I'll make a run for it.* She closed her eyes and hoped it wouldn't come to that.

"Hey, did you see anyone disembark the train?" The voice was close by, and it took a few seconds for Nora to realize another man had joined the sentry on the platform.

"What do you mean? All disembarking passengers left through

the main exit five minutes ago," the man responded, annoyance clear in his voice. "Didn't you see them leave? The others checked their papers before they left. It was all in order."

"Just wanted to make sure none of them left after we started checking the train," the other man insisted, clearly annoyed at his authority being questioned. "You're absolutely certain? If any did, the blame's on you."

There was a pause before the sentry's response. Nora felt her neck tingle and pushed herself farther into the mud. *Please don't come down here.* In Amsterdam, she would be handed over to the Gestapo. Her throat went dry thinking about it. She thought of Katja, Lars, and Arthur. *Hopefully they were more alert.*

"No, I'm telling you, nobody got off or on the train," the sentry finally said, and Nora felt herself relax a little. "Everything okay inside?"

"Why don't you just focus on what's going on outside here," the other man said, before his footsteps receded. The sentry muttered something unintelligible, then Nora heard the click of a lighter. Tobacco smoke wafted down and entered her nostrils. She held her breath, feeling the tickle of a cough at the familiar smell. *No, not now.* She closed her eyes and clenched her teeth together. At that moment, an earsplitting whistle sounded from the locomotive only a few meters ahead. Its engine let out a puffing sound, and she heard the clacking noises of coal being shoveled into the fire box. *They're getting ready to leave.* More footsteps on the platform. They moved quickly, almost running as if in a hurry. Nora remained still underneath the car. The heat coming from the locomotive's boiler was increasing.

"Sir, all passengers have been checked. All in order," Nora heard a man say in German, before clacking his heels.

"Very well. Did you check the train driver as well? They hide people in there sometimes." The other voice was deep and spoke with authority.

"We did, sir. The stokers and driver checked out. Nothing there but coal."

"Perfect. Tell them they can leave. We'll need to prepare for the next arrival."

The other man ran up to the locomotive. His words were drowned out by the engine's roar, protesting at being held back. The locomotive's door closed with a clang, and then a tremendous hissing sound emerged as the wheels on both sides of Nora creaked forward.

Nora crawled on her knees, making sure to stay clear of the tangle of wires, and emerged on the side of the train. She kept her head down as the first car slowly rolled past her. She prayed none of the passengers saw her.

The train picked up speed, and Nora realized she hadn't thought about how she would get back inside. The doors she would typically use were too high to reach. She decided to jog alongside the train as she looked for a solution. She would need to get away from the station and out of sight, no matter what happened next. Her eyes shot to the cars ahead and behind as the third car overtook her, the train quickly picking up speed.

The locomotive and the first two cars snaked into a turn, and Nora saw an opportunity. Between every pair of carriages was a buffer area. It was used to connect the cars, and the connector wires and small platform were less than a meter from the ground. From there, she should be able to reach one of the doors.

Nora swallowed hard; there was no room for error. If she misjudged the jump and slipped, she could end up underneath the train, crushed between the wheels and the tracks. But there was no time to think about that as the fifth car passed by at a worrying speed.

She broke into a sprint, no longer caring if anybody in the cars saw her, waiting for the end of the fifth car catch up. She panted, her lungs burning as she kept pace with the train, allowing it to overtake her. When the door of the car passed, the buffer area flashed beside her, the steel connector visible. The train was quickly gaining speed, and Nora pushed her legs to go faster while her eyes frantically looked for something to grab onto after jumping. Nothing but the wires around the steel part stood out, and as the train sped forward, she knew it was her last chance. She moved closer to the car, the heavy wheels so close she could feel them drumming on the rails, took one last deep breath, and jumped.

Her stomach smashed into the steel connector, almost knocking the wind from her, but she clenched her teeth and grabbed a fistful of wires, then wrapped her legs around the slippery connector. Her body slid toward the ground racing by underneath—Nora feared she might end up on the tracks after all. With every last bit of strength, she pulled herself atop the connector just as her car snaked into the turn.

She sat like this until the train returned to a straight path, catching her breath while the tracks below now flashed by at dizzying speed. *I have to get inside.* Soon, the train would be moving at over a hundred kilometers an hour, and she remembered how the bumps felt inside the car.

Nora pulled herself toward the carriage behind her, using the momentum of the train. There, hidden between the connector wires, she spotted a handle and what looked like a small platform at the back of the car. She felt weak with relief but forced herself to focus. She still needed to reach out to the handle. That meant releasing one hand from the safety of the wires. The distance to the handle was less than a meter, but it might as well have been ten times that. Nora closed her eyes for a moment and took a mighty breath. She filtered out everything around her and the sound of the clattering wheels and the wind rushing at her face disappeared.

When she opened her eyes, she calmly let go of the wires and reached for the handle with her right hand. It felt like she was floating for a second as her hand searched for the handle. When she touched the cold steel, she gripped it tightly. Next, she moved her left leg to the platform in the same motion, pulling herself toward it and pushing off the connector simultaneously. A moment later, she stood on the narrow platform, the door to the car within reach.

She collected herself, then pulled open the door and stepped inside the car, quickly closing it. Alone in the small area, her heart pounded in her chest. She stood facing the door for a moment, then turned around. Through the window in the door leading to the passenger compartment, she saw the faces of the other passengers. Some had stood while others sat and turned in their seats. All wore the same shocked expression.

A man in his forties opened the door. "Are you quite all right, miss?" he asked cautiously, keeping his distance from Nora while he held the door. "Did you just really ... umm, appear from outside?"

Nora let out a nervous laugh. "Yes, sir. I was somewhat lost."

The man's demeanor changed as he returned her smile, pointing at her clothes. "You look an absolute mess. Why don't you come in here and warm up? Perhaps you've got a change of clothes in that bag?"

As she entered the compartment, she found the other people eyeing her up curiously. Nora felt uncomfortable until the man pointed her to an empty seat next to a boy no older than ten. The boy looked up, his eyes sparkling with admiration. "Were you running away from the patrol just now? Daddy said you did." Nora frowned, but before she could say anything, the boy added, "Don't worry. We all hate the Germans. We won't tell anyone."

Nora looked around and saw kindness in the eyes of the people in the car. The man who'd opened the door for her crouched in the aisle next to her. "We don't know why you're running, but nobody in this compartment will speak a word. Let's get you safely to Brussels. Come, you can change in the toilet."

She moved to the back of the car and noticed a lone figure hunched in a seat there. As she passed by, the man raised his cap and looked up. Nora's knees felt wobbly when she recognized Lars. He gave her an almost imperceptible wink, relief palpable in his eyes. Nora closed the door to the bathroom and, as she changed out of her muddy clothes, prayed Katja and Arthur had also stayed out of the German's clutches.

CHAPTER NINETEEN

Christiaan and Lisa sat near the window in the parlor of Mrs. Green's home. Even though the curtains were carefully closed—it was dark outside, and the blackout policy was in operation—they preferred sitting here. Lisa said it gave her a feeling of staying in touch with what was going on outside. Christiaan agreed, although precious little happened in the city at night. There was still always the danger of the Luftwaffe carrying out air strikes, so most people preferred to stay within the safety of their homes. He looked at the bag near the front door and sighed.

"Are you nervous?" Lisa put a hand on his lap and slipped her fingers into his.

After returning from training in Manchester, he had reported to the offices of MI6, where he'd answered more questions about the expected resistance efforts in the Netherlands. Despite his dated information, the agents were impressed with his knowledge. For Christiaan, it had almost been second nature; in his mind, he still walked the streets of Amsterdam, working alongside his friends to fight the Germans. The only frustrating part of his visit was that they didn't give him any time frame for when he would become operational.

That changed this morning, when he was informed he would be picked up that evening and to pack only essential things.

"I'm a little nervous, but mostly about leaving you behind."

"I'll be fine. I hope I'll be able to keep tabs on what you're doing." Trying to appear stronger than she was, Lisa had a smile on her face that hardly masked her anxiety. He sat up a little straighter and stroked her hand.

"You know what helped, though? That you spoke to Somer." He still couldn't quite believe Lisa had broken into the archives room. Well, technically, she hadn't broken in, but it was clear she wasn't supposed to be in there on her own. "Did he say that he heard rumors about the SOE network being compromised?"

"Yes, but he seemed very confident it wouldn't be an issue for your mission." From the tone of her voice, it was obvious Lisa didn't share her boss' confidence.

Christiaan nodded. At Ringham his training officers had asked if he was married. He told them about Lisa, and they'd warned him she would most likely worry more about him leaving for occupied territories than he would. They explained how it was always harder for those staying behind than the agents themselves. How right they had been.

Lisa raised an eyebrow. "What's so funny?"

"Nothing. Just thinking about the queen's words in that small garden at Chester Square. It feels surreal to think I spoke with her less than three weeks ago, and now I'm waiting to get picked up for that very mission we discussed."

"Well, you can say what you want about Queen Wilhelmina, but when she wants something, she gets it done."

Christiaan could still see the regent's face. "She was so passionate when she spoke about the resistance. It almost felt as if she was testing me to see if I had enough desire to go back and carry out her plan."

“What did she say again?” Lisa stood and picked up a teapot on the far side of the room, pouring two cups. “To unite the resistance?”

“She believes a united resistance is key to liberating the country. The way it sounded, she expects to have armed partisan forces spread throughout the country, ready to rise when the liberation of Europe starts.” Christiaan took the teacup gratefully.

“Sounds like there’s quite a bit riding on you, then, don’t you think?” Lisa said, smiling as she blew on her tea. “And yet, you worry more about me staying in London.”

“I’m sure I won’t be working alone,” Christiaan said, taking a sip. The warm liquid burned his throat, but he enjoyed the sensation of it making its way into his stomach. He knew it might be a while until he shared a cup of tea with Lisa again. He looked at the woman he loved with affection. She caught his eye, and set her tea down.

“Christiaan, just promise me you’ll be safe. You need to make sure you stay out of sight when you return to Amsterdam. Too many people know you there.”

“Floris, you mean.”

“Him, but you don’t know what the situation is like right now. Reach out to Nora and Bet first. Hear them out before you make your moves. This is not the Amsterdam we left.”

Lisa didn’t share the contents of the messages that passed across her desk, but she let on enough for him to know the Nazis had become more aggressive. Even before the revelation of the SOE’s agent network possibly being compromised, it was dangerous back home.

He patted his hand on the free cushion next to him, and Lisa sat down on the couch. He put his arm around her shoulder, pulling her tight. He remembered the last time they sat like this. It was on the eve before crossing into Switzerland, in the seminary run by Amy Mae and her husband. He kissed Lisa’s forehead, and she looked up. Christiaan gave his most confident smile and said, “Don’t worry. Whatever happens, I’ll come back for you.”

The ride to the air base was done in silence. The driver navigated the quiet streets of London expertly, only having to stop twice to give way to ambulances and fire trucks racing toward freshly struck bomb sites. They were soon outside the city, and even though London was already quite dark at night, Christiaan was struck by the pitch-black sky of the countryside. It wasn't until they pulled up at the air base's front gate that he realized they had arrived.

The car halted near a building where Christiaan spotted thin streams of light filtering out between the curtains. He got out of the car and was escorted through a dimly lit hallway and into a windowless room.

"He'll be with you in a few minutes," the man wearing a RAF uniform said, before leaving the room and closing the door. Christiaan sat at the table in the middle of the room and poured himself some water. He took a gulp, washing away the tickling sensation in the back of his throat.

The door opened and Christiaan was surprised to find a tall man wearing civilian clothing enter the room. He moved with the swagger of a man entirely at ease in his surroundings and approached Christiaan, his hand outstretched in front of him.

"Finally we meet, Mr. Brouwer. My name is Colonel Somer, head of the Bureau Inlichtingen." Christiaan stood and shook the man's hand, noticing Somer's firm grip. "But then, I'm sure you've heard of me, haven't you?" He moved to the other side of the table and sat down, indicating for Christiaan to do the same.

Christiaan decided to stay coy about what Lisa had told him. "Of course, I know who you are, sir. It's a pleasure to meet you."

Somer placed a large manila folder on the desk between them and shook his head. "Mr. Brouwer, I'm about to send you off on a top-secret mission behind enemy lines. You know what the Nazis do to captured spies, don't you?" He didn't wait for an answer. "Shall we proceed without the formalities? Sans bullshit, as one would say?"

Christiaan was surprised by the man's frankness. "Of course, sir."

"I'm sure your partner has told you about our meeting the other day. I have to say, she's dedicated." The hint of a smile played on Somer's face while he opened the folder. Christiaan relaxed a little.

"You have no idea, sir. When she's worried about something, she won't let it go."

"An excellent trait, or a dangerous one. It's a good thing it was I who ran into her; there are some more overly zealous types at the Bureau. Did I put her mind at ease somewhat?"

"Somewhat, yes." Christiaan hesitated before continuing. "She still had questions, but she was pleased to hear you were aware of the rumors around the functioning of the SOE. Not meaning to offend anyone, sir."

"Yes, those rumors are rather unfortunate. The problem is that there's no way to confirm them. If the network is compromised, either the agents are sending us messages fabricated by the Nazis or, and this would be even worse, the Germans are sending us the intelligence themselves, having extracted our agents' call signs." He was quiet for a moment, letting the ominous words hang in the air. "But that's where you come in. Partly, anyway."

"Partly, sir?" Christiaan remembered Queen Wilhelmina's vision. This sounded different. He hid his disappointment, forcing himself to keep a neutral face.

"This mission will be carried out without the knowledge of the SOE." Somer picked up a sheet of paper and turned it to Christiaan. It showed a small map of the Netherlands, with a larger map highlighting a forested area known as *De Veluwe*, about fifty kilometers east of Amsterdam. "The plane is waiting for you outside, ready to take off an hour from now. It will drop you here." Somer pointed at a sandy-colored spot on the larger map. When you land, you and the two radio operators accompanying you will make your way to this safe house, where you will wait until your contacts have secured you safe passage to Amsterdam."

Christiaan studied the map, trying to mask his surprise. *How did*

Somer manage to secure a plane without the assistance of the SOE? He decided instead to focus on the mission. "Will the radio operators join me to Amsterdam?"

"No, they have a different mission," Somer said without further explanation. "Once you arrive in Amsterdam you have two objectives. You are to make contact with a group called the *Ordedienst*. Have you heard of them?"

"I have, sir." The Ordedienst, or OD, was a resistance organization with an especially high number of former military officers in their ranks. Christiaan knew of their existence but hadn't interacted with them during his time in Amsterdam. Where Christiaan focused primarily on sheltering people in hiding, the OD was more interested in sabotaging German operations, disrupting railway and telephone connections.

"The OD have traditionally been a good source of information, providing the government in London with intelligence. Recently, however, things have gone quiet. I need you to reestablish contact and find out what's happening." Somer looked concerned as he mentioned the name of a cafe in the Jordaan area of Amsterdam. "This was our previous rendezvous point for agents landing in Amsterdam. I hope it's not been compromised, and it will be the best place to make contact." He explained the procedure to make contact at the bar, and Christiaan memorized it.

"And what's the second objective?"

"We want you to reach out to your network in Amsterdam. I believe Queen Wilhelmina mentioned how dear to her heart this mission is?" Somer eyed him intently. "She feels the only way to free our country is to form some form of national resistance network. I agree with her, but I think this is only possible if we work with people who know the networks inside out. You are one of those people. You hold the key to establishing the network in Amsterdam."

Christiaan felt the weight of the words as he listened to Somer. *Lisa had been right— they do expect a lot from me.* He thought of his friends at home and felt a tingle of excitement.

"But don't worry. You're not alone. In the next few days, we're sending more agents back home, all looking to rekindle contact with their networks. Together, God willing, you will form the foundation to our national resistance network." Somer paused for a moment, then focused his intense gaze on Christiaan. "Is that all clear? Do you have any questions?"

"Sir, the way I understand it, I won't be taking a radio with me. How will I communicate with London, if not through the compromised SOE network?"

Somer leaned back in his chair, looking as if he'd expected the question. "The Ordedienst are equipped with radios and will be your connection to London."

"Sir, with all due respect, you just said you hadn't heard from them for a while. Shouldn't we consider the possibility that they no longer have access to this equipment?"

"You're catching on quick, Brouwer. If the Ordedienst are no longer able to transmit, you will continue the rest of your mission and make connections with the different resistance groups in Amsterdam. If we don't hear from you within two weeks from today, we will initiate a backup plan to get you in touch with other radio operators."

"The men I'm jumping with tonight?"

"Men like them, yes. You are to report to this address in Amsterdam and ask the woman living there if any mail has been delivered from Sweden recently. She will ask for your call sign, which will initiate the procedure from our side." He slid a piece of paper across the table. "Memorize this address."

Christiaan pushed the paper back to Somer. "Okay, sir. If there's nothing else, I think I'm ready to go." He moved to get up, but Somer held up his hand.

"There's one last thing I need to ask of you. And this would be a personal favor to me."

Christiaan sat back down, raising an eyebrow, intrigued. "Sir?"

"Just because the Brits won't acknowledge their operation isn't compromised doesn't mean I'm not worried about the young men we've sent home." He looked troubled as he drummed his fingers on the table. "I consider them my responsibility, even if they don't report directly to me. And frankly, it worries me that none of them have come back to England in the past three months. Some should've returned by now."

"I understand, sir." Christiaan wasn't sure where the colonel was going with this.

"I'd like you to ask and see if you can contact any of them. A good number were based in Amsterdam, and they must've also been in touch with men from the Ordedienst. Find out what happened."

"I would be honored to take on this personal mission of yours, sir." The man sitting across from him was hurting; he had no doubt Somer wouldn't send him on this mission if he didn't believe his network was safe.

Somer was visibly relieved as he stood abruptly and held out his hand. "Godspeed, Brouwer. I wish we had more men of your courage."

Christiaan shook his hand, more determined to make his mark back home. He couldn't wait to jump out of that plane in a few hours. He was going to make his queen proud.

It felt oddly familiar to climb aboard the narrow Whitley airplane. Christiaan was first to board, with the two radio operators—Piet and Bram—following closely behind. Christiaan met them fifteen minutes prior as they waited for the car to bring them to the tarmac. Both were about the same age as Christiaan and had spent over two months at Ringham. It wasn't without a hint of pride when Piet mentioned he was now one of the most capable radio operators at Ringham. Bram exuded the same confidence when he spoke of the mission ahead. Somer had selected confident, capable men to spearhead his new network.

Piet and Bram carried a small suitcase on board, which Christiaan knew was their radio equipment. He remembered his test with the eggs and was relieved he wasn't responsible for this lifeline—this case was a lot bigger than the bag he used in training. However, the radio operators looked confident as they strapped the suitcase to the side of the fuselage and took their seats.

The rear hatch was closed, and the airplane's engines roared to life. A few minutes later they were airborne, the pilot navigating the plane east. It was impossible to talk over the sound of the engines, and Christiaan used this time to mentally prepare for the mission ahead. He closed his eyes, imagining what it would be like to return to Amsterdam in a few days. Would the city have changed much? Would the people he left behind still be there? Nora's face flashed in front of his eyes. He last received news of his sister-in-law when he and Lisa arrived in Geneva. She was fine, but her husband—and his brother—Floris had disappeared. That was more than six months ago. A lot could've happened in that time. *Nora would look after herself, and she's got the rest of the resistance to help her.*

An hour later, the rear hatch opened and Christiaan stood with his right hand on Piet's shoulder. Ahead of them, Bram was waiting for the signal to jump. They agreed they would jump in quick succession, maximizing their chances of landing close to each other. This was no training jump anymore, and it was imperative to the success of the mission that the men stay together while making it to the safe house.

Christiaan felt his temples throbbing against the straps of his face mask, and despite having taken a generous sip of water before standing up, his throat was parched. The sky below was dark and the clouds hung close to the ground—perfect conditions for their jump.

"Approaching drop zone," came the voice of the pilot over the speaker mounted above their heads. Christiaan felt Piet tense, and he involuntarily squeezed the man's shoulder. He checked his static line, confirming it was still attached to the steel cable running down the aircraft's roof. *Only seconds to go now.* "Clear to jump. Good luck, boys."

There was no more time to think as Bram immediately disappeared into the sky below. Piet took two steps forward and followed him, instantly disappearing into the void. Christiaan put one hand over his face mask, took a deep breath, and jumped into the night sky. The wind came rushing at him—screaming in his ears and tearing at his flight suit. It took him a few seconds to find his bearings and assume the correct position: facing the ground and in a controlled descent. He looked around for the other men but it was too dark to tell where they were. He had to trust their jumps had been quick enough and none had diverted too much.

He soon broke through the clouds. Christiaan enjoyed this short, first part of the jump best. The adrenaline from the earth rushing toward him, the wind howling in his ears, and the feeling of being utterly alone in the sky for a few minutes. Due to the risk of German patrols spotting them their parachutes wouldn't deploy until the very last minute. It was a risky jump, for a miscalculation could have severe consequences, but it was necessary. He trusted the pilot had been at the correct altitude when they jumped. Christiaan suppressed the image of him helplessly dangling on his parachute while German soldiers aimed at him. *You can do this; you've practiced this plenty of times.*

A firm yank on his shoulders and an instant decrease in the pace of his descent confirmed that his parachute had opened above his head.

He looked down, scanning the contours of the landscape. Between the stretches of darkness that were forest, he could see several lighter patches of land. *I'm close to our landing zone.* He scanned the sky around him and was delighted to see two dark parachutes directly to his left, about fifty meters below him. As the ground rushed up at him, Christiaan braced for his landing, bending his knees to absorb the impact. *Four, three, two, one . . .* His feet landed on the soft sand, and he ran on for a few paces as his parachute lagged behind. As soon as the parachute touched down, Christiaan took off his deployment pack and started pulling at the cords of his parachute. To his left, he saw the other two men doing the same. Within minutes, they had packed their parachutes and ran for the cover of the trees. Christiaan finished last and caught up with Piet and Bram. It was the former who spoke first.

"We've got a problem. We lost our equipment." His voice was calm and controlled.

Christiaan looked at him dumbfounded. "What do you mean?"

"The suitcase with the radio was caught by a gust of wind."

"Wait, I thought you were supposed to hold onto that?"

Piet shook his head. "No, we used to do that, but there were too many accidents with agents having a less-than-perfect landing and damaging the equipment inside. Now, we have this rather large suitcase almost completely lined with shock-absorbing material. It has its own parachute, and as soon as mine deployed, I dropped the suitcase, which then deployed slightly below me. Unfortunately, it was caught by a gust of wind, and I had to decide whether to steer off course and follow it or meet with you."

Christiaan nodded; he would've made the same decision. "Did you see where it landed?"

"I did." There were lines on Piet's forehead. "It landed near a farm, about two kilometers east."

"It's still dark and early. Chances are we'll get there before anyone notices," Bram said, already heading in that direction. Piet and Christiaan followed him, trudging through the loose sand as they crossed one of the plains.

"It should be right behind that patch of trees," Piet said, pointing ahead.

As they cleared the trees, a large farmhouse loomed in the darkness. It was surrounded by a simple meter-high wooden fence. They climbed the fence and carefully approached the farmhouse. Bram was in the front, and as he neared the building, he stopped and raised his hand. Christiaan perked his ears and realized what had made him stop. There were voices in the air. *Shit.* Bram turned to them and whispered, "Stay close to me, and stay quiet."

They hugged the wall of the farmhouse and stalked toward the corner. Christiaan's mind was racing. Was this network compromised, after all?

Bram reached the corner of the building and peered around. Christiaan could make out the words of the voices around the corner. To his relief, they spoke Dutch. But which side did these people support?

"Do you want to open it?" a man with a surprisingly high-pitched voice said. "It must contain something valuable, considering it's locked and came from the sky?"

"It's not ours to open. We must take it to the leadership," another voice said.

Christiaan gritted his teeth and Piet shrugged his shoulders. *He's not sure, either.*

Bram motioned for them to come closer. "There's four of them just standing around our suitcase."

"Do you think they're friendlies?" Piet looked concerned.

"Don't know. But let's find out." Bram reached inside his jacket and took out a pistol. Piet did the same, and Christiaan was overwhelmed. *Why wasn't I given a pistol?* He didn't have time to contemplate his thoughts, for the radio operators turned the corner, confidently approaching the group. Christiaan followed at a distance.

"Everybody stay where you are and don't move," Bram said as he broke the cover of darkness. The faces of the men around the suitcase turned to the source of the sound, but they quickly stiffened when they saw the barrels of the guns pointed at them. "Hands up please, gentlemen. We don't want to hurt anyone," Bram said, waving his gun.

The men did as they were told. The man with the high-pitched voice spoke up, his eyes shifting to the suitcase between them. "This must be yours, then? We heard that Whitley flying overhead and came to see what was going on when this landed in our front yard. We're on the same side."

Christiaan was surprised the man recognized the type of plane and could see Bram was too. "Who are you?"

"We're with *Luchtbescherming*, the civil air defense," the man said. "Or well, we used to be, anyway. We still like to keep an eye on the skies, though. We often hear, and sometimes see, the Whitleys flying overhead, but this is the first time they dropped something here." His eyes went between Christiaan, Piet, and Bram. "Never seen paratroopers here before, though."

"Can you prove you're with Luchtbescherming?" Bram still held his gun, although it was no longer trained on the men.

"Sure," the man said, reaching into his jacket to reveal a yellow armband with the distinctive green logo of the Luchtbescherming: a man wearing a gas mask and holding a shield up into the sky. He also produced his identity papers. The others did the same, handing their documents to Bram and Piet.

"Now that we've got that out of the way," the man with the high-pitched voice said, extending an arm, "I'm Marinus, and this is my farm. Please come inside, before an overly enthusiastic patrol sees us out here. I'm sure you could use something to warm you up after your jump."

They spent what remained of the night at Marinus' house. He was eager to hear news from London, and though not given any details, he was pleased to hear the government had sent Dutch agents back home.

"The only things we hear are from Radio Oranje, and I'm sure they don't tell us everything. You know, with the Germans listening in as well. So I'm glad our queen and government are working hard behind the scenes."

"It's not easy," Christiaan said. "They're dependent on the whims of the Brits."

Christiaan was surprised to see it getting light outside and yawned. Marinus caught this and said, "If you want to take a quick nap, I have free bedrooms upstairs."

Before Christiaan could answer, Bram responded. "That would be perfect. We'll need to be on our way soon, but I suppose it's too early for us to be out now."

"It would raise suspicion to find three men walking along these parts at four in the morning, yes," Marinus said, standing up and signaling for them to follow him. "Why don't you rest a few hours, and I can drop you off at the train station when I go into town?"

"Much appreciated, Marinus," Bram said as they mounted the stairs. Marinus showed them to a large bedroom with two bunk beds and wished them a good remainder of the night.

"I'll take first watch," Bram said as Christiaan sat on the bottom bunk, undoing his boots. He hadn't even considered keeping watch. "Then I'll wake you in two hours, Christiaan."

Christiaan didn't bother undressing further as he crashed onto the bed, sleep instantly overcoming him.

A few hours later, Marinus dropped them off at the train station. Once he was out of sight, Bram turned to Christiaan.

"We will report to the safe house and let Somer know we've arrived safely." He held out his hand. "Good luck, Christiaan. I trust your mission goes well."

Christiaan shook his hand before turning to Piet. "Perhaps we will meet again when all of this is over."

"Hopefully sooner than later," Piet said.

Part Three

SOMEWHERE NEAR THE EASTERN FRONT

SEPTEMBER, 1943

CHAPTER TWENTY

The first thing Floris noticed was the sharp drop in temperature upon arrival in Ukraine. When he left Sennheim almost a week ago, the summer weather had still been pleasant. Their train had slowly made its way through Bavaria and into Austria, where they spent a night in the army barracks of the Waffen-SS training camp in Graz. It had been a welcome change from sleeping on the train. The next morning they were joined by more soldiers, a surprising number of them Dutch. Floris found out they were also joining Westland, and as the train ventured farther east, he caught up with the new recruits. Most of them had gone through Sennheim as well, and they were surprised Floris and the other men from Sennheim were sent directly to the front.

"The Russians must be giving them more trouble than expected if they're not even bothering training you in Graz." The ominous words troubled Floris. Didn't his training officer mention the combination of Waffen-SS and Wehrmacht were chalking up victory after victory?

The man opposite him laughed nervously as the train thundered across the border between Romania and Ukraine. "The Russians have been pushing us back ever since that victory in Charkov. That's a long time ago." He shook his head. "No, we'll be joining a very different war to the one you have in your head. Better prepare yourself for the worst."

"Are you all right?" Anton's voice shook Floris from his thoughts.

He nodded as he looked around, wrapping his coat a little tighter. They had disembarked the train hours ago, when their commanding officer informed them the train tracks farther ahead were no longer operational. They were still a day's march from Charkov, where the Wiking division was stationed.

The first three hours they marched at a high pace, cutting through woods and desolate plains. There had been some small settlements in the distance, but there was no sign of life. Floris assumed if there were still people in the dwellings, they were wise to stay out of sight.

"What do you think? Pretty miserable country, right?" Anton said, taking a sip from his canteen.

"The cold and overcast weather doesn't help," Floris said, looking up. "I'm surprised to see no people here."

"Not much to do here, it seems. The soil looks tired."

They had walked in silence for half an hour when the road weaved toward a small settlement. Floris' spirits lifted at the thought of a break in the monotony of their march. Perhaps they would even be able to buy something. The front of their unit passed the city gates and Floris was struck by the banners draped outside some of the windows of the houses. He didn't recognize the letters, and he looked around to see if any of the other men did. They looked on with the same fascination but didn't appear to understand what the letters meant. What they did understand was the red swastika next to the letters.

"A show of support? Of welcome?" Anton said softly as they passed the houses.

Floris looked around and was struck by the quiet of the streets. "If they're welcoming us, where are they? This feels like a ghost town." They were continuing along the narrow main thoroughfare when Floris noticed the sweet scent of smoke. *Perhaps there are people here, after all?*

The street widened and the soldiers ahead of Floris spread out a bit. The smoke intensified, but the smell was now mixed with something else. Up ahead, there were people shouting, the hissing of the fires, and the clanging of tools. The soldiers at the front slowed down as they turned the corner. Floris frowned and pushed forward impatiently.

Turning the corner revealed a modest town square. Floris' breath caught in his throat as he struggled to take in the sight. Between the group of soldiers and the church across the square was a hive of activity. Men wearing SS uniforms were busy stoking fires in the middle of the square—fueled with furniture from the surrounding shops and houses.

Floris' eyes shot across the square when he noticed something atop the church. He blinked twice, making sure his eyes weren't deceiving him. Dangling from a rope fixed to the church's steeple was a naked man, his lifeless eyes bulging from their sockets as a noose cut into his neck. On closer inspection, Floris spotted horrific burn marks across his body. He looked away, a feeling of nausea rising in the back of his throat.

"What the hell is happening here?" Anton looked just as shocked. There was no time to further contemplate as the voice of their commanding officer shouted for them to continue. They passed the fires in a stupor, most of the other soldiers looking just as shocked as Floris. He was appalled to see some of the men smiling and shouting encouragement to the soldiers stoking the fires. As they passed the church, Floris tried to keep his gaze from the man dangling on the rope above his head.

They left the square and continued on through narrow streets. It was also deathly quiet here. *Where have all the people gone?* Soon the streets made way for fields. More men wearing the uniforms of the Waffen-SS gathered around what appeared to be trenches. There were no large fires this time, only a few soldiers huddling around smaller fires.

A high-pitched wail cut through the silence, and Floris turned to see a woman—her dress reduced to rags—crawling along the side of one of the trenches. Her hair was disheveled and her face full of bruises as she pointed at the nearest group of soldiers. Her raspy voice shouted what sounded like curses in another language. One of the soldiers casually walked toward her, unbuckled his pistol and aimed it at her face. Floris was amazed to find the woman showed no reaction to the threat of imminent death. Instead, her curses only grew louder. A gunshot abruptly ended her wails. As if disposing of a rodent, the soldier stepped toward her and lifted his boot and pushed her lifeless body into the trench.

It was clear where the people of the village had gone. Floris looked to Anton, who sat crouched on the side of the road, his face pale.

Some of the men in their company shouted. "Hey, can we have a look? What do you have there? Jews? Gypsies?"

One of the men enthusiastically called them over. "Come, come; these were the last of them."

Floris felt sick as the men sauntered over. All along the edges of the graves, soldiers peered inside. Floris sat next to Anton; he had no intention of inspecting any gruesome death pits.

"Do you have any cigarettes?" a voice in German asked, and Floris looked up to find one of the men had approached him, eyeing him inquisitively. "Can you spare one? We haven't had any for a week."

Floris studied the man, who was at least ten years younger than him. His uniform was creased, lined with dirt, and let off a foul stench of smoke and something else. It was the same smell Floris couldn't place earlier, but now he knew—it was death.

"Here you go." Floris handed the man a cigarette from his pack. Even though he didn't smoke, he accepted his rations; they might come in handy later. "What did these people do?" He nodded toward the pits.

"What do you mean?" the man asked, lighting up a cigarette. "They're Jews." He took a drag and sighed contentedly as he exhaled the smoke. "Don't need another reason, do we?"

"The entire town was Jewish?" Floris couldn't contain his disbelief.

The man's eyes narrowed, and he cocked his head. "No, not all of them were Jews. But they were harboring Jews and getting ready to attack the army from the rear." The sight of the banners welcoming them to the town flashed through Floris' mind, but he decided not to mention it. "They were armed and pretending to be civilians. Did you not see their fortifications around the square? You should be thankful we got here before you did, or you might've found yourself with a bullet to the head." With that, the man turned and walked back to his companions near the mass graves, not bothering to thank Floris for the cigarette.

"You know who those guys are, don't you?" a soldier next to Anton said, nodding at the men near the pits. When Floris shook his head, he continued. "They're *Einsatzgruppen*. They operate behind the front lines; their only mission is to kill as many Jews and communists as possible." He spat on the ground. "They're scum."

"Society must be cleansed of the Jews," Floris said without emotion as he stared at the pits. "But these people were no threat, and they weren't all Jews."

"Those men over there, they are animals. They will rape, pillage, and murder in the name of the Reich. They're not fit to wear the same uniform, as they'll never see a day of combat in their lives."

From the front of the group came the command to get ready to move out. Floris helped Anton back onto his feet. His friend had regained some color in his face, but still looked haunted.

They moved out five minutes later, and as they left the burning town behind them, Floris prayed this was the last time he'd have to witness the work of the Einsatzgruppen. He was here to fight the Red Army and communism, not to witness the slaughter of women and children.

Floris' company marched for the rest of the day. As they headed east, the rumble of artillery fire became more prominent. They passed more villages on the way, most deserted, although Floris did see some farmers in the fields in the distance. They made sure to stay well clear of the marching soldiers. Thankfully, there had been no further evidence of the Einsatzgruppen having made their way through these villages. Not yet anyway.

It was late in the afternoon when the host of soldiers stopped again. They would rest for half an hour, and the men were encouraged to eat. Their final stretch would take them to Wiking division, and their commander said they might need to go into battle right away.

With their destination and the prospect of a hot meal in sight, Floris and Anton each took out a hunk of bread and stacked it with their entire ration of sausage. They sat quietly in the grass along the road and chewed furiously.

"Do you think we'll really be sent off to combat when we arrive?" Anton plucked at a piece of sausage.

"I can't imagine it's that bad. Besides, they'd need to brief us on the situation first."

"I suppose so. But how do you feel about it? We're nearly there. Are you ready to fight the Russians?"

Floris looked into the distance, where dark plumes rose from the horizon. "No matter what's waiting for us there, we're joining one of the best divisions of the German army. There will be no better men to fight alongside."

Anton took another bite of his sandwich. He didn't look convinced, his eyes scanning the men around them. He lowered his voice. "What did you think of the men joining us in Graz? They seem rather full of themselves, don't you think?"

"They did seem to think less of us," Floris agreed. "But they must've been surprised to see fresh recruits like us, less than a month at Sennheim, being sent to the front lines. How would you feel about that if you were in their shoes?"

"I guess I'd feel the same way. But we'll prove them wrong."

"That's the only thing we can do to change their minds. Besides, they'll come around soon once they find out they need us. I'm sure we're all equals once we join up with Wiking and Westland."

Anton looked more confident. "We're all fighting the same enemy in the end."

A shrill whistle sounded, indicating the break was over. Floris stuffed the last bit of bread in his mouth, stood, and picked up his field pack. "Don't worry too much, Anton." He held out his hand to his friend. "We may not have had as much training, but we'll fight just as hard once we're on the front lines."

They marched for another three hours, the air getting colder as the sun disappeared—first behind clouds, then behind the horizon. The artillery explosions grew stronger, the ground beneath their feet now shaking frequently. Floris feared they might not make it to Wiking before nightfall, and he wondered when the command to set up camp would sound, when excited voices carried from the front of the company. Feeling a flutter in his stomach, he—and the men around him—increased the pace to cross a small incline. Once he reached the top, he was astounded by the sight.

Dozens of tanks were stationed in a large clearing, with hundreds of men crowding around. Some of them leaned against the tanks, while others ran around carrying parts. Beyond the rows of tanks at least a couple of thousand soldiers were standing around. There was a semblance of a formation, and the men looked agitated but calm. They smoked cigarettes, chatted, while some had stretched out in the grass, trying to nap. Thick plumes of smoke came from large tents to the side of the gathering, where men queued up around large cauldrons. Floris' mouth watered at the thought of a hot meal.

They continued toward the assembled army, and those men had clearly experienced more than their fair share of battle. Their uniforms were muddy and tattered. Floris walked among the men and studied them. They faced the newcomers with tired eyes. Floris was surprised when he caught thinly veiled looks of scorn in his direction. He quickly looked away, not wishing to upset the weary veterans who would soon be his brothers.

"They don't seem too thrilled to see us," Anton said in a low voice, his eyes darting between the men.

"Probably has something to do with us marching in with our clean uniforms. I doubt they've had a proper shower in weeks," Floris said. A feeling of unease washed over him as he realized he was looking at his future.

The company of recruits stopped in a clearing in the middle of the makeshift camp. It didn't take long for the towering voice of their commander to boom through the ranks.

"Gentlemen, welcome to Wiking. As you probably understand, we're in a garrison behind the front lines." He pointed toward the plumes of smoke rising in the distance, to the booms of almost incessant artillery barrages. "Soon, you'll have your chance to make a difference for the Reich, but first, you must link up with your new regiments. The men gathered here will escort you to your new positions."

The commander called out the different regiments, indicating where the recruits were to report. He called out Westland, and Floris, Anton, and about fifty other men moved to their designated spot. There, they were greeted by a German officer. As soon as Floris saw the man's face, he knew this would not be a pleasant welcoming.

"So, you've finally made it," the man said with a snarl. "Well, it took you long enough. We might not have had to retreat if you'd arrived a little sooner. I'll take you to the rest of your regiment." He turned on his heel and marched off, cutting through a group of soldiers near the tanks.

Floris and the others hurried after him, stunned by this unexpectedly harsh welcome. "You'd think he'd be happy with reinforcements," Floris mumbled out of the corner of his mouth. They passed the soldiers crowding around the tanks, and Floris heard them mutter in German.

"Ah, more useless new recruits. Where are these from then?" one of them said.

"They're with Diettrich, so they're joining up with Westland."

"Ah, more dumb criminals from the Netherlands," the other man said, loud enough for everyone to hear. The men gathering around laughed and jeered at Floris' group.

"They should've been here weeks ago, I heard. But they were too scared to make it to Charkov in time. Most of them didn't even pass their training, but they were sent here nonetheless. Standards are dropping, I tell you."

"Well, at least they'll make good cannon fodder."

Floris was stunned. *What's going on? We're supposed to be on the same side.* He looked at the faces of the other recruits, but they had either not heard or didn't understand. Finally, Floris stopped and turned, ready to confront the soldiers near the tank. *Who do they think they are?* Adrenaline shot through his veins, the blood rushing to his head. Then he felt a hand on his arm.

"Don't do it, Floris. It's not worth it. Let them talk their shit. They're frustrated and tired. You can see they've been through a lot, right?"

Floris looked at Anton, then at the men near the tanks. Their attention had shifted to a group of men carrying cauldrons of soup across the camp. He looked at the faces of the German soldiers and realized they were much younger than him. Some couldn't be older than eighteen. Slowly, he felt his anger ebb away. "They simply don't know any better, do they?"

"Probably not. They might not even have had a choice in joining. And if it's true that they suffered big losses recently, it makes sense they're not exactly thrilled about us arriving now, when things appear to have calmed down." Anton's gaze moved beyond the men on the tanks. "Come, let's keep up with our group. Let's find out more from the men in Westland. I'm sure our compatriots will be happy to see us. At the very least, they'll be anxious to hear of news from back home."

CHAPTER TWENTY-ONE

The train station was just a single platform between the double tracks. There was a cramped sheltered waiting area on either end. Without the faded signs indicating this was the Solre-sur-Sambre train station, it would be easy to miss.

"Are you sure this is the right station?" Katja asked Lars as she watched the train disappear in the distance. Nora looked across the vast fields surrounding them, her eyes caught by a large castle dominating the town's outline. "Look, there's the castle Matthieu told us to watch for," she said, pointing out the structure in the distance.

The other three all looked relieved, Lars especially. There had been a short argument on the train about whether they should get off at this station or the next. Katja had insisted it was at Erquelines that they should disembark, but Lars had held his ground. Nora had sided with Lars in the end, and the other two had gotten off with them. When Nora didn't immediately see the castle their contact in Brussels had told them to look for, she had second thoughts. Now, however, they were another step closer to getting to France.

"Well, shall we just go, then?" Lars said with a smirk. "No sense in keeping the man waiting."

They had left Brussels two hours earlier. Matthieu, their contact in Brussels, had handed them papers identifying them as Belgian students residing in Paris. He explained it was the best cover they could use, considering they didn't speak French. They could claim they were still learning the language. He'd told them to revert to the best German they could muster when in doubt. The German patrols would appreciate the effort, while the French would most likely not ask too many questions. Nora was a bit nervous, but Matthieu assured her there would be few checks once they were in France. *Now there's just the small matter of making it past the border.*

They crossed the railway line, and Nora peered down the empty tracks. Following those rails, France was only a few minutes away, but they wouldn't be traveling by train.

"Say, do you know what this man is supposed to look like?" Lars said, kicking a pebble down the dusty road.

She shook her head. "No, but I doubt there will be many people waiting there. Look around, this place is deserted."

"I'll be happy once we're off the road," Arthur said, upping his pace and taking the lead. "I bet everybody knows each other in this little town. If anyone spots us, they might get suspicious."

"Oh, calm down," Lars said mockingly. "Nobody cares about us around here."

Nora frowned and matched Arthur's pace. Even though she appreciated Lars' confidence along their journey, she agreed with Arthur this time. "He's right. It's easy enough to blend with the crowds in the cities, but I feel a bit uncomfortable here as well. So let's get to the castle." Arthur shot her a grateful look while Lars and Katja caught up with them.

They reached the castle without running into anyone, although Nora thought she saw some of the curtains move behind the windows in the houses along the road. She hoped none of the people in Solre-sur-Sambre were Nazi sympathizers.

The castle looked much nicer from a distance than it did up close, surrounded as it was by a moat covered in leaves. They crossed a rickety bridge, the wooden planks squeaking. Inside, any attempts at maintenance of the gardens had long been abandoned. What must once have been a neatly trimmed lawn in the middle of the courtyard was overgrown with wildflowers and weeds. Nora shivered; it felt like she was entering a haunted castle, its occupants long gone.

"So, where do you think he's hiding?" Lars stepped onto the overgrown lawn and pulled at some of the weeds. They gave way quickly as he tore them out by the root. "We're on time, aren't we?"

Nora focused on the ornate front door on the far side of the courtyard. She stepped toward it and pushed against it. It was closed, but she felt compelled to try again. The door didn't move, but she did hear footsteps echoing on the other side. Startled, she stepped away. Seconds later it opened to reveal a man wearing a faded brown leather jacket. He towered over Nora, his eyes studying her with interest. Then he looked past her, appraising the others in the courtyard. He cocked his head and addressed Nora in French. She felt her face flush, not understanding his words. She opened her mouth, but then heard a familiar voice behind her. Stunned, she turned around to see Arthur calmly approaching, speaking French while gesturing with his hands to Nora, Katja, and finally Lars. The man standing in the doorway grinned, and he switched to Dutch.

"Well, I'm glad one of you speaks French. That will make your journey south a lot easier." He held out his hand. "I'm Pierre. That's not my real name, but that's what you'll call me."

Nora felt immense relief as she shook Pierre's strong hand. He stepped into the courtyard. "We better get moving if you want to get yourselves on a train to Paris today."

"Today?" Nora was surprised, then caught herself. She had been so concerned about getting across the border that she hadn't thought of what they would do on the other side.

Pierre looked at her curiously. "Well, of course. You don't want to spend more time than you need in that dreadful town across the border. Come, if we keep a brisk pace, you should be able to catch the two p.m. train." He was already near the drawbridge and Nora hurried to keep up. She caught a look from Lars, his eyes sparkling. He seemed amused by the situation.

Once outside, Pierre guided them away from the village, following the road parallel to the railway tracks. Pierre took enormous strides, as if he was in a hurry. She caught up with him just as he stepped off the main road and onto a narrow sandy path.

"Pierre, if you don't mind me asking, where are you taking us?"

"What do you mean? To France, of course," he said without breaking stride.

"But how, exactly? Where are we going now?"

"They didn't tell you anything in Brussels?" Nora shook her head, and he grinned. "Might as well tell you now, then." He stopped and pointed ahead. "You see the tree line beyond those fields? You can't see it now, but behind it lies Erquelines. It's the last Belgian town before the border."

"Sure, it's where our train was headed."

"Exactly. Now, if there wasn't war going on, you would get off the train at Erquelines, show your passport to the friendly *gendarmes* —border guards—and cross the platform to board the French train heading to Paris." He continued walking, not missing a beat as he spoke. "But today, we're going to avoid the town altogether. Too many Germans sticking their noses into everyone's business. We'll head south when we get to those trees and walk into France instead."

"You can just cross the border like that?"

He stopped and turned, looking at her as if she had just asked the most obvious question in the world. "*Oui*, it's as easy as that. We walk. You'll see. Come on, keep up."

When they reached the tree line, Pierre told them to wait. He disappeared between the leaves and branches, leaving them in the field.

"What do you think about him?" Lars said, looking at the others.

Katja crossed her arms and shot him an annoyed look. "What do you mean? He's helping us."

Nora frowned, and Lars held up his hands. "He seems a little too confident about this, don't you think? Don't you remember those men we ran into when we crossed into Belgium?"

"We weren't the ones walking out into the open," Arthur said, raising an eyebrow. "He seems to know what he's doing. And what else are we going to do?"

"If he's part of the escape line network, like Matthieu and Nicolas, we have no other option but to trust him," Nora added. *Why is Lars suddenly kicking up a fuss?* She took a step closer to Lars. "Hey, we're going to be fine. Pierre knows what he's doing. And Arthur is right; there's nowhere else to go."

Lars narrowed his eyes, and Nora saw some of his fiery attitude return. His gaze went between Nora, Arthur, and Katja. "All right. But let's promise each other that we speak up if something goes wrong, if it doesn't feel right." Nora opened her mouth, but Lars wasn't done yet. "And if it's too late, and we can't speak anymore, we need to look out for each other. It's just the four of us here, and we're about to be even farther away from home once we cross that border."

"But think of yourselves first of all." Pierre's voice came from the trees. "You might come to a point where you can't help each other anymore. When that happens, you run like hell and look after yourselves." The Belgian reappeared from the trees.

They looked at him in shock. *How much has he heard?* Nora studied Pierre's face but saw no malice. "Come, the road is clear. Let's keep moving. We're almost there."

They crossed the thin windbreak and stepped onto a gravel road. "This is an old logging path," Pierre explained. They walked for another fifteen minutes without running into any other traffic when Pierre stopped at a fork in the road. "The border is just five minutes from here. He should be here momentarily."

"He?" Nora's brows shot up. *Who else are we expecting?*

Pierre took a sip from his army-issued canteen and smacked his lips. "You didn't think I was going to escort you across the border on my own, did you?"

Before anyone could respond, they heard a grating sound coming from one of the roads joining the fork. Much to Nora's surprise, a man wearing an official-looking uniform approached on a rusty bicycle. He casually whistled a tune as he spotted Pierre. The faces of Nora's companions betrayed the same shock she felt.

The man parked his bike against a tree and sauntered over. He shook Pierre's hand and nodded at Nora and the others. "Ready to go?" Without waiting for an answer, he started in the direction of the French border. Too stunned to respond, Nora and the others followed.

Sensing their surprise, Pierre explained. "This is Louis, wearing the Belgian border patrol uniform. He's in charge of making sure nothing, and no one, illegal crosses into Belgium without his knowledge." Pierre winked at Nora. "He'll accompany us to Jeumont on the other side of the border."

Nora was still confused. "But what about the French border guards?"

"Don't worry about them," Louis said from the front. "This is not the first time we're doing this."

Nora found it impossible not to worry as they walked on. Oddly enough, Lars remained quiet, his face stoic. Katja and Arthur walked a few paces behind them, talking in hushed tones.

They continued, and the gravel road turned into a paved road, a few small houses appearing alongside. Then they turned, and a large overpass loomed about three hundred meters ahead. Pierre turned around and said, "France is just behind that overpass."

They had continued for a few seconds when Lars spoke up. "Wait, there's someone atop that overpass. Is it..."

Nora felt her throat constrict as she focused on the figure. "A German soldier." They were so close to France. "We can still get out of sight," she said, turning back to find Lars, Katja, and

Arthur's gazes going between her and the soldier on the overpass. *Shit!*

"Hey, what's the problem?" Louis and Pierre had continued and walked a good twenty meters ahead. Pierre's neutral expression changed to concern when he caught sight of the four refugees. "What's wrong?" the tall Belgian said as he paced back to them.

"The German soldier on the overpass," Nora said, her voice hoarse. "Didn't you see him?" She pointed at the German, who now looked in their direction. *He's spotted us. It's all over.*

Pierre glanced back at the overpass and shrugged. "What about him?"

What? Nora wasn't sure she heard him correctly.

"Just keep walking, don't worry about him," Pierre said a little more forcefully. "Trust me." He turned and caught up with Louis, who rolled his eyes and said something Nora didn't understand. She felt faint and was no longer sure what to think. *Is this a setup?* Nora looked back to her travel companions and was shocked to see Arthur moving ahead. Katja quickly followed, and Nora met Lars' eyes. He looked as torn as her but continued forward. "We can't go back, remember? You said so yourself." He gently took her arm. "Let's not draw more attention to ourselves by standing around."

Nora's heart pounded in her throat as she focused on putting one foot before another. The overpass came closer, and she forced herself not to look up. She could almost feel the German soldier's gaze as she focused on the back of Arthur's shoes in front of her. She walked into the shadow of the overpass, waiting for the command to halt. Nora stepped back into full daylight on the other side in a daze.

Only when Nora was sure they were clear of the overpass did she dare glance back. The soldier stood with his back to them, talking to a couple crossing the overpass. Pierre noticed her puzzlement.

"You know why that German soldier didn't stop us?" Nora looked at him and shook her head. "Because his job is to oversee the traffic on the overpass. Nobody's told him anything about what happens on the road running underneath."

Nora looked at him in shock, not sure she comprehended. "You mean you've never been stopped?"

"Never." Pierre grinned. "They're very particular about their orders."

Louis interrupted them, pointing to a small building by the side of the road. "Follow me, please."

They entered the building to find a man wearing a uniform very similar to Louis'. The man greeted Louis and Pierre heartily, slapping their backs as he did. Then he looked at Nora and her companions, his face beaming. *"Bienvenue en France!"*

Nora felt weak with relief. *Have we really made it?*

Pierre approached her, putting a hand on her shoulder, his eyes twinkling. "Come, let's get your papers stamped to make sure they look genuine in case anyone asks. And then, it's time to head to the train station. You can still make the next train to Paris if we hurry."

CHAPTER TWENTY-TWO

Walking around the city felt unfamiliar at first. When Christiaan arrived at Amsterdam's Central station, he'd half expected his brother and a host of policemen to spring from the shadows. Of course, none of that had happened. Nevertheless, he was careful to look out for checkpoints, even if Somer had assured him his papers would see him clear those without scrutiny. Christiaan didn't want to take any chances.

He resisted the temptation to check in on his sister-in-law, even though he couldn't wait to see her again. There would be plenty of time to catch up with Nora later. But, for now, he had a mission to carry out, and he was keen to see if the contact Somer had mentioned would be in the cafe.

Entering the Jordaan neighborhood, leaving the wide canals behind, he cut through narrow streets with modest dwellings packed close together. Where the houses lining the larger canals were grand and tall, the dwellings in this traditionally blue collar neighborhood were smaller and gave off a more authentic Amsterdam feel. Flowerpots stood next to the doors lining the street. Normally, bikes would be parked haphazardly across the street, but these had become so valuable that no Amsterdammer in their right mind would leave one outside.

Christiaan was pleased he would be meeting his contact in one of the cafes a few blocks over. Somehow, it felt fitting. The sky was overcast, adding to the cloak-and-dagger feel of his operation. Christiaan picked up his pace and soon found himself standing in front of an unassuming establishment called *De Rover*. Thin white curtains with flowery embroidery lined the bottom half of the windows, a typical feature of Amsterdam cafes, giving a sense of privacy to the patrons sitting inside.

He opened the door and stepped inside a small, cozy room. The lights were low, and the dark wooden paneling lining the walls added to the homey atmosphere. The scent of cigarettes entered his nostrils as he looked around. It was just two in the afternoon, and there were very few patrons. Only a pair of tables in opposite corners were taken, their occupants barely acknowledging Christiaan's entrance. A heavyset man was behind the bar, his face that of someone who had spent most of his life in cigarette smoke. He inclined his head as he approached and said, "What can I get you?"

Christiaan remembered Somer's instructions, and he swallowed before responding. "I'll have a *kopstoot*, if you have one." The bartender poured a shot of jenever and a glass of beer. This order wasn't out of the ordinary, but what Christiaan would request next should confirm if Somer's network was still operational. Christiaan prayed it was, and as he lifted the glass of jenever, he said, "Would it be possible to order something to eat?" In normal times, it wouldn't be an odd question, for most cafes—even the smallest ones—would offer at least a serving of peanuts, cheese, and sausage. In wartime, it was almost unheard of.

The barkeeper frowned, but there was understanding in his eyes as he leaned forward. "I wish I could offer you something, but times are hard. Between you and me, I'm happy to be able to pour you a beer. I'm only receiving shipments because some NSB men working at the coupon office down the street like to have a drink after work."

Christiaan nodded, but inwardly he was smiling. The man had mentioned the NSB and coupon office, just like Somer had said. "Do you think you could put me into contact with someone who would help me secure some goods?" Of course, to anyone listening, the sentence would mean nothing.

"Matter of fact, I can. He should be arriving within half an hour from now. Why don't you take a seat over there." He pointed at a small table next to the bar, separated from the main room by a small wall. "I'll have him come to you."

Christiaan stood and reached for his beer. The barkeeper grabbed the shot glass and poured him another jenever. "Here you go." His eyed went to the occupied tables on the other side of the room, and he spoke softly. "You can't imagine how long it's been since I've had someone coming in here speaking those words."

Christiaan nodded his thanks and sat at the table while sipping his beer. On the train into Amsterdam he had thought about his companions, and he'd come to the conclusion there was more to Piet and Bram than met the eye. This hadn't been their first jump into enemy territory. Piet had remained icily cool when he'd lost his equipment. Bram's response when approaching the people between their equipment and them had been equally experienced. Whoever they were, they knew exactly what they were doing. It gave Christiaan confidence to know he was working in a network with capable people, and he was looking forward to meeting the men of the Ordedienst.

He hadn't thought of a way to unite the different resistance factions in the city yet, which gave him slight anxiety. When Queen Wilhelmina and Colonel Somer talked about it, it sounded so easy. Christiaan would swoop in, tell the different factions about their plans, and they would all fall in line. But as Christiaan had time to think it through, he remembered the factions were fractured for a reason. It made it much harder for the Germans to bring down the operation if the factions weren't aware of each other's activities. The hard truth had hit Christiaan as he stepped off the train; he would need to find a way to gain their trust, and that would be supremely difficult. *But I'll be damned if I don't try.*

The scraping of a chair brought him back to the present. A man in his early forties with a pockmarked face sat across from him. The man put his hands on the table and observed Christiaan for a few seconds. Then he extended a hand. "I'm Bob. Henry over there," he said, pointing at the barkeeper behind him, "Henry said you have something you want to ask me. Something about the NSB and the coupon supplies?"

Christiaan shook the man's hand. Meanwhile, he felt adrenaline coursing through his veins. Bob had mentioned the code words. His voice thick with anticipation, Christiaan responded, "I've heard they've had some setbacks recently." He leaned back in his chair, now studying Bob's face for the correct response. For a good ten seconds, Bob didn't respond, returning Christiaan's stare. Finally, their standoff was broken by Henry, who placed a beer in front of Bob before quickly returning to his spot behind the bar. Bob raised his glass and took a sip, and when he put it back on the table, he leaned forward, his face relaxing.

"You know, when Henry told me you were here just now, I could hardly believe it. Do you know how long it's been since anybody from across the Channel walked in here? When did you arrive?"

Christiaan felt a weight lift from his shoulders. "We landed last night."

"We?" Bob raised an eyebrow. "Never mind, I don't want to know. Did you all make it out all right?"

"We did, but I'm operating alone. The others should be establishing contact with London soon."

"Bloody hell, you sound confident," Bob said, staring at Christiaan. "I'm sorry, but I'm surprised. The past month has been filled with doom and gloom, and here you are, all fresh and optimistic about reporting back to London." He took another large gulp of his beer. "I almost gave up on coming here every day, but I guess it shows you should never give up, huh?"

Christiaan listened to the man with interest. Even though he'd expected to find the Ordedienst welcoming, this man seemed mostly relieved to find him here. "So, what's next? Where do I go to let London know I've arrived safely? Do you have any radios?"

The man swirled the remaining beer in his glass. "You should come with me. The leadership will be very interested to hear of your arrival." He looked at the clock on the wall behind the bar. "In fact, the big man should be at the church right now."

The church? The big man? Christiaan was intrigued. He stood. "Take me to them."

It was only a short ten-minute walk to the Koepelkerk, located between the Jordaan neighborhood and Amsterdam's Central station. Christiaan had passed the imposing church many times, but he was surprised when Bob nudged him toward the domed church's entrance.

"Your headquarters are in the Koepelkerk?" Christiaan asked as he stepped inside the house of worship. Imposing paintings covered the bottom of the dome. The large, high windows lining the walls let in an incredible amount of light; it was almost brighter inside the church than outside.

Bob was already halfway down the aisle and urged him to follow. "Come on, we don't want to miss the Esquire."

Esquire? Christiaan frowned. A church was an odd place for an esquire to reside, but he caught up with Bob, nonetheless. He led him through a door behind the pulpit, revealing a large stairwell. They mounted the stairs and, at the top, reached a narrow hallway. Bob knocked on a door, and a muffled voice responded. He opened the door and indicated for Christiaan to enter first. Bob closed the door behind them, and Christiaan found himself in another bright room with smaller, more modest windows still allowing plenty of daylight to stream in. A man reading from a file sat on the far side of the room.

He didn't immediately acknowledge his visitors, and Bob moved toward him. Christiaan followed at a slight distance.

"Esquire Six," Bob said, scraping his throat. "I believe you'll want to speak with this man."

The man looked up, placing the file on the desk. Christiaan estimated him to be in his late forties, perhaps early fifties. He took off his glasses, placing them on the file. His eyes showed intelligence, and his face had an openness Christiaan found instantly disarming. He looked at Christiaan, then Bob, and then appeared to remember something, as a slight smile appeared on his face. "Thank you, Bob. It's been a long time since you brought an outsider into my office. Can I assume he brings good tidings?"

"Yes, sir. He was waiting for me at De Rover this afternoon."

Six's eyebrows shot up at the mention of the cafe. "Where did you come from?" he asked without preamble.

Christiaan's eyes went between the man behind the desk and Bob. *Who is this man?* "I'm sorry, sir, but I'm a little confused. Where am I?"

Six looked annoyed for a moment, then appeared to catch himself. "Of course. I haven't even introduced myself yet. My name is Piet Jacob Six, but most prefer to use my noble title, Esquire. Please don't ask me why; consider it a nickname. I'm the leader of the Ordedienst." He stood and held out his hand. "And if I understood what Bob told me correctly, you have just arrived home from England?"

Standing behind the desk, Six was taller than Christiaan had estimated from him sitting down. The man made for an impressive sight, and when Christiaan shook his hand, he could feel confidence and power radiating from the man. "Sir, I was sent to contact your organization by Colonel Somer."

Six looked momentarily taken aback by the mention of Somer and sat back down, indicating for Christiaan to do the same. Then, with a flick of the wrist, he dismissed Bob, waiting for him to leave before continuing. "Did Bob tell you anything about what's been happening here?"

"Only that he was very surprised to see me in the cafe earlier. He said he couldn't remember the last time he met someone from across the Channel, sir."

"That's because we haven't had any agents reporting in for months now," Six said with a sigh. "Is Colonel Somer still with Bureau Inlichtingen?"

"He's leading the Bureau, sir."

"Right. Very well." Six was quiet for a minute, seemingly pondering his next words. "To be perfectly honest with you, I'm surprised you made it here today."

"How so, sir?" An uncomfortable ball was forming inside Christiaan's stomach.

"We've been in touch with the British and the Dutch governments since the start of the war. We've supplied our government with valuable intelligence, and the communication lines have always been good. We've helped Dutch agents sent by the Special Operations Executive find their feet in the Netherlands. That's what Bob was talking about earlier; he would wait for them to make contact. But that all changed recently. The agents stopped coming, and we assumed perhaps the operation had been paused or even halted."

"Would they not inform you about this?"

Six let out a deep sigh. "They may well have tried. It is wartime, after all, and we are a resistance faction. Messages get lost along the way sometimes. I didn't think much of it, until about three months ago."

"What happened?"

"We received word that several prisoners had escaped from Haaren seminary in the south of the country. The Nazis converted it into a prison for political prisoners. Two men escaped and contacted us. What they told me changed everything I assumed about the SOE's operation in the Netherlands." He paused, but Christiaan already knew what he would say next. "They informed us the Germans had infiltrated the SOE's Dutch network, transmitting false intelligence to London, while the agents are held in Haaren."

"So the rumors were true," Christiaan said softly.

"You knew about this?" Six looked incredulous. "I sent word to London as soon as I heard, letting them know they needed to stop sending agents to the Netherlands and that their network was compromised. Despite this, I received word from my connections in German intelligence that they apprehended at least four more agents in July."

"Before I left, there were rumors that several people at the SOE knew something wasn't quite right. However, the official line was that everything was fine, and they were receiving valuable intelligence." Six shook his head, and Christiaan continued. "But Colonel Somer was worried, sir. None of the agents had returned to England for months. He told me it is customary for agents to return after they've spent time behind enemy lines. That's why he sent me and two radio operators."

"Are you saying Somer is operating outside SOE directives?"

"He is, sir. And listening to you, I believe that's the only reason I'm sitting here with you today instead of in an interrogation room in Haaren."

"It's good to know we still have some capable people in England. But we should let Somer know you've arrived and confirm his suspicions about the SOE network."

"You mentioned you were sending messages to the SOE, sir. Do you still have a working radio?" When Six nodded, Christiaan added, "We should send a message to him directly, using my call sign. Then he'll know the message is genuine. The SOE don't have to know anything about it."

"And the Germans won't be able to pick it up, either."

"Exactly. Can we broadcast tonight? Somer's people will be waiting for my message."

Christiaan left the Koepelkerk fifteen minutes later. He had spoken with Six about his mission, and the leader of the OD had been very receptive to the idea, especially after Christiaan mentioned this mission came from Queen Wilhelmina herself. He informed Christiaan the Ordedienst was already working on a national communications network that would be ready to use once the liberation started. Six had even offered to reach out to some of his contacts within the other groups.

Christiaan had a spring in his step as he headed east, crossing through the city center. The canals were deserted as the weather had turned a bit colder. The people passing by wore their fall jackets, avoiding his gaze as they rushed home. Christiaan could feel the change in the air; his beloved Amsterdam had changed even in the six months he had been away. People were more distant, more detached—the occupation had hardened people's souls as they prepared for another miserable winter. Nevertheless, he comforted himself in the knowledge that he was part of a growing number of people working to end the occupation. His meeting with Six had strengthened his resolve—they could do this.

He turned onto the Zeedijk, his pulse increasing as Cafe 't Mandje came in sight. He was pleased to see light shining through the curtains, a faint humming of the music and crowd inside filtering through as he reached to open the door. The main room was busier than he'd expected, with half a dozen people crowding around the bar while all tables were filled. Behind the bar he saw the familiar face of one of his best friends, Bet van Beeren. Christiaan stood near the door, observing as she struggled to keep up with the orders. He joined the queue at the bar and marveled at her efficiency as she cleared the crowd within a few minutes. She held out a beer to the man in front of Christiaan, then almost dropped it when she caught sight of him.

"Well, look at this!" Her voice was shaking as she put the glass down and ran to the opening on the far side of the bar. Seconds later Christiaan felt Bet's strong arms around him, squeezing him like a mother would a long-lost son. "Christiaan! I did not expect to see you here!" She looked at him with misty eyes, which she quickly wiped. "Look what you're doing to me! When did you get back?"

"Hey, can I order another—" came the voice of a man next to them.

"In a minute!" Bet practically hissed at him, and he cowered back. "Bar's closed for a few minutes." The man walked away, returning to his table.

"I see you're still ruling this place with your iron fist, Bet." Christiaan's eyes were stinging a bit as well; he was just as happy to see Bet. "We have a lot to catch up on, but I see you're a bit busy. Perhaps I should come back later."

"I'm one of the few cafes that still secures a good supply of booze. Pretending to be a Nazi supporter helps, I guess," she said, before adding in a lower voice, "As long as they don't know about my extracurricular activities, right?" She turned to the bar and grabbed two small glasses and a bottle of jenever. She poured them both a generous portion and held up her glass. "To you returning home. I don't care what the reason is."

They clinked glasses, and Bet sat on a stool next to him. Christiaan decided he could discuss details about the resistance later when there were fewer people around, but he needed to know something urgently. "Do you know how Nora is doing?"

Bet's face darkened, and the sound of the people around them faded. "I suppose you haven't heard." She quickly shook her head. "Of course not; how could you have?"

"What is it, Bet? What happened?" Christiaan's throat constricted. Did something happen to Nora? Had Floris finally caught up with her? *Am I too late?*

"Nora left Amsterdam."

"What? Why?"

"Long story short? Right after you left, your brother confronted her at the crèche. He was going to take her in and bring down the whole place. Thankfully, some men from the school next door intervened, and they caught Floris."

"What do you mean, caught him? Last I heard, he disappeared?"

"He did. To a basement cell run by the resistance. They kept him there for months, and he was about to be executed." Christiaan's expression must've betrayed his horror, for she quickly shook her head. "He escaped, Chris. Your brother murdered one of the guards and escaped."

"You're not serious."

"As a hangman. When that happened, Nora knew she had to leave. She took a train south, about two months ago."

Christiaan put his hands on his knees, struggling to breathe. "And Floris? His bosses must've been delighted to have him back?"

"They were, at first, when he told them about the crèche. Raided the place on the day he escaped, he did. But then, he disappeared as well."

"He what? How?"

"Nobody knows what happened." Bet shrugged. "But he hasn't been seen anywhere around town for months. Disappeared shortly after Nora did."

"Do you think he went after her?" Christiaan was alarmed at the thought.

"I doubt it. Your brother wouldn't give up his position at the Bureau of Jewish Affairs so easily. I think there are two possibilities. He was offered a promotion somewhere else, or he upset the wrong people and got transferred."

Christiaan considered the two options. "I suppose the most important thing is that he's no longer here." Even though he was shocked by Bet's revelations, the absence of his brother from the city was welcome news. He wouldn't have to worry about running into Floris. Yet, the news about Nora made him feel dizzy. She was one of the reasons he came back, and now she was no longer here. He prayed she didn't take the route to Geneva, and his heart went cold at the thought of the Gestapo getting their hands on her.

"Look, Chris, I would love to catch up more, but I've got a lot of thirsty customers waiting," Bet said, nodding at the increasing number of impatient patrons behind her. "Why don't you come back tonight after closing time? Do you have a place to stay yet?"

Christiaan realized he didn't, and he accepted her invitation gratefully. "I'll be back tonight. Thanks, Bet."

"Don't mention it. You're family." She gave him a kiss on the cheek and moved back to the other side of the bar. Christiaan stepped outside. He needed a walk to clear his head before heading back to Esquire Six later. Lisa's words in London echoed in his mind. *This is not the Amsterdam we left.*

CHAPTER TWENTY-THREE

Lisa hurried into the office a little after eight, surprised to find all but one of her colleagues already at their desks. She frowned as she sat opposite Femke.

"You're all in early. Did I miss anything?"

Femke shook her head. "Not really; I suppose we just all wanted to get a head start on the day." She pointed at the stack of papers next to her typewriter. "Much activity on the wireless last night. I wonder if something big is happening. I haven't had a chance to talk to the other girls yet, but it seems I'm stuck with messages from the consulates." She talked while her fingers danced on the keys of her typewriter.

Lisa's desk was empty, which was odd. Her supervisor would normally have placed the thickest stack on her desk. She knew it was partly because she was the best typist and because he appeared to enjoy overloading her with work. *I guess I'll have to ask him what's going on.* She sighed and headed for her supervisor's office. He was reading a newspaper, sitting with his feet on his desk, as Lisa knocked on his open door. She suppressed a remark on his relative comfort compared to the women in the typists' room. "I hear there's a lot of work for us today, sir. I didn't find anything assigned to me."

"Ah, yes, Lisa. I'm glad you finally decided to show." Bakker glanced up from his newspaper, not even pretending to feel slightly uncomfortable about getting caught with his feet up. "The boss wants to see you right away."

Lisa raised an eyebrow. "The boss?"

"Colonel Somer. I was told to send you to him as soon as you came in. Better hurry, his assistant came asking for you more than half an hour ago. It seemed urgent." His face disappeared behind the newspaper, and Lisa turned into the hallway, slowly heading toward Somer's office. Had something gone wrong with Christiaan? There could hardly be any other reason for the Bureau's chief to talk to her, especially after their chat in the archives room. Christiaan had left two days ago; by now, he should've confirmed he arrived safely. Lisa had kept her eyes peeled for messages coming in from the Netherlands, and the other typists would surely let her know if anything came in.

Her legs felt heavy as she stopped before Somer's closed door. She took a deep breath, which did nothing to steady her nerves and, hands shaking, rapped her knuckles on the door. A voice called to enter, and she pushed open the door.

Somer looked up from behind his desk. His face was neutral as he told her to close the door. "Please have a seat, Miss Abrahams. I'm glad you're here. There have been some developments in the matter we spoke about the other day."

Lisa sat with apprehension. She had a sinking feeling in the pit of her stomach and instinctively folded her hands in her lap. "It's about Christiaan, isn't it?"

"Yes, and I thought you would want to know as soon as possible." He paused, and Lisa was unable to read anything from the expression on his face. She sucked in a sharp breath and braced herself. "He reported back last night from Amsterdam. He's made contact with the resistance."

Lisa blinked hard, unsure she'd heard the colonel's words correctly. "Christiaan is all right? He's alive?"

"Very much so," Somer said, his expression showing concern. "I'm sorry. Did I scare you?"

"Just a little, sir." Lisa's voice was strained, and she cleared her throat. "When Bakker said I needed to report to you, I prepared myself for the worst. But you're saying he's made it to Amsterdam already?"

"He did," Somer said, raising a finger. "What I'm about to tell you must stay between us." He didn't wait for her to affirm. "Agent Brouwer made contact with the Ordedienst, as was his mission. But I didn't call you in here to discuss his mission."

"I appreciate you letting me know he's safe, sir." Lisa moved to stand but to her surprise, Somer held up a hand.

"Please remain seated, Miss Abrahams. Agent Brouwer sent us new intelligence we can't ignore."

Lisa frowned. *Why is he telling me this?*

"The OD confirmed our suspicions around the Special Operations Executive's Dutch network." Somer's face went a shade paler as he spoke the words. "I'm afraid you were right to worry, Miss Abrahams."

"The Germans have infiltrated the network." Lisa focused her eyes on her hands. "What does that mean for Christiaan?"

"Well, since he's successfully made contact with the Ordedienst, he'll continue his mission as instructed."

Lisa looked up at Somer. "He's not in danger? How can you be sure it was really him sending the message?"

"Because he used the correct call sign. Before he stepped on the plane, I gave him two call signs; one in case he was captured, the other if he was safe. Nobody but Agent Brouwer and I knew about these call signs. Trust me, Miss Abrahams, he's safe," Somer said confidently. "But we don't know how much of the network has been compromised. More importantly, we need to ensure we don't send any more Dutch agents across the North Sea."

Christiaan got lucky.

"I need your help."

She closed her mouth, dumbfounded.

"Naturally, I must raise this with my peers at the SOE."

"Yes."

Somer shifted in his chair, looking uncomfortable. "But before I do, I want to make absolutely sure that I have all possible information at hand."

"How much more information do you need, sir? Are you questioning the intelligence from the Netherlands?"

"I'm not. I trust our contacts back home are operating in best faith with the information at hand." He fervently shook his head. "But it's only one source, and I know the men at the SOE will demand more proof that something is awry. This is a very political organization, and the revelation that their carefully built-up network is compromised won't be met with enthusiasm. I've tried to bring this up before, and they assured me all was well."

"With all due respect, sir, if you were having trouble getting through to these people, how can I make a difference?"

"I'd like you to reach out to someone within the SOE. From what I've heard, this man has rocked the boat before but has gone quiet since. Too quiet, to my liking."

"You think he's been told to keep his mouth shut?"

"Yes, although perhaps not so boldly. If I were to approach him, it would set off alarm bells everywhere. So, I was hoping you would meet with him and find out what he knows. He sounded like the kind of person who wouldn't just let this go." He smiled at her. "A bit like you, I suppose."

Lisa couldn't suppress a grin. "Who am I reaching out to, sir?"

It hadn't been difficult to locate Leo Marks. In fact, Lisa was surprised at how quickly she had been connected to him when she called the SOE headquarters. Perhaps the fact that she called from the Bureau Inlichtingen under the ruse of needing assistance analyzing recent messages helped, and the operator didn't ask any further questions before putting her through.

At first, Marks has been evasive, insisting he didn't know what she was talking about, claiming she had called the wrong person. Lisa had panicked for a minute, almost giving up, when she thought of the men back home in German captivity. When Marks was about to hang up, she'd told him she had proof from the Netherlands that the SOE network really was compromised. He had gone silent, but then indicated he was willing to listen to what she had to say.

She looked around the pub. It was almost five, and Lisa was glad she had arrived early to secure a table as those around her quickly filled. The bar staff struggled to keep up with the demand, and Lisa was—not for the first time—impressed with the resilience of the British people. Despite the hardship, their pub culture steadfastly remained a pillar of everyday life, a symbol of defiance and a safe haven from an uncertain and volatile world. Even Lisa managed to relax a little as she took a sip of her bitter and listened in on the conversations around her.

"Miss Abrahams?"

She looked up to find a diminutive man around her age standing by her table. He looked apprehensive; his shoulders hunched ever so slightly forward. Despite that, his eyes studied her curiously, intelligence shining through. Lisa decided she liked him and waved to the seat opposite. "Lisa, please. It's nice to put a face to a voice." He sat down, and she continued. "Thank you for meeting me right away. I understand what I said on the phone might've overwhelmed you."

He took off his coat and placed it on the seat next to him. "Not at all, Miss Abraha—Lisa. To be honest, I was surprised to receive a call, from none other than someone at Dutch intelligence. I imagined the operators must've put me on a blacklist." His voice was a bit shaky, and Lisa realized he was nervous.

"How so? May I call you Leo?"

He nodded. "Well, because I've been demoted to my own little office, if you can even call it that—it's more like a broom closet in the basement of the SOE. I wasn't sure the telephone was connected until you called this morning." A waiter rushed by, and Leo barely managed to order a drink. "When you started about the Dutch network, I thought it was a test at first."

"A test? How so?"

"Well, the last time I brought up my concerns about the network, I was told I was wrong and to leave it. When I insisted and showed them the messages I considered iffy, they told me troublemakers didn't have much of a career at the SOE."

Lisa gasped. "So, they considered you a nuisance?"

"I suppose that's the right way to phrase it. But I didn't give up. I was certain something was amiss, and I typed up a memorandum with my findings. I was summoned by one of the higher-ups, a brigadier by the name of Gubbins. He made it abundantly clear I was not to speak a word of my findings to anyone and that my memorandum would stay with him. A few days later, I was moved from the country section, where we analyze the messages coming in from the continent. I now work on overall coding deciphering."

Lisa listened open mouthed. Someone from inside the SOE confirmed what she and Somer suspected. The waiter appeared and placed a pint of lager in front of Marks, who immediately took a large sip. "Leo, do you know what this means?"

"Of course. If I'm right, all those men sent to the Netherlands were in grave danger. Matter of fact, they still are. Are they still sending new agents to the Netherlands?"

You have no idea. "Yes," she said softly, before taking a sip from her own drink. She tried to process Leo's words. *This must be enough proof for Somer.*

"You said you tried to convince a number of people within the SOE about your findings, right?" When Leo hummed his agreement, Lisa continued. "And the men who dismissed you, do you think they simply didn't believe you, or did they not want to hear what you were saying?"

Leo pondered the question, his eyes focused on his beer. After a minute, he said, "A bit of both, I suppose. You must understand, these men had a lot to lose if it turned out I was right. Big decisions are made based on the information coming from our foreign agents. If one of our agents in the Netherlands reports a weapons shipment, or an important Nazi visit, we act on it. Can you imagine what would happen to the people responsible for this organization if it turns out the Germans have duped us?" He whistled softly. "Not a pretty thought."

"I have to ask. Does anyone else in the SOE know that the Germans infiltrated the Dutch network? That they were feeding you —us—false intelligence?"

"And willfully sending young men to certain death?" Leo's eyes locked onto hers. "Lisa, I can't say for certain, and I haven't seen any recent messages. Nobody in the SOE will ever admit to knowing about this, but if you were to ask me, it was clear as day."

Lisa leaned forward. "What makes you so certain?"

"Do you know how the codes between the agents and us work?"

"On a general level, I do. I know about the safety checks."

He shook his head. "The safety checks are only superficial. They are as easy to crack for the Germans as they are for us. No, it is more complicated than that. Every agent has their own handwriting, if you will. I analyzed every message coming in from the Netherlands and became very familiar with how the different men communicated. They had their little tells, errors if you will. It's not easy sending these messages under the constant threat of being found by the Germans. These men had to hurry and had no time to resend their transmissions."

"I understand. You're saying you could pick out the agent based on how the message was composed?"

"In a sense, yes. But that's not what alerted me to the problem.

After a while, I noticed most of the messages had the same handwriting. They all sounded the same, written in the same tone."

Lisa gasped. "They were sent by the same person."

"Exactly. And what made it even more suspicious was the lack of mistakes. Whomever was sending these messages appeared to be in no rush, sending perfect messages every single time."

They sat in silence for a minute. Lisa struggled with the realization that those in charge at the SOE knew their network was compromised but continued to send Dutch agents. She looked at Leo, who sat nursing his beer. She considered what he had told her. *Is he reliable?* Then it hit her. Leo was young, and most likely quite junior in his organization. Listening to him, she understood how damaging his bosses considered his findings. A small mistake meant missing out on promotions for a considerable time. A catastrophic one like this would be enough to derail a career. It would've been much easier to move the problem—Leo—to a different position.

But Christiaan's recent intelligence changed everything. Combined with Leo Marks' revelations, Somer could take this to the leadership of the SOE and change things. Lisa knew his approach would depend on how she would report back on what Leo had just told her. She eyed the man opposite her again and made her decision.

Half an hour later, Lisa sat across from Colonel Somer in his office. After leaving Leo Marks in the pub and assuring him that she would take this to her superior in confidence, she returned to the office. It was nearly seven in the evening, and most people had gone home. Somer was waiting for her in his office, and she told him everything Marks had shared with her. When she finished, her heart was beating frantically.

Somer stood and left the office. He returned with a tall glass of water and placed it before her. "Here, you look like you could use this."

He remained standing, leaning on the side of his large desk. Lisa drained her glass in one go while he stared out the window. Oddly enough, the silence between them didn't make her nervous. Instead, she felt at peace. *I've done everything he asked me to do.* It's up to him now. From the corner of her eye, she glanced at the boss of the Bureau Inlichtingen. She didn't envy his position; he had to decide whether the information supplied by Christiaan and Leo Marks was convincing enough to risk a political bombshell.

He turned back to her. "What do you think, Lisa? Do you believe the SOE analyst?"

"I do, sir," Lisa responded without hesitation. "Not once did I feel he was making things up. I also didn't think he had any reason to."

"It's a shame his original report was confiscated. I wonder what his superior did with it."

Having a copy of the memorandum would've made Somer's approach much easier. Now, he was only operating on what Brits would surely consider hearsay. "For what it's worth, sir, you could still mention it. They might have archived it somewhere." Even as she spoke, she heard the lack of conviction in her words. If Leo's fears were swept under the carpet, she was sure that brigadier had buried the report somewhere as well.

"Hmm, perhaps." Somer stood and paced the room. "Thank you for this, Miss Abrahams. I'm sure these have been trying days for you. You must be exhausted."

"Sir, I'm happy to be involved in any way that I can. I came to London because I wanted to do something, anything. I'm grateful I've been placed here in the intelligence agency." She shuffled on her feet. "There's just one thing that's been on my mind since this morning, sir. And after speaking with Leo Marks, I still can't quite figure it out."

He looked up. "What is it?"

"Well, if the Germans know about the operation, how did Christiaan make it through? The way Leo spoke, it seemed like the entire network has been compromised. I would imagine all agents would be intercepted as soon as they landed. But you seemed so confident when I spoke to you before he left. You told me not to worry about the rumors."

Somer was silent for a moment, then he closed his eyes and a chuckle escaped from his lips. "I suppose I might as well tell you now. You're so involved it doesn't really matter anymore." He sat on his desk. "I was confident because there was no way the Germans could know about Christiaan coming. He's not part of the SOE operation."

Lisa frowned. "What do you mean? Aren't all foreign agents in contact with the SOE?"

"I have my connections," Somer said with a grin. "Let's just say I didn't want to take any risks with Christiaan. He did tell you his mission is very dear to our queen's heart, didn't he?" Lisa nodded; Christiaan had been delighted. "Well, part of his mission back home was to make contact with the agents. It was a stroke of luck that the Ordedienst provided us with this information as soon as he landed."

"So, the SOE is completely unaware of Christiaan's existence?" Relief fluttered in Lisa's stomach.

"Not completely unaware, but they're in the dark about his current whereabouts. For all they know, he could still be somewhere in England. He reports directly to me. No British interference." He looked at her with an almost fatherly gaze. "Does that ease some of your concerns? I realize the last time I asked you this, I kept you in the dark, but I promise you know everything this time."

Lisa couldn't suppress a laugh. "All right, sir, I'll take your word for it. But yes, I feel much better knowing Christiaan isn't part of the SOE network. Are you going to speak to them about it?"

"I must. It will be hard for them to dismiss the evidence, even if we have nothing on paper. This should, at the very least, suspend the sending of Dutch agents through SOE."

"And at best?"

“They realize they need to be careful with the intelligence coming in through the network and act on it.” He looked at the clock. “It’s getting late; it’s been an eventful day. You should go home and get some rest. Please report to me tomorrow morning.”

“Sir?”

“I think we’re wasting your talents in the typists’ room. I’ll have a new assignment for you in the morning. Good night.”

“Good night, sir.” Lisa stepped into the hallway, closing the door behind her. As she walked down the hallway, past the dark typists’ room, she let out a little shriek of excitement.

CHAPTER TWENTY-FOUR

Floris loosely held his rifle as the stream of *Panzer* tanks and troops crossed the bridge. The faces of the battered and bloodied Wehrmacht soldiers were strained; most kept their eyes fixed firmly on the ground.

The soldiers were part of a Wehrmacht division retreating from the front near Charkov. The Red Army had surprised them with a much larger force than expected. Backed by heavy artillery, the Soviets had pushed the Germans back, and they had no choice but to retreat. Floris' initial optimism when setting out to join Wiking—the division had racked up an impressive number of battle victories—had been subdued somewhat. This wasn't the first column of retreating troops he'd witnessed since arriving.

"Look at them. Useless, all of them." Floris turned to find Willem had moved next to him, eyeing the column of soldiers with contempt. "Can't trust them to carry out a job. We always need to bail them out."

Floris met Willem when Floris reported to the Westland regiment two weeks ago. A few years older than Floris, he had welcomed him and Anton the moment they arrived. It had been good to hear kind words from his compatriot after the frosty German reception. Willem assured them that the men of Westland were happy to see reinforcements. When Floris asked him if the German soldiers of Wiking were like this to everyone or just newcomers like him, Willem responded with a shrug. "Even though we're considered Germanic brothers according to Hitler and Himmler, the German soldiers will always feel superior to us. They treat the Belgians and the Danes the same, despite all of us volunteering, just like them. Don't let it bother you. Ultimately, they'll be fighting alongside us, dying just the same." Willem's words were meant to make Floris feel better, but the condescending attitude was present in all ranks.

"They appear to be a pretty big division, huh?" Floris said to Willem as he peered across the water, where a seemingly endless procession of Panzers stretched into the distance. "You'd think they wouldn't have to flee?"

"You haven't seen the Russian tanks yet." There was respect in Willem's voice. "The T-34 is built in Charkov. I'm sure they have plenty of those in these parts. They are magnificent pieces of machinery, and you don't want to run into a division of them unprepared. Or be ambushed by them, like I'm sure those sods were."

Floris had only heard of the Red Army's prized tank, for he'd been stuck behind the lines, not involved in combat yet. But, watching the demoralized army retreat, he wasn't too unhappy about that. He shook his head. *What am I, a coward? I should be fighting those Bolshevik bastards!*

"So, what does this mean for us? Will we be deployed to take back Charkov? Or will the Russians come after them?"

Willem shrugged. "Impossible to know. Intelligence is spotty at best; either way, we'll be last to hear about what's really going on. If we're lucky, they'll tell us where we're going an hour in advance." He tapped his helmet, then the MP40 casually hanging on a strap in front of him. "Just make sure you're always carrying these, ready to go. There will always be a failing Wehrmacht division to bail out."

Floris focused on the other side of the bridge. One of the tanks had stalled, delaying the convoy. Several soldiers hurried around as they tried to get the tank's engine started again. Floris considered how this would be a perfect time for the Soviets to launch a counter-attack. He scanned the perimeter and was relieved to see no sign of an advancing army. *Perhaps they're taking a breather as well,* he thought optimistically. Perhaps they were preparing for a larger assault on the retreating German army. Even though Willem was right about the men not being given a lot of intelligence, there was no mistaking that the entire eastern front was steadily shifting westward.

"Brouwer," a voice behind him said, and he turned. He didn't recognize the lanky man. "You're to return to your unit immediately. Urgent orders from battle command. Come with me."

At first, Floris wasn't sure he'd heard the man correctly. He gave Willem a quick salute and followed the messenger, who was already a good ten paces ahead of him. Floris felt his hands shaking as he struggled to catch up. *Battle command?* This was the first time he'd heard those words, but he knew what they meant. He was being sent to the front.

An hour later, Floris was part of a ten-man party crossing the bridge in the opposite direction. The stream of Wehrmacht soldiers and tanks continued at the same pace, and he caught several admiring glances from the soldiers moving away from the front lines. For the first time since arriving at Wiking, Floris felt a hint of pride. He clasped his MP40 a little tighter as he marched on.

When he had arrived back at the field garrison, Anton along with eight other men of the Westland regiment were waiting in a small tent. Their squad commander explained what he needed from them, and Floris had been surprised to be included. For as much as he could tell, all the men selected—but Anton and himself—were experienced regiment members. This was an opportunity to show his worth to the Westland regiment, and the Wiking division as a whole.

They left the bridge behind, and soon their leader signaled for them to divert from the road and into the adjoining forest. The softer ground and cover provided by the trees gave Floris a sense of security as they marched single file. Floris loosely cradled his MP40 submachine gun as they stalked through the forest. One of the more experienced members of his squad had told him to be ready to encounter enemies at all times. Keeping his finger close to the gun's trigger was the best way to survive an ambush, the man had said, before adding that the area beyond the bridge was likely crawling with Bolshevik bastards.

The squad navigated the forest in silence, and for the first two hours there was no evidence that a battle had been raging in this area for months. The forest felt serene as they followed the course of a gentle stream flowing east. Floris was surprised, disappointed, and perhaps a little relieved when their squad leader signaled for a break. *Where's the front line?*

The men sat down on the rocks near the stream while refilling their canteens.

"Quieter than I expected," Anton said as he took a sip of his water.

"You'd think the Russians would keep some big guns in place, right?"

"It's probably why we're on this mission. They must be moving their artillery."

"Their whole army, I suppose," Floris said, watching the water near his feet. He then looked to their squad leader, standing a little distance away, poring over a map. "I wonder what we'll run into once we break the cover of these trees. Must be thousands of Russians nearby."

"I'm sure most of them are celebrating another victory," Anton said, his eyes on the experienced men around them. "Getting some rest while they prepare to attack our fleeing army."

"Well, let's make sure we find their artillery before they can get it in place." At the front, their squad leader folded his map while he conferred with the man next to him. The man nodded, and the squad leader gave a quick whistle, signaling the men to get ready to move out. Floris felt a burst of energy as he got up. The cold water from the stream had revived him, and he was keen to complete their mission.

The forest opened onto a small ridge to reveal a lunar-like landscape. Making sure to stay low and under the cover of the trees, Floris let out a silent gasp. The plains ahead were scarred by neatly dug trenches running as far as the eye could see. The soil between the trenches was bare of vegetation, the only aboveground cover provided by hastily built, rickety-looking fences. Witnessing the actual destruction made him shudder. He squinted to look for movement within the trenches, but they had been abandoned. *These were our trenches.* They had reached the front lines, but no soldiers remained.

He peered across the plains, where a similar line of fortifications was visible. It was impossible to miss the frenzied movements and activity on the other side, even from a distance. On both sides of the Soviet trenches columns of vehicles—primarily tanks—were moving toward the German lines.

"Look at the big trucks at the back," their squad commander let out a chuckle. "That's their artillery. Or parts of it, at least. They're already moving it."

"What do you want us to do, sir?" one of the other men asked.

The commander checked his watch. "We're going to stay here a bit longer to see if we can get some numbers on the artillery. It looks like they'll take that road through the forest to our left. Find a spot along the ridge but stay out of sight."

Floris found a spot between a pair of trees, giving him a good overview of the battlefield. The Soviet army crept closer, and soon the first tanks rolled past the German lines. They were a good four hundred meters away, but Floris could see why the men at Westland spoke about the Russian T-34 tank with such awe—it was much more graceful than their own Panzers. They glided along the plains, their turrets pointing forward, and a number of soldiers sat on their roofs, seemingly without a care in the world. Flanked by the tanks was the oncoming artillery. The soldiers pulled some of the smaller guns while tractors pulled the heavier pieces. Despite their heavy loads, the soldiers appeared in good spirits, a number of them smiling and jostling with each other as they followed the tanks.

"They seem confident," Anton said in a low voice. His friend was positioned only a few meters away.

Floris nodded. Nothing like the Wehrmacht men ahead of them. He wondered when their commander would give the signal to head out again. From what Floris could see, the Soviet army was heading out in two columns; one was taking the same road the Wehrmacht had followed and the other was veering off slightly north. Even though Floris didn't know where that would take them, he imagined they would try to flank the German army. He looked to his commander, who was peering through binoculars, evidently not ready to move yet. He sighed and scanned the trenches below.

Out of the corner of his eye, he saw movement farther along the ridge. He pressed himself to the ground and looked again. He met Anton's eyes, and his friend immediately followed suit, burying his face in the ground. Floris reached for his MP40 and quickly looked behind to where the other men of his squad were. They were all focused on the Soviet convoy in the distance. He turned back and scanned the ridge. Nothing. *Perhaps I'm imagining things.* He looked to Anton, who turned his head from the far side of the ridge to Floris. He gave Floris a questioning look. Floris shrugged his shoulders in half apology. *Is this what the front lines do with a man's mind?*

He focused on breathing just as the world around him exploded. Fine sand was blasted into his face, momentarily blinding him. His surroundings went quiet as his ears popped, the earlier peaceful silence replaced by a loud ringing noise blocking out everything else.

Floris tried to open his eyes. They felt as if they were clamped shut, and he only managed to open them slightly, revealing nothing but dark shadows obscuring his vision. He grabbed his canteen, furiously unscrewed the top, and poured it over his face. He sighed as the cold water brought relief to his stinging eyes. More importantly, his vision cleared. The situation on the ridge had changed dramatically. His squad was no longer focused on the situation below, but on what was happening in the forest behind them. They lay on their stomachs, their guns out. Floris heard distant shooting, then saw the muzzles of his comrades flash. Without another thought, he crawled behind one of the nearby trees.

He was now breathing hard, the sound of gunfire intensifying in volume and tenacity. His ears popped, and the full force of the firefight overwhelmed his senses. He heard cries of pain as the men along the ridge fell rapidly, one by one. The commander shouted, "Fall back, fall back!" before he, too, was silenced by a Soviet bullet. Floris swung his MP40 around the tree and took aim. He was about to pull the trigger when he realized none of the Soviet guns were aimed in his direction. *Did they not see me?* He quickly returned to his safe position in back of the tree and checked on Anton, behind him. His friend was ducking behind a tree as well. The shooting stopped. Floris was horrified to see the bodies of the other men in his company sprawled out on the ridge. He could hear the Soviet soldiers talking. Their voices were nearing. *They're going to make sure we're all dead.* Floris looked to Anton, who had clearly come to the same conclusion. Floris pointed down the ridge, toward the trenches.

Without hesitation, Anton nodded. *Run.*

Floris took a deep breath and pulled his MP40 close to his chest. The ridge was steep, but if they dashed, they had a chance to make it to the cover of the trenches before the Soviets could reach the edge. Or he could trip, and it would all be over. The voices were getting louder, Floris was running out of time. Then a thought struck him. He looked to Anton, who gave him an impatient look. Floris held up a finger and reached for his belt. He pulled out a grenade, closed his eyes for a second and yanked the pull cord, triggering the fuse. He leaned from the tree and saw the Soviets were about fifty meters away. *Damn. So close already.* They hadn't spotted him yet, and he threw the grenade their way, his arm shaking as he did. Then he rose and sprinted toward the edge of the ridge. As he did, he heard cries of surprise behind him. Bullets whizzed by his head as he jumped over the edge, and he prayed he wouldn't trip on the way down.

CHAPTER TWENTY-FIVE

The decline was steeper than Floris expected, and he struggled not to trip over his feet as he ran down. There was an explosion at the top of the ridge. *The grenade.* Floris thought he heard anguished cries, but he didn't dare look back as he continued down the hill at breakneck speed. To his right, he saw Anton, his arms flailing as he fought to keep his balance.

The trenches were only twenty meters away, and the decline started to smooth out. *We're going to make it.* Floris pushed his legs harder, anxious to get to the safety of the dug out maze below. They had covered half the distance when the first shots rang out from atop the ridge. Floris instinctively ducked his head but forced himself to keep moving. Within seconds, more shots rang out and he heard the soft thumps of bullets burying themselves in the soft soil around him. Only five meters to go, the edge of a trench almost within touching distance. He remembered his training and started to run in an unpredictable pattern, praying it threw off his assailants. Perched on the ridge, they were in a perfect vantage point. A skilled marksman would have no trouble taking them out at this distance.

The gunshots became more frequent, and several bullets flew past them, throwing up small explosions of sand near the trenches.

Floris reached the edge of the trench and didn't hesitate. He dived headfirst into safety. The trench was deeper than expected. He landed upside down in the soft middle of the trench, his hands and feet immediately submerged in a sticky layer of mud. Stars danced in front of his eyes as Anton landed next to him an instant later. The gunfire from the ridge stopped and was replaced by angry shouts. It was enough to bring Floris to his full senses, and his vision cleared.

"We have to keep moving!" he said, louder than necessary.

"Where to?" Anton looked shell-shocked, holding onto his gun tightly.

Floris quickly assessed the situation. The Russian army was moving toward the German positions behind them. The route they had taken getting here would be blocked, and he suspected there would be plenty of squads patrolling the woods directly adjacent to the column. They needed to warn their brothers of the impending danger, but they could only do that if they made it out of here alive.

"We need to lose those guys up there first. That way!" He pointed down the trench, away from the Russian army. Anton disappeared down the path. Floris had no idea where the trenches led, but he heard the voices of the Russian soldiers as they made their way down the ridge. Anton was already far down the trench when Floris peeked over the edge. The Russians had sent five men down the ridge. He considered firing a few shots at the soldiers but decided against it; it would only give away his position. The trenches were a maze, and once they were out of sight from those looking down from the ridge, it would be impossible for the Russians to find them. He just prayed they wouldn't get lost themselves.

He followed Anton's path and was relieved to find his friend waiting at the first intersection. The trench split three ways ahead of them, one heading toward the front lines, one going straight and the other turning back, seemingly adjacent to the trench they came from. Floris looked to his right, where the canopies of the trees were still visible.

"If we want to return to Wiking, we need to keep close to the trees. We need to get some distance between the Russian army and their escorts before we can try to double back." Floris pointed in the direction of the path going straight, which he prayed continued adjacent to the tree line. "Let's go this way. And keep moving; I'm sure those Russians won't give up that easily."

They slogged through the trenches for another ten minutes. Floris was horrified by what they encountered along the way. It was clear the Wehrmacht had made a hasty retreat, judging by some of the equipment and bodies they left behind. Finally, they reached a makeshift field hospital, where they found a small medical kit in the mud. Floris didn't hesitate and slung it over his shoulder. A little farther, he found a shattered field radio. A map was attached to it, and Floris stuffed it in his pocket. *Might come in handy later.* The trench snaked away from the trees, angling toward the Russian lines. Floris was nervous about losing the tree line; it was his only orientation point. Now, he feared they might stray off course, and he stopped. Anton looked at him with nervous anticipation, and Floris lifted a finger in front of his lips. He was breathing hard, and he had trouble keeping his gun steady as he aimed it down into the trench behind them. Controlling his breathing, Floris listened carefully for the sound of approaching soldiers, slowly counting his breaths. When he reached thirty—his breathing returned to normal—he lowered the gun and turned to Anton.

"I think we might have lost them."

"We've passed plenty of intersections along the way. Perhaps they gave up?" Anton suggested, his face looking hopeful. "Decided it's not worth it?"

"Perhaps." He looked at the gray sky above, the darkness of the impending dusk in the distance. "Or they didn't fancy ending up in the trenches at night. Can't blame them, really."

"So, what are we going to do? I don't fancy staying out here myself."

Floris scratched the back of his head. Nighttime temperatures dropped close to freezing point, and they would be fully exposed to the cold and potential rain if they remained here. Floris remembered the map and pulled it out. He was relieved to find it covered the current area, and he soon pinpointed their position. He carefully looked over the top of the trenches and saw the woods only two hundred meters away. "Look, there are some settlements directly behind the woods," he said, pointing at a few small dots. "We should be able to make it there before nightfall."

Anton lifted his head above the edge, scanning the area between the woods and the trenches. "It doesn't look like anyone's followed us."

"I doubt they'd go through the trouble of setting up an ambush for just two soldiers." Floris shook his head. "Either way, we need to get back to the division and warn them about the approaching force."

"I agree. Let's make for one of those houses on the map and stay the night there. They'll be abandoned anyway, this close to the front lines." Anton sounded confident and a little impatient, but it strengthened Floris' resolve. *We really can't stay here.*

They both took generous gulps from their canteens, and Floris put his hand on Anton's shoulder. "No matter what happens, keep running toward the tree line. We only change course if the Russians are waiting in the trees." *There's no plan B.*

"Let's go." Anton put his hand on the muddy wall and climbed over. Floris quickly followed, and soon they were sprinting toward the tree line. Floris ran as fast as he could, his legs aching from exhaustion, the precarious sprint down the ridge earlier still fresh in his memory. He expected to hear gunshots ringing out behind him or soldiers to appear from the tree line, but there was only silence. It took them less than a minute to reach the cover of the trees. They didn't stop until they were well clear of the tree line.

Floris was sweating and reached for his canteen. Anton did the same, and they sat hunched on a fallen tree for a minute, both catching their breath. Floris kept his ears perked for any unusual sounds. But, apart from the rustling of falling leaves, it was quiet, and Floris felt his heartbeat returning to normal. The sky beyond the treetops was steadily growing darker, and he stood. "Let's keep moving. The closest farm should be a kilometer away. Let's hope it hasn't been burned down yet."

Floris frequently checked his compass. They couldn't afford to get lost and lose valuable daylight. The trees around them were already looming in semidarkness, and Floris was careful where he put his feet. He didn't want to rush and injure himself. He also stayed alert for any odd noises. Anton did the same, turning his head to constantly scan their surroundings. Floris was thankful Anton had survived the ambush as well; besides being his best friend, Anton was also a competent soldier.

Their careful approach meant it took twenty minutes before they reached the other side of the forest. It ended abruptly, a vast stretch of fields spanning the horizon. Of course, the fields were bare, and Floris wondered whether they had been razed intentionally by the Soviet army to deny the German invaders potential food or if the farmers had fled and abandoned the fields. He suspected it was likely a bit of both. The farmhouse stood some two hundred meters away, its silhouette visible in the faint glint of the full moon rising. Anton and Floris looked at each other.

"Shall we see if we can break into the house?" said Anton, taking a step in the direction of the house.

Floris shared his enthusiasm for finding the farmhouse intact. He remembered the burning villages on his way here. The farm was probably far enough off the main road to have been left alone.

"Yes, there might even be some food left. One can hope, right?"

They followed a dirt path between the fields and soon reached the farmhouse. The path turned into gravel, and the soft crunching underneath his boots unnerved Floris somewhat. He felt exposed with nothing but the fields around him. *What if there are Russian soldiers inside the barn?* The windows next to the door were boarded up, dark curtains blocking out anything potentially happening inside. He stopped and listened but heard nothing but his own breathing. He looked at the thick wooden front door and realized a squad of soldiers could be waiting for them.

"What's wrong?" Anton stood next to him and spoke in a low voice.

"I can't shake the feeling the place might not be as abandoned as we think. It might be a trap." He turned to his friend. "But I'm probably being too paranoid."

Anton lifted his MP40. "Why don't we play it safe and approach from the back door? I'll go first, and you can cover me while we enter. If there's Russians in there, we'll shoot first and ask questions later, okay?"

Floris raised his gun as they carefully circled to the back door. It was eerily quiet as the last daylight faded. The dark fields around them were only faintly illuminated by the moon. Anton reached the back door and turned, an eyebrow raised as he silently waited for Floris' confirmation to proceed. Floris gripped his MP40 tighter and nodded.

Anton reached for the door handle and Floris held his breath. He noticed Anton's surprise as the handle yielded and the door opened. Things moved very quickly after that. Anton stormed inside, and Floris followed. They entered the kitchen, and the first thing Floris noticed was the flicker of a candle in his peripheral vision. He turned and aimed his gun at it while Anton moved farther into the room. A large wooden table dominated the space. There were four plates; two empty, the others half-empty. *They left in a hurry.* While Floris inspected the table, Anton moved toward the next room. Floris was about to follow him when he saw Anton had stopped. He stood frozen in the doorway, his eyes and gun barrel focused straight ahead. Something was wrong.

"Anton, talk to me. What's in the next room?"

"There are people in here," Anton said hoarsely.

"Soldiers?"

He shook his head. "A family. Two kids. The father is holding a gun."

"Tell him to drop it." Floris slowly moved closer to the side of the doorway. *If he tries anything, I'll shoot him and his family.*

Anton moved the barrel of his gun up and down, while telling the man to drop the gun in German. The man responded in Russian, and from the tone it was clear he wasn't going to comply. Anton glanced at Floris, who now stood to the side of the doorway, still out of sight of the people in the other room. "What now?"

Floris thought quickly. The man had to know he didn't stand a chance against two soldiers. So, what was he trying to accomplish? The answer was obvious. *He's protecting his family.* Floris lowered his weapon and stepped into the open doorway. Anton looked at him open mouthed. "Keep your gun trained on him," Floris said as he lifted his hands and turned toward the people in the other room.

He was surprised. The man was smaller than he'd expected, and he immediately saw the man's grip on his small revolver was wrong. His hands were shaking, and there was fear in his eyes as they shot between Floris and Anton. The mother held onto two children, the boy protectively standing in front of his younger sister. *Brave boy.*

Floris made a soothing gesture with his hands, slowly and carefully moving them up and down in front of him, palms out. The man swung his revolver to him in panic, then realized Floris was unarmed, and quickly trained the gun back on Anton. Floris realized the man wouldn't understand German or Dutch, but he knew he had to try to get him to lower his weapon.

"Sir, please lower your weapon. We are not going to hurt you." He put on his most disarming voice, as he did when he still worked as a policeman back home. "We are only looking for a place to stay the night." He clasped his hands together, raising them to his slightly tilted face. He hoped the man understood the sign of sleeping. He then pointed to himself and Anton.

There was understanding in the man's eyes, and Floris felt encouraged. Quickly, he repeated his promise of not hurting them. He pointed at the man and his family and waved his hands, shaking his head and pointing first at Anton's gun, then the man's. Then he waited, his heart in his throat. He kept his eyes trained on the man, the air in the room heavy. A trickle of sweat ran down his back.

Then the woman spoke. Her voice was calm as she addressed her husband, pointing at the children in front of her, and then at Anton's gun. The man listened to her and responded calmly, shaking his head and waving his revolver. Anton tensed and readjusted his grip. Floris held up his hand. For a moment, it looked like the man wasn't going to back down, but then he knelt and placed the revolver on the floor.

An hour later, Floris and Anton sat in the barn next to the house. The woman, who introduced herself as Gisya, had handed them a large stack of blankets. Boris, the man with the gun, had escorted them outside. The barn was surprisingly comfortable, and the men had created sleeping spots in the hay.

"When you stepped out of cover without your gun, I wasn't sure what you were thinking," Anton said when the man had left, leaving them in the darkness.

"I didn't think my message would come across if I was also waving a gun at him," Floris said with a grin. "Besides, these people were no threat to us in the end, were they?"

"Sure, but you didn't know that when you did that. That was a bold and brave move, my friend."

Floris shrugged it off. "How would you have felt killing civilians?"

"That's not what I came here to do. But if Boris had shot you, I would've taken him out without hesitating." Anton spoke with confidence, and Floris believed him.

"I counted on that. But I also knew he wouldn't risk his family getting hurt. It's a good thing his wife forced the decision in the end. I was a bit worried."

"I was surprised they shared their dinner with us. Do you think we can trust them?" Anton leaned back against a few bales of hay.

"We don't have much of a choice. Why don't we take turns keeping watch? You never know what might happen during the night. And keep your gun close. I'll take the first watch; I'm not tired anyway."

"Thanks." Anton stretched out and yawned. "Just wake me in a few hours."

It didn't take long until Anton was snoring softly. Floris settled in near the door and wrapped an extra blanket around him. The area surrounding the barn was quiet, and his thoughts drifted back to the dinner they had with the young family. After Anton had also lowered his gun, the family had invited them to sit down. Gisya quickly produced two extra plates and served them a portion of the same stew they were having. Floris was ravenously hungry and finished his plate within a minute. They had communicated mostly using sign language, but it had been enough. After dinner, the boy showed Floris a magic trick, and he was genuinely impressed. Misha wasn't much older than ten but had been confident enough to approach him with a stack of cards and cheekily produce the card Floris had picked out.

He wondered how the family had survived for so long, so close to the front lines, and he wished he could ask them. It was nothing short of a miracle. He shivered, grabbed another blanket, and settled in for his watch.

Floris opened his eyes to Anton shaking him, his expression full of concern. He was instantly awake. "What's wrong?"

"Movement near the house. Come," Anton said, gesturing impatiently as he walked toward the door.

Floris stood and followed his friend. He peered through a small crack in the wall, giving him a good view of the area in front of the house. What he saw made his blood freeze. A squad of six Soviet soldiers stood at the front door of the house. One of them knocked on the door and stood tapping his foot, waiting impatiently. Floris turned to Anton.

"Shit! We're trapped," he said as he hurried to his sleeping spot and picked up his gun. "I'm not going to surrender. You've heard what they do to prisoners of war." He checked the magazine of his gun.

"Me neither. But let's not make hasty decisions. There's Boris."

Floris squeezed next to Anton and watched Boris step out of his house and talk to the soldiers. He looked remarkably composed as he shook his head. *He's used to talking to them.* On the other hand, the leader of the group looked agitated as Boris kept shaking his head. At one point, Boris held up his hands and then pointed toward the forest.

"I don't think he's giving us up," Floris said, no small amount of surprise in his voice. He could hardly believe his eyes.

The soldier turned around one more time, but Boris again held up his hands in apology. It appeared to appease the soldier, for he signaled for his men to head out to the west.

"They're really leaving," Anton said with a sigh. "I can't believe it."

Anton and Floris peered through the crack until the Russian soldiers disappeared into the forest. Half an hour later, Boris came into the barn, carrying bread and water. Floris didn't know how to thank him, so he pointed in the direction of the soldiers and clasped his hands together as if in prayer, bowing slightly. "Thank you," he said in Dutch.

Boris understood the gesture, and he lowered his eyes and inclined his head. As he did, Floris noticed something he hadn't seen the previous night. Boris wore a small cap on the back of his head. *A kippah?* Floris was stunned. *Boris and his family are Jews?*

He felt overwhelmed with conflicting emotions. These people were supposed to be the enemy, and surely they knew what the Nazis did to Jews. Even in their remote area, they must've heard about what happened in the nearby towns. Floris turned to Anton, who seemed less shocked. "Did you see his kippah last night?"

Anton calmly shook his head. "No, he wasn't wearing one. He must've put it on this morning."

Floris looked at Boris, whose eyes glittered as he observed Floris with a curious look. *He knows I know.* Boris looked more confident than the night before. Then Floris understood. After Floris had risked stepping from cover unarmed, Boris decided he was no threat. *No, he decided I was not the enemy. And then he risked his own life by keeping us hidden.* He looked at the young Jew and, for the first time in his life, questioned his beliefs and everything he'd been told before. *This man could have easily turned us in and collected a reward.*

Unsure what else to do, Floris held out his hand. Boris hesitated only for a moment before shaking it.

CHAPTER TWENTY-SIX

The house was larger than Nora had expected. She peeked through the curtains to the dark Parisian street below. It was only five in the morning, and there was hardly anyone about. She tiptoed back to her bed, passing Katja, who was still fast asleep. Nora crawled back under the covers and took a torn book from the small wooden bedside table.

She started reading but the words jumped around the page. Nora found it impossible to concentrate and put the book away. She swung her legs out of bed and changed into some of the warm clothes their host had provided. The comfortable pants and oversized sweater were nothing to look at, but it had been a long time since Nora cared much about that. At this hour, she knew the downstairs would be quite chilly. Heating at night was a luxury they couldn't afford. She slid her feet into the wool slippers and sighed contentedly as the soft fabric caressed her feet. Their host, Madame Dufort, handed them to her on arrival a week ago. Nora had been shivering and hadn't let the slippers out of her sight since. She was grateful; Madame Dufort had welcomed the four strangers into her home without any hesitation. The woman fussed about them all day and was keen to hear of their travels. Between their host's passable Dutch and Arthur's decent French, they had been able to exchange stories of the war. Nora had been impressed to learn Madame Dufort had sheltered people like them for over a year now, despite seeing many of her friends hauled off by the Gestapo. "It's a matter of duty," she had told them.

Nora slowly opened the bedroom door, careful not to wake Katja. Her companion didn't stir, and she quickly slipped into the hallway. The floorboards creaked as she made her way toward the stairs. Even though the blackout curtains were drawn, she knew her away around the house by touch, and was soon downstairs. She froze as she heard soft voices coming from the kitchen. That was unusual; Madame Dufort didn't usually rise until six thirty. A faint flicker of light came from underneath the door, and Nora approached while her ears pricked up. She picked up a deep tone from the other side—a man's voice, but the door muffled his words. She stood in the darkness of the hallway trying to determine who was there. Then, much to her relief, she heard Madame Dufort's voice. Her tone was relaxed, as if she were talking to a friend.

Nora knocked on the kitchen door and opened it. Madame Dufort was leaning against the counter and appeared surprised to see her, but she quickly gave her a reassuring smile. Nora found a man she imagined about ten years older than herself sitting at the kitchen table, an open notebook in front of him. His neatly combed hair accentuated the sharp features of his face. Nora stepped inside, still holding the door.

"Sorry to disturb you. I didn't think there would be anyone downstairs at this hour," she said to Madame Dufort. She stood uncomfortably in the doorway, and Madame Dufort indicated for her to enter.

"You're not disturbing us at all; please come in and close the door before you wake anybody else," she said. "Why don't you take a seat, and I'll make you some tea. You look like you could use some."

Nora sat opposite the man, whose eyes studied her curiously. He looked amused, and Nora wasn't sure what to make of him. Then, on impulse, she held out her hand. "I'm Nora." He didn't immediately return the gesture, and she sat with her hand uncomfortably outstretched until he reached out and shook it.

"Jean, nice to meet you." To her surprise, his response was in accentless Dutch. "I trust Madame Dufort has been taking good care of you?"

Nora glanced at their host, who had filled the kettle and placed it on the stove. "She's been great. How do you know her?" She studied his expensive clothes. He looked out of place in Madame Dufort's safe house.

His mouth widened into a smile that matched his twinkling eyes. "I've known Liliane for many years. I'm glad to hear she's taking good care of you." He turned his eyes to the notebook as Madame Dufort sat down next to Nora. She put a hand on Nora's wrist and patted it reassuringly.

"You weren't supposed to see Jean, actually," she said in Dutch. "He was just about to leave. But now that you're here, it makes sense to at least share a cup of tea with him." The eyes of the man across the table quickly scanned the scribblings in his notebook.

Nora frowned. *He was just about to leave? Where does one go at five in the morning?* She bit her tongue as Madame Dufort stood to pour boiling water in three large mugs. Nora studied the man across the table. He crossed out some words, closed his notebook, and then leaned back in his chair. He appeared completely at ease in his surroundings. He met her gaze, the smile returning to his face.

"You must be wondering what I'm doing here."

"Maybe a little."

He sat a bit straighter, leaning on his elbows. "That's fair. You've been here for a week now? Close to two?" The tone of his voice made it obvious he wasn't really asking.

Nora's eyes shot to his notebook. "Week and a half."

"And before that you were probably in Brussels, right?" He

caught her look, and he drummed his fingers on the notebook. "You've been on the road for a while now."

Nora looked at Jean for a moment. It was clear he knew more about her than she about him. Madame Dufort placed two mugs of tea on the table, but held onto her own, not joining them.

"I suppose you would like some time alone with Nora?" she asked Jean, who promptly stood and embraced her. He spoke in French, and even though Nora couldn't understand everything, she picked up on the tone. *Definitely not a Gestapo man.* Madame Dufort left the room and the man sat down, returning his attention to Nora.

"The waiting," he said while blowing on his tea. "It's the hardest part, isn't it? Sitting around, unable to go anywhere and just hoping for good news?" He spoke in a soft voice.

"It can feel like an eternity. We haven't been in one place for this long before."

There was a look of understanding between them, and Jean took a sip of his tea. "When you receive news that the papers or the transportation have been sorted out, it feels liberating at first, right?" *Whomever he is, he knows what he's talking about.* She started to feel more comfortable. "It's a bit exciting, even, I suppose. Having that feeling of moving on to the next step?" He looked at her expectantly.

"I guess so," she said. She thought back to Antwerp, where they had to leave unexpectedly, abandoning the man who'd risked—and probably lost—his life to save them. *Poor Nicolas.* "But it's also terrifying to step out the door into the world where there could be an enemy around every corner."

"I understand." He looked at her with a serious expression but remained silent as he cradled his mug in both hands.

Nora couldn't stop herself and heard herself ask, "Who are you exactly, Jean? Are you also on the route south?" As she spoke the words, she knew he wasn't.

He put his mug down and shook his head. "I'm always on the route, but never just in one direction. I need to ensure that people like Liliane are taken care of and have enough money to look after the people coming through." *People like me.* "But most of the time it's more than just the money, food coupons, or train tickets. They need to know the rest of the network is still there."

"The network?" Nora felt a tingle of excitement in her stomach.

"Those people you've met so far are all part of it. From Amsterdam to Geneva, Madrid, Lisbon, and every little place in between, they're all connected. And even though they only know the other people closest to them, you can rest assured they're all playing their part in getting people like you to safety."

"And where do you come in?" She had a feeling the man speaking so passionately did a little more than check in on Madame Dufort every so many weeks.

His eyes shifted to the door, and he was silent for a few seconds before he returned his attention to her. "Let's just say I facilitate wherever I'm needed most."

She wasn't sure if she understood correctly. "Across the entire route?"

"Yes." He raised his mug to his mouth and took another sip. "Although it's been a while since I've been back in the Netherlands. It's a bit too small for me. Too easy to be spotted by someone, and then I'll never make it back across the border."

Nora understood; it was why she hadn't hesitated in leaving Amsterdam herself. A thought struck. "I guess you know most of the people in the cities across the network?"

"You could say that, yes. Although I try to keep the number of people who know my face to a minimum."

"When were you last in Geneva?" The words came from her mouth before she could stop herself. *I have to know.*

He looked thoughtful for a minute. "Four weeks ago, actually. Why do you ask? You're not headed for Geneva, are you?" He glanced at his notebook again, and Nora wondered how much he knew about her. He appeared to read her mind. "Don't worry. I don't have your name, or those of your companions, written down anywhere. Only numbers, and even if the Germans got hold of this, they wouldn't be able to make heads or tails out of my scribblings."

"We're not going to Geneva, but someone very dear to me did. I know he arrived in February, but I haven't heard anything from him since that."

"And you were hoping I would know more about him? Many people arrived in Geneva earlier this year. That was until the Germans made it almost impossible to cross into Switzerland. What's his name?"

"Christiaan Brouwer. He arrived with a young Jewish woman, Lisa Abrahams. He's my brother-in-law."

For the first time that morning, the man across the table looked at a loss for words. His eyebrows shot up and his mouth lifted a little in surprise. He looked at her without speaking for a few seconds, his eyes scanning her face as if looking for a hint that she was trying to trick him. Nora held his gaze, unsure if she should feel hopeful or discouraged by his response.

"You're *that* Nora? Christiaan Brouwer is your brother-in-law?" he finally said. "Are you the policeman's wife?" Now it was Nora's turn to be speechless, and she only managed a weak nod. *Who is this man?* The air in the room felt heavy as neither spoke for a minute. Then Jean cleared his throat. "I'm sorry, I'm a little surprised to be running into you like this. Christiaan spoke about you many times, but I never imagined I would meet you. He told me about what you did in Amsterdam, your work for the resistance, and your relationship with your husband." He looked at her with respect. "I suppose the time finally came for you to run as well?"

"Floris, my husband, found out about what I did." She told Jean about what had happened in Amsterdam, and he listened attentively.

"You were right to leave, even though I'm sure it must've been hard for you. He would've found you in Amsterdam, eventually."

"Is Christiaan all right?"

"He was the last time I saw him." Nora let out a sigh of relief, but then Jean raised his hand. "But that was over two months ago, just before he left."

"Left for where?" Nora's relief instantly disappeared.

"He wasn't happy to stick around in Geneva, and he constantly asked me for a new assignment, to be more active in fighting the Germans. He wanted to go to England."

"And did he?" Nora held her breath.

"Last I heard, he made it to London safely, yes. Along with Lisa."

Nora felt ecstatic. Christiaan and Lisa had made it to London. A warm feeling spread through her body at the thought of their safety. "This is wonderful news."

"I imagine you'll be looking forward to meeting up with him as soon as possible," Jean said, and Nora nodded. She couldn't think of anything better. He reached into a small bag on the floor, produced four sheets of paper, and placed them on the table. "These are tickets for tomorrow's train south. It will take you to the northern part of the Pyrenees, close to the border with Spain. From there, you will cross the mountains on foot."

"On foot?" Nora looked at him in shock. "Won't it be too cold?" She imagined the snow-covered mountains, then thought of the clothing she'd brought with her. She could survive the valley's cold, but she wasn't at all prepared for a trek through the mountains.

"Don't worry. You don't have to be concerned about the cold; your *passeur* will provide you with the proper clothing."

"What's a passeur?"

"Your guide through the mountains."

Nora felt lightheaded as she listened to Jean explain how to get to the starting point. His revelations about Christiaan and Lisa had shocked and delighted her, and the thought of seeing them filled her with joy. But as she listened to his instructions, she realized the passage into neutral Spain would be the most dangerous part of their journey yet.

CHAPTER TWENTY-SEVEN

Christiaan and Bet sat in the deserted main room of Cafe 't Mandje together. It was only nine in the morning, and it wouldn't open for a few more hours. Bet had fixed them each a cup of ersatz and some bread for breakfast. It was simple, but Christiaan appreciated her efforts. He had been back in Amsterdam for almost a week, and it had felt odd not being able to go home in the evenings. Instead, he slept in the basement of Bet's cafe. The first night he'd found it almost impossible to get to sleep. Thoughts of the captured agents kept him awake as he considered their fates. When he'd transmitted the message to London with Six, he'd asked about the Haaren seminary-turned-prison. Six said the escaped agents reported they had met only a small number of agents in the prison. When Christiaan asked if that meant there might still be agents out of the clutches of the Germans, Six had been pessimistic. "It's more likely they have already been sent to the concentration camps in Germany or Poland," Six had said. "Most likely for further interrogation before they are no longer of any use to the Germans."

Christiaan wondered how the news had been received back in London. He hoped the new information had provided Somer with enough ammunition to convince the SOE to stop using their compromised network. Even though he was certain the SOE would push back, he was grateful Somer seemed to be taking the situation seriously. It couldn't have been easy for him to procure an airplane without the approval of the SOE, and Christiaan was sure if anyone could do this back in London, it would be the head of the Bureau.

Christiaan took a bite of his bread and thought of Lisa. She had been right to question the messages coming in from the compromised network, and she had even dared to do something about it. Christiaan wasn't sure if he would have done the same, snooping around the archives and standing up to Somer. But, in the end, she had set things into motion, and Christiaan had heard the admiration in Somer's voice when he spoke about Lisa. Christiaan was glad; there wasn't a better place for Lisa to be. Despite the dangers lurking around him, it gave him comfort to know she was in a safe place.

Lisa and Somer's suspicions had been confirmed, but despite the setback that the compromised network presented, Christiaan still had important work to do. Queen Wilhelmina's mission of uniting and preparing the resistance networks in the country was now his only priority. He'd met with Esquire Six twice more in the last week, and he'd been encouraged by the Ordedienst's progress in setting up the national communications network. Six explained he wanted to use the network only once the liberation efforts in the Netherlands started. Christiaan knew Somer wanted the different factions spread across the country to communicate in preparation ahead of the liberation efforts. Six conceded he understood Somer's stance, but he was worried about the Germans intercepting the network's messages. He told him of German radio cars driving around the city, searching for signals to intercept. Christiaan didn't push Six yet, deciding he would talk to the other resistance factions first and worry about the best approach to get them all in line later. Besides, from what the radio operators that jumped with him had said, Somer would send more radio operators of his own as well.

"How are you feeling? Looking forward to meeting with your old friends?" Bet's voice brought him back to the matter of the day.

"Yes, I'm glad you were still in touch with them. With Nora away, I'm not sure I would've been able to reach them without your help." Christiaan looked at his friend with respect. "It's impressive how you're able to run your operations almost under the noses of the Germans."

She snorted. "Well, there's not many Germans coming into this place. They deem it beneath their standards, but they've been happy to sell me alcohol. They've left me alone since I staged that little performance about being a secret Nazi."

When the Grüne Polizei raided Bet's cafe, she had professed her loyalty to Hitler and the Reich in a dramatic display that convinced the German leading the raid. Since then, they left her alone. Cafe 't Mandje continued to be a popular meeting place for members of Amsterdam's resistance, and Bet was happy to facilitate.

"I think my brother was onto you, though," Christiaan said. "But he was never able to prove anything."

"I'll be honest with you—I stopped storing those weapons upstairs for a while after that. If they had found those, I would've been done for."

Christiaan finished his cup of ersatz and placed it on the bar. "Thanks, Bet. I better get going. Gerrit won't be pleased if I keep him waiting."

Two hours later, Christiaan left the house on the Amsteldijk. He shivered as a gust of wind from the Amstel River, opposite him, hit his face. A tram passed as he turned north, and for a moment, he was tempted to head in the other direction. The tram depot where he used to finish his shift every day was only a few hundred meters in that direction. He would love to catch up with some of his old colleagues. He shook his head and resisted the temptation. It would be better if as few people as possible knew about his return. Besides, he wasn't sure they would still be working there. Quite a few of them were involved in the resistance as well, and from what Gerrit had just told him, the Germans had been quite successful in infiltrating resistance groups in the past few months. It had been good to see him alive and well, and Gerrit had assured him he would try his very best to get Christiaan an audience with the leadership.

He reached the end of the Amsteldijk and turned left onto Stadhouderskade. He walked along the edge of the canal. After speaking with Six, he had been certain the other resistance groups would follow suit, or at least be open to working on the Somer plan. He had left for this morning's meeting with Gerrit with high hopes, only to be met with hesitation and caution. He rubbed his eyes; not all hope was lost yet. Gerrit could be persuasive, and Christiaan was certain his friend would come through for him.

Christiaan was so caught up in his thoughts that he didn't notice the queue of people until he almost walked into them. He stopped and looked up to find the street ahead blocked by two trucks—Christiaan's heart skipped a beat when he saw six men wearing the green uniforms of the Grüne Polizei. *Shit.* He had run into a checkpoint. He glanced over his shoulder but was dismayed to see two similarly dressed officers keeping an eye on anyone looking to back out of the inspection. He was trapped. Christiaan joined the queue and was relieved to feel the papers in the inside pocket of his jacket. He forced himself to calm down; the Bureau issued these papers in London. *They would know a thing or two about forging documents, right?*

The queue moved swiftly, and Christiaan studied the men inspecting the papers. They were young and most likely very junior. They looked bored as they casually leafed through the papers, allowing everyone to pass. Christiaan remembered the careless way he used to approach these checkpoints. His Dutch papers never caused the men to look at him twice, and he needed to act the same as usual once it was his turn. *Then why am I feeling so bloody nervous?*

He shuffled forward, and now there was only one woman ahead of him.

The woman looked back at him with a nervous glance. "You never get used to this, right?"

Before Christiaan could respond, one of the officers said in a loud voice, *"Nächste, bitte!"* The woman shuffled forward in a hurry. The officer farthest from Christiaan finished inspecting an older man and called him over. He managed to control his shaking hands, handing his documents to the man. Christiaan stood in silence as the man glanced up at him, his eyes going between the photo on his papers and his face. He raised an eyebrow. "That's interesting, Mr. Peters." Christiaan felt a chill run down his spine as the man addressed him by his false name.

"I'm sorry, sir?"

The officer tapped his finger on the paper. "You're wearing the same jacket in this photo. And your hair is about the same length." He rubbed the papers with his gloved hand. "Did you get these papers only recently?"

Christiaan hesitated. He hadn't expected such a meticulous inspection of his photo, but he cursed himself for not being more careful. He remembered the state of his old papers; faded and with small tears at the sides. A brand-new, shiny set would always stand out. He answered calmly, "My old papers were falling apart, sir. I had them replaced only last week."

The young man eyed him for a few seconds, and Christiaan felt himself flushing underneath his coat. He hoped the officer didn't notice anything as he concentrated on keeping a straight face. The man looked one last time, then shrugged and handed the papers back to Christiaan. "Very well. All is in order. You can proceed."

"Thank you, sir. Have a good day." Christiaan controlled his trembling hands as he replaced the documents in his pocket. He suppressed the desire to hurry through the checkpoint, deliberately taking calm steps toward the opening. Two officers were chatting and only glanced at him for a second as he approached. Christiaan found himself holding his breath and lightly exhaled as he walked between the trucks. There were no officers on the other side, and he breathed easier, taking a gulp of the fresh air that tasted like freedom. He upped his pace a little, keen to get away from the checkpoint when someone called out behind him.

"Excuse me, sir!" Christiaan initially kept walking, and the man repeated himself, louder and more persistent. "Sir, a word, please!" Christiaan stopped and looked at the people around him. There were only women. A feeling of unease crept into his mind as he turned to the source of the voice.

As he did, his heart sank. The man approaching him didn't wear a uniform, but approached him confidently, as one used to wielding authority did. "I thought you looked familiar, but I could hardly believe it was you." Christiaan's eyes scanned the area, but with the canal to his left and only houses on the right, there was nowhere to run. The man caught his look and shook his head, placing his hand on the holstered revolver on his hip. "Don't even think about running, Christiaan. You're coming with me. I think we're due a little chat, don't you?" Two men in uniform approached from the checkpoint, alerted by the shouting.

There was no sense in denying his real identity. He had run into one of the few people left in Amsterdam who would recognize him no matter what his papers said. He realized his best chance was to cooperate, insisting he had done nothing wrong.

"All right, Hans."

CHAPTER TWENTY-EIGHT

Floris sat in the cramped living room with ten other soldiers. When their regiment arrived the day prior, they had been relieved to find most of the houses intact and the village abandoned. It had become a familiar sight when marching through the countryside, civilians fleeing their homes from the approaching armies. The Soviet army was just as murderous as the Germans in their encounters with those suspected of aiding the enemy. It made him even more grateful for what Gisya and Boris had done for them, now almost a month ago.

When they returned to their regiment, they reported on the Soviet positions. There they found out they weren't the only squad sent out to inspect the Soviet artillery movements. Wiking's commander, Herbert Gille, had sent out half a dozen squads like theirs. Of those six, only two had returned at full strength. The others had suffered the same fate as Floris' squad; Soviet patrols had ambushed them. Two squads never returned.

The Red Army's superiority in numbers and, more decidedly, artillery firepower, meant Wiking spent the next month retreating farther west. After crossing the Dnieper River two weeks ago, Wiking was pulled from combat for some much-needed rest. It was the first break from the front lines in months for many of the men, and their spirits had lifted with every step west. They had spent the past night stationed in a cluster of villages well into Poland.

Floris opened his last can of *Wurst*, canned sausage, and spread it on some stale rye bread. He took a bite and chewed furiously; the bread was even tougher than expected. Anton sat next to him.

“I’ve heard we’re moving out this morning.” He took a bite of his own piece of bread and pulled a face. “Here’s hoping we stick around long enough for them to set up the field kitchen.”

“I almost expected them to do that last night, but then the rain came pelting down. It feels like we’re in a bit of a rush these past few days.”

“Yeah, do you think the Russians might be advancing on us?”

“I hope not. Those boys relieving us at the Dnieper seemed fresh enough. They should be able to slow them down, don’t you think?”

“Whatever it is, I think we might find ourselves back in combat sooner rather than later. And the odd thing is, I’m ready for it.”

“Really?” Floris frowned. Even though they marched over fifty kilometers a day in rapidly deteriorating, wintry conditions, Floris was happy to head west. The conditions—and not just the weather—were much preferable to those in the east. The more battle-hardened soldiers in his regiment had shared their experiences of the last winter on the eastern front, when they were deployed south of Stalingrad. There, they had to endure temperatures of 40 degrees Celsius. They spoke of men freezing to death while keeping watch during the night. After seeing the strength of the Soviet forces firsthand, Floris had no desire to return to the front lines. He had just put the last of his simple breakfast in his mouth when the door to the house opened. One of the messengers informed the men they would be moving in half an hour. Some asked where they were going. The messenger said today would only be a short walk. Cheers went up when he revealed their destination. They were headed farther west to the city of Lublin.

The march to Lublin was still a good fifty kilometers, and they didn't arrive until late in the afternoon. Despite that, the clear skies above their heads and decent roads meant the walk was pleasant enough. More importantly, they had been promised a hot meal on arrival. It was enough for even the weariest of soldiers to march with a spring in their step.

On the city's outskirts, they passed hundreds of people digging what looked like a network of trenches. Floris thought that was odd; the front lines were far away.

His first impression of Lublin was better than Floris had expected. While it was clear the city had suffered during the early fighting of the war, there was plenty of activity as they marched through the streets. People hurried along the sidewalks, carrying small bags with groceries. They kept their eyes averted from the soldiers. There was also plenty of German presence in the streets. Soldiers and men clad in German police uniforms stood on corners, keeping their eyes on the little traffic and people passing by. It was the first time in months that Floris found himself in an actual city, and even though Lublin was nothing like Amsterdam, it gave him a sense of familiarity, putting his mind at ease.

They were stationed on the city's outskirts, where Floris' regiment was assigned to a surprisingly well-equipped barracks. The men sat down on beds with actual mattresses, and the temperature in the room was comfortable. Floris placed his heavy field pack down and stretched out on the bed, sighing contentedly as he savored the softness of the sheets. *I could sleep all day.* He closed his eyes, but the sound of the men chatting while settling into their bunks made it impossible to drift away. Finally, he overheard a few of them mention drinks in the city, and he opened his eyes. They turned to him.

"Are you joining us? Commander said we're off tomorrow morning, and we can enjoy a night out."

Floris got up from the bed in an instant. The last time he'd enjoyed a beer was during training in Sennheim. That felt like a lifetime ago. The past two months had been spent in trenches, drafty field tents, and abandoned houses in varying states of decay. Worse, the threat of a Soviet attack had been looming over their heads every minute of every day and night. Not thinking about the war for a few hours would do him good. He saw Anton was part of the group, too, and he hurried to catch up with them.

The barracks were quiet the following morning. Almost all the men in the Westland regiment—along with the rest of the Wiking division—had been out in the city until late. Floris awoke among some of the first and, much to his surprise, felt quite fresh. After taking a hot shower, another rare luxury, he found the mess hall and enjoyed a cooked breakfast. He left feeling reborn and decided to get some fresh air. He wouldn't need to report for another two hours.

Lublin's architecture was nothing like Amsterdam's. The city would have been beautiful before the fighting, as many buildings were shot up or damaged by bombs and artillery. Crossing the main square, the colorful houses surrounding the square lifted the wintery day's gloom. Very few people were out, and those who were hurried by without making eye contact.

He returned to find the barracks lively as the rest of the soldiers prepared for the day. Westland regiment was due at a briefing in half an hour, and everybody was anxious to know what would be next. They were all keen to stay in Lublin a bit longer.

"You were up early." Anton appeared next to him as Floris was organizing his bag. "No hangover?"

"I took it easy," Floris said, not without a hint of pride. Some of the men had let themselves go the night prior, and he could tell from some of the faces in the room that many were still struggling. "You never know what they come up with the next day, right? Things can change in a heartbeat even when they tell us we'll have the day off."

"Sure, sure." Anton looked a bit worse for wear himself. "Let's go, shall we? I could use some fresh air."

It was only a short walk to an open space in the middle of the camp. Floris was surprised to find the other regiments there as well. "Did they summon all of Wiking?"

"I guess we're moving out soon," Anton said, not doing anything to hide his disappointment.

Floris couldn't deny feeling a little discouraged himself, but he put on a brave face. "Let's see what they have to say." They found the rest of Westland and it wasn't long before their commander, *SS-Gruppenführer* Herbert Gille, appeared in front of them. He tapped on his microphone, and the men in the open space went quiet.

"Gentlemen, good afternoon. I trust you've all had a good night's sleep." His voice boomed through the speakers. Even though Gille did not have a particularly impressive appearance, his pale face and almost white hair contrasting sharply with his uniform, when he spoke, people listened. "Although some may have slept more than others," he added with a smile. "I'm pleased you've regained a bit of color in your faces. I realize we've had a difficult few months, and I'm sure you'd like to stay in Lublin a bit longer. Well, I have some good news. You'll have the rest of the day off to do as you please." Murmurs went up in the crowd, the men smiling. Gille held up his hand. "But keep in mind tomorrow will be an early start. We won't be marching, but I need all of you to be rested and ready for duty at five in the morning, sharp. No exceptions. Make sure your guns are in operational order. You'll need them."

Floris looked to Anton next to him. *What does this mean?*

"Report to your regiment commanders before leaving the field, gentlemen. Dismissed." Gille saluted the men, handed the microphone to a soldier standing next to him, and walked off. A cacophony of voices exploded almost immediately as the assembled men all started talking simultaneously. Floris could hear they were all just as curious as to what tomorrow's mission would be. As he searched for Westland's commander, he decided he would turn in early that day. The mention of a five a.m. start was enough for Floris to suspect he would require all his energy and wits the next day.

Floris marched out of the city at an almost leisurely pace. His breathing produced small vapors, the morning temperature only a few degrees above freezing point. He was thankful for his warm coat and rubbed his gloved hands as he turned in a southeastern direction. The regiment was complete, with none of the men making the mistake of not being ready at five. SS-Gruppenführer Gille's words hadn't missed their mark. Apart from a few men chatting under their breath, Westland marched in silence. They still didn't know what the morning's mission entailed, and the faces around Floris were tense.

It didn't take long to reach the trenches they had passed on their way into the city. Floris frowned: Were they going to do drills in the dark? Was that what all this was about? He scanned the dark horizon beyond the trenches; there was no sign of advancing Soviets. Besides, if there was, they wouldn't be marching this casually. Floris was confused as their commander confidently led them toward the trenches.

As they got nearer, he saw the trenches were dug in an odd zigzag pattern. Even more startling was the lack of connections; there was no way to move between them. Either they were testing something new today, or whoever was responsible for these had made a mistake. *What if we are here to fix these trenches?* He wasn't looking forward to digging trenches.

The men ahead of him stopped, and Floris looked around. Apart from Westland, there were two other regiments. *Where's the rest of Wiking?* He didn't get much time to ponder this as his commander started issuing orders to the squad leaders.

"I want five of you on the edge of the trench." He pointed at the nearest trench. "The others will wait in line. Once the first five run out, they're replaced by the next five. And so forth."

Run out of what? Floris wanted to ask, but he decided to wait and see. The squad leader picked out five men and moved them into position. Floris wasn't one of them, and he stood a short distance away, Anton next to him. All along the trenches, the situation was the same, and before long, three regiments were neatly aligned around the trenches. It resembled nothing like a battle formation, especially with the men standing around, instead of inside, the trenches.

"Okay, now we wait. They'll be here soon," the squad commander said as he pulled out a packet of cigarettes and lit one. He seemed at ease, evidently one of the few men in the field aware of the operation's purpose.

"It's all a bit odd, isn't it?" Anton said in a low voice as his eyes scanned the fortifications. "Why aren't we in the trenches? What kind of exercise is this?"

Floris felt his fingers go numb. "I'm not so sure this is an exercise."

The words had only just left his mouth when he heard voices from beyond the darkness in the distance. He spotted movement from the corner of his eye. Emerging from the veil of darkness was a column of people. He recognized the soldiers escorting them on the sides, wearing the same uniform as him. Their faces were focused on the people between them. Floris blinked hard, unsure if his eyes were deceiving him. The people herded by the soldiers were naked. Men, women, and children trotted along in the near-freezing temperatures barefoot. The panic in their voices became clearer as they neared. Floris couldn't understand their words, but they were terrified. He turned to Anton, who looked on with morbid fascination.

Suddenly it all made sense. These weren't trenches. They were graves.

The first of the column arrived, and when the naked people caught sight of the trenches surrounded by soldiers, they panicked. Two men in the front stopped in their tracks, resulting in those behind them also stopping. Suddenly, the procession became unorganized. The soldiers escorting them noticed, and they were on the men in the front in a flash. They butted the stocks of their rifles in the men's faces, shouting at them to keep moving, or else. Stunned, the men did as they were told.

The first people were herded down wooden ramps at the ends of the trenches. The soldiers harried them down, telling them to keep moving toward the ends of the trenches. "*Schneller, schneller, Judenschweinen!* Faster, faster, Jewish pigs!" They indiscriminately kicked the terrified souls struggling down the ramp for additional effect. When the first people reached the ends of the trenches, they looked up, unsure of what to do. There, the executioners stood looking down at them from a few meters up. Floris watched the faces of his fellow soldiers, and he was unnerved to see a good number of them wore savage os. A minority looked troubled, but most looked at the people at their feet without emotion.

When people could no longer move down the ramp, the soldiers stopped those waiting at the top. Floris saw there were still hundreds coming down the road. Although Floris couldn't see the people in the trenches, he could very much hear them. Howls of despair filled the air. Women sobbed while children cried. Floris found himself in a daze, unsure if the terror around him was real or if he would soon wake up.

Suddenly, loud music filled the air, almost blocking the cries of the people in the trenches. Floris looked around and saw a dozen loudspeakers set up around the trenches. They faced the city of Lublin.

It was as if the music triggered another group of uniformed men to spring into action. Their uniform was unfamiliar to Floris, but as they approached the trenches, it soon became clear what their purpose was. Standing next to the killing squads, they yelled at the people in the trenches. Floris couldn't understand their words, but a few seconds later, the sound of dozens of rifles exploding into action drowned out the sound of the music from the loudspeakers. Floris flinched and closed his eyes as the second salvo filled the air. The volume of the loudspeakers was promptly turned up. A few more isolated shots filled the air, then, for a few seconds, there was only music. Floris looked in the direction of the city, where plumes of smoke indicated its citizens were slowly waking up. He wondered if they could hear the music, and if any of them would be foolish enough to inspect what was going on. Most unlikely, he decided. They knew better.

The music was soon interrupted by the voices of the soldiers at the tops of the ramps. More people moved down, and Floris felt sick. This time, it took a bit longer for the people to reach the ends of the trenches. After the salvo of death sounded around the trenches for a second time, the first batch of executioners turned around, their rifles empty. Floris felt someone push on his back. Reluctantly, he shuffled forward.

He reached the trench and took a deep breath before looking down. The sight that greeted him was even worse than he'd expected. He tasted bile and, before catching it, found himself hunched on his knees, the contents of his stomach pouring out over the lifeless bodies in the trench. He closed his eyes in defeat as his body convulsed, trying to block out the lifeless eyes looking up at him. Finally, his breathing returned to somewhat normal, and he stood, barely able to keep his gaze averted from the fresh corpses below. He heard some men farther down the line snigger, but he ignored them.

"Are you all right?" Anton said, putting a hand on his shoulder, his face now full of concern.

Floris nodded weakly. "What the hell are we doing here?" Out of the corner of his eyes he saw people struggling across the layer of corpses. The next group of condemned were making their way down the trenches. Floris closed his eyes and shook his head in disbelief. His head was spinning, and he took another deep breath, trying to ignore the sour taste still lingering in his mouth and nose.

The first people lumbered past him below. Floris kept his eyes averted, but it was impossible to block out the crying, the pleading, and the sheer horror of parents carrying their children toward their deaths. Movement stalled to his right, which meant the first person had reached the end of the trench. A minute later, a man no older than Floris stopped in the trench below. He stood with his head bowed before him, mumbling what Floris assumed was a prayer. The man made no move to face Floris, seemingly oblivious to his surroundings. Next to him, a woman stood looking around fearfully, her eyes scanning the trench as if searching for someone.

Then came the command in Polish. Most of the people in the trench understood and first crouched to their knees, then lay down on their stomachs. A few didn't understand—or didn't want to—and remained standing. The man in front of Floris sat with his knees in the back of the man who was shot before him. Floris gripped his rifle, then met the man's eyes. He was surprised to see no emotion. He had expected him to plead, cry, or lash out in his final moments. But the man appeared almost at peace with his fate. Floris heard the command to take aim, and in a haze, his arms moved the barrel of his gun into position almost automatically.

Floris looked at the naked man with pity. What horrors had this man endured to go to his death like this? Without fighting, without resisting? In the background, Floris heard the command to fire, and rifles around him exploded almost in unison. The bodies of the people who had refused to lie down were violently forced to the ground as the bullets did their deadly work. A few more shots echoed around Floris as some soldiers required a second or third shot to get the job done. Finally, they moved away from the trench, relaxing their grips.

Floris stayed rooted in position, his rifle still pointing down. The man below looked back at him. The expression in his eyes had changed to one of surprise. Floris' finger was on the trigger, but he couldn't pull it. Something inside him had revolted against shooting a truly unarmed man. His mind flashed back to the moment in the barn, where he and Anton were spared. The man below could just as easily have been Boris. Or Floris if the Soviets had gotten their hands on him instead.

"What do you think you're doing?" The words shook him from his thoughts. He looked into the face of an unfamiliar officer pointing at the man in the trench. "Why is he still alive?"

"I'm not sure I can do this, sir." Floris spoke without thinking. "This is murder, sir. I'm a soldier, not an executioner."

The officer looked shocked, then his eyes bulged, and his cheeks flushed red. He stepped uncomfortably close to Floris and hissed in his ear, "You are a soldier of the Waffen-SS. You will obey orders. Shoot this Jew vermin. He's not human."

Floris felt his hands tremble as he clasped his rifle tighter. He looked at the man below, who still hadn't moved, but was following the proceedings above with interest. *I can't believe how he remains so calm.* Floris turned his face to the officer. "With all due respect, sir. I can't. It's criminal."

The officer huffed and drew back his face as if slapped. Floris saw the man reach to the side of his belt. He unholstered a pistol and cocked it. A second later, Floris felt the cold steel pushing against his temple. "Shoot the fucking Jew, or I'm shooting you for insubordination."

Floris felt his body go cold as he met the officer's eyes. There was pure evil there, and Floris knew he would follow through on his threat. He looked down at the man in the pit, who had tilted his head somewhat. As Floris looked at the bodies strewn around the man, he knew there was no stopping what was going on around him. His one act of resistance would accomplish nothing; the Jew would die seconds after Floris.

"What's it going to be, soldier?" The voice of the officer sounded in the distance.

Floris turned to Anton, who looked at him wide eyed. Floris looked down at the man in the pit, meeting his gaze. To Floris' shock, the man gave him an almost imperceptible nod and closed his eyes. Reluctantly, Floris raised his gun and pointed it down into the trench.

CHAPTER TWENTY-NINE

Nora stepped outside the house in the morning. She took a few steps into the garden, crushing fresh powder under her feet. She eyed the narrow road running through the village in the distance and was pleased to see it covered in snow. There wouldn't be any cars making their way up into the village this morning. Taking a deep breath of mountain air, she closed her eyes, savoring the cold on her face.

Nora, Lars, Katja, and Arthur arrived in the small village of Cier-de-Luchon three days ago. The landscape was so different from what they were used to that they sat in silence for most of the bus ride from the train station. A single winding road crawled through the valley, making Nora a little nauseous on the way up. She had been relieved to get off the bus and step into a picture from a fairy tale. Snowy peaks surrounded the small village on all sides, the lower slopes dotted with snow-covered pine trees.

Their contact, Marcel, was waiting at the bus stop and quickly took them to their safe house. He'd made it clear they would need to stay inside the house most of the time but that they could get some fresh air in the garden in the early morning and evening. People in the village were very much on the side of the resistance, but they did have patrols come through occasionally. Today, however, the snowed-out roads would make that impossible, and Nora enjoyed her carefree stroll through the garden.

"Can I join you?" Lars caught up with her, properly bundled up in a thick coat, his leather boots making fresh marks in the snow. "I could use some fresh air."

Nora nodded, pleased to have him along. On the train from Paris, they shared a compartment to make it appear they were traveling as a couple. Nora hadn't shared all the details of her conversation with Jean Weidner, but she had told her travel companions they would be trekking through the Pyrenees. That alone had been enough for them to be anxious about the trip, and that was before the reality of the snow-covered peaks rose before them.

"It's beautiful, isn't it? Marcel told me Spain is just over the ridge between those two mountains." She pointed at the two highest peaks in the distance. "I wonder when he'll decide the time is right to go."

"Maybe today?" Lars said with a confidence that made Nora stop and turn. "It would make sense, wouldn't it?" Nora looked at him in surprise, and he continued. "I don't know, the patrols must come from somewhere, right? And if the roads through the valley are blocked by the snow, this seems like the perfect time for us to trek up the mountain."

Nora considered his logic. "I suppose you're right. We'd be trekking through the snow regardless. I doubt it'll clear anytime soon." They crossed the small village square, deserted but for a couple of people coming from the small bakery. They greeted Nora and Lars and continued on their way. *They know we're outsiders, but they don't seem to mind.* Even though Nora had been hesitant to believe Marcel when he said the villagers could be trusted, a few days in Cier-de-Luchon had convinced her she had nothing to fear from these people.

"You seem confident. Did you speak to Marcel about this?" Nora asked, poking the toes of her boot into the snow as they turned back to the house. Despite her warm clothing, it was getting chilly. *I'll ask for more layers before we make the trek.*

To her surprise, Lars nodded. "Last night, after you and the others had gone to bed. I asked him when we would head out, and he said we were waiting for a small group of Americans to make it here."

Nora's ears perked up. "Americans? Really? Pilots?"

"He wouldn't say. What's important is that they arrived during the night. Made it in just before the snow came down hard. I suppose they were lucky."

"And we might be, too." Nora felt a flutter in her stomach and looked to the mountains on her right. Were they heading out today? Was it really going to happen? Lars was looking in the same direction. "Does it scare you?"

"What, crossing those mountains over there? Maybe a little bit, yes. I'm a city boy. I've never crossed anything higher than the bridges over the Maas River. And I've never seen snow quite like this." He looked up at the thick layer of snow on the roofs of the houses lining the road. "If we've got snow like this, imagine what it'll be like up there."

"I'm sure Marcel will have a safe path to follow. Did he tell you anything about how long it might take?"

"At least twelve hours. A full evening and night. But I wonder if this snow will make it harder and longer."

They returned to Marcel's house, and Nora was surprised to see through the window several people gathered in the living room. Lars had seen them as well, and he chuckled softly. "Looks like something's happening. Let's hear what they have to say."

Lars had been right. After they stepped inside, Marcel outlined his plan to leave for Spain that evening. The four Americans turned out to be downed pilots and appeared in good physical condition. Marcel then revealed that another six people hiding in nearby villages would also join them. It meant their party would consist of fourteen refugees and Marcel. It sounded like a large group to Nora, and she wondered if they could make it across the border unseen. When she raised her concerns with Marcel, he agreed there was a risk, but there was no other way.

"The people in this group are fit enough to cross the ridge before the moon reaches its highest point. After that, we should be fine."

"What does that mean?"

"We need to cross the ridge before two thirty in the morning. That's when the moon rises above the peaks and makes us visible to German ski patrols."

The house sprang to life when the sun disappeared behind the mountains at four thirty. The Americans wore their flight suits underneath the heavy coats provided by Marcel. As Nora put on her own clothing, she scanned the other faces. Lars had returned to his usual confident self, even conversing with the Americans at one point. They seemed happy to talk about their experiences and were impressed by Lars' recollection of his journey. Katja and Arthur were quiet, and Nora thought the young woman seemed a little nervous. She looked out the window at the dark silhouettes of the Pyrenees rising in the distance and couldn't deny feeling anxiety creeping into her head. Then Marcel appeared; he carried a small, bulging backpack and looked around the room, counting and inspecting them. When he appeared satisfied with their preparations, he whistled sharply, drawing everyone's attention.

"Listen up. This is going to be a tough night. It will be cold, and at times you may feel so tired you just want to sit or lie down in the snow for a few minutes." His face hardened when he spoke the following words. "You cannot do this. We only stop when I say it's safe to do so. German patrols are on the route; if they spot us, we won't make it to Spain. This is why we'll need to keep moving until we reach the ridge. If you've looked up in the direction of Spain, and I'm sure you have, you will have spotted two peaks. We can't rest before we've crossed those."

Nora remembered his words about the moon rising high enough for the German patrols to spot them, and she suddenly felt impatient. *Let's get going.*

"If anybody feels sick, weak, or otherwise like he can't make it through the snow for twelve hours, this is the time to speak up. We can't carry anyone across the border." He silently made eye contact with everybody in the room, allowing the words to sink in. "It wouldn't be the first time I've had to abandon someone because they couldn't keep up, unfortunately." There was sadness in his voice as he spoke, but his face was stern. Finally, when everyone remained quiet, he opened the door. "Well then, let's go. And try to be as quiet as possible during our trek. Voices carry far in the valley and up on the mountain." With those words, Marcel stepped into the darkness outside.

They struggled through deep snow on the lower slopes for three hours before Marcel called for the first stop. The village had disappeared behind the pine trees, which provided welcome shelter from the wind. Nora took a sip of water and saw Lars eat one of his sugar cubes.

"Take one as well," he said in a low voice. "It warms you up and gives you a bit of energy. I think we're going to need it."

Marcel hadn't been joking when he said the journey would be tough. Their guide had set a brutal pace, with even the American pilots struggling to keep up. Nora took out one of the sugar cubes and put it in her mouth. The sweetness of the sugar and the kick of the brandy in which it was soaked instantly revived her. A warmth spread across her mouth as she let it melt on her tongue. Soon, the warmth spread to her stomach and the rest of her body. When Marcel handed out the cubes earlier that day, she had been hesitant, uncertain about having alcohol on such a strenuous trip. But Marcel had insisted, and she was glad to have listened.

"How are you feeling?" she asked Katja, who leaned against one of the pine trees. Even in the darkness, Nora could see she was pale as a sheet.

Katja put on a brave face. "I'm okay. Just glad to have a breather for a few minutes. I'll be fine in a minute." She took off her hat and a bit of steam escaped from her head.

"Put it back on or you'll freeze!" Marcel approached from a distance, looking annoyed. "Don't take off any of your clothes, especially farther up the mountain. I've seen people black out because of the cold." Katja hastily put her hat back on.

A few minutes later they were climbing again. The snow was getting deeper, and their pace slowed. It did nothing to lessen the intensity of the trek, as the party huffed and puffed, following Marcel's steps. Soon, nearly every step sank them knee deep into the snow. The going was slow, and Nora worried they might not be moving fast enough. She looked at Marcel, who was a few meters in front of her. Heat was rising from his cap, and his jaw clenched in determination. In the distance, the peaks slowly grew as they got closer. After an hour, she could even see the ridge Marcel had mentioned. It was easy to spot against the clear sky, and she felt optimistic they would be able to make it there before the moon exposed them. She glanced into the sky behind them and saw no sign of the moon, as the mountains still obstructed it.

Two hours later, Marcel announced another rest, much to the relief of everybody. The pine trees had thinned and they were about to enter a more exposed part of the mountain. Marcel signaled for everyone to gather closer.

"The snow up there will be waist deep in some places. There is a trail, but you need to follow my exact steps. If you divert from the trail, you'll sink so deep into the snow that there is no way we'll make it to the ridge in time. Is everybody clear on that?" There were murmurs of understanding across the group. Despite the warm clothes, everybody was cold, their faces pale, some shivering as they stood in a small semicircle. Around them the wind howled, and Nora's teeth were chattering. She reached into her pocket and took another sugar cube. The effect wasn't quite as strong as earlier.

"We're running a little behind schedule," Marcel said. "So, I suggest we keep moving until we cross the ridge. It's still a good five-hour trek. Let's go."

Nobody needed any further encouragement as they gritted their teeth and fell in line behind their lone guide.

The ridge was only a couple of hundred meters ahead when a slight hue illuminated Lars' silhouette. The snow shone a little brighter, the little crystals sparkling. Nora looked over her shoulder and saw the moon creeping above the peaks behind them. Anxious faces around her did the same, and she tried to catch Marcel's look in the front. He didn't as much as acknowledge what was happening behind him, stoically marking their ascent with his walking stick. Nora, following his path, was impressed by his ability to avoid the deeper snow. To her, the endless fields of snow all looked the same. She marveled at the stories of people crossing the Pyrenees on their own without any local knowledge. She was certain very few made it to Spain alive.

For the next half hour, Nora kept her head down, focused on Lars' boots in front of her, carefully stepping into his footprints. She felt a pang of hunger but ignored it. *We need to get to the ridge first.* Even though Marcel hadn't shown any signs of distress about the moon revealing them on the mountain, his pace had increased since, and Nora was panting, her calves burning from the effort. Despite this, she was encouraged to see the ridge nearing with every step. She had just lifted her foot when she felt a slight tug on her coat. Surprised, she turned to see the procession behind her had halted. *Shit, what are they doing?* Without another thought, she hissed to Lars, "Tell Marcel something's wrong in the back." Lars frowned, took a quick look, and passed the message on. Ten seconds later, Marcel came down, worry etched on his face. Finally, he reached the people in the back, who sat in the snow. Marcel addressed them in a hushed but determined voice, gesticulating with his arms. The rest of the group used the unscheduled stop to drink and eat whatever they still had left. Arthur climbed up and joined Nora and Lars. He was shaking his head, his eyes wide.

"Two of the Austrians can't continue. Marcel is trying to convince them to go on, but I don't think they will."

"How can you be so sure?" Lars asked as he peered at the scene below.

"They've been lagging behind for over an hour now. Some of their friends have been helping them, but now they've just sat down in the snow, unable to continue."

The wind direction changed and carried Marcel's words up the mountain. The Austrians needed to get up now, or they would be left behind. Nora shuddered at the thought of leaving people behind. *Don't these people realize they will die if they don't move?* There was snow all around them, and Nora was already feeling the cold creep through her coat after standing still for a few minutes. *Sitting down is suicide.*

"This is your last chance. We must move, now." Marcel's voice rang out clear as day. Nora held her breath. The people in the snow didn't respond, their heads bowed, their arms clutched around their chests.

Marcel shook his head in exasperation, then looked up, meeting the gaze of the rest of the group. His eyes showed defeat, and Nora knew that, despite his chilling warning at the start of the trek, he needed to decide for the good of the group. She felt for him as he walked away from the two people in the snow. No words were needed as he climbed past the group to return to his position at the head of the procession, his face lined with agony.

When they started moving again, Nora looked back. The two figures sat hunched in the snow, while their two friends stood by, desperately trying to find the words that Marcel hadn't. The couple in the snow no longer responded to their companions' words. Finally, they too gave up and rejoined the group.

When they reached the ridge thirty minutes later, Nora saw the two Austrians hadn't moved. Their heads hung limply on their chests. The wind picked up, and Nora shivered. Even though she didn't know the men, she felt her eyes sting. She felt a gentle tug on her sleeve. It was Lars.

"Come on, let's go. There's nothing we can do for them."

Nora saw the pain in his eyes as well. She stepped onto the ridge. Marcel was waiting, and when the last of their group made it to the top, he spoke for the first time since leaving the people behind.

"This is not the first time this has happened," he said in a shaky voice. "But there was no other option. It was either them or us. I hope everybody understands this."

He was met by silence, but looking at the faces around her, Nora could see nobody blamed Marcel for what had happened. She certainly didn't.

"The good news is that we've reached the dark side of the ridge without running into patrols," Marcel said as he pointed at the other side of the ridge. "It doesn't mean the trek will get much easier, but at least we won't be sitting ducks in the moonlight. Everybody can take a minute to eat and drink something quick, and then we head for Spain."

Barring a few places where some of the group found themselves waist deep in the snow, the trek along the ridge was uneventful. Nora kept her eyes peeled, expecting German patrols on skis to emerge from every corner. When Marcel started descending, the confidence of the group grew steadily. They seemed to find a last bit of energy for the final stretch, and Nora was surprised when she spotted the contours of buildings rising in the distance.

Thirty minutes later, they reached a village, just as the first rays of sunshine appeared behind the mountains ahead of them. Marcel stopped in front of one of the houses with a triumphant look. “This is Bausen. We are now in Spain.”

A cheer went up from the group, and Lars turned around, throwing his arms around Nora. She was surprised at this sudden show of affection. It felt good. They had made it. They were free from the Nazis. Katja and Arthur caught up with them, and together they cried. Nora looked around at the rest of their group, relief prominent on their tired faces.

Marcel stood patiently waiting for a few minutes, a hint of a smile on his face as well. Then, when everybody calmed down, their attention focused back on him. “Follow me to our safe house. It’s in the next village. We’ll be able to rest and wait for transportation farther south.”

Nora had a spring in her step as they walked into the village. She could hardly describe the excitement at finally being free again. The houses in the village were identical to those on the other side of the border. She wondered how the Spanish would welcome them. They were refugees in a neutral country, after all. Her mind quickly went to the next challenge. How would she get to England? As her mind went into overdrive, she didn’t realize the people in front her had stopped. Parked in the middle of the road was a dark green car, its engine rumbling. The emblem on the doors left no doubt about the purpose of this vehicle. *Guardia Civil.* Next to it stood a simple truck, its tarp open, revealing simple benches on either side.

The doors of the car opened and four men in uniform stepped out. Guns swung loosely on their hips. They approached the group with confidence, and the tallest of them addressed them in Spanish. Marcel calmly responded in the same language, and the man gestured toward the truck. Marcel turned back to the group, no longer smiling.

"I'm sorry. It appears these men were aware of our arrival. This is the Spanish border police. We're going to have to go with them."

The ride to Lleida had been in silence. Would Spain send them back to France, back to the Nazis? The thought terrified Nora. It meant their entire journey had been for nothing.

Upon arrival in Lleida the truck stopped in front of a small prison, and it took less than an hour to process them. Nora had been surprised to find they weren't given any prison clothing, and she waited in a large holding cell while the last of their group were processed. She sat next to Lars, whose eyes kept darting between the group in the cell and what was happening on the other side of the bars.

"They don't seem too bothered about us being here. In fact, they've been quite cordial, don't you think?" said Lars as two guards approached their cell. The last two of their group followed the guards. Even though Nora didn't understand the guards' words, it was clear they were to follow them. She stood and stepped out of the cell.

The group was then split up into groups of four. They were placed in smaller cells, and Nora was relieved to find Katja would be confined with her. As the guard closed the door, the women embraced.

"At least we have each other," Katja said with a sob. "What do you think will happen to us?"

Nora shook her head and stroked the younger woman's hair. "I don't know, but I'm sure we'll find out soon enough."

The last of the cell doors was closed and the guards left. It was soon obvious they were the only prisoners. It became oddly quiet, with no sign of the guards anywhere. Something felt off, and Nora moved to the door. To her surprise, she saw one of the Americans in the hallway. He looked around in a perplexed manner, then said something in English. The other Americans entered the hallway, and Nora frowned. She tried the handle of her cell door. The door gave way, and she pushed it open and stepped into the hallway. Nora turned around to Katja and the two other women.

A minute later, their entire group stood outside their cells. *Is this a trap?* Slowly, one of the Americans walked to the far end of the hallway. He tried the door, and it, too, swung open.

"What's going on?" Lars said as they followed the pilot. "Did they forget to lock the doors?"

They were still waiting for an answer, and they walked through the area where they were processed. There were no police officers here, either. It was as if they had simply vanished. They hesitantly stepped out of the station; the cold air hitting Nora's face had never felt more welcome.

No police officers. There was only a slight, older man standing across the street. He motioned for them to cross. The Americans were the first to approach him. When they did, he reached into his jacket pocket. From it, he produced a stack of papers. The Americans took them, eyeing the papers in disbelief. When Nora received her piece of paper, she looked around, struggling to comprehend what she was holding. Finally, the elderly man pointed down the street, toward a building with a clock prominently on its facade.

Nora checked the piece of paper in her hands again. She almost cried with relief. It was a train ticket to Barcelona.

CHAPTER THIRTY

The stench was overpowering. It hit Christiaan as soon as he was dragged down the basement stairs. Sweat, unwashed bodies, excrement, and cigarette smoke mixed together. It was the epitome of human misery around him as he passed the masses of people locked up in cages. They stared at him with hollow eyes, with a disinterest he couldn't place. When the door to his cell was opened, he was surprised to find it empty. He was roughly pushed inside, the door almost slamming into the back of his head when they closed it.

The first day and night nothing happened. He fell asleep to a chorus of wails and pleas outside his cell, as men begged to be let out, protesting their innocence. Occasionally, guards came down to pick out an unfortunate soul. They were taken from their cell to be returned bloody, battered, and silent a few hours later. The horror stories about the basement of the Sicherheitsdienst's headquarters on Euterpe Street weren't exaggerated.

The next morning, Christiaan woke up with a parched throat and a grumbling stomach. He waited for the guards to come for him, but noon came and went. Christiaan soon found himself tempted to join the chorus of pleading voices outside. He was about to do so when there were footsteps in the hall. Keys jangled there before the door opened, revealing two large guards wearing the green uniform of the SD. One of them stepped inside.

"Get up and come with us," he said in German. Christiaan didn't need to be told twice and followed the man out of his cell. Outside, the population seemed to have increased overnight, with some men unable to sit down in a number of the cells.

Christiaan was escorted from the basement, and he felt a hint of relief for a moment. Perhaps he wasn't going to be interrogated in one of the notorious basement cells after all?

They entered a long hallway on the side of the building. None of the doors had windows, and he soon found himself in one of the rooms. The guards chained his hands to a table bolted to the floor and left. Christiaan looked around the bare room. There was nothing but a table and a chair opposite. He was relieved to see no tools of torture.

He had sat for a few minutes when the door opened. A tall man carrying a briefcase walked in and calmly set it on the floor in the corner. Christiaan was surprised to find the man wearing rather casual clothes, in sharp contrast to the uniformed men he'd encountered so far.

The man sat down across from him and leaned back. "Well, well. I have to say I'm surprised to find you here, Mr. Brouwer." He spoke in heavily accented Dutch, his raspy voice making Christiaan's skin crawl. "We've been searching for you for a while now. And then you reveal yourself near a checkpoint. I suppose you didn't think anyone would recognize you, now that your brother is no longer in the city?" The man sported an evil grin as he spoke the last words.

Christiaan wasn't sure how to respond, and kept his mouth shut. Everything about the man screamed danger. He fidgeted in his seat and tried to rub his wrists. The guards had fastened the handcuffs just a little too tight. *On purpose, no doubt.*

The man caught his discomfort and leaned forward. "Would you like me to loosen those a bit? How about you tell me about your work for the resistance, and I can make you a bit more comfortable." He reached into his pocket and produced a pair of keys. "This doesn't have to get more uncomfortable."

Christiaan eyed the keys while his mind went through a host of possibilities. *How much does he know?* With as much confidence as he could muster, he said, "What resistance?"

The man scoffed and replaced the keys in his pocket. "We're going to play it like this, are we?" He opened the briefcase, produced a sheet of paper, and placed it on the table. Christiaan's photo was at the top, his personal data neatly typed out below. "Let's not pretend you don't know what I'm talking about. We know you started out as a courier, using your job as tram driver to distribute messages and illegally obtain food coupons all over the city."

Christiaan kept his face straight as he listened. This wasn't nearly enough to keep him locked up on his own in the basement. There had to be more.

"And from there you climbed the ranks to become one of the leading men in the Ordedienst." The man looked up, an eyebrow raised. "Quite how you managed to do that without any military experience is beyond me, but I suppose there's more to you than meets the eye."

Christiaan had to suppress a chuckle. "I have nothing to do with the Ordedienst, nor am I involved in the resistance. And to think I would be leading anything is beyond me." His surprise was genuine, but his response was mostly fueled by fear. *If they really think I'm a leader of the resistance, I'm in even more trouble than I thought.* He forced himself to meet the eyes of his interrogator.

"Hmm," the man said as he placed the file back on the table. "You know what I find most fascinating about you?" He didn't wait for Christiaan to respond. "That you somehow managed to disappear for over half a year, while your brother was held by the resistance. And only a few months after your brother is sent off to the Waffen-SS, you return. It's like you were waiting for him to leave?"

Christiaan's head was spinning. *Floris has joined the Waffen-SS? Is he lying, trying to trick me?*

"Did you think the heat would die down, now that your brother is gone?" He whistled between his teeth and got up. "Well, you're wrong about that." He slammed a fist on the table, making Christiaan jump in his chair. *What the hell?* "You're going to tell me everything about your organization, or I swear you won't leave this room alive!" He reached into his briefcase again, retrieving a pair of shears. "You know what we do with these?" He roughly grabbed one of Christiaan's fingers and placed the shears around the tip. "I can either use this to cut off parts of your fingers." He squeezed the shears and Christiaan felt the sharp edges biting into his skin. "Or I have another one which first extracts your nails. One by one."

Christiaan felt himself shaking as he looked up into the man's eyes radiating pure, raw evil. Christiaan's cheeks had turned red, and he could feel the blades tightening their grip around the tip of his finger. Christiaan was terrified, but he couldn't admit to the accusations. He wasn't a leader of the resistance.

The man's gaze went between Christiaan and his fingers. Christiaan closed his eyes, expecting to feel the sharp blades of the shears to cut through the tip of his finger soon, when the door opened again.

"I'd like a word with Mr. Brouwer, if you don't mind." A familiar voice filled the room, and Christiaan could hardly believe it when his interrogator-turned-torturer stepped away from the table, releasing the pressure on the tip of his finger.

"Certainly, sir. I'll be right outside," the man said as he took his briefcase and left the room without another word.

Hans sat across from Christiaan, wearing his police uniform. He folded his arms and looked Christiaan up and down for a minute. "You know, he'll be happy to return later and finish the job. He might not seem like it, but he's an absolute psychopath."

"Could've fooled me." Christiaan looked down at his finger, blood trickling onto the table. Hans made no move to help.

"He probably told you we know about your role in the resistance, right? About being part of the Ordedienst, helping all those Jews in hiding?" Hans spoke in a confident manner, and Christiaan felt something was off. *Why repeat what the other man had already said?* Christiaan remained silent. "That's hardly news, and I don't think you've been involved in any of that for the past six or seven months. I mean, even before Floris was snatched by the resistance, he suspected you. Turns out he was right." Hans smirked at him. "Right about Nora, too, in the end, but she somehow set a trap for him. Funny how your brother escaped, killing some of your men in the process, eh?"

Christiaan shook his head. "I had nothing to do with that."

"I know you didn't. You were gone by then. I was there that evening when we searched your house. Floris was furious he couldn't find anything, and he insisted we leave everything the way we found it. Didn't want you to find out we were there. But you knew, didn't you? Because the next day, you were gone." He leaned forward. "What I wanted to know was, where did you go? And what did you do? I don't believe you went into hiding at all. Amsterdam is small; we would've found you sooner or later. We always do."

They sat in silence while Hans twirled the shears between his thumb and index finger. After a minute, Hans put the shears down. "Would you like to know what I think?"

Christiaan just looked at him.

"I think you somehow escaped the country and linked up with the resistance there. Maybe Belgium, somewhere nobody knows you. But then you decided you wanted to return home, make a difference, maybe come back for Nora?" He smiled as he mentioned her name. "You know what happened to her? She had to run when your brother escaped. Last I heard, she was headed south. I can assure you there's very little chance she actually made it. The Gestapo have become very adept at catching illegals across Belgium and France. I would know, I see the reports coming in at the Bureau. My guess is she's probably been caught somewhere in

France, and her arrest report will filter back here soon enough." His smile turned into a smirk, and Christiaan felt his head spin. He remembered the reports of people trying to use the escape lines to Geneva while working at the consulate. He prayed Nora hadn't tried to get to Geneva; that escape line had become especially dangerous.

"That was my first idea, anyway," Hans continued, interrupting his thoughts. "But then I went through your papers yesterday." Christiaan felt a chill run down his spine. His unease must've shown, for Hans started smiling. "Yeah, thought you were clever with those papers, didn't you? Of course, you would've gotten away with it, as well. The regular officers don't pay that much attention to the identification papers as long as they look genuine. Which yours do, of course." Hans got up from his chair and placed his hands on the table, leaning forward. "But here's the problem, Christiaan. Those papers were just a little too perfect, and I had my friends at the Sicherheitsdienst take a closer look." His expression turned triumphant. "Imagine my surprise when they came back to me this morning; your papers were identical to the ones carried by the Dutch agents sent from England."

Christiaan's mind was racing. Even though Hans was onto him, the papers alone didn't prove anything. Certainly not that he was a spy sent by the Brits. He met Hans' eyes and shook his head, even managing a faint smirk while he spoke with just about enough surprise in his voice to make it sound authentic. "Is that what you think I am? A British spy?"

"How else would you have gotten those papers?" Hans sat back down and crossed his legs. "It doesn't seem like a coincidence to me." Despite Hans' confident exterior, Christiaan detected a trace of doubt in his voice. This was his chance.

"Come on, Hans. Only minutes ago, your colleague thought I was in the top of the Ordedienst, then you claimed I ran off to Belgium to help the resistance, and now I'm a British spy? I'm having trouble keeping up." Christiaan's wrists were getting sore, and his finger was still bleeding, producing a small puddle on the table. "Do you think I could get a bandage for my finger while we're here?"

Hans' relaxed demeanor changed, his eyes showing annoyance. "You'll get treated when you help me. And right now, that means telling me where you've been since they took Floris. I can make your life very uncomfortable. We know Nora was involved in his abduction, but she didn't operate alone. Now that she's fled, I think you were working alongside her."

"I already told you; I know nothing about that."

"And you also said the Brits didn't send you," Hans said, leaning forward in his chair, his eyes on Christiaan's bleeding finger. "And I don't believe you." He was quiet for a moment, then abruptly stood. "I see we're not getting anywhere today. I'll invite our friend back inside. Let's see if you prefer talking to him instead." Hans walked toward the door, and Christiaan fought to keep his back straight. Hans was closer to the truth than he realized, but he appeared hesitant to push Christiaan at this point. *Why?* It would be easy for Hans to use the minimal evidence he had to claim that Christiaan had been the mastermind behind Floris' abduction. He could even add his suspicion that Christiaan was a British spy, which would be enough to see him executed. So why was he hesitant to do so? Hans neared the door, and Christiaan turned his head.

"Can I ask you one thing?"

Hans stopped and turned back to him, looking amused. "Sure, why not?"

"What do you want from me? You know I will never admit to any of the fantastical things you accuse me of. What's the point?"

Hans took a step closer, rubbing his hands. He looked pleased with himself. "Ah, but that's where you're wrong. One way or the other, I will find out what you've been up to. And I'm quite certain you were involved in what happened to Floris. And I'll prove it."

"But why? Floris got out, he's with the Waffen-SS now, as you said."

"You answered your own question. The Waffen-SS was a demotion for Floris, a dishonorable discharge from the police force." Hans' eyes narrowed, his voice turning to ice. "This is not for me. This is about justice for Floris. And you're going to give it to me." Hans held his gaze a while longer, then turned around, opened the door, and left. As Christiaan found himself alone in the room again, he realized this wasn't about the resistance or British intelligence at all. This was personal.

CHAPTER THIRTY-ONE

Lisa walked through the hallway. It was almost noon, and she was looking forward to her lunch break. Since taking on her new job of Somer's assistant, her days had become quite a bit more hectic. Not that she was complaining. If she thought she had access to a lot of information as a typist, it paled in comparison to what came across her desk now. It was fascinating when Somer asked her to sit in on meetings and keep minutes. She had been especially pleased when he told her the SOE had agreed to stop sending Dutch agents through their network, even if they didn't acknowledge the network was compromised. No more young Dutch men would be parachuting into captivity. That was a victory, regardless of the political maneuvering of their British allies.

She entered her small office across the hall from her boss' and was surprised to find Femke waiting for her. Her friend from the typists' room looked excited as she held a small piece of paper.

"Isn't Christiaan's last name Brouwer?" she asked without preamble, her eyes expectant.

Lisa frowned in surprise, her eyes moving between the piece of paper in Femke's hand and her friend's unusually animated face. "It is. Why? What's going on?" *Did something happen to him?*

Femke handed her the sheet of paper with its list of names and pointed at one at the top of the page. "Any chance this woman is related to him?"

Lisa gasped and looked up at Femke. "When did you get this?"

"It came in this morning from the Madrid consulate. I only found out because one of the other girls mentioned that the name sounded familiar. So, you know this Nora Brouwer?"

"She's Christiaan's sister-in-law." She read the words again, hardly believing her eyes. *Nora is in Barcelona?* Lisa shook her head as she handed the paper back to Femke. It was no use speculating. "I assume they've already requested a visa to travel to Portugal?"

"Most likely, yes, but the Spanish government is in no hurry to process those, as you know."

Even though Spain was neutral, the Franco government maintained friendly relations with Nazi Germany. Franco was concerned the country's neutrality would be questioned if Spain offered safe passage to Britain. Portugal, another neutral country, did not have these reservations, and offered direct passage to Britain. Dutch national airline KLM even offered a daily flight between Lisbon and London. The problem was getting to Portugal. Spain would only supply an exit visa when Portugal provided an entry visa. And neither country would supply one without the other. Lisa scratched her head in frustration; Nora had come so far but was stuck in Barcelona.

"Anything we can do about this? To move things along?" Lisa asked out loud.

Femke gave her a curious glance. "Well, maybe not you and I, but ..." Her eyes drifted to the door across the hallway. "You could always try."

"You're right!" Lisa exclaimed, a burst of energy shooting through her veins. *Why didn't I think of this right away?* The solution was so obvious.

"Look, I've got piles of work, but good luck. I hope you can convince him." Femke disappeared down the hallway, leaving Lisa to ponder her approach. She sat at her desk and focused her eyes on Somer's closed door. Ever since she became his assistant, he had involved her in practically everything. Sure, not quite like when she met SOE agent Leo Marks, but Lisa was well aware of her boss' modus operandi. He liked to be creative in how he got things done, operating in gray areas when required. She tapped her fingers on her desk, then realized how she could convince him. She jumped up from her chair, headed across the hallway and knocked on her boss' door.

Colonel Jan Somer listened without interrupting. Lisa quickly explained Nora's situation, and how she was related to Christiaan.

"And with everything we know about the Franco government, I'm not too optimistic about her making it to Portugal, and then London, anytime soon," Lisa said, her heart in her throat. Somer appeared deep in thought, his eyes a little glassy as he rubbed his left cheek. Lisa shifted her weight from one foot to the other, feeling more anxious with every passing second.

"And you said she was in the resistance in Amsterdam?"

"She played a big part in smuggling Jewish children from the city to the countryside. She's also the reason I'm here. Nora provided the connections for Christiaan and me to make it to Geneva." Lisa paused for a moment before adding, "I owe her my life, sir."

"She's clearly important to you, and I understand you'd want her here as soon as possible. But, unfortunately, it's not as easy as just asking our friends in Spain to allow her to travel to Portugal. They're not so keen on this."

"I know, sir."

"But if it weren't for this young lady, I wouldn't have you as my very capable assistant, nor would we have an agent setting up my communications network across the North Sea. And that's even without considering that she would most likely provide us with recent information about the situation back home. About how the resistance functions, most importantly."

Lisa nodded.

"That would be enough to secure a visa from the British authorities, but that leaves us with the problem of getting her from Spain to Portugal." Somer looked doubtful as he stood and paced the room, and Lisa felt discouraged. *If Somer can't force this through, no one can.*

"Sir, with all due respect, you've done this sort of thing before, haven't you?"

"Hmm?" he asked absentmindedly, still on his feet.

Lisa chose her words carefully. "Finding creative ways to get people to the places they need to be."

Somer stopped and turned abruptly; his sharp eyes focused on her. *Did I go too far?* Then he burst into laughter, and Lisa couldn't help but join him. When he recovered his composure, he said, "You don't miss a lot, do you, Lisa? I suppose I could've expected as much when I hired you. And I think you're right about Nora Brouwer as well. Based on what she's already done, I think she could be a valuable asset in London. We have to devise a way to get her out of Spain, into Portugal, and then on a plane or boat to England." He paused, and a cheeky grin Lisa had never seen before appeared on his face. "Sounds easy enough, don't you think?"

She returned his smile. "I'll do whatever it takes to get her here, sir."

"Very well. Why don't you grab your notepad. We have work to do."

CHAPTER THIRTY-TWO

Floris had no idea where he was. He only knew to keep his shoulder pressed to the wall. The sounds of battle were all around him. Gunfire mixed with the yells of men—either commands or from pain—and Floris looked to the small team gathered around. They had been separated from their squad when a Soviet ambush forced them to make a quick decision. In the city's narrow streets, Floris and the other six men had turned south while the other half went north. When he had looked back, he saw the Soviets had gone after the other team. He hoped they found adequate cover.

The Soviets started their attack in the early morning, when it was still dark. Wiking was fortified in a city Floris had forgotten the name of as soon as they arrived. It didn't matter anymore; every city and town looked the same. Piles of rubble alternated with half-bombed-out buildings. Whenever they arrived somewhere, the soldiers scrambled for a building providing at least partial cover. The city's center was still somewhat intact, and Floris' team had positioned themselves overlooking the main street. That was until the Soviet attack and the order to pull back.

Now he found himself behind the only remaining wall of what used to be a house.

Floris looked to his left, where his squad commander, a man by the name of Simons, was in discussion with his second-in-command. They appeared to disagree on the direction, and even though Floris had a lot of respect for the man, he was worried. The nearby gunfire intensified, and he feared the rest of Wiking had retreated farther west.

"They're looking to cut us off!" said Floris to Anton, who was crouching next to him. His friend risked a peek through one of the many small holes in the wall.

"I think we may already be. I can see them on the far end of the street. If my sense of direction is correct, we must pass them to link up with Wiking." Anton looked as worried as Floris felt. "I hope Simons has a plan because there's no way we're going to fight our way past them. They're properly barricaded." Anton had barely finished speaking when a piercing whistling sound screamed over their heads. A second later, the wall of the building a few meters behind them exploded and came crumbling down. Floris ducked but still felt the force of the impact, with little pieces of stone raining down on his helmet.

"Shit!" someone shouted. They couldn't stay in place any longer. The Russians were aiming their small artillery at their position. The first shot had barely missed, but the men in the distance were already adjusting their aim. He looked to Simons, now shaking his head furiously at his second-in-command. The other man looked resigned; then Simons turned around. Another explosion, this time a few meters ahead of their position.

"We're going to loop around them! We can't beat them in a gunfight; there are too many." He pointed at Floris and Anton. "I want you two to provide suppressive fire. You've seen their position, right?" Floris and Anton nodded, both reaching for their MP40s. "At my signal, blast away at them, okay? The rest of us will make for the other side of the street over there." Simons pointed at a small side street. Floris swallowed hard; he estimated they needed to cross about twenty-five meters to get to safety. He moved into position and gave the sign to Simons and the other men that he was ready. Anton did the same, and a moment later, he heard Simons shout, "Now!"

Floris leaned slightly to the side of the wall, sticking the barrel of his gun ahead of him. He didn't hesitate and pulled the trigger, aiming at the Soviet position. From the corner of his eye, he saw the first men of his squad running. An instant later, Anton's gun burst into life, and Floris held his fire for a few seconds. There was no need for them to shoot at the same time. He might need the bullets later. Floris narrowed his eyes and looked for movement in the Soviet position. He thought he saw the tips of some of their helmets, but it was clear Simons' move was working; the Russians were taking cover.

Anton stopped shooting and pushed Floris back behind the safety of the wall. He pointed toward the alley. The rest of the team had made it and were in position. Simons lifted three fingers, and Floris and Anton moved close to the side of the wall. Two fingers. Floris' eyes twitched as he eyed the Soviet position. A number of the helmets had moved. One finger. *Are they getting into position? Shit!* Simon finished his countdown, and the guns in the alley exploded into fire.

"Flo! Let's go, what are you waiting for?" Anton's voice sounded oddly distant. Still, Floris didn't move. Then he felt Anton shaking his shoulder, his face filled with impatience. "We need to move, now!"

Floris nodded, but Anton was already gone, sprinting from cover. Floris felt in a daze as he watched Anton get closer to safety. Then he snapped back to his own reality. He was alone, and the Russians' next artillery round could well end him. He looked to the alley, where Simons was waving at him furiously. Anton was halfway across the street, and Floris realized he only had one option. Without another thought, he left the relative safety of the wall behind and ran as fast as his legs would take him.

The sound of the suppressive gunfire faded into the background; all he heard was his heavy breathing. Anton was a good five meters ahead of him, and Floris kept his eyes on the ground before him to avoid tripping on the scattered debris. Finally, he heard the encouraging shouts from the men in the alley.

The gunfire intensified. Floris was confused only for a second, until he heard the familiar sound of bullets whizzing by in close proximity. The voices in the alley grew more frantic. He didn't need to look up to know the Soviets had opened fire on him. *Fuck! I'm a sitting duck.* The adrenaline kicked in, and he pushed his legs harder, trusting his feet to land in the right places. *If I fall now, I'm a dead man.*

Floris was catching up with Anton, and his friend was now only a few paces ahead. "Keep going!" Floris shouted as he overtook him. They had crossed halfway to safety, and the sound of bullets zipping intensified with every step Floris took. But, fueled by an overpowering will to survive, Floris ignored the whizzing of the deadly projectiles and ran without thinking.

He reached the safety of the alley a few seconds later. As he ducked behind the wall, he turned to check on Anton. He still had five meters to go when a bullet struck his left leg. Time slowed down as the explosion of blood combined with Anton's scream. His leg gave out and he crashed to the ground, clutching the wounded leg. He writhed in pain. Amazingly, he went quiet, aware any sound would only draw more attention.

"Keep your head down!" Simons shouted before turning to the men around him. "Hold your fire."

What? Floris wasn't sure he'd heard the commander correctly. The soldiers complied, and a few seconds later, it was oddly quiet as the Soviets did the same. He looked at his friend. The scattered debris now worked to his advantage, as it would be near impossible for the soldiers on the other end of the street to have a clear shot. Until a sniper caught sight of Anton. Floris felt himself shudder at the thought.

"Can you crawl our way? It's only a few meters!" Simons shouted to Anton, who immediately shook his head.

"I can't feel anything below my waist," he managed to croak, his voice sounding oddly weak. Floris felt his heart sink. It wasn't just a wound to his leg, after all. He turned to Simons.

"Let me go get him."

His commander shook his head. "Absolutely no way. I'm not going to lose two men."

"Excuse me, sir?" Floris looked at Simons, dumbfounded. A fury was building up inside him, and he only barely managed to suppress it. "I'm not sure I understand." He stood up and moved toward the edge of the alley.

Simons took a step closer to Floris, and with a look of resignation repeated his order. "You will not step into that street. You know they are waiting for one of us to do so, right? They will shoot you to pieces as soon as you do."

Floris stared at his commander and struggled to comprehend the man's words. His best friend was lying wounded and helpless in the middle of the street. Wounded, yes, but not dead. *He can still be saved, damn it!* He turned away from Simons, focusing on Anton instead. This man had been with him for the entire journey and had been the only friendly face at Sennheim. They had survived the Soviet ambush on the ridge together. Floris clenched his jaw. He wasn't going to leave his best friend out there. He knew what happened to captured soldiers, if they even bothered to catch him. A sniper might be making his way toward them now, climbing up to a nearby vantage point to finish Anton off. Floris turned back to Simons.

"Sir, I respectfully decline your order." He unslung his MP40 from his shoulder and placed it against the wall. Two of the other men looked at him with shock. He didn't wait for his commander's response as he peered around the wall and saw no activity on the Soviet side. He knew they were there, watching and waiting, but he didn't care. *Anton is my brother.*

He heard Simons' voice in the distance as he broke cover and sprinted toward Anton. His friend's eyes showed surprise as he clung to his bleeding leg. Floris waited for the inevitable sound of the gunfire and the force of the bullet—or bullets—hitting him. He could almost feel the sniper focusing on him.

Floris reached Anton and hit the ground next to him. He was surprised at the silence. *Had the Russians not seen him? Impossible.* At least one of them must've been keeping an eye on Anton.

"Are you out of your mind?" Anton said, wincing. "Those boys on the other side are just waiting to finish me off, and now you're screwed, too."

Floris managed a dry chuckle. "Shall I leave you here, then? Come on, I wasn't going to let you die here."

"You're a crazy bastard, Flo. But I'll take it."

Floris got to his knees and gently reached underneath Anton's shoulder. His friend groaned as he put his other arm around his waist. "Sorry, this is going to hurt a bit. Hang tight." He felt the strain on his own legs as he lifted Anton. There were muted cheers from the alley, but Floris didn't dare look. For a moment, he considered the possibility the Russians were letting him save his friend. He stretched his arms, straining his knees as he held Anton about half a meter above the ground. Floris quickly turned and took a step toward the alley.

A second later, he heard the familiar whistling sound above his head, and he knew there was no time to duck, not while carrying Anton like this. So instead, he closed his eyes and braced for impact. The force of the explosion seemed to move the ground beneath his feet, and an instant later, he was on the ground. Anton howled in pain as he collapsed on top of his friend, his hands still wrapped around him.

Floris opened his eyes to a silent world covered in an otherworldly red-and-gray hue. The distant gunshots and shouts were replaced by a deafening ringing in his ears. More explosions shook the ground around him, but Floris could barely look beyond his outstretched hand, the smoke and dust reducing his surroundings to shadows, depriving him of any sense of direction. Small flashes shot through the air around him. *Bullets.* He looked down at Anton and saw his friend was still alive but in even greater pain. "Don't worry, I'll get you out of here."

It was then that he felt the sharp pain in his shoulder. He reached out with his other hand. His uniform was torn, and there was something sharp sticking out. He turned his eyes and was horrified to find a small piece of shrapnel lodged in his flesh. As he moved his arm, pain radiated from his shoulder down his spine. He tried to pull it out, but the pain was too great. *We still need to get out of here.* He cursed himself for leaving his gun in the alley. *Where is the bloody alley?* He frantically scanned the area but saw nothing beyond the smoke and dust.

His ears popped, and he was overwhelmed by the sound of gunfire from seemingly all directions. Men shouted words he didn't understand, nor could he make out whether they were five, ten, or twenty meters away from him. For a minute, he lay next to Anton, pondering what to do. He couldn't blindly make for any direction, for the chances of running into the enemy were significantly higher than the likelihood of linking up with his Wiking brothers. *But I can't stay here, either.* Then he realized the explosions had stopped, and he felt a slight breeze. Slowly, the explosion-peppered fog started to lift. He could make out movement to his left and reached for his sidearm. He wouldn't stand a chance against a couple of soldiers wielding rifles, but he'd be damned if he was going to make it easy for them. The men disappeared in the fog again, and Floris decided to wait a little longer.

Then he heard the sound of men running, and to his relief and delight, they were shouting in German. They moved in shadows to his right, and he got up. "Are you ready? We're getting out of here." Anton just groaned, and Floris bent down to lift his friend once again. As he did, his shoulder protested. Pain tore through his body like a hundred burning knives. He closed his eyes and gritted his teeth like never before. *I can't abandon him.* With an immense effort, he managed to lift Anton and slung him over his good shoulder. He took a step in the direction of the German-speaking shadows. He hoped his mind wasn't playing tricks on him. He took another step, his shoulder protesting again, but he blocked out the pain and took one step at a time.

Around him, the fog was clearing, and he saw Waffen-SS uniforms running around the corner about ten meters ahead of him. He didn't look back—he couldn't—but he knew the Soviets must be near. Instead, Floris focused on taking one step at a time.

There were footsteps next to him, and he glanced to see a couple of men wearing the same uniform as him racing by. "Hey! A hand?" Floris shouted. They looked at him but didn't slow their pace as they ran toward the end of the street. Floris was furious. "I'll find you, assholes!"

He was only a few meters from safety when he heard a crunching sound behind him. A metallic, wheezing noise cut through the air. It was a sound Floris had heard many times before, and he felt all energy drain from his body. He turned around to see the armored beast a mere twenty meters behind him. *A T-34 tank.* A loud click confirmed that the barrel of the devastating 74mm gun was locked into position. Floris felt every muscle in his body tense, and he was rooted to the ground, unable to move.

Resignation and acceptance flowed through his body as he eyed the tank, looking for a face beyond the machine of death. For a few seconds, all was quiet as he faced off with the unseen man inside the tank. Then fire erupted from the barrel, and Floris closed his eyes, ready for darkness to take over. *At least I died trying to save my best friend.*

To his surprise, he felt nothing. No shell designed to pierce tank armor reducing his body to a mangled heap of blood and muscle. No descent into nothingness to finish it all. The thunder of the tank's gun echoed between the buildings, and Floris opened his eyes. For a moment, he felt ecstatic. The tank had missed. He still had a chance. But then he heard a rumbling sound behind him. He turned just in time to see the adjacent building shaking on its foundations. The tank had blown away most of the lower floor, and the rest of the building was collapsing into the street. As the first bricks fell, Floris looked down at the face of his friend, who seemed oddly calm, and said, "I'm sorry, brother. I failed you."

Anton opened his mouth, but at that moment, a crushing weight overwhelmed Floris, knocking him to the ground. The last thing he remembered was the taste of dust filling his lungs. Then his world went dark and silent.

CHAPTER THIRTY-THREE

Christiaan had lost all sense of time as he shifted on his hard bunk. He licked his cracked lips as he listened to the silence around him. He had just been returned to his cell after spending an uncomfortable few hours with a new interrogator.

After Hans had left the interrogation room a few nights ago, the first interrogator returned. Even though he hadn't gone through with his threat of severing Christiaan's fingertips, he had made it clear he would do so on his next visit. Oddly enough, he hadn't seen the man since.

Not that this evening—or was it night?—the experience had been much better. The new interrogator, Rainier, had clearly been instructed to take a more forceful approach. Christiaan winced as he rubbed his swollen face, feeling the dried blood caked around his nose and mouth. But even though his head was throbbing, Christiaan was pretty certain nothing was broken.

Rainier had battered him for what felt like an eternity, asking the same questions repeatedly. Where have you been these past six months? Who are you working for? Are you connected to British intelligence?

Christiaan had kept his mouth shut, but he started wavering near the end. After a blow to the side of his head that sparked stars in his vision, Rainier had stopped. He had given Christiaan some water and waited. After Christiaan gulped down the water, Rainier had spoken in a controlled voice, promising him he'd spare his life if he answered his questions. Christiaan had been too stunned to respond, and Rainier must've taken his disoriented look for refusal, for the next thing Christiaan remembered was being back in his cell.

He sat up on the bunk, a sharp pain shooting through his head, momentarily blinding him. *I must have a concussion.* The pain subsided after a few seconds, and he carefully stood, waiting for another jolt of pain to strike him down. Nothing happened, and he shuffled toward the door. He put his ear on the door, trying to make out any sounds in the hallway. It was silent, and he walked back to his bunk. He hadn't seen daylight since being hauled into the Sicherheitsdienst's headquarters, but he estimated he'd been here for three, maybe four nights now. What else would they do to get a confession?

Christiaan heard footsteps in the hallway. The door opened abruptly, and two guards entered, filling the room.

"Get up, you're coming with us," the tallest said. He scanned the rest of the cell, confirming Christiaan possessed nothing but the clothes on his back. Before Christiaan could respond, the guards grabbed his upper arms and pinned him between them.

"Wait, where am I going?" Christiaan struggled to keep his balance as the men dragged him into the hallway. "What's happening?"

They ignored him as they headed toward the stairs at the far end of the basement. Christiaan felt dizzy, his head spinning as he passed the other cells. It was quiet, and he assumed the other prisoners must be sleeping. *Nighttime, then.* Finally, they reached the stairs, and Christiaan mustered enough strength in his legs to mount the stairs himself. The alternative would've been getting dragged with his knees clipping every step.

When they reached the top of the stairs, the dizziness threatened to turn into nausea. Christiaan was panting, and the other guard turned to him. "Don't even think about making a mess here or in the car. Get yourself together." Christiaan took deep breaths as the guards strengthened their grip on him, pulling him along faster.

They were now on the ground level, and the contrast with the dark basement couldn't be greater. The hallway was brightly lit, and they passed empty offices. He could see through the windows that it was dark outside. He was about to ask the guards what time it was, but another wave of nausea hit, and he swallowed a couple of times, fighting his mutinous stomach.

Ten seconds later, the guards opened a large door, and they stepped into a courtyard. The cold air hit Christiaan's face, and he took a deep breath. He hadn't tasted fresh air since being locked up, and the sweetness of the air revitalized him. Nausea faded and the throbbing in his head became less prominent as he was manhandled toward a parked car. One of the guards opened the door while the other tossed him in the back seat. The door slammed shut, and the guards took their seats in the front. Thick metal bars separated Christiaan from them. It was clear why the men hadn't bothered with any additional restraints; Christiaan was surrounded by metal, an animal locked inside a cage.

The car started moving, and Christiaan looked outside. They pulled out through a simple gate leading to Euterpe Street. Two SS troopers stood guard, facing the street, briefly acknowledging Christiaan's car. The guards didn't speak as they drove through a dark, quiet, sleeping Amsterdam. The narrow city streets made way for the broader lanes of the suburbs, and Christiaan wondered where they were headed. The dimmed headlights emitted just enough illumination for the driver to make out the road ahead of them, but Christiaan soon gave up trying to identify landmarks alongside the road. Even if there were any, it was too dark to make out anything.

He sat in the back and closed his eyes. As soon as he did, he felt sleep tugging at him and quickly opened them. *I need to keep my wits about me. Where are they taking me?* The large prison in Scheveningen —mockingly called the *Oranjehotel*—was his most likely destination. It was clear Hans and the interrogators were convinced he was part of the resistance, one way or another. That he hadn't admitted to anything meant nothing to them; Hans had been quite explicit about that. The prison in Scheveningen was where all known resistance fighters were incarcerated. Christiaan swallowed hard; many of the men and women held there were kept as collateral. These people were executed in retribution whenever the resistance assassinated a prominent German. The most recent ratio Christiaan had heard was twenty-five Dutch prisoners to one German. He remembered thinking of those men and women when he was still part of the resistance in Amsterdam, smuggling the food coupons obtained by raiding distribution offices. He'd never expected to end up on a "death list" himself, but here he was, on his way to the Oranjehotel.

They continued in silence for another hour, and Christiaan felt restless. They should've been there by now if they were headed for Scheveningen. Thick woods surrounded the roads, and there wasn't a hint of the dunes surrounding Scheveningen. When they crossed a large bridge, Christiaan realized they weren't heading toward the coast. He knew this bridge; they had just crossed the Lek River. They were headed south. He closed his eyes. This could only mean one thing: they were taking him to Camp Vught.

Half an hour later, the car slowed as they approached a gate. Christiaan scanned the surroundings. A high barbed-wire fence separated the densely forested areas on both sides of the gate. The driver stopped the car and held out some papers to another man approaching from the gatehouse. He quickly inspected them, then waved them through. Leaving the gate behind, Christiaan looked out the window as the driver slowly drove on. The forest had been cleared on either side of the road, but something was off. Instead of administrative buildings or barracks, the area resembled a garden. Neatly cut bushes, empty flower beds, and bare fruit trees lined the road. After a minute, he was surprised by the sight of a large castle-like building ahead. *This can't be Camp Vught.* He could no longer contain his curiosity. "Where are we?"

The driver shut off the engine and turned around with a smirk. "This is your new home. For now, anyway." The other guard chuckled, and they exited the car, slamming the doors. For a few seconds, Christiaan was alone. He searched furiously for an explanation. *What is this place? And why wasn't I taken to Scheveningen or Vught?* An uncomfortable feeling built in the pit of his stomach.

He didn't have much time to contemplate his position as the door was opened and he was told to get out. When he did, the guards grabbed him again and escorted him to the front door. There, another man opened the door into a spacious hall. He wore the uniform of the Sicherheitsdienst, and Christiaan realized with a sinking feeling this meant the interrogations weren't over yet. The man in uniform continued into a narrower corridor, where he snapped his fingers. Two new guards appeared almost instantly, cuffing his hands. The guards who escorted him from Amsterdam left without a word, and he looked at the SD man. "Please tell me where I am."

The man cocked his head, and then, without warning, punched Christiaan square in the face. The unexpected force of the blow had Christiaan seeing stars, and the nausea finally overpowered him. His body convulsed, and he jerked forward, the SD man barely jumping out of the way in time before Christiaan sprayed the contents of his stomach on the marble floor. It gave him a short feeling of relief, as if the pressure he'd felt for days was finally released. The sour taste of bile followed, and as he looked up into the glowering eyes of the SD man, he knew his relief would only be temporary.

"Hold him steady." The man's words sounded distant, as if he was in another room, despite Christiaan seeing his scowling face less than a meter away from him, his lips moving in slow-motion. He couldn't understand the words and felt himself floating outside his body for a moment. Christiaan was only barely aware of the guards tightening their grip. Then he saw a flash in the corner of his eye and heard something crack, followed by a searing pain on the side of his face. He slumped forward, the voice drifting into nothingness as strong arms dragged him down a dark hallway.

Christiaan opened his eyes. The first thing he felt was an agonizing pain on the left side of his face. He instinctively rubbed his jaw and flinched; the pain intensified, and his skin felt raw.

"Hey, he's awake." Christiaan turned to find two men wearing regular clothes looking at him from the other side of the room. They sat around a small table, a stack of cards in front of them.

"Where am I?" His head felt heavy as he sat up, and he held it in his hands as he closed his eyes, catching his breath. *What happened?*

"Are you all right? Take it easy." Christiaan heard one of the men get up and shuffle toward him. "They hauled you in here in the middle of the night, and you've been out since. Looks like they gave you a warm welcome." His voice was close, the man was speaking Dutch. Christiaan opened his eyes and looked around. He was in a prison cell. Again.

"What is this place?" Christiaan repeated. "The guards wouldn't tell me."

The man shrugged. "They tend to do that. Best keep your head down. You're in Haaren now."

Christiaan felt a chill at the mention of the location. *Of course I'm in Haaren.* His thoughts went back to his meeting with Esquire Six in the church in Amsterdam only a few weeks ago. He had mentioned the escape from Haaren. It all made sense now. *They've decided I'm a British spy, after all.* He thought of Hans and wondered how much his brother's friend had to do with his transfer. He looked at the man in front of him. "Why are you here?"

The man sighed. "Same reason most of us are here and not in Vught or Westerbork. This place is run by the Sicherheitsdienst, not the SS. It means they want more information from whomever ends up here."

Christiaan's head was spinning. The man hadn't answered his question. "And have they succeeded?" He also looked over the man's shoulder, where the other man was shuffling the deck of cards.

"Well, in our case, it was pretty clear why we were here. And since you were placed in this cell with us, I suppose your fate was the same. When were you dropped?"

Christiaan didn't immediately answer. Instead, he studied the man's face. The look in his eyes was calm and calculated. His mouth was relaxed, and he stood with his arms hanging loosely by his sides. Despite that, Christiaan felt a tinge of doubt. What if the Germans placed him in this cell to get him to admit to being a British spy? "What do you mean, dropped?"

The man flashed a quick, humorless smile and pulled up a chair next to Christiaan's bunk. "You think I'm working with the Germans? All right, then I'll go first. My name is Max de Ruijter. I did my training at Ringham about six months ago, together with him." He motioned at the man on the other side of the room, who had finished shuffling the cards and sat silently looking on. "His name is Johannes, and we jumped about three months ago." Christiaan listened but kept his expression neutral. "When we landed, all seemed fine, and we packed up our parachutes. Then, when we were ready to head out, to get to Amsterdam, they appeared. There must've been at least thirty to forty of those damn Krauts surrounding us. They knew exactly where we'd be. They took us straight to this place, and we could do little else but confirm what they already knew."

"What did they know?" Christiaan held his breath.

"That the Special Operations Executive sent us," Max said. "They even knew our code names. The next day they *introduced* us to the other agents. That's when we knew the operation was blown." The man looked genuinely downcast, his eyebrows dropping, sorrow in his eyes. Christiaan wanted to believe him but needed to be sure.

"At Ringham, what planes did you use to practice your jumps?"

"Why, Whitleys, of course. What else?" Max answered without hesitation.

Christiaan felt relief wash over him. Max was telling the truth. He held out his hand. "I'm sorry for grilling you like this, but I've had a very uncomfortable few days. I'm afraid I'm having trouble trusting anyone right now."

Max shook his hand. "Not at all, I completely understand. It's why you're still alive. Now, tell me, did you jump recently?"

"I did." Christiaan recapped his journey since jumping from the RAF plane almost a month ago. Max and Johannes listened silently, not once interrupting him. When Christiaan finished, Johannes spoke for the first time.

"At least you managed to let London know the network is compromised. Did you hear back from Somer?"

"I was arrested before I could speak to Six again." He thought of Lisa, and he hoped she had seen his message come in. *She must be so worried.* He wondered if he'd ever see her again. A stab of pain shot through his heart. Of course he'd see her again. He'd find a way to get out of here. He turned back and looked Johannes in the eye. "I know the people back in London will make sure no more Dutch agents are sent through the SOE's network."

"I hope you're right," Max said, folding his hands together. "Because when we arrived, the agents already here told us about the escape in June. We should never have been sent." His tone was bitter and accusatory, but he caught himself. "We knew there were risks, of course. But to think people in London knew something was wrong and still went ahead with our mission..."

"What happens next? You said you've been here for three months?" Christiaan dreaded the answer, but he needed to know what to prepare for. If it was more interrogation and torture, he needed to be in the right frame of mind. "More interrogations?"

Max and Johannes exchanged a quick look. They looked uncomfortable, and it was Max who spoke in the end. "Well, yes, normally I expect that would be the case."

"Normally?" There was something in Max's voice that made Christiaan feel a little woozy.

"Listening to you, I think this Hans in Amsterdam has either decided you really are a spy, or someone else in the Sicherheitsdienst has." Max looked at him with an odd, resigned expression. "It's no coincidence you were brought here in the middle of the night."

Christiaan was getting flustered. "How so?"

"The guards have been talking about all of us getting relocated soon. The Dutch spies, they call us. And last evening, we were told to pack our bags and be ready to leave." Max looked out the window above Christiaan's head, where the first rays of the morning sun filtered into their cell. "And I think today might just be the day."

"And you think I was sent here to join you."

"It would be the only logical explanation for them to transfer you here in the dead of night. And from what you told me, they will feel they have enough proof to consider you a spy."

A deep sense of dread overcame Christiaan as he listened to Max's words. He thought back to the interrogations at the Sicherheitsdienst headquarters and racked his brain. Had he unknowingly shared details of his mission, training, or even his journeys across Europe during those interrogations? Christiaan realized—with dismay—that he couldn't be sure. His head was spinning. *I must've shared information. otherwise I wouldn't be here.* He turned his attention back to Max, who patiently observed him. "Did they say where we'll be taken?" In his mind, Christiaan could see himself on a train headed to Germany, to be taken to the Reich's best interrogators in Berlin or Munich. They would extract information from him until he was no longer useful.

Max looked at him with an expression that was a mix of resignation and compassion. "They never do. You want my advice? Try to get some rest while you can. You look like you need it. And you'll never know when they'll come for you next."

Christiaan's head suddenly felt very heavy, the weight of their words straining on his mind. He placed his head back down on the hard bunk and closed his eyes. Lisa's face flashed in front of him. He heard his promise before leaving England. *No matter what happens, I'm coming back to you.* Lisa smiled and gently placed his head in her lap. He looked up at her. Her lips were moving but he couldn't make out the words. He opened his mouth to ask her to repeat herself, but his throat felt like cotton, and no sound came from his lips. Then the vision of Lisa started to slip away, her dark brown eyes never leaving his as she faded into darkness. Christiaan fought to hold onto her, but he felt himself falling as exhaustion overpowered him, and sleep took him from consciousness.

The crash of the door and bright lights tore him from his slumber. Christiaan opened his eyes, feeling like he'd fallen asleep only seconds earlier, his mind barely processing his surroundings. *Where am I?*

"Get up! Out, out now, you piece of filth!" The words were barked centimeters from his ear, and when he didn't immediately jump to attention, the blow to the side of his head made the world go blinding white for a few seconds. The next words sounded like he was hearing them underwater: distorted, distant, and spoken at half speed. "Are you deaf? Get up or I'll finish you off right here!"

For a second, the alternative to getting up sounded acceptable, if it allowed him a few more seconds in his bunk. It wasn't to be. Strong hands roughly lifted him, and as he was forced upright his brain started putting the pieces of his surroundings together. He was in his cell in Haaren. Max and Johannes stood against the wall opposite. Max shot him an urgent look, and Christiaan's senses returned with a start.

"Too bad you're leaving today." The same voice now came through at full volume. "I would've loved to teach you some discipline." Christiaan kept his face straight ahead, avoiding the guard's gaze, but unable to ignore his foul alcohol breath. His nostrils twitched in disgust. "But it doesn't matter. Where you're going you won't last a week like that." A sharp stab of pain shot through Christiaan's head and he flinched involuntarily, closing his eyes for a second. He clenched his jaw, partly because of the pain, partly in anticipation of the inevitable next blow. As the pain subsided, he opened his eyes to find the guard at the door.

"Follow me, and no funny business. If you try anything, you'll be sorry." He stepped into the hallway, where more prisoners passed in a single file. Christiaan followed Max and Johannes and they joined the procession. As they emerged from the basement, they were greeted by a corridor of guards wielding rifles. The show of force was excessive.

Two trucks stood outside, and the fifty or so prisoners were harried into their backs. They found their places on splintered wooden benches and soon the tailgates were closed, the engines roaring into life. Two *Kübelwagens* guarded the rear of the column as they pulled away from the prison.

The prisoners were silent on the drive over, and it took less than fifteen minutes for the trucks to reach the front of a small train station. More guards stood waiting, and as the tailgates were lowered, the screaming started.

"Everybody out, single file, hurry up! Now! Come on!"

Christiaan joined the rest of the prisoners as the guards hustled them through the station's deserted waiting area. They had made sure there would be no curious onlookers today. They turned onto the platform seconds later, and fear gripped Christiaan's throat when their train came into view. It wasn't the imposing locomotive with small puffs coming from its smokestack that caused his heart to skip a beat. It was the single boxcar behind it. He knew what that meant.

The door of the car was open, and the first men reluctantly boarded. Christiaan saw the same realization on their faces, but one look at the guards made it clear there was no alternative. They held their rifles at the ready, their fingers close to the triggers, ready to use them. Christiaan was one of the last to reach the boxcar, and there was so little space left that a few of the other men had to squeeze in to allow him to board. When the last man boarded, Christiaan felt he could barely breathe without inconveniencing the men around him.

Two guards stood in the door opening, one of them grinning as they shut the door without another word. A heavy clang confirmed it was locked from the outside, and with it Christiaan's hope all but disappeared. The train slowly pulled away from the station, and as he peered through the small gaps in the car's walls, he knew his chances of survival had just taken another turn for the worse. Christiaan closed his eyes and felt all strength drain from his body. The boxcar was the prelude to hell. The only uncertainty was which hell they were being taken to.

CHAPTER THIRTY-FOUR

Nora entered the small waiting room. She clutched the papers tightly to her chest as she approached the desk at the end of the room. The simple chairs lining the walls were filled with people waiting nervously. She caught the eyes of a man shifting between the woman behind the desk and a doorway leading to a corridor next to her. Nora reached the desk and waited for the woman to look up from her papers. When she didn't, Nora softly cleared her throat, drawing the woman's attention.

"I'm sorry, I didn't see you there," the woman said without sincerity. "You're here for your application, I assume?"

"I was told to come back today. I applied a week ago," Nora said hopefully. "My name's Nora Brouwer." She passed her papers to the woman's outstretched hand. Her finger went down the list, then she frowned at Nora's papers. She turned in her seat and opened the filing cabinet behind her, thumbing through the folders. Nora's anxiety grew with every sigh and groan. Eventually, the woman appeared to find what she was looking for.

"Why don't you take a seat? Someone will be with you shortly." The woman focused on the papers on her desk again.

Nora looked at the others in the waiting room. There had to be at least thirty people there. "I'm sorry, but are they all waiting for the same thing?" she asked in a soft voice.

The woman put down her pen and rolled her eyes at Nora. "You're just going to have to wait your turn like everyone else, Mrs. Brouwer. Take a seat."

Nora found a free seat in the corner and scanned the people in the room. They were mostly young men, and she assumed they had taken journeys identical to hers. Even though the clerk had been rude, she knew the people at the consulate were doing their best to arrange visas. The woman was probably stressed about the number of applicants in the waiting room.

Since arriving in Barcelona, Nora had quickly learned she could be in for a long wait. When she had reported to the consulate with Lars, Katja, and Arthur and asked about their chances of getting to Britain, they were told to put in the two requests. One to leave Spain, another to enter Portugal. They had been warned the process was set up to delay their exit, and after speaking to several people in the same situation, Nora's hopes of a quick reunion with Christiaan in London had been tempered. Lars had tried to lighten the mood by mentioning they were at least safe, but Nora had been bitterly disappointed. It was why she returned to the consulate this morning. Even though the other Dutch refugees told her there was no way her application had been processed within a week, she decided she would show up every week until she had her visas.

"Nora Brouwer."

She was surprised to find a young man holding a thin manila folder scanning the room. "Nora Brouwer?" She stood and approached him, and he inclined his head. "Follow me, please." He guided her to a small room in the back, sparsely furnished with a table and four chairs.

"Would you like something to drink? Water, maybe?"

"I'm all right, thank you." She sat down, intrigued by how quickly she was called. *Maybe this trip wasn't a waste of time after all?*

"Very well." The man closed the door and sat down, placing the folder on the table between them. It contained only a few sheets of paper, and Nora didn't know what to make of it. "My name is Meyers, and I'm a special consular officer here in Barcelona." He flashed a modest smile. "Special in the sense that I'm not officially trained as such. I arrived in Spain much like you, albeit a year earlier."

Nora returned his smile, already feeling more connected with him than with the woman in the waiting room. "How did you get here, if you don't mind me asking?"

"I was one of the first people to take the route directly to Spain. Like you, I crossed the Pyrenees, but I did so in August when the trails were more accessible. And we had way fewer German patrols back then." There was admiration in his voice. "When I arrived, it was almost impossible to get to Britain, and I was asked if I would be willing to stay in Barcelona and work here instead. I decided it would be a good job. I could look out for the new arrivals; who knows, it might be easier to get to England later in the war. Turns out, it only became harder, but the number of people coming through has only increased, so I feel I'm doing useful work here."

"I'm sure you are. I'm grateful for the way we were received." Her words were sincere. When they arrived in Barcelona, the Dutch consulate assigned them hotel rooms, provided fresh clothes, and even gave them a weekly stipend for essentials. But, despite the new, safe surroundings, Nora couldn't wait to make for London.

Meyers opened the folder. "I'm afraid I'll have to start with some discouraging news. The Spanish government has denied your initial application for an exit visa. We haven't heard from the Portuguese yet, but from experience, I can tell you they will automatically deny the entry visa as well."

"One doesn't go without the other, right?"

"Yes, and unfortunately, there's not much else we can do but appeal and try again," Meyers said, sliding a sheet of paper across the table. Nora scanned it and saw it was the Spanish rejection letter.

She felt a pang of disappointment. None of the people she had talked to this past week knew of anyone receiving their visas without going through the drawn-out process of appeals. She set aside her disappointment.

"What do you need from me to start the appeal process? And how much longer does it normally take?"

Meyers took the rejection letter and replaced it in the folder. "There's no set time, and I'll be honest with you: there's no guaranteed approach to speed things up. However, I also have good news." He pulled another sheet of paper from the folder and slid it toward her. "It appears you have friends in high places in London."

Nora raised an eyebrow as she picked up the paper. On the surface, it looked like any other official letter, bearing the royal crest of the Netherlands in the top right corner. However, this came from the Dutch government in London, and as she read the short letter, she felt her heart in her throat. She looked up in disbelief. "Is this real?"

"Very much so, Mrs. Brouwer. I've never seen this before, but I think you'll agree the plan is quite brilliant."

Nora was speechless, still struggling to believe the words on the paper. Finally, she managed, "When?"

"Tomorrow morning."

Nora looked out through the tinted windows of her train car as it slowed down yet again. It was surreal to think they were about to make their way into Portugal, barely twenty-four hours after leaving Barcelona. The journey had been long, but Nora hadn't cared one bit. Nora, Katja, Lars, and Arthur had met their fellow travelers at a small train station on the outskirts of Barcelona, where they were directed to a waiting freight train. At first, Nora had been confused, but when they reached the front of the train, they found a single passenger car attached. Its windows were tinted, and as soon as the last of their party boarded, they were told it would be sealed until their arrival in Portugal. They would receive further instruction upon arrival. The man guiding them wished them safe travels and shut the train doors. Nora had been anxious for the first couple of hours as they slowly made their way west. But as the Spanish countryside raced by outside her window without incident, she relaxed.

Now, the train had stopped, and two men in official-looking uniforms approached. The train driver climbed from the locomotive and greeted them. The men held clipboards. They looked amicable enough as they chatted with the driver.

"Are you nervous?" Lars sat next to her, his eyes following the men outside. "They look an awful lot like customs officers, don't they?"

Nora let out a nervous chuckle. They had seen their fair share of border guards and officials in the past few months. "There's nothing we can do but wait. I'm sure the consulate in Barcelona made sure our papers are in order. No sense in going through all this trouble only for us to get sent back. Besides, you have to admit you can hardly make this up."

Lars glanced at the bags in the baggage compartments above their heads and grinned. "I've never played a game of field hockey, so I hope they don't ask us to demonstrate our skills."

"I doubt they will." Nora giggled and instantly felt better. She was glad Lars was with her. Despite their challenges, he hadn't lost his optimistic outlook. It wasn't the first time he'd lightened the mood when she was feeling particularly worried or gloomy. She reached for her small bag and checked her papers for the umpteenth time. They indicated she was a match official for the Dutch field hockey team, due to officiate an important game in Portugal. The twenty-odd men in the car with her made up the team. It was plausible enough; they were all in their early twenties and looked the part. Nora had spoken to a number of them on the way, and they all possessed skills that would make them fine additions to the Dutch government-in-exile. Three of them were pilots, and they were confident they would be assigned to the Royal Air Force. She knew Lars was looking to join them as soon as they arrived; he hadn't given up on his dream of flying yet.

"Looks like they're coming to say hello," Lars said as the door to their car was unlocked. A moment later the customs officers stood in the aisle at the front. Now that they were closer, Nora saw their uniforms were slightly different. One sported a Spanish flag, the other wore the colors of the Portuguese flag. The Spanish officer addressed them in broken English.

"Please have your papers ready for inspection. This should only take a few minutes." He even managed something resembling a smile as he held out his hand to the men in the front. Nora kept her eyes on the officials as they leafed through the papers. This was the moment of truth. If they were satisfied with the first bits of paperwork, everybody on board the train was in the clear.

The officer took his time, double-checking the man's face and photograph. He frowned, then asked, "Hockey, huh? So, this is important enough for your country, despite the war?" He rolled his eyes, then turned to his Portuguese colleague. "And for you, too?"

The other officer shrugged. "I care more about football anyway. But what do I know? Might be good for morale, I suppose."

The Spanish officer handed the papers back to the man. "Well, good luck with the game. Give them a beating, eh."

Nora's body relaxed. The papers were good. It took the officials another fifteen minutes to check everyone's documents, and they soon disembarked. The train driver locked the car again, and the customs officers placed a new seal over the door handle. Nora supposed that was more for show than anything; they were about to enter Portugal.

The train started moving again, and Lars spoke up as they passed the small customs building. "They didn't look like they cared too much about why we were going to Portugal, did they?"

"They didn't. Do you think they've seen this before?"

"I'm sure this isn't the first time they've seen such an interesting delegation pass the border. I think it's mostly window dressing for the Nazis. This way the Spanish and Portuguese can claim all the paperwork was in order, even if our hockey team disappears somewhere along the way."

"What do you think will happen next?" Meyers at the consulate hadn't shared anything beyond the instructions to get onto the train in Barcelona. "Do you think we'll be spending much time waiting around when we arrive?"

Lars looked thoughtful. "It wouldn't surprise me. But to be honest, I wouldn't even be too upset about it. It's just a matter of time until we're sent to England, one way or another."

"I hope you're right." Nora didn't share his patience. They had made it to Portugal, and England now felt within reach. She couldn't wait to see Christiaan and Lisa. Even though she couldn't be sure, she suspected Christiaan played a part in getting her onto this train. It was too much of a coincidence that she had been picked to travel to England. She longed to tell him about what had happened in Amsterdam since he left, and of her journey across Europe.

The train rolled on slowly through the Portuguese countryside for another two hours, and Nora was growing restless. She wished she could ask someone how much longer it would take, but in the end comforted herself with the thought that they were getting closer to freedom with every minute.

The open plains made way for small villages, and soon enough they found the train halting at a terminal station, the locomotive letting out a long, content sigh. They watched the driver climb down from his cab and, to Nora's delight, move toward their car. He removed the customs seal and opened the door. Nora was sure she detected a hint of excitement as he shouted, "*¡Vamos, Desembarca!*" They all knew enough Spanish to understand what that meant and grabbed their bags, some whooping as they jumped down the steps and onto Portuguese soil.

Nora was one of the last to disembark and looked around. The train station was tiny, just a track on either side of the single platform. It was surrounded by small buildings housing shops on the ground floors and, judging from the plants hanging down behind the windows on the second floors, apartments. From the slightly elevated position of the station, Nora could see the deep blue of the Atlantic glittering beyond the houses. The area surrounding the train station was deserted, and the group looked around in a bemused manner. *Where to now?*

The train driver climbed out of the car, holding a bag containing hockey sticks. He handed them to the man standing nearest. The man asked him something in Spanish that Nora couldn't understand. The driver pointed toward the ocean.

"He says we should make our way to the harbor; that's all he's been told," the young man said.

"Might as well, then," Lars said, slinging his bag over his shoulder. "Maybe we can also get something to eat. I'm starving."

Nora followed him, and as they walked through the small town, the pungent smell of fish entered her nostrils. They were clearly in a fishing village. *Are we going by ship?* Looking at the water filling the horizon, she felt excitement; the ocean was freedom. Not just to the people of this small fishing village, but also to her.

It took less than ten minutes to reach the harbor, where half a dozen small fishing boats were unloading their catch. The fishermen looked up at the party of strangers approaching the docks, then quickly resumed their work. They didn't seem bothered by their presence at all. Nora was intrigued; she couldn't imagine too many tourists making their way to this village, and certainly not in December.

One of the men in the front pointed at what looked like a lone restaurant on the far side of the crescent-shaped harbor. "Why don't we go there and see if we can get something to eat? Perhaps someone is waiting for us there?"

"It doesn't look like there's anywhere else to go, anyway. If anyone's expecting us, I'm sure they'd be at the restaurant," Lars added. The others murmured their agreement, and the group continued along the water. Nora eyed the men unloading fish; then her eyes were drawn toward the harbor entrance, where waves crashed against the piles of stones protecting the docked ships. In the distance, she saw a speck on the horizon, just another returning fishing boat.

"Do you think we're in the wrong place? Not much happening in this town," Katja said softly, then nodded at the fishermen. "Although they didn't seem surprised by our appearance."

So Katja had noticed it, too. "Maybe they're our next ride?" She caught the nervous crack in her voice. "I don't know, Katja. Let's wait and see what happens next. We've only just arrived. Maybe Lars is right, and someone's waiting for us in the restaurant."

Lars overheard them. "Whatever happens next, we'll be in England soon enough, I know it," he said confidently. "You must be looking forward to seeing your family again."

"You have no idea. And I'm sure you and Christiaan will get along just fine."

"Oh, I have no doubt about that. If what you said about him being involved in all of this"—he waved his arms at the harbor—"is true, then your brother-in-law and I are going to be the best of friends."

The first of their group entered the restaurant, and Nora turned to take another look at the ocean. The fishing boat on the horizon had closed the distance surprisingly quickly. She shielded her eyes with her hand and squinted at the vessel, which was making its way toward the harbor at an unusually high speed. "Hey, Lars, do you see that ship over there?"

"What's that?" Lars was already halfway through the door but turned back. He peered out at the ocean with her, and she could feel the tension build as she heard him hold his breath. "That's no fishing boat."

The ship grew against the horizon as it raced toward them, and some of the others joined them outside, staring at the vessel.

Nora wiped her clammy hands on her pants as the ship's details became clearer. It was unlike any of the small fishing boats in the harbor. Its slim bow cut effortlessly through the water; the waves appeared to have little impact on its course. The sunlight reflected on the hull's grayish-green paint, and it was now close enough to see the shapes of sailors milling about the front deck. They wore white sweaters, and despite their best efforts at concealing them with large gray sheets, the shapes of cannons pointing out in the middle of the ship were unmistakable.

"That's a ship of war," one of the men beside her said under his breath. "A destroyer."

"Yes, but of what country?" Lars said.

The ship was moving so quickly that it was hard to identify the flag hoisted above the bridge. A flash of red. Nora's heart skipped a beat. She looked again, waiting for the swastika to appear and confirm her fears. A large wave splashed against the hull, spraying the sailors at the bow. Nora felt her knees shaking. Had they really come all this way to be caught at the very end? How did the Germans know about their trip? Who had betrayed them?

One of the men next to her let out an excited scream. "It's the British navy! Look at the flag! They're flying the Red Duster." He slapped the shoulder of the man next to him. "They're pretending to be a British merchant vessel!" Nora looked at him, dumbfounded. *It's not a Nazi warship?*

The ship entered the harbor, and Nora was overwhelmed by its size. It had to be at least eighty meters in length, dwarfing the other boats in the harbor. The fishermen paused what they were doing and stared and the monstrosity entering the harbor, rapidly slowing down. The sailors on the fore and aft decks were moving about quickly, holding mooring lines. A few of them shouted at Nora's group, frantically waving their arms.

Lars didn't hesitate. "Let's go! That's our ride!" He sprinted toward the destroyer, where the first sailors had jumped onto the dock, quickly securing the massive ship. The engine was still rumbling; it was clear they weren't staying for long. Nora sprinted after Lars, as did Katja and Arthur. She was panting hard when she reached the ship, and two of the sailors held out their hands as she climbed one the ladders dangling from the ship's deck. She grabbed them, and strong arms lifted her up and over the ship's railing.

"Welcome aboard, ma'am!" one of the young sailors said, his face beaming. It took less than five minutes for the dock to clear. "I suppose that's all of you, then?"

Nora was overwhelmed by the activity, as sailors busied themselves around the refugees. She spotted Katja and Arthur on the opposite side of the deck. "I'm not sure. Did you count us?" *Where's Lars?*

"Twenty-one of you, ma'am." The sailor's answer came instantly and confidently. "Can't imagine any of you lingering about after we made our entrance," he added.

Nora was relieved to see Lars talking to another sailor a few meters to her left. He turned to her and winked, a relieved smile on his face. She turned back to the sailor. "Then that's all of us."

"Thought so, ma'am," the sailor said. "If you would excuse me, I'll be right back. Don't go anywhere." He rushed off, barking commands at the men on shore, who sprang into action, undoing the lines, quickly jumping back on board.

A few minutes later, the destroyer exited the harbor. As it reached the open sea, the roar of the engines intensified, and Nora felt the bow rise as they picked up speed. She stood on the stern and held onto the railing, watching the harbor entrance merge into the coastline within minutes. All around her, sailors sprang into action, removing the covers from the ship's cannons and guns. The Red

Duster flag was replaced by a white flag with a red St. George's cross sporting the Union Jack in its top left corner.

"That's the White Ensign." Lars stood next to her, shouting over the wind and engine noise. "The flag of the British navy. Looks like they're done pretending."

Nora marveled at the efficiency around her as the British navy men took their positions, one strapping into the seat of a large gun nearby. His eyes immediately went skyward, scanning for threats from above.

"Ma'am?" Nora turned to find the sailor that had welcomed her standing behind them. "Would you mind coming below deck with me? We'll be reaching cruising speed soon, and well, you don't want to be above deck when we hit some serious waves farther ahead. Plus, you might want some hot tea and a bite to eat, perhaps?"

The mention of food made Nora realize she hadn't properly eaten since leaving Barcelona. The sailor led them down into the ship, and Nora savored the warmth as they reached the ship's mess hall. It was larger than she'd expected, with at least fifty people, some from her group, eating and chatting away. The sailor pointed at the far side of the room. "You can get something from the galley over there. Eat as much as you want, we've got plenty. I'll come find you in about an hour to show you your berths." He turned but Nora stopped him.

"Would you mind telling me where we're going? This has been quite overwhelming."

"Why, of course, ma'am. We're on our way back to Gibraltar. This was quite an interesting assignment for us—we've never docked in such a small harbor before. Someone must really want you back in Old Blighty."

Nora looked at him in confusion. "I'm sorry?"

"England, ma'am. You're going to England."

AUTHOR'S NOTES

For this second book in the *Orphans of War* trilogy, I wanted to focus on the journey and influence of the Dutch refugees and resistance fighters that made the trek to England. In Dutch, they are called *Engelandvaarders*, or England sailors. It's a piece of history that's relatively well known in the Netherlands, but less so in the rest of the world. I can imagine those reading the story might wonder why they didn't just cross the North Sea, instead of trekking all the way to Spain and Portugal. The shortest possible distance, as the crow flies, between the coastlines is 180 kilometers, or 112 miles.

Of the 136 attempts to cross the North Sea, only 31 were successful, amounting to 172 Engelandvaarders. Apart from the treacherous sea with its unpredictable weather, would-be Engelandvaarders had to avoid German patrols on Dutch beaches before they had a chance to launch their various crafts. While some undertook the journey with small motorboats or sailboats, there are also plenty of stories of Engelandvaarders attempting to cross in canoes or kayaks.

For those that managed to make it out to sea, the next challenge was staying clear of German patrols, which consisted of airplanes, regular *Kriegsmarine* vessels, and, of course, the feared U-boats lurking underneath the surface. If they were "lucky," Engelandvaarders would be picked up by these ships, but plenty were sunk.

This made the overland journey a relatively "safer" undertaking, and a documented 985 men and women successfully made it to England using the southern escape lines covered in this book. Nora's journey is based on the incredible material collected by A. M. F. Dessing in her dissertation *Tulpen voor Wilhelmina. De geschiedenis van Engelandvaarders*—Tulips for Wilhelmina: The History of England Sailors—published in 2004. I would not have been able to write this book without her efforts, and I thank her profusely for writing what is, in my opinion, the most comprehensive overview of the history of Engelandvaarders available. Many of Nora's experiences are based on snippets of memoirs in Dessing's dissertation.

Which brings me to the Mother of the People, Queen Wilhelmina of the Netherlands. Her official role in leading the Dutch government-in-exile and making regular broadcasts on Radio Oranje is well documented. Her involvement with the Engelandvaarders less so. I loved reading how she welcomed new arrivals by serving them tea, and I couldn't resist including this version of the queen in the book. She was also passionate about the resistance back home, and she played an active role in the plans to have a network of partisans ready to strike upon liberation. More on that in the final book of the trilogy, I promise. Having Christiaan accept and undertake a mission on her Majesty's orders was so much fun to write.

Lisa's uncovering of the compromised Dutch network run by the British Special Operations Executive is, unfortunately, based on actual events. Known as *Das Englandspiel*—the England Game—or *Unternehmen Nordpol*—Operation North Pole—it was one of the German *Abwehr*'s most successful counterintelligence operations during WWII. From September 1941 to May 1943, 54 Dutch SOE agents were dropped in the Netherlands, only to be "welcomed" by German troops upon touching down. Despite numerous warnings by, among others, Leo Marks in January 1943, and the RAF's observation that flights to the Netherlands felt too easy on the way over but involved fierce attacks on the return, it wouldn't be until May 1943 that the last agents were dropped. The two agents escaping from Haaren prison in June 1943 were initially arrested on their return to Britain, for the operators of the Englandspiel in Germany had announced their return, claiming they had turned and were now German double agents. The reality of the compromise finally became indisputable in April 1944, when the German operators sent a mocking message to Britain, confirming they had been played, stating any future agents would be welcomed with open arms.

Finally, I want to touch on Floris' journey. If you thought you knew him from *Orphans of War*, I hope his recent exile to the eastern front gave you even better insight into the evil brother of the series. Having lost his job and his role in sending Dutch Jews off to faraway camps, he now had to get his own hands dirty.

During the war, plenty of young Dutch men volunteered for the Waffen-SS. In fact, with an estimated 25,000 Dutch recruits in the period between 1942 and 1944, the Netherlands was responsible for the largest absolute number of foreign Waffen-SS soldiers. Of those, 20,000 were sent to the eastern front, where they experienced the true horrors of war. Floris' journey in the Waffen-SS is based on memoirs of these soldiers, as documented in the exhaustive book *Veldgrauw* by Evertjan van Roekel. Without his research, I would not have been able to describe Floris' experiences on the eastern front in such vivid detail.

If you've read other books written by me, you probably noticed the first installment of *Orphans of War* was comparatively low on war atrocities and graphic violence, except for Floris' domestic abuse of Nora. I can imagine some of the more gruesome scenes in *They Bled Orange* came as a surprise, but I felt it was important to show the war crimes committed by the Waffen-SS near the eastern front.

The scene where Floris initially refuses to shoot the Jewish man in the ditch refers to the massacre at Majdanek. Part of Operation Harvest Festival, this systematic butchering of an estimated 43,000 Jewish prisoners of the Majdanek, Poniatowa, and Trawniki concentration camps occurred on November 3 and 4, 1943. That's no typo. It took just two days.

I hope you're itching to know what happens to the Brouwer

family next. The final part of the trilogy will be out in September 2023. I promise it will be worth the wait. In the meantime, I'd love to hear what you thought of *They Bled Orange*. You can reach me at michaelreit.com or on Facebook (MichaelReitAuthor).

A NOTE TO THE READER

Dear Reader,

I want to thank you for picking up your copy of *They Bled Orange* - the second book in the *Orphans of War* series. Readers mean everything to authors, and I appreciate you more than I can say.

As an author I depend on you to leave an honest review on Amazon, Goodreads, or your favorite (online) bookstore. If you've got the time to do so, I would be very grateful.

If you would like to reach out to me with questions or comments, please feel free to contact me via my website – michaelreit.com or reach out to me on Facebook – www.facebook.com/MichaelReitAuthor. I love hearing from readers, and look forward to hearing what you have to say about *They Bled Orange*!

Warmly and with Gratitude,
Michael Reit

ABOUT THE AUTHOR

Michael Reit writes page-turning historical fiction. His books focus on lesser-known events and people in World War II Europe.

Born in the Netherlands, he now lives in beautiful Vienna, Austria, with his partner Esther and daughter Bibi.

Connect with Michael via his website:
www.michaelreit.com

Or via Facebook:

facebook.com/MichaelReitAuthor

ALSO BY MICHAEL REIT

Beyond the Tracks Series

1. Beyond the Tracks

2. Tracks to Freedom

Orphans of War Series

1. Orphans of War

2. They Bled Orange

3. Crossroads of Granite

Stand-alones

Warsaw Fury

Made in United States
Orlando, FL
05 June 2024